Something Special

CARRIE JADE REIDINGER

ISBN: 1502939231
ISBN 13: 9781502939234
Library of Congress Control Number: 2014923009
CreateSpace Independent Publishing Platform
North Charleston, South Carolina

PROLOGUE:

Darkness is essential. As is the light.
They cannot survive without each other.

I need to learn to embrace both.

But darkness can be evil. And light can be evil.

Nothing is as clear as it seems.

A certain kind of light is needed to see pure beauty.
A certain kind of darkness is needed to see the stars.

Corrupt light can make you blind. Blind to the truth.
Blind to everything, morally right or wrong.

Corrupt darkness can make you numb. It can make you
unfeeling and heartless. It can make you hateful, brutal, ruthless, vicious, and blood thirsty.

Both can make you evil.

I *need* the dark and the light in order to fulfill my destiny.

But can I stop them from being polluted by the world?
Can I keep them innocent of corruption? *Can I keep them pure?*

Or will I be consumed.

I don't know.

1

3 days to my birthday

I remember the darkness. The darkness that came out to play just before the stars lit up the sky, sparkling like small diamonds.

The stars are the suns of night. They are the light in the darkness. They are beautiful and strong, and resilient. They are fiery and hot.

I sit here, now, staring at these distant balls of fire, as the warm wind blows through the trees. The breeze sighs and dances and swirls, tangling my hair and kissing my face.

I sigh. The air was never this fresh in the city. It was never this pure.

It could never be as pure as it is here, in the country.

My fingers curl around themselves as I pull my knees up towards my body. Though the movement could have easily unbalanced me, I stay perched and steady on my private spot here on the roof.

Voices escape from the house. I can tell that there are more than the usual two of my grandparents. My grandparents are in the house with some guests that I have no interest in meeting. Gramps says that I should make some friends, since I am to stay here for the whole summer. But sometimes, I just prefer to be alone, in peace. Alone with my thoughts and the stars and the memories that always threaten to make me want to either cry or laugh or do both at the same time.

The painful memories are the ones that led me to take up writing, reading and dancing. My hobbies help me to forget, to escape. And nothing is better for this than riding my horse.

My horse was given to me by my father as a birthday present. He had said, "This is Ruby," I remember his smile and the crinkle in his face as his eyes sparkled. "Take care of her. She'll always be there for you, especially when you're most lonely. As will I." His face fills my vision. "I love you sweetheart. I'll be back soon."

But that was a lie.

He never came back.

It's been two years. And I can still remember those painful last words. Those last words that never came true. No fourteen year old would ever dream of her father saying anything but the truth. My dream was broken.

Tears prickle my eyes, threatening to overflow... I shake my head.

No. No. Usually I am good at blocking out memories that hurt. But now, it's almost as if my brain wants me to recollect, almost as if it wants my heart to hurt again.

This country air is messing with my head. Making the foundation of the walls that I have built around my heart weaker.

I can't let it break. I can't.

I look up at the sky, at the stars sparkling and burning in the distance, and wonder whether my dad can sense me thinking of him.

Mom had gone to look for him when he didn't return that night, when it got late enough for her to worry. But she never found him.

We don't know for sure where he'd gone; many think he's dead. I heard them whispering, I could feel their eyes on me as they glistened with pity.

"Dead."

I heard that word whispered so many times. It probably should have driven me crazy.

But I know he's not dead. I can feel it.

But Mom is not so sure... those months were depressing, and mom was hardly ever home. When she was home I tried everything to reach out to her, but she always had a blank but strangely aware expression on her face, as if she were only half there, as if she were seeing something else. And she always left with a swift "Buy pizza for dinner tonight, I'll be home late my dear. Don't wait up. Love you." and just walked out the door.

I miss my dad who is not here physically, though I feel like he is here with me in my heart, and I miss my mom who is with me physically but is not with me mentally. Both have deserted me in some way.

I feel abandoned.

Something trickles down my cheeks. Funny, I didn't know I was crying. I wipe my tears away, feeling weak. This country air really IS making me do some deep thinking. I don't want to feel this pain anymore. And just as I decide that, I hear Gramps calling.

"Veronica, come in here, I'd like you to meet someone!"

I sigh; I guess my alone time is finished. Maybe it's for the best. After all, I'd probably end up crying into the night if I continued thinking about my dad.

"Coming Grandpa!"

I jump down from the roof, my soft boots meeting the wooden deck with no sound and no weight: as if the deck came to me. Ten years of dancing has taught me to be agile.

The door creaks as I open it, I can hear voices and laughter coming from somewhere in the house, but the living room is vacant. Hmmph, I guess everyone is in the office. I hate that room; all of dad's stuff is there… It still brings back loving but lost, and therefore, painful memories.

I step into the office with the sense of nostalgia hanging on my back. It is warm in here, warmer than outside. The three extra bodies are at fault. It is a little bit too crowded for my liking; I debate walking out again. I am just about to step out when something strange hits me. I realize that I can sense something… the atmosphere in the room. It's cheerful. It engulfs me as if I could actually feel the emotions radiating off the three new comers.

This is weird. Maybe my mind is messing with me, because this is definitely not normal. I've never felt anything this strong before. I could always tell if someone was upset or happy, but I was never able to sense it to this level before.

I push it to the back of my mind. It's starting to bother me. Maybe I'm losing it.

I take another step away, another step towards the door. Gran notices the movement. She smiles and waves me forward.

I sigh; my hesitation gave me away. I walk towards the group, plastering a smile on my face, not wanting them to think I'm unfriendly. I guess that it couldn't hurt to say hello.

The three newcomers turn to greet me; smiles brighten their faces as they see me. I feel the change in their emotions as if I could taste them and name them. My head buzzes. What is happening? It's almost as if I can actually sense what they feel, sense their emotions… But that's not possible…

I'll deal with it later.

"Hey," I say and give them a small awkward wave. That's me. Awkward.

But as I see their warm smiles, I feel myself relax. Perhaps it couldn't hurt to have a friend.

I study the three newcomers.

There is a woman, a man and a boy. I'd guess the woman and man to be around forty, while the boy seems more or less my age. The boy sees me looking and his mouth stretches out into a grin while one of his eyes closes and opens. A wink. Jeez, he's friendly... *and* a looker; that is as much as I can think without blushing.

The woman speaks, bringing my attention back to her.

"Hello Veronica, I'm Alicia Blanchard, and this is my husband, Tom." She smiles a warm smile that brings a bigger smile to my lips. "You can call me Aunt Alicia. And this is our son..."

"I'm Jake," He smiles, dimples and all.

"Hey Jake" I smile back, I can't help it. I am a sucker for dimples.

His smile grows wider when he hears my warm welcome. His eyes sparkle just like Dads...

Out of the corner of my eyes I see Gran, Gramps and Mr. and Mrs. Blanchard exchange delighted looks and I feel their smugness. Oh brother... It seems that I have a new friend. He seems nice enough though. Well, perhaps one friend wouldn't hurt.

"Well," Gramps says, "I'll show Mr. and Mrs. Blanchard around. You two should get to know each other," and he leads them out of the room.

Once they are gone I turn back to Jake. He is studying me, so I do the same to him. He has dark blond hair and startling bright blue eyes. They seem to burn with a blue fire, which keeps his eyes warm looking. His nose is not too long and not too sharp, almost flawless. His mouth is amazingly even, his lips almost symmetrical. His face is nearly perfect.

After scrutinizing his whole face, I bring myself back to looking at his eyes and realize that he is staring at me with a mixed expression of curiosity, open friendliness and something else I can't distinguish. And I realize that I like him already.

"So how long are you planning to stay here Veronica?" He asks, one of his eyebrows lifting.

Cool, I always wanted to be able to do that eyebrow thing.

"I'm staying for the whole summer, plus one more month." I smile. I hope I don't sound hostile. That's my habit. Usually, when talking to people I don't know, I sound shy and unwelcoming.

The corners of his mouth lift and his eyes turn playful.
"I guess we'll have plenty of time to get to know each other."

I can't help but laugh; he is easy to be around and talk with. And his sense of humor isn't too bad. "Yes, I guess we will" I say. I can almost feel my eyes sparkling with real enthusiasm. I might actually want a friend...

I study him more; He does seem my age, but he could be older. His body is lean but he looks muscular even with a shirt on. I am honestly getting quite curious about his age.

I open my mouth to ask him but he beats me to it.

"So how old are you Veronica? You look like high school age, but somehow, the way you act makes me think otherwise. It makes me think you're much older." He asked this in a friendly manner, but a memory I have try to forget hits me like battering winds during a hurricane.

Ice cold rain, the smell of metal and rust, aching arms from dragging the kid up, the loud boom, the heat of fire, and the broken body of a man I was unable to save...

"Veronica?"

His anxious tone brings me back to reality. I can feel his worry and feel worry myself that I can sense his emotion so clearly. How could I feel what he's feeling? It's not natural. Not right. My heart pumps with rising alarm. I attempt to force it down.

I try not to think about it. I don't want Jake to tell my Grandparents that I'm acting strange again.

"Oh ya, erm, I'm turning sixteen in three days." I smile sincerely. Sixteen! "It's the 1ˢᵗ of July," I add, sensing what he might ask next. "How 'bout you?"

Jake smiles when I answer his next question before he even asks it.

"Cool. My birthday's in September and I'll be seventeen." His eyes twinkle like he's enjoying some joke. His eyes twinkle and I know that I can keep staring at them and not get enough.

We both stand there staring at each other; I know that he isn't feeling awkward. But I sure am.

"So, do you want a tour of the house? Or should I leave that to later?"

He chuckles. "What would we do if we aren't touring?"

I feel my eyes getting wide with unexplained excitement and I can also feel my mouth stretching out in the huge smile that I only use for close friends. I seem to have already placed my trust in him. Getting familiar isn't something I do a lot, but this guy really makes me curious.

"I could make us hot cocoa and we could go to my favorite spot in the house!" I tell him excitedly.

"Sure, I'd love that" He grins down at me and we walk like old friends, side by side, towards the kitchen.

While walking there, I ponder on my newfound knowledge of my weird sixth sense. It would seem that I am able to interpret what others are feeling. I know that this should probably scare or shock me but I only feel annoyed. As if something I've been waiting for has finally come, but showed up late. Weird.

I make the hot cocoa fast, adding two huge marshmallows to each of our cups. He takes his cup and sniffs.

"Wow, it smells real good, Rose." Jake says and he takes a sip.

I stare at him in shock. What did he call me? No one calls me that anymore... No one. Not since mom lost dad. Her name is Viola Rose and she always used to call me Little V-Rose or just Rose since both our first names started with a V and we have identical middle names. I think she liked the idea of me being another her. But when Jake called me Rose, I can't help but feel like he already seems personally attached to me.

And it's true, I trusted him faster than I've ever trusted anyone.

But it still seems a little too early for nicknames. What I also wonder is: Did anyone tell him my middle name? Because I certainly didn't... I wonder if he saw it somewhere... How else would he know?

"That's my mom's second name… and my middle name. How did you know?" I question, raising both eyebrows since I can't do the cool raise-one-eyebrow-thing.

His eyes turn guarded. And I can sense and feel that his emotions are that of one who has given too much away.

"I just call all beautiful girls I meet some types of flowers. And Rose just seems to suit you, you know, since your cheeks are so rosy, and your skin looks as soft as a flower petal. Not to mention the fact that you smell like roses" He winks, and smiles playfully.

He isn't lying. I now know that I can sense a lie because fear and anxiety always accompany a lie. However, I also sense that he is hiding something. Oh well, he'll tell me when he's ready. And for some reason, I know that he will.

"Haha," I say sarcastically, I am NOT beautiful. I never thought I was, and still don't think I am. My skin is way too pale and my lips too small.

I look at his face and burst out laughing, I'm not sure why. He joins me, of course, though he has nothing funny to laugh about.

"What are you laughing at?" My bottom lip pulls out in a pout, my fake attempt of dismay.

"You; silly girl. Your laugh is so cute. You should laugh more." He says it with such kindness that I know that Gran and Gramps had told him that I haven't laughed in a long time.

Surprise. That's what I feel when I realize that I had just laughed. I had laughed? How long has it been since I did that? Whoa… I am liking this Jake dude even more; he makes me happy again.

I smile back at him; now I really want to show him the roof.

"So you wanna see my favorite spot? Or are we just gonna stand here drinking chocolate?"

Jake rolls his eyes, and grins. "Of course. Lead the way Princessa."

I giggle; I am nothing like a princess anymore, but dad used to call me his little princess. Though it hurts a little, the reference doesn't make me sad, it makes me cheerful.

As we pass through the house, I stop to tell him about some of the things that we see.

We pass Great Grandmama's mirror, and I get a short look at my reflection.

My curled waist length brown hair trails behind me, and my small mouth is pulled up in a grin. My nose is not big but quite little and not too pointed. And my eyes, which have been a dull brown since dad disappeared, seem to be sparkling with happiness.

Now my eyes look like a chocolate brown.

But here's the thing, I've got weird eyes; they reflect color. So if a surface is red, and I was close to it, my eyes would look a little brownish orange; the same thing happens with other colors. Blue becomes navy and green becomes olive. So sometimes no one knows the true color of my eyes. It's interesting, but some people find it weird. My eyes ARE brown though, and 'that's the warmest color you can get'. That's what dad always told me. But dad has bluish grey eyes; his eyes were beautiful no matter what. I got mom's brown eyes; her eyes used to shine... well, not so much anymore.

My face is small and even; the color of my skin a light cream shade, usually colorless and pale, and I have a rather high cheekbone that sometimes makes me look gaunt. Today, however, color creeps into my cheeks, making them look healthy and rosy, just like how Jake said.

It makes me look less pale. Different. Happier.

I push the door open and the cool summer night air blows into the house with the breeze. I can immediately hear the river, and can smell the trees.

Jake and I walk to the deck and just take in our surroundings for a minute, enjoying the freshness of the natural and beautiful mountain area.

Jake turns to me.
"So this is your favorite place? I can see why. It's really peaceful."

I look back at him. If he thinks this is nice, he's going to love being higher.

"No, we're not quite there yet." I grin when his mouth pulls down in a confused frown.

I motion him towards where we will be able to climb up.

I pass him my hot cocoa and jump to reach the gutter, and then I pull my body up onto the roof in one swift motion and sit there looking down at him.

He stares at me in amazement. I can almost hear his thoughts: *"How did she do that? She ain't the soft indoor girl I thought she would be."*

I laugh internally; it's nice to be good at something.

"Now gimme that hot cocoa and get yourself up here," I challenge him. It should be easier for him since he is tall, but he has to be strong to be able to get himself up to where I am.

Jake passes me both drinks and rubs his palms together.

He jumps, and before I know it, he is next to me. Whoa. How did he do that?

I stare at him in amazement as I pass him back his hot chocolate.

"What?" He asks. I can feel that he is a little self conscious under my hard stare. Oops, I should soften up a bit.

"It's nothing… just that… *How* did you do that?"

"Do what?" He sips his cocoa, all innocent looking.

"How did you get up so fast?" I set my mouth; he **is** going to tell me this.

"I just followed you, Rose. I copied you exactly."

He copied me? But I didn't practically fly onto the roof… did I? No, I couldn't have.

"So you're saying that I practically flew onto the roof?"

He grins. "It sure did look like it"

"Whatever" I have had enough weirdness for the day. Any more and I may explode.

I turn my attention to the sky.

It is breathtaking. More stars are out now than they were previously, and the Milky Way is visible. The warm summer breeze ruffles my hair, tangling it into small knots.

"Wow, it's beautiful. I see why you like it" Jake's voice is a whisper, as if he doesn't want to disturb the stars.

"Yeah, I love it..." I murmur. "Hearing the river, listening to crickets, watching fireflies pass... sometimes animals come by here too. These are the best things in life, the natural things. They belong here. It's beautiful"

We just sit there, neither one of us breaking the silence. I decide that Jake will be a good friend. He can appreciate true natural beauty. We have something in common.

I turn to peek at what he's doing. His hair looks silver in the moonlight, and his face, normally tanned, is shimmering pale and strangely beautiful. Then I meet his eyes and see that he is staring at me with an unexpected intensity. The emotions rolling off of him are both unfamiliar and familiar to me and I decide to shut them out. I don't want to feel that. Yet.

"Veronica! Jake! Where are you? Come in!" I hear my grandparents and his parents calling from the house.

Jake slides, with unexplained grace, down the roof first. I go after him, and just as before, the ground comes towards me and there is no sound of my landing.

Jake and I walk back inside, shoulders touching; I can feel new friendship blooming. But I have no idea yet how much I am going to need him.

2

Jake and I are sprawled across the carpeted floor; a deck of cards lie in the center of our little circle. Some cards are in our hands. The adults are sitting around the dinner table, discussing agriculture in Bali. Before that, they had started talking about politics; that's when Jake and I left them. The smell of roasted potatoes and chicken stew lingers in the air. That was one of the yummiest meals I have ever eaten, and I think everyone who had it would agree with me. Gran's cooking is always delicious.

During dinner, Jake, his parents, my grandparents and I surrounded the table. It was really cheery, and the emotions coming from everyone were so bright that I couldn't help but smile and laugh along with whatever they were saying. Gran and Gramps looked happy with the new brightness on my face, and laughter was in the air. We had talked about childhood times; it seems it is always the elder's jobs to embarrass their young. Luckily for me, all the embarrassing stories happened before I was even aware of what was considered embarrassing. And nothing funny happened in my family after Dad had gone.

Gran and Gramps also bragged about my many hobbies; not that I am very good at any of them, but the hobbies take up the time that I would have spent thinking about Mom and Dad. My hobbies keep me distracted from the pain.

During dinner, I also learned that Jake can play the guitar and drums, and that he has a nice mellow baritone voice. His parents asked him to sing. I was enchanted. It was another thing that we had in common: a love of music.

Now the atmosphere is a lot more peaceful with Jake and I playing cards on the floor, and the adults chatting away and drinking wine.

Jake looks up from his cards the same time I do and our eyes meet. Some silent communication seems to happen and I know that he wants to do something different. Well, that and the fact that I could feel his boredom… it almost speaks to me, telling me that he wants to do something else.

This whole emotion sensing is really getting on my nerves and freaking me out. But I will figure out my new

'Sixth Sense' later. For now, we've got to find something more interesting for us to do.

An idea comes to me.

"Jake?" I ask.

He smiles. "Yes?"

"Erm, would you like to hear me play the piano?" I question shyly, I feel the heat making it's way up to my face. Why am I blushing? Ha. "Well, that's only if you would sing while I play. I'd like to hear you sing more."

His grin widens. He sets down his cards, gets up, and holds out his hand for me. I let him pull me up, but he pulls a little too hard and I lose my footing on the ground. I don't fall but he still has to help balance me out. Our arms intertwine for a second before I swiftly let go. Inner fire burns from where his hands had touched to my cheeks and down my neck.

I clear my throat and step away. Jake laughs at my expression while I roll my eyes at his idiocy. We are already like old friends.

I lead the way to the piano and set it up. I can feel his gaze boring into my back and I wonder what he's thinking.

Experimentally, I open up my mind. The intensity of his emotions almost knocks me down. It seems that I am also able to hear and smell more clearly too. That doesn't make sense though, why should I be able to do any of that? It's crazy. Not normal… and just plain weird.

I place my fingers delicately on the ivory keys and start playing some warm up chords. I feel his body heat as he moves closer to me so that he can watch my hands. I start to feel self-conscious… I don't want to mess up. I am also aware that the dining room has suddenly become very quiet. Great. Is everyone listening? Well, I might as well make the best of it.

"So, what song do you want to sing?" I ask.

"How bout 'In the arms of an angel' by Westlife?" He suggests, his blue eyes softening, the fire in them decreasing into slow churning blue molten rock. I feel warm inside.

"Sure" and my fingers gently dance across the keys, making beautiful resonances, even to myself. I improvise; secretly hoping it sounds good. "You sing the first verse and second chorus and I'll do vise versa" I add.

And that's when I completely lose track of time. It is so fun to just sing and play and build harmonies. I have no idea how many songs we sing or how long we stay there, enjoying the music. But when I stop I realize that sometime during our little musical numbers, Jake had moved to sit next to me on the piano stool. And he's not the only one who moved. Gran, Gramps, and Mr. and Mrs. Blanchard are also in the room. Their expressions are one of admiration and delight. The emotions that I feel from them are pride, joy and peace.

Jake is staring at me with a very gentle expression, but it is also a very determined expression. I can't make sense of it.

"You sing beautifully, Veronica," Uncle Tom comments in his deep mysterious and calming voice, which has a magical quality to it. "A voice like yours could cure a broken heart." His voice holds unwavering clarity. I look up at him, surprised. His eyes embrace intensity so deep, I feel like I'm being knocked over.

"Yes... You've got something special" Jake says. I look back at him; his blue eyes are burning.

I look away from Jake. I have to, or else I know I wouldn't want to anymore.

"Thank you Uncle Tom," I say, I can hear the warmth in my voice. I am flattered; no one has ever given me a compliment like that before. I like these people very much; they make me feel like I belong. I decide to return the compliment "Well, even though you didn't sing Uncle Tom, your voice is very magical too." I grin at him.

Jake chuckles softly, and Aunt Alicia and Uncle Tom exchange humorous glances, their mouths turning up into smiles, as if I didn't know the full meaning of what I had just said. This family seems full of secrets, but they are good secrets, I can't sense any bad. I'm hoping that they will unmask themselves once I get to know them better. Once they trust me.

"Well we've got to go," Aunt Alicia announces. "I've had a wonderful time Natasha; your cooking is divine! And Paul, you still haven't made me steak!"

Gran and Gramps get up and hug the leaving guests.

Jake turns to say good night, I can tell that he is reluctant to leave. I don't want him to leave either; for the first time in a long time I am having fun.

"Goodnight, Rose," He says softly.

"Night Jake!"

He leans closer to me, and I am suddenly engulfed with the scent of mint, sweet men cologne, and hot cocoa. I return his hug happily; he is warm. And the hot chocolate scent just makes me want to laugh, at least I left my mark: HOT CHOCOLATE!

I bid Jake's parents goodnight and watch as their car fades down the driveway. That family has awoken something in me. I can feel the change but I can't tell what it is.

The things that I can list with certainty, though, are: 1) Jake got me to laugh. 2) Their presence initiated my emotion-reading ability and sharpened senses. 3) My voice has suddenly turned 'special'.

4) I am happy.

I am also sure of one other thing. Hope. For some reason, I feel hope. I feel hope that I will see my dad again, hope that my mom will be happy, and hope that I will live to see that happen.

I wonder how I will sleep tonight…

■ ■ ■

Rain splatters onto my face; the droplets are cold and angry. This is going to be a bad storm; I have only about a mile to go before I reach home. I wish I took a cab… it was stupid to be cheap, especially when it had looked like a storm was gathering. I look around: the roads are deserted of cars and people, which is rather strange.

I walk on, counting my steps, not paying attention to my surroundings. Thirteen, Fourteen, Fifteen, Sixteen…

I think I get to about two hundred and twelve steps when I hear it. The loud ear-splitting noise of tires screeching and a loud bang as a large object hits something. All this is followed by a scream.

My head jerks up. It takes me about a second to process the scene before I am running; I have to reach the accident. I know. I can sense it. This is not the end of a bad accident; something even worse is about to follow.

I reach the area of the car crash: a silver Toyota had hit a lamppost. It doesn't look serious at a first glance, but then I see the leakage of oil from the car, and the sparks from the lamppost that was hit. I have to get the people out of there.

"Hello! You okay? Can you move? You've got to get out!" I scream.

But the windows of the car are not broken, and they can't hear me properly. I look into the car: there is a little girl and a man, presumably her father; and he is hardly moving. The girl is crying. The car door is locked. It won't budge open even when I pull my hardest. Even when I ask the little girl to unlock it.

I have to break the windows to save them.

I put my hand over my eyes: an attempt signal of cover. They understand what I am trying to communicate and shield their faces.

My elbow slams into the window on the passenger side with hard force and breaks it at first try. My fingers fumble for the lock of the car door, but it is jammed. The air bags are getting in my way!

"Take her!" The man wheezes. I am wrong about how serious it is. The car isn't damaged badly, but the people are. The man has a long gash across his head, which is bleeding, and his nose looks broken; he

must have hit his head on the wheel really hard. The little girl appears unharmed. "Save her! Save my baby! Please!" he seems to have trouble getting the words out.

I don't need to be told twice. I reach into the broken window and unbuckle her seat belt. But reaching in was the easy part, pulling her out is hard. I need to avoid the broken glass so as to not cut her, but I give myself some deep cuts in the upper arms, which I brace against the sharp edges of glass, as a result of protecting her.

I can feel warm blood, my blood, trickling down my arms. I get the little girl out and carry her safely away. Placing her where she will be safe. This all takes about a minute.

Time seems to slow down as I run back for her dad; saving him is not going to be easy.

I reach the car and try opening the driver's door. It is locked shut.
"Try to unlock it!" I say desperately. We don't have much time left; I need to hurry.

"I can't, I've tried," says the man. His wound is bleeding badly. "I'm sorry…"

"Don't say that!" I scream back at him. "Don't give up! Your daughter needs you!"

The determination in my voice and the mention of his child must have awakened him. Because his eyes suddenly narrow and sharpen, he *tries the lock again and I will it to work. The car door opens, but his anxious fingers are unable to unbuckle his belt. I reach over to do it for him.*

He lurches out of the car and practically collapses on me.

"Sir please, I can't carry you, I'm not strong enough!" My voice is desperate now. "Please try to walk!"

We stagger a couple more steps with his arm around my shoulders and half his weight bearing down on me. But this seems too much for him; he must have hit his head hard and be losing a lot of blood because he slumps against me, falling on top of me before I can manage to catch him and myself.

I lay him on the ground and rip off part of my shirt to staunch the blood flow in his head. I am still not comfortable with this distance from the accident; we are too vulnerable.

"Miss… Save yourself. Take my daughter back to her mother. She knows where to go," he whispers, eyelids drooping. He doesn't even have enough strength left to stay conscious.

"No please, I've got to get you out! I need your help to do it!" I am crying now, I feel the tears running down my cheeks, making little streams of salt water.

"Go! Listen to me, young lady. I'm dying; it's no use. I'm not going to get you killed as well!" He shoves me with his last remaining

strength; strength I didn't know he had, and I stumble away. My usually sure footing is muddled with fear. He looks at me with intense pleading eyes. "Take care of my daughter. Tell her I love her." And he passes out cold.

This is my last chance… perhaps I can drag him? He won't feel any pain now.

I grab him by his arms and try to pull him across the gravel.

But then time seemed to slow down. And I see the electrical spark falling into the oil and igniting. Then human instinct takes over and I dive for cover. Leaving the man, who I was just trying to save, in the streets. I hear the explosion and feel the blast and heat of fire, only realizing then that I am curled into a small protective ball around that man's daughter. She has gone unconscious; that may be better for her. I stay there for the next five minutes shivering with fear and pain.

When my ears stopped ringing, I uncurl myself and lie next to her. I can see the man on the road. Fire burns in spots around him but none seem to be touching him. But I don't go any closer because I know he is gone. I can see the puddle of blood around him and sharp debris.

I could have saved him.

I should have.

Instead, I saved myself. Selfish.

Why did I leave this little girl without a father?

I can't even call 911; I don't have the strength. I just sit next to the child, my arms aching and bleeding. I can smell metal and rust. And blood. And though it is still raining, the fire does not die. I move closer to the little girl protectively. Hopefully someone had heard the commotion and called emergency services; for I know that I will be unable to speak or call for help.

The last thing I remember is sirens wailing before I slide into the abyss of darkness.

■ ■ ■

I gasp awake in the night, shivering from the nightmare. No… it wasn't just a nightmare… it was a memory. The day that I saved myself instead of a child's father still haunts me. I have regretted that day for almost a year now. How could I have left that little girl fatherless when I knew what it was like not to have one?

Sobs rack my body as I unintentionally punish myself with the guilt of the memory. A memory that is so painful and so vivid that it is impossible to forget. No matter how much I want to. It is like a loyal friend, it will not abandon me, even when I tell it to go away.

I make a silent promise to myself: next time, I will save the other, even if it means that I die. I will do it.

That is the last thought I have before my eyes close and I fall into a mercifully dreamless sleep.

3

2 days to my birthday

I wake up in the morning to the sound of birds chirping outside my window. My room is still relatively dark since my curtains are drawn. I get out of bed and stretch my arms and legs.

As I walk over to the window to let some sunlight in, I catch the scent of eggs and sausages. Gran's making breakfast! Gran's breakfast is absolutely amazing; it's been a long time since I've had it. I've been in my Grandparents place for about three days now and it's already made a big difference in me.

Ithaca is just thirty minutes away from Gran and Gramps house. And New York City is just three hours away from Ithaca. That's where my mom and I live, in a tiny apartment in the Bronx. We live there because of her job; if it were up to her, and dad if he was still here, we would be in Brooklyn. But that's not a choice when you are living on one paycheck.

The quiet of the country is really different than the busy noise of the city. I'm glad mom sent me here for the summer. I could get used to the silence of the mountains; with only the noise of animals and nature to be heard.

I take a shower and get dressed, my wet hair curling around my face and dripping down my back.

Feeling refreshed, I bound down the stairs. Despite the nightmare from the night before, I am jumpy and happy. I can't wait for the events of the day to unfold. Plus, my birthday is in two days!

I pass Great Grandmama's mirror just as I had the night before, catching a glimpse of myself. I am surprised by how joyful I look.

"Good Morning!" I say while skipping over to give Gramps a kiss on the forehead. Gramps looks up from reading the newspaper with delighted surprise, his emotions radiate love.

I smile at him affectionately; I really do love my pops. His face shape and features are like Dad's but his hair is a blondish grey while Dad's hair is brown. Gramps also has pretty hazel eyes, full of wisdom and compassion.

I then hop over to the kitchen to offer to help Gran with the cooking. However, when I reach the kitchen, she is already coming out with a steaming pan of scrambled eggs and sausage; it looks and smells divine.

"Morning Gran!" I give her a little pat on the shoulder as she passes. Gran is a small little thing; I am already a head taller than her. She has brown soft curly hair, like me, but her hair has streaks of grey in it. Gran's eyes are a stormy grey blue, and they are beautiful like Dad's.

"Good morning sweetheart," Gran smiles at me, her expression showing the same love that I can feel from Gramps. My family is amazing, and I love them all. I hope to see it complete again, because without Dad, there is always an empty chair.

"I'll get the table set!" I say while walking to the kitchen to get the plates and silverware.

I walk out of the kitchen with my hands full of plates, forks, and spoons. I have just set the plates down when the phone rings. Gramps answers it.

"Hello?" He says. "Oh, hey Jake!" Gramps looks at me. "Yes, I'll pass it on to her," Pause. "Okay, we'll see you then!" Another pause. "Yes, yes, of course! Bye now." He hangs up.

"That Jake?" I question curiously. Is he coming to the house again?

"Yes, it was," Gramps eyes me with amusement; I can feel it from his emotions as well. I decide to get used to being able to sense emotions. Perhaps if I embrace it, it won't drive me insane with fear. "Jake saw your horse on the way down yesterday, and he is wondering whether you want to ride with him today."

Gran starts serving the eggs; it smells amazing. My stomach growls.

Gramps chuckles "Well, why don't you eat breakfast and I'll do the talking." He must have heard my tummy.

I sit down and straightaway scoop the food into my mouth. The eggs and sausages are bursting with flavor. It is just as I remembered, like a delicious piece of heaven.

"Well, Jake is interested in riding with you. Says he knows how." Gramps pauses. He must be watching me inhale my eggs. Gran is watching me too, her eyes sparkling with pleasure. "And he asked whether it was okay for him to tag along. I told him yes of course, you guys seem pretty close already." Gramps looks at the clock. "He'll be here around two."

I am reaching for a second serving before Gran and Gramps have eaten half of their food.

"Hmm… Okay," I say while piling my plate with more eggs. "I'd love that. He can ride? Cool." And in the food goes.

"I don't know where you put all that food dear girl." Gran mumbles. "You don't gain any weight either. Lucky baby." She smiles. Gran has the sweetest smile; it makes you want to protect her.

I finish chewing my food only to pour myself some orange juice, gulping it down immediately and pouring more. I drain the second cup just as fast as the first.

"In a hurry?" Gramps inquires.

"Nope, I just love Gran's cooking." I reply with a grin.

Gran's eyes appraise me. "Why thank you, my dear."

I take my dirty dishes to the kitchen, rinse them off and put them in the dishwasher. I drag the iron pan from the stove and turn the tap of hot water on. The pan steams as it makes contact with the water; I scrub all the excess food off and clean the pans. I don't want Gran or Gramps to have the trouble of doing the dishes.

I look out the window and have a sudden urge to go outside and enjoy the sunlight. Finishing off the dishes, I wipe my hands dry as I make my way to the door.

"I'll just be outside, okay?" I shout into the house.

My foot makes contact with the grass outside, and I'm running before I know it. Running through the front lawn, into the beautiful meadow just a few yards away. I don't get too tired while running, and I never trip. I feel my heart accelerate while I fly across the ground.

I stop in the center of the meadow to enjoy the scenery. The sky is a beautiful clear blue with white fluffy clouds filling the empty space up above. The trees seem to speak and radiate my joy. Birds fly above me, and butterflies fly around me. Animals of all kinds are in the forest, I can sense them, but they seem to be keeping their distance. The forest is alive and healthy and beautiful. I lie down on the grass, relaxing into the soft bed.

I stay there for a long while, not keeping track of time. I don't want to get up; it's so serene and it fills me with peace. I start singing very softly to myself; it makes me happy. But time passes quickly, and the sun is now in the center of the sky. I hadn't realized that I had stayed out so long. I have to get back home or Gran and Gramps will get worried.

As I get up, I realize that there are animals around the meadow, watching me. I stand very still, not wanting to disturb them. The animals seem to be looking at me, but they show no fear of me, not like how they should show fear of a human. This is very strange.

I can almost feel their amity. And then one by one, they disappear back into the forest. I walk away from the meadow and towards the house, wondering what all of that was about. I push aside my confusion because I don't want it to cloud the happiness that now fills my heart. I got to see the animals that live in the woods. And I am glad for the good start of the day.

■ ■ ■

I walk into the kitchen of the house; I had taken the back-door instead of the front. Gran is cooking again; it looks like chicken broth and toasted buttered bread. I love Gran's soup; just like everything she creates, it's wonderfully delicious.

"Hey Gran, any of that for me?"

"Yes, of course, dear." Gran looks over at me "Most of it is for you, I figured that you would want to have plenty of food in you if you are to go out riding with Jake." She brings out a bowl and pours some broth into it, takes two pieces of toasted bread and places the bread and the bowl of soup on a plate. The bowl is filled to the brim. Yum. I am hungry despite how much I ate during breakfast.

I take my time eating lunch, savoring the aroma of chicken in the soup and the creamy taste of buttered toast, which I dip in the broth. It's tasty, as usual.

As I am finishing my food, the phone rings. I pick it up while taking the last bite.

"Hello?" I mumble, my mouth full. Very ladylike. As usual.

"Hey Veronica" Jake's voice replies from across the line.

"Hey Jake, what's up?" my voice revealing the happiness I feel. Much to my surprise, I miss him already.

"Do you want to meet at the field instead of me coming over and saddling up with you? We could get going more quickly, and that would give us more time to ride!" Jake sounds excited about our day out riding. His husky but clear voice sounds good even over the phone.

"Sure!" I agree readily. "See you there at two?"

"Yep," I can hear a smile in his voice. "See you."

The line beeps as he disconnects. I put down the phone and run up the stairs.

I quickly strip off my shorts and put on my riding jeans and run back down the stairs.

"Bye Gran, Bye Gramps! I'm going to go riding now!" I say as I pass them, giving each of them a kiss on the cheeks before I race out the door.

I am out of the house and running down the driveway towards the field where Ruby grazes. I don't want to be late.

I put two fingers in my mouth and whistle loudly. I hear a neigh as Ruby comes galloping towards me, her mane blowing with the breeze, while her hoofs pad softly on the ground. She's a fast horse, with a little white streak down her forehead to her nose; the streak stands out against the chocolate brown pelt. She canters the last couple feet towards me and dips her head.

"Hey Ruby," I say as I pass her an apple. She takes it whole and chews it down, making crunching noises with each bite. She's the most spoiled horse ever, I think with a smile. I lead her to the little shed, where I store all my riding supplies, saddle her up gently but quickly, and climb on.

Riding my horse is like flying through the air with no limitations; I can't even explain it. I don't feel any resistance while Ruby and I soar across the fields. I feel like nothing can compare to Ruby's speed. It is extraordinary to me and I have no idea how she manages it. She is a special thing. The last thing I have from my dad.

I think we travel about less than half a mile when I see someone astride another horse, waiting in an open field. Ruby flies across the field before slowing down to a trot.

"Jake!" I call out.

A huge smile breaks out on his face. It looks like the sun has just come out from behind the clouds. His dimples are showing and his blue eyes are warm and sparkly. His emotions are a strong mix of relief and joy, and I can't help but feel the same. My heart drums unevenly, I seem to be aware of his presence a great deal more than I should be. I'm not sure what it means, but it makes me feel vulnerable. And I suddenly know that he has made it to the list of people that have the power to hurt me because I care for them.

"Hey Veronica!" His voice is welcoming and sunny. I smile as I realize how familiar his voice is to me. Already.

"Hi Jake!" I bring Ruby up to stand next to his horse. I can almost hear a silent greeting between the animals.

"Let's ride around the valley. We should get back before six." He suggests, his eyes twinkling with excitement.

"Sure!" and we start at a slow trot; both of us looking forward to getting to know each other. The valley is a beautiful green, and the mountains reach towards the sky as if they could touch the heavens.

4

Jake and I walk into the house in fits of laughter. I hear my higher pitched squeals matching his lower pitched guffaws. My laugh is different, and some people find it annoying, but Jake likes it; and that's all that matters for now.

Today's outing has made my feelings for Jake even more confusing than they already were. He is very understanding and easy to talk to and I opened up much more than I usually do. It's like I'm a locked door, and only he has the key to unlock me.

Ruby and Jake's horse, Flash, are grazing in the field near the shed. Jake and I had raced up the hill towards the house, and to my surprise, I was faster. I can't tell whether he was holding out on me, but I enjoyed the wind in my face and the slight burn in my muscles as my feet pushed into the ground.

I am built rather small, the top of my head reaching Jake's chin; but I am muscular and fit from years of dance training.

As I pause in the midst of laughter to catch my breath, I glance over at Jake's face, which is flushed and radiant. I let out a muffled giggle as I am reminded once again of the reason for our laughter:

Jake and I were play-fighting and I had aimed a punch at his left cheek. He had caught my knuckle and pulled me closer to him. But just as I was about to touch his body, I turned on my toes with what seemed like the speed of light and elbowed him in the gut. I am not the strongest thing, but I am quite fast. He had let out a breath when my arm made contact with his stomach. I wasn't sure whether I had even hurt him though; I think I might have actually bruised my own elbow instead, for his middle section is protected with hard lean muscles. We stayed in the position; he was holding my left fist and my right arm (which I had used to elbow him) with my back to his chest. He had started to loosen his grip and I took that opportunity. I clutched both his arms and spun in a way that enabled me to move behind him, bringing his arms with me. He rolled out of my grip only to turn around and move closer to me. I had given him a light push away, but since the ground was extremely uneven, Jake had stumbled backwards and landed on the grass. I ran to him immediately, afraid that he might actually be hurt, but he had gotten up with grass in his hair, on his shirt and on his pants. His face held an expression of surprise and disbelief; I bet he didn't know that I could defend myself that way. His emotions showed surprise and respect. But it swiftly changed to humor when I fell on the ground laughing.

Trying to contain my laughter, we got up and we stumbled along, shoving each other lightly, while walking the remaining steps up to the house.

Jake's eyes meet mine and I can tell that he knows the reason for my sudden giggle. He smiles a huge smile, which dimples his cheeks and brings twinkles to his eyes. He gently shoves me and rolls his eyes.

"I can't believe a girl beat me in wrestling," He mutters in mock disbelief. I can tell that he meant me to hear because he fist bumped my shoulder playfully.

Jake and I walk to the living room and plop ourselves onto the couch; the smell of homemade pizza comes from the kitchen. My stomach growls.

"What were you both laughing about?" Gramps asks as he walks into the room, his eyes bright with humor. "Sounded like a pack of hyenas had just stumbled into the house! I was getting my gun out!" He grins. "Not that we get hyenas here," He mumbles softly, as if as an after thought.

"Veronica tackled me and I got grass on my hair," Jake answers. I grin at him and ruffle his dark blond hair. He catches my hand and holds my wrist; electricity sparks between the little space between us, and my skin tingles from his touch.

I pull my hand away, afraid of the unfamiliar emotions radiating from both him and myself. I put my hands to my cheeks and feel warmth. I laugh silently to myself.

"I did not! I was defending myself; thank you very much!" I can't contain my laughter as I add, "And it's not my fault I'm faster than you" I say to tease him, I'm pretty sure he could be faster than me if he actually tried.

Gramps looks between us, his hazel eyes shifting from Jake to me, seeming to just notice the spark between us.

Jake looks at my Gramps, humor showing on his handsome face, then back into my eyes. He winks at me, as if guessing the direction of Gramps's thoughts. I clear my throat.

Gramps seems to finish his train of thoughts and smiles at me proudly. I guess he likes the idea of his little granddaughter being able to defend herself; especially against a strong guy like Jake.

"Well, I guess my little Ronnie ain't a baby no more." He says, sounding happy. "She'll be able to defend herself whenever necessary… And she'll know how to fight for those she loves." He adds last minute, his eyebrows crinkling together in deep thought.

I don't know why he said that; it is a little intense for my taste. Of course I will always fight for my loved ones. I decide not to dwell on that, shifting my reply to a much less sensitive subject.

"Aw, Gramps! You know I don't like that nickname! Ronnie sounds so babyish!" I feel a pout forming on my lips. "Plus, you don't like me calling you Pops! It's the same thing!" A smile replaces the pout on my lips as I remember my childhood days; Gramps had explained to me why he hadn't liked the name Pops. I grin in amusement, as Gramps eyes turn mischievous; making him look like a little boy instead of a seventy year-old man.

"Well, I have an edge, dear girl," Gramps beams, the side of his eyes crinkling up. "I'm sure you don't want me to go all tickle monster on you!"

I smile with him as I am engulfed in a childhood memory of my cousin, Lana, and I hiding from Gramps, who would have tickled us until we couldn't breathe through our laughter. Lana couldn't come this summer because she is going to camp, but I'm sure that I will see her sometime soon, maybe during Christmas. Maybe after Mom comes up from the city.

"Now, now Grandpa," says Gran as she appears in the living room; she walks over to Gramps and gives him a small peck on the lips. It is a sweet and affectionate gesture and I feel my chest expand with love. I want that for myself when I'm older; growing old with someone who I love and who loves me back, both of us knowing our true selves.

I look away from Gramps and Gran, for the scene seems too private, and catch Jake staring at me with the same intensity as he had the first night on the roof. I meet his gaze with boldness; I don't want to show him my vulnerability. We remain like that, just staring into each other. I can't look away.

His eyes turn very soft and I know that he can see through the wall I built. His hand reaches up to touch my cheek. His palm curves and seems to fit my face perfectly. I can't breathe. I can't look away. I can't move.

"Breathe, Rose," He says those words very quietly; his mouth turns up in a charming crooked smile.

I take a breath and close my eyes. Then Jake's hand leaves my face and I feel a sense of loss. All these feelings are very confusing to me and I have no idea what to make of them. What exactly is Jake to me? I've only known him for about a day, and yet...

My eyes open and I realize that he's staring at my Grandparents. I follow his gaze and the butterflies, made of warmth and fire, fly out of my stomach, go all over my body, and finally reach my cheeks.

Gran and Gramps are staring at us; they share a small smile. I look back at Jake; he doesn't look embarrassed or uncomfortable. In fact, he looks very pleased with himself. Maybe he thinks that placing his hand on my face and cradling it was a bold act. Or maybe he is showing my grandparents that there is more going on between us than I am letting on.

My cheeks burn with new embarrassment at the direction of my thoughts. Jake can't like me like that... right? There are so many more beautiful girls out there for him, so many more better and more interesting girls. To me, I'm plain and boring. I became closed off and glum after dad went MIA. I've been like that for two years, and the people in my school in the city don't talk to me much anymore.

But as I think about that, I know that it isn't completely true. I've caught people watching me during lunch or when I passed them in the corridors. Some stares were bold and curious, and some stares didn't last more than a second. But all stares held admiration and a question. Perhaps I intrigue people; I have no idea. Or maybe I amuse them with my quiet and reserved way, though I always tried to be nice when talked to. But I sit alone at lunch, and I would go to the dance room and just lose myself in the music and movements. Or just find myself a corner where I could get lost in a book.

"Jake," Gran starts, pulling me away from my own thoughts. "I've called your parents and invited them over for dinner. They'll be here any minute, and I suggested that they bring fresh clothes for you just in case you want to change out of your riding clothes."

I smile internally; Gran is one of the least selfish people I know. She doesn't do anything for herself; she always put other people before her.

"Thanks, Aunt Natasha," He says Gran's name with familiarity and I catch her giving him a cautioning look, her eyes flickering briefly to me. I see Jake nod very slightly; the movement may not have been noticeable if I wasn't so aware of everything he does now.

But before I can ask any questions, I hear tires making contact with the gravel road of Gran and Gramps driveway. The Blanchards must be here. Gramps gets up, and reaches the door about a second after it rings.

I hear Aunt Alicia's ringing and Uncle Tom's calming voice bubble greetings to Gramps. Then they are in the living room, filling it with a great earnest presence that I didn't notice before. It is very similar to how Jake holds himself; calm, cool and collected. But mixed in with that, the Blanchards, including Jake, have a loving and warm air about them. The atmosphere in the room is always pleasant with the Blanchards around; and I suddenly remember how instantly I liked them the first time we met. Not that that means much, I just met them yesterday.

"Hello!" I exclaim to them.

"Hello Veronica," They pause, look at their son and smile brightly.

Their eyes shift between Jake and me, just like Gran and Gramps had. A grin is breaking out on both their faces and I look away. I can tell that they sense a different kind of friendship between us after a day together. I can also tell that they know that we are closer already. I'm not exactly comfortable under their gaze; even though I know that they mean no harm. Jake chuckles and I turn to look at him.

"What?" I ask him, blood rushing to my face.

Jake grins. "You're red Veronica!"

I dip my head and pull my hair over my face. The heat of my blush burns my eyes, the smile on my lips widening even as I try to push it away.

I feel a hand, Jake's hand, reach out to brush the hair behind my ears. The fingers, though strong, are very, very gentle.

"Don't hide your face." He says softly, his blue eyes burn with fire. He moves closer to me, and I can feel his breath.

My heart kicks into fourth gear and I can hear it beating. I want his hand to be on my face forever. I don't want him to move away. But he moves away, grinning. His emotions seem determined, and his eyes darken with promise.

■ ■ ■

The night is surprisingly cold for summer, but the stars burn on in the sky. Jake and I are huddled close together on the roof, looking up at the blackness above which is decorated with blazing diamonds billions of miles away. There is no moon to shadow the stars tonight, so all of the stars are visible.

Dinner ended about half an hour ago and Jake and I had come up on the roof while the elders stayed inside and talked.

"You know something?" Jake suddenly questions.

I look at him to show that I'm listening.

Jake continues. "I never noticed the stars so much before that first night with you. They seem to burn brighter when you're around." I expect him to be joking, as I would normally expect people to be joking. But there is no humor in his voice.

I don't know what to reply. How could you reply to something like that?

So I just snort. How adequate of me.

Then, as if on some deep soul impulse, I open up my mind and let my senses go free. I don't know what I'm doing, but it feels right. Suddenly, I am able to smell the woods and the grass and the soil. I can hear the crickets and the rustles of leaves in the wind. I can almost taste the air. Yet above all else, I can smell his scent: mint, sweet cologne, hot chocolate (which seems to have stayed with him thus far) and something new, something that was not there before. Is that lavender? The scent clings onto him. But instead of making him seem girlish, he turns the scent manlier. All those scents together are lovely. They are intoxicating. They are faint. They muddle my mind.

The wind blows fiercely, making my hair fly all over the place; I shiver. Jake wraps his arms around me to keep me warm. But all I can think of is the fact that he's touching me. I look gratefully at him and draw myself closer. I don't know what our relationship is, but I am comfortable with him.

We stay there, looking up at the twinkling sky. With Jakes' arm around me, I can't deny that everything else seems more beautiful and clear. I look at him from the corner of my eye; he's looking up at the sky. My heart, my heart, my heart won't stop running. I turn away, feeling nervous.

"Veronica…" He says in a soft, melodious voice.

I look at him, careful to not touch his skin. He's looking at me, his eyes burning with the same look of promise as earlier this evening.

I hold my breath.

His face is closer than I had anticipated. Slowly, he bends his head down; placing his face closer to mine, our eyes leveled. He has captured my eyes, my heart and my body. I can't move away. I don't want to. I want to be closer. But I am not brave enough to move.

Laughter comes from the house, muffled by the glass and wood but loud enough to disrupt the serenity of the moment. Jake leans away, the grin I love appearing on his face.

I let out my breath. My heart continues its marathon.

He doesn't continue what he was going to say. And I don't know whether I want to find out what was and probably still is on his mind, even though part of me is still aching for him to continue.

We hold each other's gaze for a long moment; our faces still irresistibly close. I have an urge to close the distance between us. And I realize that my gaze had drifted from his eyes to his lips. I look away as soon as my brain realizes what I am doing. But Jake doesn't look away, he leans closer and I feel his forehead press against my temple. My breathing becomes uneven as I feel his mouth near my ear, his whispers tickling my skin with each word.

"I know you don't realize it, but you are something special," He whispers, his lips leaving the shadow of a kiss against my ear. "Even though I've only known you for a couple of days, I feel like I'm worth something when I'm around you. Like every vein in my body is burning with fire every moment I'm with you."

And suddenly, it is like MY veins are on fire. I can't move, but I feel like leaping into the air. The electrical current running between us is stronger than ever. The only problem is that I have no idea what to do. But as all that passes through my mind, a deeper part of me is doubtful. Why would Jake like me? I'm not anything amazing. I am a damaged mess with issues that can't be easily fixed. God... I haven't even smiled for most of the past two years. I am nothing special, not in the way that he means. But, he makes me feel differently.

Jake leans away; he probably senses my conflict between desire and reservations. I feel a pang of pain when I no longer feel his breath on my skin, but at the same time, I feel unwelcome relief.

I don't want to hurt him by not answering, and I can't speak for fear of saying something wrong. So I just lean closer to him, placing my head on his chest: Listening to his heartbeat. He strokes my hair with smooth and tender motions. My chest expands with an emotion I've never felt before and I am content to just stay there.

But nothing lasts forever, especially good things. So I savor the moment while it lasts.

5

(1 day to my birthday)

I lie in bed, enjoying my soft haven of pillows and quilts. I am warm in my fort of blankets and feel too lazy to get up. I keep my eyes shut, replaying the events of last night in my head. It seems like a dream, too perfect to be real. Jake and I are closer than ever; I've almost got his face memorized. I feel myself smile just thinking about him, and an aching in my chest appears because he is not here with me.

Nothing intimate happened between us. Well, at least not by modern standards. But the closeness between us is more than I've ever experienced with anyone else. All of this is new to me. After all, I'm only fifteen. Still.

After staying still for what feels like forever, I decide to get up. Nothing is planned for me today so after I have my bath I wear loose grey track pants and a black tank top. This is what I usually wear when I am being lazy and going around my house dancing and singing. I put my hair up in a messy bun away from my face and put on my 'hip hop' shoes. I am just going to slack off today and save my energy for the big day tomorrow.

One day till I turn sixteen!

I can feel in my heart that things are in motion. I'm not sure what to make of that feeling, but I sense something gathering: a powerful force waiting to be unleashed the moment I turn sixteen years of age.

I head downstairs. My soft steps haven't slacked off like the rest of me, and I still have my senses about me. The house is quiet. Gran and Gramps must have gone to the nearest town for groceries, so I just get myself a bowl of cereal and eat breakfast quickly.

I look out the window; the clouds are grey in the sky, covering the sun. I can feel the emptiness in the woods, as animals get ready for the coming storm. Hmm… I step out onto the porch, inspecting my surroundings. It is too quiet. The house, which is usually warm and welcoming, feels empty and deserted.

I shudder and rub the bare skin on my arms with my hand, goosebumps appearing. It isn't cold yet, but I am pretty sure that this storm is going to be bad. I go back into the house and shut the door.

The sky darkens rapidly and I hear the rain pattering against the roof. The storm starts, first as a light drizzle then gets heavier. The winds begin to howl and the trees sway furiously.

Gran and Gramps won't be able to drive in this. I hope they realize that point and stay safe themselves instead of coming home because they are worried about me. Part of me wants them to come home, so that I would have someone by my side for comfort. But I push the thoughts away as soon as they come.

Why should I be afraid of a storm? It's just a storm.

But as thunder booms and lightning cracks the sky, my will power fades. I'm not afraid of a lot of things, but storms scare me. It is like an angry child that you can't tame, and you just have to let it run its course until it's all worn out. Storms are unpredictable and not knowing the outcome of an event scares me.

As I stare out the window, I remember not knowing whether dad would come back, whether he was alive or dead. I remember not knowing whether I could save that man and his little girl. If I could go back to that moment, would I have saved him and not myself? I keep telling myself I would have tried harder to save him. I'm not so sure. Not knowing what I would do differently is what scares me.

The storm carries on. I'm not afraid of the storm itself, because it is natural and part of the earth, and it's innocent and not evil. That's what I know.

As my fear melts away, I start to see the beauty behind the organized chaos of the vicious winds and angry bullets of rain. So instead of worrying about the unknown, I focus on the little things about the storm to help calm myself down. Lightning flashes and I see the woods light up briefly. The leaves look white in the electrical light and the texture on the leaves is visible. Thunder booms and I listen as the sound echoes off the mountains around me; like nature making its own drumbeat.

I close my eyes and think about the following day. Immediately, I feel the unknown force again. With the storm covering whatever energy might have been outside, I realize that most of the force is dwelling inside of me. I press my lips together while trying to figure out what this feeling is.

It is like I am a butterfly, wrapped and trapped in a cocoon, getting stronger by each day, and finally, when the time is right, I will emerge and spread my wings. But it is not a feeling I understand, and I am not a butterfly, so I bet that when I do break free of my cocoon, it won't be pretty and definitely won't be as easy. Nothing is. If it's easy, it's not often right, not true. Not sincere.

My eyes open as I hear the storm die down. The howling winds turn into soft whispers and the thunder and lightning cease. I have no idea how long I've sat on the couch watching the storm. But as the rain turns into soft pitter-patters against the windows, I drift to sleep, the smell of wet clean air in my lungs.

■ ■ ■

I honestly didn't think it was possible, but the air and sky looks and feels cleaner here in the countryside than ever before, shining with the last drops of rain. That is my first thought when I step out the door onto the lawn the moment the rain had stopped completely.

There is dew on the wet grass, droplets of water roll off leaves and plunge down from the trees. The warm sun is just coming out from behind the clouds, startling me with its warmth. It makes everything so much brighter. As the rays of sunlight reflect off little droplets of mist, a small barely visible rainbow forms in the air. The colors are beautiful, forming an arc from one end of the sky to the other. I continue to stare and reach out my hand as if to touch it. My arm just goes through space.

I lift my face towards the source of warmth, close my eyes and smile. It feels good. I can smell the air. It is clean. My lungs sigh with contentment. A soft breeze whispers past me, whisking my hair and making it dance. I spin in circles with my arms outstretched; face still up towards the sky, eyes still closed. A laugh escapes my lips as I twirl around myself. Sometimes being alone is good. Sometimes, when there's no one around, you don't have to feel pressure, or responsibility, or even weakness. Being alone, alone with nature, has crumbled the walls that I have built these last two years to dust. Every moment I spend here seems to change me and make me more like myself: the fun loving, caring, tough-natured girl that my father brought up. She had disappeared with my father two years ago. But now she's back. And Dad is here, all around me, within me, in my heart. And being back here, where he grew up, has made me grasp the fact that he never left.

A tremendous weight lifts off my shoulders and I jump with new lightness. I can almost see dad giving me an approving smile, beckoning me forward to see what other new discoveries I can make about myself, and about those I love. And somehow, in that moment, I know that he is still alive.

■ ■ ■

I take an apple from the kitchen and munch on it on the way up to my room. My stomach isn't complaining so I skip lunch. I turn on my laptop, open up ITunes and play my dance album. Then I turn the volume as loud as it can get and dance around my room to my favorite tracks of music. Yes, I know I'm weird. I make random dance moves to the music. Any type of dance: Ballet, contemporary, hip-hop (though I'm not very good at it), lyrical, and just crazy dancing. When I move, I know my body and my body knows my soul. And for a short period of time, my mind and heart are released from their cage of worries. It makes me feel more relaxed and released;

it makes me feel like I have no reins and no chains. It makes me feel free.

I dance around for fun at first, bobbing my head from side to side, taking occasional bites of my apple, and making stepping spins with my arms going up around me.

My friend, Josh, had once caught me dancing like that in my room when he came by to say hello. Oh my, I don't think my face has ever been redder! I smirk at the memory; I am one strange person.

Jakes' words come back to me from the night before. *"You are something special"*

I stop twirling, the wheels in my head spin as I think about what Jake had said. Though I do not believe his compliment, a hidden part of me doesn't want to be just strange or normal… I really do want to be special. I want to make a difference somehow. I don't care if it's a small difference; I just want to do something that helps people. Somehow.

I throw the core of my apple into the trashcan and start dancing for real. Putting all my passion into my moves, letting them flow with grace and force. I do love dancing.

After an hour of dancing I hear the front door open and close. I mute my music quickly and open my door. My body is damp with perspiration from the small workout.

"Gran? Gramps?" I call down the stairs. No reply. I call again. Nothing.

Cold sweat starts to break on my forehead. Who is there?

I creep past Gran and Gramps room and look in.

Empty.

Well, I'm not going to go downstairs while an unknown person lurks in my living room. I search through Gramps' stuff, looking for a gun, or whatever I will be able to use to defend myself. But I don't know how to use a gun... well; perhaps I'll get lucky. But I don't want to hurt anyone either.

I find a Swiss army knife instead. That's better than nothing. I take out the blade section, hold it before me and walk down the stairs.

My footsteps are silent, and my breathing is even, to my surprise. I may look calm on the outside, but my heart races with fear.

I get to the bottom step and look around a corner, holding the knife before me, its blade ready to dig into whatever might harm me.

I don't hear or notice when someone comes up behind me. I let out a soft shriek when warm hands take hold of my waist from behind.

I probably should have held onto my knife, but instead, I drop it.

I jump and let out a little yelp. My heart threatens to fly out of my chest. I probably would have bit into the hand of my attacker if he hadn't spoken.

"Jeez Veronica, calm down…." Pause. "Were you going to stab me?"

I sigh with relief as I recognize Jakes' voice. Oh My God, that ass! He scared me to death! I was about to stab him!

I spin around and shove him away lightly, but he doesn't budge. I think he can sense my shock because Jake supports most of my weight and leads me over to the sofa, not letting me out of his arms. Cradling me against his chest like I was a baby. I hide my face in the curve of his neck.

"Veronica? Are you okay? I'm sorry I scared you." Jakes' voice sounds worried, and I realize that I'm trembling.

I exhale, making sure that my voice won't be shaky when I reply.

"Yes, I'm fine. You jerk! You frightened me!" I glare up at him. "I could have hurt you! I was armed!"

He chuckles at my expression. Jake is not the type to be fearful of a knife.

But behind the adrenaline rush and fear, I feel the happiness of him being here with me. I am in sloppy clothes, my hair a mess, and my face is bare of make up; but I don't care. He is here, and I'm not alone anymore.

I am very aware of his arms around me. I feel like he's my shield, my protector. My heart rate slows immediately. I am safe with Jake.

6

(my birthday)

I wake up early on the morning of my birthday.

The sun is not yet up. Silver moonlight shines through the cracks of my curtains. I feel a tugging in my gut, dragging me up.

I sit up on my bed and blink. I'll be sixteen today!

I get up and decide to wear one of the nicest dresses I own; I have no idea what is going to happen today, but I feel like whatever it is, it is going to be big.

The dress flows down to my ankles; the fabric as soft as silk, as free as the river. The dress twirls around me whenever

I turn or spin. I decide to leave my face free of make up; I like it better this way. It is more natural. More pure.

I have no idea why I am dressing up for my birthday, but it seems appropriate; as if my soul knows something important is going to happen.

I tiptoe down the stairs, not wanting to disturb the house. It wouldn't make a difference anyways; my footsteps are always silent. I still don't know why. Sometimes I wonder what's wrong with me, but other times I'm just grateful. I grab a glass of water and look out the window, taking small sips from my cup.

As I stare out the window, the tugging sensation in my gut grows stronger. I can almost see a pathway of light that leads me into the forest. I open the door slowly. I'm not scared, but I am very cautious. Wild animals could be up and around at this time. My feet take the first step out the door, and suddenly I can't go any slower. I run across the front lawn and into the trees, floating across the grass.

I reach the clearing of the meadow and stop in the middle. It is the most magical and extraordinary thing that I've ever seen. Dawn is just breaking, so the soft sunlight seems to make the meadow glow. Fireflies are still out and butterflies are all around. It is so peaceful and beautiful. I lie down on the soft bed of grass just as I had two days before and close my eyes. I love this place. My skin illuminates gently as the soft morning sunlight touches it, making it glow along with the meadow. My cream-colored dress fans out around me like a shield.

Suddenly, the forest stills. It's like all the animals have gone to hide, and the trees gone to sleep. The sun light dims, and the air turns cold. I sense something dark and unwelcome approaching. I look around as I sit up. What could be so wicked and cold that nature itself is frightened?

Some sort of darkness is polluting the innocent forest and turning joy into fear. I can almost feel the life seeping out of the meadow. What is this? Anger seeps into my veins like poison as this darkness forces the creatures away. I push away the feeling; anger and hate are not emotions I want to feel; they make people irrational and stupid.

"What are you?" I ask the emptiness. My voice, strangely enough, sounds calm and collected. I have no idea why I am talking into space, but I know that somehow, I am not alone. All I am sure of is that this someone, or something, is watching my every move. And all I want is for it to go away.

Just as the thought crosses my mind, the presence vanishes. No proof, no evidence is left to show that the meadow was ever defiled by the strange darkness. The trees awaken and the forest comes back to life.

Weird... I wonder if I had imagined it all.

I lie back down on the grass, a little more alert than before. My senses sharpen, as I will my mind to open. The smell of the forest is warm and moist. I can hear the birds cawing in the distance. I lie down, relaxing back into the bed of grass. I shut my eyes while taking in the warm sunlight

Crunch, snap.

My eyes fly open. What was that? I am on my feet in an instant. My gaze sweeps across the meadow, looking for signs of anything out of place.

I see a brown figure on four legs with a magnificent crown of horns emerging from the trees. I hold my breath. I don't want to scare it away.

It walks with steady pace towards me. So steady. So calm.

With a shock, I realize that I can sense its emotions. The glorious stag comes to a stop about an arms length in front of me. He's so close. Close enough to touch. I reach out my palm hesitantly, my fingers trembling with the feeling of amazement at what I am just about to do, of what I'm being allowed to do. I know that the stag will let me touch him, so I'm not afraid.

The tip of my fingers touches the stag's head, just above the eyes. It is staring at me with such intensity that I think that the stag can sense my emotion just like I can sense his.

My hand traces the velvet hide of the stag's neck. I am so absorbed with this amazing creature that I do not realize that animals from around the woods have come and gathered around the meadow. They are watching me with curious eyes.

I am in absolute awe.

Usually animals run away from people, but these creatures seem to be coming towards me. I don't understand. But I don't move either. My instinct tells me to wait. I hold my breath. Hold. Hold. Hold.

The stag dips its head, as if it's greeting me. I hear a whisper in my mind, so soft that I'm not sure whether it's my own thought or not.

"We have been waiting for you for a long time, little one."

I am at loss for words. The stag is staring at me and I know that it has spoken into my mind. For some reason, I don't question my sanity. I don't question whether or not this is real. It feels real. But I don't know how to reply; no words could ever be suitable for a moment like this.

So what escape my lips are simple words. Two simple questions that could never suffice for this moment, but that could soothe all the thoughts hammering inside my mind.

"What? Why?" I ask in a whisper as soft as the voice in my mind. Yes, I know, stupid questions.

"The World is darkening. It stands on a knife-edge between the light and falling into the dark. One heart may be the key to tilting the balance of the knife. One broken heart. Save the broken heart, and the world may have a chance to grow towards the light. Let the broken heart continue to crack, and the world will fall to the dark." The stag cocks its head to one side. *"And as for why it's you to receive this task, I don't have a clear answer. I just know you're special. You will pass darkness into the light. You will see them for what they truly are, and will judge them both equally. You are destined to this task."*

With every word I hear in my mind, I feel my jaw crashing towards the ground. I snap my mouth shut before I start speaking gibberish.

What is happening?

Yesterday I find out that I have a sixth sense that I absolutely don't understand. And today I am told that I am special, though I still don't believe it.

Sure, I am different and abnormal, but special? No. And what is this about me healing a broken heart? No… it was THE broken heart; whose? None of it makes sense. Insecurity washes through me. I can hardly manage myself; I have just recently picked myself up off the ground. And now I have to save someone?

Suddenly, and very unwillingly, a memory pops up in my brain from my early childhood, when nothing had gone wrong in my life, and when everything was perfect.

I was with my dad and mom by the beach. They were holding hands and walking while I ran ahead picking seashells.

"Look Mama! I found a white one! It's for you and Dad!" I ran up to my mom, she opened her arms for me just as I went into them. Dad hugged us both. "You will be the best releaser anyone could ask for." He whispered into my ear. "Love more, and hate less. Use what you've got wisely." Dad had kissed my hair before Mom let me down. We walked and laughed down the beach, a happy family.

I, of course, had no idea what he was talking about at that time. But now, it was starting to make some sense. And if my dad believed in me, that's all that matters, even if I don't believe in myself.

The memory fades.

Heal a broken heart. Heal a broken heart. Heal a broken heart. Those words repeat in my brain. Uncle Tom and the stag had said those words… They had said that I have to cure a broken heart. I try to make sense of that. But how could I do that? How how how. I'm not ready for this. Not capable of it. I'm not strong enough. I'm just a teenage girl for crying out loud!

I am brought back into reality when I feel something brush my shoulder.

I look up; the stag has bumped its head against my arm. I hear his voice in my head once more.

"Today is the day of your blooming. Sixteen is the age when you come to your powers. You must learn to use them properly. Use them wisely. With great power, comes great responsibility."

I process this with difficulty. I think I remember Aunt Alicia whispering something about my blooming in three days to Uncle Tom that first night they visited while I was singing. I had dismissed it then. Now I wished I had paid more attention. I'm not ready, at least not now. And I have absolutely no idea what to do. I am only human. I want to help… But this? This is so much bigger than anything I've ever imagined. I don't know what to do.

"Who knows?" I question, already having guessed the answer. I just want to be sure.

"Your Grandparents know, the Blanchards know, and your mom and dad know. They are all behind you if ever you shall fall." The stag's brown eyes shine with kindness. *"There are many who will aid you, whether they know or don't know who you truly are. Trust is essential. You must place it in the right people."* The little animals around the meadow are starting to thin, all of them making their way back to their homes. *"Many will guide you. Find the heart to make*

whole again, and with that, love will grow more in the world. Do not be afraid, dear child. Do not give into your anxiety. Stay strong. Good luck, little one, beautiful Roza."

I watch as the stag walks away from me with swift flowing movements. I know that he is telling the truth. This is the truth. This is my destiny. But I don't know whether I'll be able to live up to it.

■ ■ ■

I walk through the front door in a daze. It is around seven in the morning, so I still have till noon before Jake and his parents arrive to celebrate my birthday. I have five hours to make sense of what had happened in the meadow. Five hours to decide whether or not it was real or whether I imagined it. It feels like a dream to me now.

I climb silently up the stairs to my room. Once in, I shut the door. Beams of sunlight stream through the windows, highlighting dust particles as they swirl around me. Thanks to my heightened senses, I can see each and every one of the particles, but only when I focus very hard.

Am I going crazy and seeing things...? Wouldn't be the first time. Or is this actually happening? I fight the bubble of fear that is expanding in my chest. I don't want to question Gran or Gramps for fear that this isn't real and that they will make me see a doctor, like last time. So I plan to ask

Jake about it since it seemed like he and his parents knew a couple of things about this yesterday. Suddenly all the mysterious comments that his family had made are starting to make sense. Jake is going to tell me everything he knows. He has to. I will make him.

I gaze out the windows, my eyes sweeping the front lawn. I can almost feel the animals secretly watching me.

My eyes rest on a tire swing, which is tied to a tree branch. That tire should have a single name carved into the rubber. Alec. That name is Greek and means 'the protector and helper of mankind'. It is my fathers' name. I always believed that he was, and still is, my protector. The name suits him well.

As I think about Dad, I realize that he knew about who I really was, and what I am supposed to do. Could that be why his name was Alec? The name Alec means the protector and helper of mankind. Was it by chance, or was the reason he was named Alec because he had to protect me while I grew up? I don't know… I have no answer for that. But after the last three days, I am starting to believe that anything is possible.

I hear someone walking up the stairs, and across the hall. I am so confused about all the things that have been happening. But I am also exhilarated. The ability to hear so much clearer is amazing. But it's unhinging… I don't know if I can act normally around anyone right now. Not until I can get myself in order. I am not used to this. It makes me feel unstable.

The footsteps stop in front of my door, the handle turns. My bedroom door creaks open and Gran's face appears.

"Good Morning, Honey! Happy Birthday! Would you like breakfast now?" She asks pleasantly.

I clear my thoughts, trying to focus on the present for now. These strange occurrences seem like something out of this world. I have to focus on earth.

"Yes please Grandma." I smile. "I could make it myself, no need to trouble you."

"Oh please darling, I always love making breakfast for you. Especially on your special day." She winks, and in that moment, I realize that she knows that I have found out the truth. The sparkle in her eyes shows that she is proud to be my Grandmother.

Something in my chest expands rapidly and reaches my throat. My eyes feel moist; I'm getting a little too emotional. I blink the tears away before they escape. Gran's eyes turn a little sad, and I feel worry seeping through her veins. She must be happy that I found out that I'm 'special', but she's probably also scared of how much it will cost me. I'm scared of that too; but I try not to think about it.

I look over at the clock; it's almost nine.

"Sure Gran, I'd like to eat more of your delicious food."

I follow her down the stairs; her footfalls making soft thumps while mine make no sound. I almost wish that I could hear myself.

But at least now I have a reason for all my quirkiness and difference. I am able to feel other people's emotions. My senses are sharpened and I can react more quickly; my reflexes are now faster than usual. I always thought this was normal, and now I am sure it is not. I am different. And I was born to bring darkness into light. To help take away some darkness by this one task. It is important. It may determine whether the world falls into darkness or light. I will do this, whatever it costs me. It is too important; it is worth any sacrifice.

I feel the certainty of my statement go through my body, giving me strength enough to continue.

7

Serenity fills the depths of my heart, pouring through my veins like warm honey. I feel my mind clearing. The shock and fear are still there, but I'm getting used to it.

I know what I have to do.

But knowing what to do and actually doing it are entirely different things.

Jake and his parents walk through the door, making me forget about my fear. My heart does a little leap in my chest as Jake picks me up and swings me in circles, wishing me a happy birthday. Laughter bubbles from my throat and all I see are his eyes. But the corner of my subconscious focuses on my Grandparents and his parents. Gran is talking with the Blanchards, and from their hushed whispers, I can guess what it is about. Gran is telling them that I've found out. She is telling them that I know everything now. Well, not everything...

I look back at Jake, and see him scrutinizing me. I can tell that he notices the difference in my face. I noticed it as well when I looked in the mirror. My face and skin still holds the glow and radiance from the meadow, and my eyes are bright and shining with life. So even though part of me feels frightened, the other part feels awake and extraordinary. I prefer the positive feeling, so I try to push away the negative while Jake is here. It works, but only to an extent. Because I can still feel the fear trying to break through the barrier I had built to protect my mind.

But I know that he sees through my walls because his expression changes from excitement to one of anxiety; I feel his worry. He sees my fear, and probably knows the reason behind it. His eyes soften as they look into mine and I immediately feel better, my fear temporarily forgotten. I will question him later; when we are alone. And he is going to answer; he has to. I need him to. But for now, I feel the security and comfort that I always feel when I'm with him. With him with me, nothing can hurt me; I feel myself calm further. A smile spreads from my lips and reaches my eyes. I feel his relief.

"Later," Jake whispers into my ear as we turn back to our families.

"Promise?" I ask back. My voice is quiet and shaky. I clear my throat, embarrassed.

Jake turns me to face him; his blue eyes look into mine with clarity and conviction. He isn't in his normal joking mood, but I like him both ways. He knows something has happened. He knows that something needs to be done, that it is important and has to be taken seriously.

"Promise," He replies. I can see it in his eyes. He will keep his promise.

Jake smiles at me reassuringly. I feel his emotions pulsing out from him: anxiousness, happiness, fear, calmness and love. Or are those my emotions? And what does that love mean? Because I know what loving family feels like, and I know what loving friends feels like. But what I feel for Jake? Well… it is different; and I do not recognize it. Butterflies swim inside me and I don't know what it means. What are my feelings for Jake?

Whatever goes through my head should stay there. I push the thoughts away and focus on reality. I smile back at Jake, my mouth curving into a huge grin. I am happy he is here. He seems to take my fear away; he spreads warmth through my body just by smiling.

We turn our attention back to the rest of the family and start talking about the activities of the day. My worries are temporarily forgotten.

■ ■ ■

After a few hours of horse riding, cake baking and laughter, we finally sit down for dinner. Gran made lasagna for my birthday dinner treat, and all of us had helped with the cake one way or another. We are all exhausted, our stomachs aching from so much laughter.

Now I sit down on my chair, with the hem of my dress reaching the floor and shimmering against the red embroidered carpet. I stare at the food, hungry; I want to start eating, but I know I have to wait for everyone else to get settled. Gran is the only one not at the table so I get up and walk to the kitchen, planning to offer my help.

I feel Jake's eyes on me as I make my way out of the dining room, burning holes into my soul. Permanently etching my form, my self, into his mind. His gaze makes my back tingle. I feel lightheaded. I have an urge to turn around and look into his eyes, but I fight it off.

My footsteps are silent as ever but I seem to have trouble making my legs move forward; I feel like I'm about to fall. Then I realize that it is not Jake's stare that's making me feel faint. It is something else, staring at me from afar. I realize that I actually do feel light headed; something is probing my mind, like it's trying to invade my soul and tear it apart.

My head spins around and around and I want it to stay still.

But it doesn't. It doesn't.

Instead

It starts to burn.

My legs give way and I collapse.

My mind isn't aware of much after I fall; I'm too busy resisting the pain that seems to go through my whole body. I hear chairs screeching and alarmed voices. I vaguely feel my cheek pressed against the hard wooden floor. Hands wrap around my waist and pull me closer to something soft and warm. I smell mint, sweet cologne, and lavender. I know who is holding me, and yet, I can't think about that, I'm too busy thinking about the agony inside of me. I feel my blood turn cold and the light going out of me. It reminds me of what happened at the meadow, and how the dark presence seemed to invade its serenity. Something clicks in my brain behind all the pain and I realize that I recognize this. It IS the exact same feeling, the exact same coldness that I had in the meadow; only now it is more concentrated. It is concentrated on me. I feel like writhing in pain, but I can't, or my family will be worried. I feel like screaming, but I know that my screams would pierce their hearts. So I don't.

They can't help me. They can't. So I just endure this alone.

Better to not let them feel what I'm feeling. So I just lie still and motionless, muscles and teeth clenched through the blinding pain.

Out of the darkness comes a voice, a voice so chilling and malevolent that it can only belong to the one who is torturing me.

"So weak." The voice laughs. The voice belongs to a male, it sounds young. The laughter is deep and grating and unpleasant. It is as if each cackle is fingernails and knifes scraping against my skin. I can feel myself falling, getting lost in the darkness. I sink deep into the depths of my own mind, my skin getting as cold as nothingness.

I slip.

I'm drifting towards oblivion when something soft and warm presses against my cold forehead and I feel cool breaths against my face. The breath clears my mind enough for me to hear a soft voice.

"Come back to me," I hear Jake whisper against my mouth; His lips gently brushing but not quite touching mine. But it is enough. His voice brings me back to myself. I am no longer lost in the darkness, I am no longer drowning, but I'm floating. My

will becomes strong again and I feel the anger of the dark presence; I hear him growl. Then something ignites in my heart and rage churns deep in me; something that I've never felt before. It is a horrible feeling, but it gives me vigor and power. I can sense the presence right outside the house, and with all my might, I force it away. I feel his surprise at my strength and his unforgiving wrath. His voice speaks in my mind once more.

"You have not escaped. I will see you soon. Next time, you will not be so lucky." The evil voice shakes with fury.

I shiver with fear, but answer back resolutely.

"We'll see about that." My mind's voice does not shake, and I am satisfied to sound so much braver than I feel.

The presence vanishes altogether, just like it had in the meadow.

I groan and my eyelids flutter open.

"Oh, thank God," I hear someone say, the voice sounds like Gramps. I raise my head and look over to see Gramps and Gran clutching each other on the carpet, not too far away from Jake and I. Jake's parents are also there, their hands are clenched tightly on Jakes shoulder as if they didn't want him to be dragged away by something. It looks like it hurts. I squint at their white hands; puzzled.

My air supply is suddenly cut off when Jake gathers me in his arms more tightly and closer to his body. I feel his breath down my neck and tremble.

"You saved me," I say in a soft whisper to Jake. Tears of relief spill down my cheeks before I can stop them. Jake pulls away and puts his hand on my cheek; he wipes away my tears. His eyes kiss my heart with their softness.

"He will never hurt you like that again," Jake says in a firm strong voice. His mouth is set in a thin line as he adds, "I won't let him, or anyone else." His eyes blaze.

I don't like this… Jake said *he*? As in, a male? Does he know the person behind that voice? And I don't want him to get hurt trying to protect me. I would rather feel that pain from the presence a thousand times over than for Jake or anyone else I love to get hurt helping me.

"I won't let you or anyone get hurt over me," I say back, though I can't help but feel warmed that he wants to protect me. I see his lips pull together, his eyes glint and I know that he is going to argue. So before he can start, I interrupt him.

"Thank you though, Jake… That was terrifying. I swear I was… dying; well, it felt like that." I can't quite catch the word 'dying' before it slips out of my mouth, I just didn't have any other word to describe what it felt like. When it came out, Gran and Gramps gasp. Aunt and Uncle Blanchard exchange worried and angry glances. Jake's eyes soften and I feel that his relief is almost as strong as mine.

"You are welcome... That must have been horrible, and on your birthday as well." His arms tighten around me protectively, as if what he said could have triggered some reaction.

"Yes," Uncle Tom suddenly said. "It does seem quite strange. Jake? Do you think Nicholas could know that she would bloom today?"

Jake's eyes had wandered over to his fathers as Tom started talking. Jake tenses at the name 'Nicholas'. I place my hand on his arm, and he immediately relaxes. Jake looks back at me and presses his forehead to mine; his breath is a little shaky as he breathes in and out. I feel fear, and anger course through him; he seems to be trying to calm himself down.

"Jake," I ask hesitantly. My voice still sounds weak. I'm not even cut out for this. How am I supposed to heal a heart? "Who's Nicholas? And my blooming, what's that? The deer said something about it but I still don't know what it is. Can you tell me?"

I sound like a child asking a question that she is afraid might sound stupid.

Jakes' eyes open as I am talking, our noses are almost touching, my eyes only a few centimeters away from his. He doesn't answer me; he just keeps staring into my eyes. His eyes seem to have darkened from their light blue. I'm drowning, drowning, drowning, consumed in him. I almost forget what I wanted to know, but someone answers me.

It is Aunt Alicia who answers my questions; well the first question.

"Nicholas…" Aunt Alicia seems to have difficulty getting the name out. "Is a lost soul. He was once my nephew; but a few years ago; darkness corrupted him. He became evil, around the same time that your dad went missing. We don't know what happened but we tried to help him." She draws in a shaky breath. "And over the last two years, Nick has been learning how to use his own gifts. For you see, Veronica, you are not the only child with special abilities. There are a few like you; mostly from family bloodlines from the ancient past, in our case with Greek backgrounds. Your family is special, though the abilities and so-called 'powers' can skip two or three generations. However, each of you kids with abilities has something special of your own. Your abilities are always different, except for the increased senses and faster and better reflexes.

"You, Rose, can move with great agility and sense when things are going to happen. Perhaps you can do something else that is not so obvious or easy to spot. Jake can bend people to his will, though that only works on some. Nicholas is much more dangerous for he can bring pain and crush your will instead of bending it. And from what I can see, Nick's presence brings coldness and darkness and it follows him like a magnet. You can't find Nicholas unless he wants to be found, and those who try… well, things don't work out so well for them." She pauses, letting me absorb the information.

Jake is like me, we are different, abnormal, and capable of strange things. But so is this Nicholas guy. And one thought forms in my mind. One thought so repellent and horrible that I want to push it away, but I can't, because it also brings hope. **What if Nicholas has my dad?**

Aunt Alicia continues, her voice thoughtful.

"And it seems that all three of you have your five senses, sight, hearing, touch, taste, and smell heightened."

I nod; I know that.

"I can also sense emotions," The words make their way out of my mouth before I even have time to think it through.

"Really?" Aunt Alicia asks, her eyes wide.

I nod.

"Can you influence emotions?" Gran speaks for the first time. Her eyes are on me and they look at me like I am the elder one now. I don't want that, I want Gran to be the one taking care of me. But I know that now, it is going to go both ways. She has my respect, though I think I haven't yet earned hers enough to be given that look.

"I've never tried... I was always too scared. I didn't know what was happening to me." My voice quivers, showing my insecurity at last.

Jake hugs me tighter.

"Whatever you can or cannot do," He whispers in my ear. "You'll always be amazing to me, and I'll always help you and be there for you."

I turn to look at him; my throat suddenly tightens, I can't reply. But I hope that my eyes show all the things that I want to say, and all the feelings I want to show him. They do. His eyes lighten with understanding and protectiveness. They always hold love, but I don't know what kind.

"And about the blooming..." Gramps starts.

Bad Idea. As soon as the words come out of Gramps's mouth, I am no longer part of my body. My soul is floating over their heads. I see my head slump against Jake's shoulder. He is shaking me, gently at first, then harshly and panicky. His eyes turn wild, showing the pain inside. Gran and Gramps move closer to my body, they touch my chest, looking for a heartbeat; but I know nothing is there. How can it be when my soul, me, is above and watching them? My soul aches at the pain I see in Jake and my grandparent's faces, and at the loss painted across their faces. Grief starts to cover me like a blanket, suffocating me.

I can't watch my family go through this; I have to get back, I cannot die. I need to live for their sakes.

But this doesn't feel like dying.

What is happening?

Aunt Alicia and Uncle Tom do not look panicked. They seem to be expecting something; they seem to be waiting. Watching them calms me down; the Blanchards know what is going on. They are watching my body; observing. Then I see it: a small mark appears on the right side of my neck, and another on my left wrist. Pain flares through my ghost self and I look down and see the source. On my wrist, just as it appeared on my physical body in front of me, is a carving of a rose. It is like a tattoo pierced onto my skin; except it looks and feels like a burn mark, it's been scorched onto me. The mark is just the rose flower with a thorned-stem and a leaf. And next to it is a tiny yin-yang sign. I feel a burning pain on my neck and guess that something has appeared there as well. Then in the same second, the pain ends, and I am dragged back into my body.

I sit bolt upright gasping for air. This is just too much. I was just a ghost. Now I'm not. Did I die and come back to life? No. Way.

My hand lifts up, I see the burnt mark on my wrist: A red rose and yin-yang. I reach to the side of my neck and feel the sign; I can't make out what it is. Then I realize that Jake is staring at me in shock. The Blanchards are smiling; whatever they were waiting for has just happened. Relief radiates from them.

I look at Jake; he is staring at my neck, at my wrist, at my face, and into my eyes. I reach up to touch his face. His eyes close and he covers his hand over mine. I smile up at him, because I know what's happened. I feel different, out of place. But I also feel awake and *strong*.

I have bloomed.

8

Five minutes pass and I can already feel a big difference. However much my senses had heightened before my blooming has increased another ten-fold. It seems that I can move even faster, with more strength and agility than before and still be silent. My ability to read emotions remains the same but for some reason I sense that I will be able to influence them as well. This idea doesn't scare me as much anymore. I've come to expect the strange and to accept it as it hits me. That is the only way that I'll keep from going crazy.

The room is silent except for everyone's quiet breathing.

"Why is everyone so quiet?" I ask. Even my voice sounds different, clearer. "I think I've bloomed right? What do these marks mean? Do you have one Jake? How come I feel so much more aware now?" I pause to catch my breath, and decide to add. "And why is everyone just staring at me like I'm some weird alien?"

Because they are, they just keep on staring at me. I start to feel self-conscious and pull at a lock of my hair. Jake practically explodes with laughter. I feel it vibrating through his chest. Since I am still on his lap, I try to move off because I'm afraid I'm heavy, but Jake just pulls me closer to him. His body is still shaking with suppressed energy. Everyone cracks a smile, including me. I prefer this Jake, the Jake that's not in pain but happy, especially because of me.

"Now what's so funny?" I ask, raising both eyebrows. I still can't do the cool one eyebrow thing that Jake does.

"You!" He chuckles again. "You're so full of questions, and are bursting with energy. It's strange because you kind of just died and came back to life with two new inks to show for it. But they kind of look more like burn marks."

Then his expression turns serious; he reaches up and strokes my cheek. The blue of his eyes burn, melting my insides and warming me up the longer I look into them.

"I thought you left me…" His voice cracks. Jake looks down.

"Never," I reply. I force him to meet my eyes. "I will never leave you." I face my family. "I will never leave any of you."

Jake smiles at me, and stands up with me still in his arms. He carries me like I weigh nothing. He walks over to the couches and settles down on one of them, with me still on his lap. Gran, Gramps, Aunt Alicia and Uncle Tom follow his lead. They are all still staring at me in amazement.

"Now," Jake starts. "Yes, you have bloomed. The marks on the skin are symbols that represent what's on the inside. So roses usually symbolize love and beauty, and heaven and harmony in the world. Which could mean that you will bring love, light, beauty, and harmony wherever you go." He smiles at me knowingly, and smugly adds, "I knew it." Making me flush.

"As for the yin-yang sign," He murmurs. "That's a very Chinese oriented symbol. But since you are half Chinese, it makes sense. But the meaning… It's interesting. It basically symbolizes the dark and the light uniting and that's why they sort of join and curve together. They are opposites, but they cannot survive without each other. So maybe that means that you can unite the dark and light?" He shakes his head. "The meanings to the symbols that we get are never clear and this one is even more confusing."

I just stare at him. After a moment, I realize that my jaw has dropped. I snap it shut.

Jake winks as I roll my eyes. Even though I do believe him, I don't exactly understand. How do I bring all the things that he had said to the world when I don't have any of that to begin with? How can I love enough? How can I bring beauty when I don't know how to create any or spread it? How can I bring harmony and heaven's grace when no one will possibly listen to me? And what is this about dark and light uniting and being unable to survive without each other?

"Well, I don't possess any of those traits…" I mutter, suddenly feeling very disheartened. "I have no idea what the yin-yang thingy means and I don't have beauty, harmony or heaven."

How could I?

Jake shakes his head, a secret smile playing on his lips.

"Veronica, when will you ever see yourself clearly?" His eyes twinkle like stars, and for an instant, I see myself through them. It's nothing like how I see myself and I'm grateful and a little bewildered that someone sees me in the way that Jake does. For through his eyes, I shine.

"And as for me having one, yes I do." Jake says as he lifts up his shirt to reveal the side of his body. When I manage to focus enough, and not look at the layers of muscle on his abdomen, I see what he is trying to show me. On the skin of his ribcage, is a burn, a tattoo; the mark is of a bear.

"What does that symbolize?" I ask, it's interesting, and I am curious. My fingers reach to trace the bear on his skin.

"It symbolizes many things. But the main ones are: Healing, Natural strength, Creature of dreams, wisdom, transformation, and death and resurrection." He replies in a soft murmur.

"You are the amazing one Jake," I say to him, wink and giggle. He smiles back at me, his features softening with emotion.

A thought occurs to me and my fingers reach the spot of my second marking on my neck.

"Jake, I have two... What's this one?" And I show him the mark.

"It's a dove..." He whispers. His eyes find mine; I see fascination in them. He continues his explanation under my expectant stare. "Erm, Doves represent peace, love, spirit messengers, Feminine Energies, and prophesy. You have very strong symbols... Doves and Roses both have love, beauty, harmony, peace and strength. And maybe the yin-yang symbols mean that the energy you have will be used to the purpose of uniting opposite sides and bring the balance to the world. After all, one cannot survive without the other." His voice is like a chant. It makes me want to fall all over him.

The room is hushed as everyone listens to Jake as he gives me an explanation of all of this. But he still hasn't answered the most important question, the questions about the further enhancement of my abilities.

But before I can open my mouth to ask, he is already speaking, telling me what I want to know, but not what I want to hear.

"Your ability enhancement seems to be a sign of your strength, and the sign that you're the one we have been waiting for. You can capture darkness and carry it to light or release it. And there are many people like us, with special abilities out there, and I've met some of them. But never have I met anyone with as much potency as you, and never has anyone been given more than one mark. Perhaps with two sides of you, you'll become one, and stronger than the sum of both. The markings will turn invisible if you wish them to."

I think about it; I don't like tattoos. I will my markings to go away, and they fade a little bit, but they are still visible, looking like a darker shade of brown against my skin. It looks like someone drew on my arm with the Indian henna; I decide that it looks okay like that. It isn't too bad.

Without warning, pain flares on my hipbone, and I curl up in a ball, trying to get as small as possible. But this pain isn't the same as the mind-splitting pain in my head caused by Nicholas. This is the burning sensation that I felt when the markings appeared. The pain ebbs away and I uncurl myself and unzip my dress just enough to reveal the burning area, avoiding the worried looks that Jake and everyone else is giving me. Because my attention is focused on the new marking that has appeared on my hip. Dread fills me as I recognize the shape of the animal that will now forever be etched on my skin.

"A crow..." I whisper as Jake leans in to study the new marking.

"Another mark?" He whispers in astonishment and confusion, looking at me in a way that I can never fathom. Still lost in thought, he continues. "Crows... They are Carrier of souls from Darkness into light, trickery, boldness, skill, cunning, eloquence, and working without fear in darkness..." For once, shock fills his features completely. Then worry makes it's journey across his face. "It is both good and bad. Unpredictable." He looks like he wants to say more, but he doesn't, as if he is afraid to scare me.

I know why: Because unlike most good heroes, I have a dark side. Unlike others like me, I have three markings while they only have one. Unlike most people, I'm ruled by more than one clear ethic. And unlike my own self, my crow self is not afraid of the darkness.

■ ■ ■

We finish eating the cake we made. While munching on the delicious chocolates, all my worries are temporally forgotten.

And as I have time to digest all that Jake, the Blanchards and my family had told me, my fear ebbs away. What replaces it is a confidence that I have never felt before. This confidence isn't one of snobby quality, it is the type of confidence that you get when you have a goal that you want to reach, and you'll do almost anything to achieve it. For me, my immediate goal is to take care of this Nicholas guy. He is bringing pain and sorrow to many people, and I have to stop him. I don't want to hurt him, but perhaps it's his heart that I have to heal as well.

I see Jake look at me curiously when my head bobs. He doesn't know that I'm thinking to myself and nodding, so he must think it's something else.

"Are you tired Veronica?" Jake walks over to me and puts his hands on my waist, giving me support.

Heat rushes through me, beginning from where his hands touched, and spreads all over my body. There's fire, warm and hot everywhere. Though he doesn't touch my skin, I can feel the heat of his palms through my dress. He is so close. So close. My skin tingles with each breath. He smells nice.

"You smell nice," I say suddenly, the tone of my voice very matter-of-fact. I pause and add, "Have I ever told you that?"

"No," His eyes twinkle, and his dimples show as he smiles. "You haven't told me that. I'm happy that I do smell nice though. It makes me more attractive right?" He winks.

I can feel myself blushing; Jake is still holding my waist, and he's really still too close to me. My mind goes foggy and I can't think straight. I only see his eyes, they are startling and blue as always. His eyes are gentle as they hold mine. Jake appears to be thinking about something because his expression turns thoughtful. Then he seems to have made a decision because I feel nervousness, eagerness, confidence and excitement radiating from him. His eyes do not betray his feelings, but I can sense them. And those feelings send a rush through me. My heart beats faster. It's racing, leaping and jumping, and yet, nothing is happening.

"Wanna go to the roof?" Jake asks. His eyes are smothering mine with their deep blue flames.

"Sure," I answer breathlessly.

We are going to be alone on the roof. I am excited and nervous. Thoughts go through my mind as my feelings match his. What can he be thinking?

The door creaks as we push it open and walk out. Warm air blows past my face as the wind from outside whisks into the house. It is so inviting, I can't stay indoors any longer. I move out of the house like I'm being swept away. Jake follows me, and in no time, we are both on the roof.

The stars are not out yet as the sun is just setting. It is one of the most beautiful sights I have ever seen. The best birthday present that nature can give me: A beautiful sunrise from the meadow this morning and a remarkable sunset from the roof now. The orange and golden rays dance and play across the sky, highlighting both my and Jake's face and hair. The warmth of the setting sun spreads across my body.

I feel Jake touch my fingertips and I turn my head to him. He has reached over to hold my hand, our fingers intertwining together. They seem to make an unbreakable lock. I stare at our hands, stare into his eyes. They burn with the intensity of what he is feeling. Jake places his hand on my chin, holding it gently in place, he leans closer and my breathing accelerates. I want and don't want him to come closer. He touches his forehead to mine; our noses are touching. I close my eyes. His breath touches my face. His lips. His lips are so close. I feel them press against mine very gently. I open my eyes in surprise then close them again as the softness of his mouth covers mine. They are soft and warm, so warm. I don't know what to do. I stay still but I want to wrap my arms around his body. He presses his lips against mine again, a little harder this time. Then he pulls back a little, and I hide my disappointment. His lips are still very close to mine when he whispers, so I can feel his mouth brush against mine with each movement of words.

"I'm sorry I didn't get you a present," He breaths, a smile forms on his lips. "I hope this is enough." Jake leans in again and touches his lips to mine once more. His emotions are so raw, so intense and filled with love and happiness that I get overwhelmed.

With his lips, he forces mine open. My mouth moves with his like it is natural; the shape of our lips fit each other's like we were meant to be. His hand moves from my chin to the back of my neck, and his other hand finds the small of my back. His hands, his hands, his hands are so warm as they trace my skin. Jake pulls me closer to his body; he is very warm. My heart pounds madly, I'm sure he can feel it. This is all new to me. I have no idea what I'm doing. I don't care. I want to be closer to him. My hands find his shoulders and I draw myself closer than we already were; I want to get rid of any distance between us. His hands wrap around me and my hand finds his hair; I grip. He gasps and presses me closer to him. Then he breaks away; and though I am disappointed, I am a little thankful. I don't think I could have continued kissing him without ending up in a faint. My head feels light, almost as if I am floating. Though our lips have parted, his face is still really close to mine, and our arms are still around each other. I'm surprised we haven't fallen off the roof.

"I have wanted to do that since I met you…" Jake murmurs hoarsely, his usually velvety voice rough with emotion. "When I first met you, you enchanted me. And the more you stayed here; you seem to have become more pure than you already were. Being out here in the country has changed you. I can see it. You wear less make up and yet your face is more bright now than it was the first day. But you don't need make up; your face is perfect to me. Just like your heart." Jake kisses me again, but tenderly and not so insistent this time. My head buzzes; I can only see, feel, and smell him.

My heart is fluttering as fast as a hummingbird's wings, trapped in a cage made of bone, flesh and muscle. But the rest of me feels free. I am flying. Happiness and love wraps around me like a shield. Jake likes me; he wants me. And though it seems impossible to me, it's true. I smile to myself and look into his eyes.

"I've wanted you too…" I whisper back to him. "Though I've only known you for three days, you're the first person I've felt this way about."

Jake's eyes soften and stir with his feelings. His lips touch mine again. And this time, neither of us breaks away. We continue like this for quite a while; until I notice that there is no more sunlight and that what is keeping the skies bright are the stars.

I turn to Jake to show him the stars but he's gazing at me, incredulously. I look at myself and gasp. My skin is glowing; there is an aura of soft-gold light around me. It clings to my skin and follows my movements; it lights up the night dimly just like the stars light up the skies brightly.

My eyes rip themselves away from my shining body and focus on Jake. I place a glowing hand on his cheek and he lights up as well; the light goes through him making him glow. His aura is light silver; not as warm as my gold, which is like my own sun, but his color burns with heat, just like his eyes. When I touch him, he seems to transform. His skin glows with health and his eyes sparkle with life. He looks at me with surprise.

"When you touched me," Jake speaks in amazement. "It was like every wound I ever had, every unseen scar I ever collected, went away." His gaze drops down from my eyes to my lips and back again. "You healed whatever unknown injury I had, just by touching me. But when you placed your hand on me, I FELT your love flow through me, it warmed and awakened me."

This is overwhelming. It's impossible. It's an incredible gift. It seems that I mended deep wounds in him; wounds that he didn't even know were there; just by touching him with love. My touch spread through him like fire and healed him. I can cure wounds with my touch, my fire touch.

9

Warm water runs from my head and down my body. Steam rolls from the hot water coming out of the faucet and drifts up to the lights, illuminating the droplets. It mesmerizes me. Every time I'm in the shower, I just watch the little swirls of tiny water vapor in the air moving around. They fly, dance, twirl, swirl and swim unreservedly through the air. So free.

It is the night of my birthday after everything crazy had happened. Jake and his parents have gone home. Mr. and Mrs. Blanchard looked happy and proud that I had bloomed, and they seemed willing to leave me alone. Jake however, was a different story. He didn't want to leave me at all! I couldn't hide my joy; he even asked his parents to sleep over at my house. He said something about me being "unprotected" and was going on and on about how it would be unsafe because Nicholas could try to attack again. But they declined, and even though

I was disappointed, I was also a little relieved. I really did need alone time to think about the events of the day. So much has happened. Plus, I don't think Nicholas will attack, and if he does, I don't think he can hurt me. This is partly because Aunt Alicia taught me briefly how to shield my mind from unwanted forces. It seems to work because I do feel more sheltered. And I don't feel weak. If he attacks, I'll fight back.

Shampoo drips off my hair; I am almost done rinsing myself clean. The water is turning cold, and I don't want to waste water. I step out of the tub, my wet feet leaving watermarks on the mat on the floor as I reach for my towel to dry my body. Once dry and dressed in my PJ's, I tie my still wet hair into a bun.

I stare at my reflection; nothing about the girl in the mirror shows how tired I feel inside. The person staring back at me with wide eyes seems alive and excited; waiting for more things to happen. Her cheeks, which are flushed from the heat of the shower, seem to glow.

If I had to picture myself right now, I wouldn't see myself looking this healthy; in fact, I imagined a pale face with bags under the eyes. But it is totally the opposite. I feel drained, but at the same time I feel like I could run miles and not be tired. I am all right physically, but on the inside, I feel like I need an extra long nap but I can't even let myself slouch…well, I never was one to slouch; but slouching would show some of the exhaustion I feel.

I want to seem more human.

Even though I feel fatigued, I feel alive. Today has been the best and the most confusing day of my life.

My hands reach up to touch the glass reflection. The girl in the mirror mimics my moves perfectly; her lips pull up in a curve. Hmm… weird, I don't remember smiling. My fingers touch the side of my lips and prove that I am. My eyes move down the mirror to look at the rest of me. The PJ's that I randomly picked happen to be rainbow checkered shorts and a hoodie jacket shirt. These are my comfort PJ's… I guess my actions reflect what I feel inside. Hopefully I'll be able to sleep better tonight.

Tap. Tap. Tap.

I spin around to find the source of the sound. My heart nearly jumps into my throat.

Outside the bathroom window stands a large shadow. It looks sharp but curved, and there is something glinting in that shadow. The darkness outside doesn't help distinguish this figure; the shadow is black. Then it moves, and I realize what it is.

It is a crow.

A huge crow: with a long sharp black beak. The feathers look smooth and shiny; nothing that speaks of any imperfection in the creature, nothing about it seems dark even though most people associate this bird with evil. It also seems to be intelligent.

It seems to want to come in.

Tap. Tap. Tap.

The sound bounces off the windows as the crow pecks at the glass again. Is it trying to tell me something? My hands are reaching up for the window handle before I can help myself, as if I'm no longer in control of my actions. Something in my brain is screaming at me: My subconscious.

No, no, no. It says. *Do* **NOT** *open that window.*

My fingers close around the handle, turning it halfway. This whole time I am unable to take my eyes off the crow. It is looking at me with cleverness that no normal animal should and could have. Its eyes flash with eagerness as the window clicks to show that it is unlocked. The crow's feet steps closer to the window seal, its talons scraping the glass. I stare, captivated, stunned, unable to look or move away from the crow.

My mind is fogging up. This is not normal. *Un-natural!* My conscience yells at me. *Fight! Fight! Mind control! Evil!*

I blink. What *was* that?

"Veronica? Dear, may I come in?" I hear Gramps' calling from outside my bedroom door. I quickly come out of my daze and look back at the window. The crow is glaring at me, the expression so full of irritation that it looks almost human. It hops off the windowsill and takes flight. A shudder goes through me as I stare after it.

"Yes Gramps." I answer back. My voice is clear. Good. I can't afford to look weak. I need to be strong for Gramps; he is so strong himself.

Gramps steps into the bedroom, just as I click the small window shut, and walks towards me. The window is going to stay shut. Nothing, no one, is going to make me open anything and I'm not going to let anything in.

"Happy Birthday, Veronica," Gramps says as he steps forward to hug me. His arms wrap around my body, engulfing me in a warm bear hug that has always been so familiar. Gramps is very huggable; hugs are nice, cozy and they feel like home.

"Thanks Gramps!" I smile; he can't see the smile since we are still hugging. But I hope that he is able to hear a smile in my voice. Gramps pulls back.

"You're welcome baby girl." He leans forward and kisses the center of my forehead, his hands resting on my shoulders. "Stay strong darling. We're here for you."

Tears threaten to spill over. No, no. I have to be strong. I sniff and quickly wipe my hand over my eyes just in case.

If Gramps noticed, he doesn't comment. I love him for that; he understands that sometimes thinking strong makes you strong. He has that in common with dad.

"I will Gramps. I'll stay strong for you and Gran and everyone. I'll try to make you proud."

Gramps' eyes twinkle with love, his lips pull back into a grin. It makes him look younger, almost boyish. He really does look like Dad; or Dad looks like him.

"You already have, sweetheart." He walks out of my room. "Good night." The door clicks shut and the tears I had fought back before spills over my eyes as I slide down to the floor.

Get a grip. Don't be weak.

That's what I keep saying to myself as streams of salt-water slip down my cheeks. I wipe them away before they can fall down my chin. I should be stronger than this. I should be. But I know why I suddenly feel unconfident. I know why I feel weak.

It's because I'm afraid.

I suddenly realize that I'm afraid because I have a feeling, a dreadful feeling. It's a feeling that I'm being watched and stalked. Watched and stalked by an animal with jet-black feathers and a sharp, long beak. An animal, who isn't an animal at all; but a person. A person whose name I know. A name of fear to those who know:

Nicholas.

■ ■ ■

It is late at night when I call Aunt Alicia. The phone rings three times before Aunt Alicia picks up on the other end of the line.

"Hello?"

"Aunt Alicia!" I breathe out in a soft whisper. "The mind shield doesn't work! I was compelled, in a way! I almost opened my window to a huge black crow! I seriously don't think that it was a normal animal. It acted too... strangely."

Silence.

"What?" Her voice sounds nervous. "A black crow? Did it seem more intelligent than an ordinary animal?"

"Yes," My hands are shaking. "Yes it did. At first it seemed all right, it seemed good... but then it looked greedy and eager. It wanted very much to come in. And I couldn't make my hands stop, and I couldn't take my eyes away."

"Oh dear…" Aunt Alicia's voice sounds strained over the phone. "My, my… He has gotten stronger."

He has gotten stronger? What? Fear courses through me, as my theory is proven right. The crow was Nicholas. A chill goes down my spine but is quickly taken away and replaced by relief as Aunt Alicia continues.

"Stay there honey, I'll speak to your Grandparents and send Jake over there." She sighs. "You'll need someone to help you until you learn to fully shield yourself against him."

My chest lightens and I feel like I can breathe again. Jake is coming back. I feel safer already.

"Bye Hun, Take care."

The line disconnects before I can say my farewell. My footsteps are silent as ever as I make my way down the corridor back into my room.

My bed is so soft that I'm not able to resist.

The pull of sleep drags me deeper and deeper into the chasm of dreams. I drift off into a quiet silence.

Wings brush against me, soft and comforting. Wings capture me in their cage. I smell something that I can't distinguish but will never forget. Something sharp seems to be poking at my neck, at my torso, at my arms, and at my legs. It doesn't hurt at first, but then stinging pain starts wherever the wings are touching me. I can't move, I can't thrash; I am paralyzed. This dream is turning into a nightmare. Warm wet liquid trickles from my eyes down my face. A moan escapes my lips as the sharpness pricks at my neck again; stinging sensations are all over my body. Then out of the darkness comes a shout.

"Get out! Get out! Be gone!"

There is a commotion and I am shaken, consciousness coming back to me in pieces. But the sharp beak and wings are gone. Warmth seems to wrap around me like a blanket, arms cradle me against a soft chest. I open my eyes.

"Jake," I manage to croak out.

He is looking at me with an alarmed expression. He's cradling me against him on my bed; rocking me back and forth as if I were a child. His hands reach down to my neck and arms and legs. I follow his hands and stare at my scratched and slightly bloodied body. The dream was real. The nightmare actually happened.

"Shh…" Is all Jake says as he traces my wounds. They aren't deep enough punctures to cause serious damage, but they tell of the attackers weapon: a long sharp black beak.

"Black Crow? Nicholas?" I ask in a flat whisper. I feel weary to my bones.

"Yes," Jake mumbles. His hands are now on my face, tracing my features. "It was Nicholas. But he's gone now, I got here just in time." His voice cracks.

"What was he doing?" I ask. My voice trembles, I am not sure if it's from fear, or from rage. I can't hide it any longer.

"He was hurting you," Jake's eyes harden. "He was in animal form, but if he were human, I would guess that it is the same as tracing you or scratching you. No matter what, he was hurting you. Touching you in a way that should never be allowed." His hands curl into fists, his knuckles turning white.

I reach up to touch his face, to reassure him. I don't tell him how much it alarms me. I don't tell him that I think that I let Nicholas in.

"I'm fine now. Really." But as the words come out, I know they are not true.

I am not fine.

I am frightened, angry and irritated out of my mind. Even though the fear of Nicholas being there with me scares me to death, the irritation and rage I am beginning to feel with the fact that he was in my room and pecking me is so strong that I start to feel hate boiling in the pit of my stomach. I don't like the emotion hate. In fact, I absolutely hate feeling it. I know. It's ironic. But the emotion is horrible. And I feel it against Nicholas.

"No, you're not." Jake's eyes soften. "You don't have to be so strong you know… You're already one of the strongest people I know. But you should let it out."

"How?" I ask.

"By learning how to fight him." He says matter-of-factly. His eyes shine, his lips pull back in a mischievous and playful grin.

"What?" I question. And even though it sounds ridiculous, I want to do it. I want to learn how to fight. "Teach me. Do you know how?"

His grin widens and stretches across his face, it makes his dimples more noticeable and brings my own smile to my lips.

" 'Course I know how to fight." He winks. "I'll teach you everything I know: how to fight in a hand to hand combat, how to hold a knife, use a gun. Well… maybe not that last one. Not that those would be much use against Nicholas. Which is why I'll also teach you some stuff about our special abilities. So that you can protect yourself better."

I raise both eyebrows in question.

"Nicholas is powerful because he can fight and use his powers. And now it seems like he's learned how to shape shift. I don't know how he did that, but it must be part of his special ability. But I can teach you how to shield, how to control and how to move. We don't have more than what's given to us. So you only have your ability with emotions, agility, more speed, more strength and enhanced senses. Since you seem to have spoken with animals, you might have some effect on nature. It's not hard to develop; I learned how to use my skills very quickly. I also don't think you and I will be able to shape shift like him."

As Jake is speaking, hope fills me and I feel much better. Jake will teach me how to protect myself. Jake can teach me how to protect others. Jake will teach me how to fight and defeat Nicholas.

But do I fight Nicholas? Or do I heal his heart? He needs to be healed of the darkness inside of him. Could he be a good person underneath all that wickedness? If that's the case, maybe I can help him; I could show him love and make him good. I don't have to defeat him; I just have to defeat the evil in him. My heart does crazy drumbeats in my chest. How would I do that? No idea.

Suddenly out of nowhere, a question pops into my mind. It was probably pacing around the corners of my brain, trying to get its way past all the other questions; and it finally made it though it brings doubt with it.

"Jake?" My voice sounds unsure. Like I didn't really want to know the answer to what I am about to ask. "Why is Nicholas's animal a crow?"

Jakes' eyes turn darker, the color looking more like the dark blue of the night sky than like the blue sky of morning. It still burns with fire though, and it still makes me warm inside. But there is something different about his expression. His lips are pulled down in a troubled frown that I've never seen on him before. Even with the frown he is handsome, but it makes him look older and less like the Jake I know. It isn't a bad thing; it is just... unusual.

"I don't know what it means..." Jake's eyes move to mine; his expression softens. "But it doesn't matter. We can deal with it some other day."

With that bit of comfort, a huge yawn escapes my lips. Jake chuckles at me. I really do feel like a baby since I am still wrapped in his arms and yawning.

"But first," Jake's dimples show briefly. He seems to be trying to hide a smile. "I think you need to go to sleep."

Fear grips me unexpectedly. Jake can't leave. If he leaves, the crow might come back. I don't want the crow to come back.

"Don't go..." My voice shakes, showing how worried I am. Strange, I shouldn't be worried about myself... I clear my throat and start talking but Jake interrupts me.

"Don't worry, I'm staying. I'll sleep on the couch right there; you've got a big one in your room. Convenient." Jake winks at me. "I won't ever leave you, I'll stay to protect you. You'll be safe with me."

I want to tell him that he doesn't have to take the couch. That it won't be comfortable. That he is welcome on the bed. But my mouth won't move to my command. Maybe that's because the flush that makes its way to my face stops me from asking.

Jake sets me down and pulls the blanket over me as my head sinks into my pillow. It is so comfortable that my eyes won't stay open. Even with closed eyes, I know that Jake's face is still close to mine.

"Good night Veronica," He whispers, his breath soft against my face as he speaks. I feel his lips touch my forehead in a tender gesture. I drift off into a deeper sleep. Then I feel something soft and warm touch my lips. But I can't be sure that the kiss that Jake gives me is real for my brain is already in dream mode.

Then a multitude of shifting colors appears in my head, like the Auroras in the northern sky. Dreams like these are beautiful, peaceful and natural. They are also safe. And that's how I will always feel with Jake. Safe.

As long as Jake is here, Nicholas can't mind control me. He can't hurt me or come in. As the pull of deeper slumber drags me further into emptiness and color, a question comes to my mind. It is troubling, I can't think straight in my dream. The question itself is also worrying. How did the crow, Nicholas, get into my room? Did I open the window for him? I thought I was asleep on my bed.

Before I am completely gone, I hear a voice, deep and echoing, in my head.

"Once I'm let in, I can always come in, my dear. You unlocked the window before… an invitation, letting me in. Your enchantments around the house only work for unwanted guests. It would seem that you want me to come in." The voice seems to laugh. *"And since you want me in, I'm in. But don't worry my Rose. I want you too."*

Sleep overpowers me before I can make sense of the thought that was not my own. The only thing that keeps my dreams from turning into a nightmare is the soft sweet voice that seems to carry a tune. I realize that Jake is singing me to sleep very softly.

I roll and feel his arms around me. I know his arms, I know him. He'll stay and keep me sheltered. Safe from everything.

"Not me…" The voice whispers, breaking into my peace. A deep bottomless chuckle seems to consume everything except for the sweet humming of Jake's voice.

10

I wake to the sound of chairs scraping the floor and laughter from the kitchen. My room is dimly lit by the streams of sunlight that manages to escape through the shade of my curtains. The light shines, already promising a new day. My room smells like roses; the candle incense seems to be working. Jake gave me a rose scented candle for my birthday; he seems to know that I love roses. Jake is not in the room so that means he must be in the living room. He's probably the source of the laughter; I can recognize his melodious laugh from a mile away. It is so distinct.

I smile to myself as I throw my legs over the bed. Not bothering to change, I put on warm boots and make my way to the dining room. No one notices my entrance. I think they hardly ever do; I am so silent when I walk. It seems, however, that people notice my presence, because it only takes a second for them to sense me in the room. It happened the first day I met Jake as well; they didn't notice me when I walked into the room so I debated turning away, but then after a second they seemed aware that I was there. It perplexes me that others seem to feel my presence.

I stand silently at the doorway, absorbing the morning mood and the cozy scene of Gran cooking, Gramps reading the paper, and Jake standing with a plate full of French toast in his hands.

They all turn to face me when they realize I'm watching. Jake's eyes shine and the smile he already has on grows wider. Gran and Gramps come over to me to give me a little hug as Jake sets down the plate of food.

"Good morning darling," Gran says to me, giving me a peck on the cheek before she goes back to the stove to cook more food. Gramps's eyes twinkle; he seems to find something funny.

"Someone's lazy today isn't she? One day of sixteen and already forgetting how to change." Gramps shakes his head in joking disappointment. "It ain't that old, young lady." Gramps laughs merrily under his breath.

I let out a sarcastic sigh and hop over to give Gramps and Gran a kiss on the cheek before I sit down.

"I'm not lazy. I just didn't want to miss a moment of breakfast." My eyes shift to Jake. He has settled down on the seat next to mine. "I could hear you guys from my room. How loud you all are!" I click my tongue together like a parent would do to a child who has done wrong. My humor is usually not very good; I hope this time it would make them laugh.

They do, thankfully. But I have a feeling it's just to make me feel comfortable. I've never been funny. Jake reaches for my hand and squeezes it lightly, an acknowledgement. I guess we can't hug or anything in front of my grandparents.

"And it's good to have you here." Gran says as she comes into the dining room carrying a plate full of sausages. She sets it down next to the French toast. "The room seems to have lightened up with just you being here." She winks at me.

I know that she means that lightly, but I ponder it. Jake seems to be doing the exact same thing as me. He has a thoughtful expression, as if what Gran had said gave him an idea.

I give Jake a meaningful look; he will have to share whatever he is thinking with me sooner or later. Jake smiles and gives me a little nod, his eyes look brighter, probably with whatever new found knowledge he has just acquired. Grr… Now I'm really curious.

"Well, dig in!" Gran says cheerfully. "Jake has always loved my French toast. I use to make it for him when he was younger."

My mouth forgets how to chew; it won't move or let me swallow the delicious food that I have put in it. Gran has known Jake since he was young?

"How long have you known each other?" I ask, astonished.

"Well, I've known Jake ever since he was a baby!" Gran smiles at me. "Whenever you and he were both here at the same time, your parents would meet up and hang out and let us take care of you two kids. You guys had such fun together! I was surprised that you didn't recognize him Veronica!"

My heart takes three large hurtles. What? I've met Jake before? Surely I'd remember if I did. Then I think over it again and realize how horrible my memory is. I tend to not remember things that don't stick in my brain in an extremely painful or extremely happy way. But it's weird. Wouldn't anything associated with Jake be extremely happy? Or maybe not. But…

"I knew Jake?"

"Yep! You did! I recognized you as soon as I laid eyes on you." Jake winks at me, his dimples are appearing. "You had forgotten me, but I made you remember. Or maybe just made you know me. That's probably why you trusted me so much faster than you usually trust someone. But even when we were younger, I was already your protector." He winks and chuckles at a memory.

"Remember the time when an apple fell from a tree and dropped on your head?" Jake suggests.

I have to think hard before a vague picture of me rubbing my head and a laughing boy appears in my mind. He looks younger, maybe about eight years old, but very much the same. His hair is a little lighter in the memory but his eyes are the same… they still held the same deep blue fire. Hmm, I guess I do remember him. No wonder I trusted him so easily and as soon as we met.

I smirk.

"Ha, 'protector'! That's a real funny way of putting it. You laughed at me when that apple made a bump on my head!" I playfully punch him. "You jerk."

Jake grins at me. "I'm happy you remember, love. I was starting to feel hurt that I didn't imprint myself into your brain. Surely my charm and charisma was excellent even when I was a boy?"

I roll my eyes but can't stop the smile from widening on my face. Jake has the best sense of humor. He is cocky in a humble and playful way that can always turn a frown upside down.

"But what about our parents?" I probe.

"His parents were friends with your mom and dad. The pair of them had met in Ithaca during vacation." Gran replies before she starts to eat.

"Ithaca? You mean here?"

"No, no," Gramps cuts in. "We mean the actual Greece Ithaca. It is a beautiful and mystical place; that is, it seems to be filled with ancient magic. You were born there, did you not know?"

I was born in Greece? In Ithaca, Greece? I didn't know that… Weird. But cool. And what is even stranger is that I live in Ithaca New York now. I wonder if there is some deeper link or meaning behind this.

"It seems like we must always return to our origin." I add casually. "Born there and now live here. It's interesting." In my mouth goes another piece of sausage.

"Hmmm…." Jake is silent, contemplating something.

All eyes move to him; I sense that Gran and Gramps are curious and eager. Jake knows something. Would Jake say it in front of them? Of course he would. Everyone here knows about the special abilities. And I would like it to be explained.

"Jake?" Gramps mumbles. "Tell us. Please."

I am still staring at Jake, his eyes lift from his plate and are looking at Gramps, at Gran, and then finally, they rest on me. His eyes stay there, keeping me under the power of his fire.

"Ithaca…" Jake begins. "Is a place filled with ancient power; or so I learned. And my great, great grandfather was from there, and his fathers before that. So I have an Ithacan bloodline." He pauses. "Were any of your ancestors from Ithaca Greece by any chance?" Jake's blue eyes are piercing; they won't release me. Though he is looking straight at me, I know that he isn't addressing me; so I don't even bother to try to answer.

"Erm, not from my side." Gran says, clearly confused.

"There is some Greek from my side." Gramps supplies. "But I don't know whether it is from the province Ithaca. It could be from anywhere in Greece."

"No…" Jake murmurs. "I think it is Ithaca. At least, I'm pretty sure it is. It would make much more sense if it were, because then you would be part Ithacan."

"Why would it make sense, Jake?" The question manages to escape my mouth without sounding like gibberish. I cannot really think very well with him staring at me like that.

"Because all the people with special abilities I've met so far seem to have some sort of relation with Ithaca. It has never occurred to me before, but after you brought it up, everything kind of clicked in place." Jake appears to be following and speaking his own train of thoughts out loud. "Well, it is a very ancient place, full of powerful and unknown things. Perhaps our heritage from there is what gives us these special abilities. Or maybe it's Ithaca that is the source of our power," He keeps on speaking, almost chanting. None of us want to disturb him for fear that he will lose his train of thoughts.

"And what you said about the room seeming lighter when Veronica was around, I think that's because she replaces darkness with light, therefore making us feel more pure. I felt that when she touched me. It was like I immediately felt healthier, restored and stronger. I think her presence brings that to people and her touch enhances whatever her presence has already brought. That's why everyone notices and is drawn to her. Plus, she seems so pure that no blackness can breach her."

The table is silent.

My cheeks bloom with heat and color; I look down, overwhelmed. They are talking about me like I'm some sort of phenomenon. But that is not true. I'm just a normal girl with problems as well as unreal abilities. The number of imperfections in my body, mind and soul are practically unbearable to count.

Jake has stopped speaking, probably thinking more. But no one breaks the silence; nothing disturbs the quietness. I stay hushed. Just in case Jake isn't done, I don't want to disrupt him.

Then Jake finishes his speech with a perfect ending; an ending that summarizes his whole point. This time, he is talking directly to me. This time, every word is for me. And though I don't know whether it's true, I find myself mesmerized by his every word.

"Life and light, more than her own, follow her, and she gives them away freely. Remaking people into their light vital self as she goes. Her love renews us."

■ ■ ■

"Did I really know you since I was a child?" I question Jake, nudging him with my elbow. We rock back and forth on the swinging chair outside on the deck. The sun is high in the sky, but the day is cool.

"Yep, you did…" Jake replies, grinning. "We met up for several years, but then the schedule didn't work after I was about 9. That was the last time since…" He stops himself and gives me a look.

He doesn't need to finish his sentence; I know why we haven't seen each other more recently. Dad went missing and things kind of got messed up. Mom and I also never visited Gran and Gramps in those two years; I think the house, and Gran and Gramps, reminded Mom too much of Dad. So this year when she sent me up here, I was quite pleasantly surprised.

"Well, we remember each other now!" I say back to Jake, trying to break the tension. It works.

"Ha! I never forgot you!" He smirks. "That's why I might have seemed so familiar with you on that first day or two. I was actually surprised that you didn't remember me."

"Sorry." I mumble.

"Don't worry, I almost didn't recognize you either!" Jake grins; his eyes sparkle. "You were always a cute little girl, missing a tooth, large bright baby eyes. But since then you have bloomed into a gorgeous young lady. I was pleasantly stunned, because you changed from a cute little baby bud rose to a fully-grown one. And you know how beautiful those are." He winks at me again.

I find myself laughing. Jake speaks as if I am actually pretty; I never thought I was pretty. Sure, I'm not ugly. But pretty? I don't think so. To believe otherwise would be... weird. Different.

"Why do you keep saying that? I can't actually be that good looking. Unlike you." I smile at him.

Jake shakes his head in disagreement.

"Veronica, you are the most beautiful girl I have ever known." His eyes grow thoughtful. "And to add to that, you're beautiful inside and out: amazingly talented, kind, smart and powerful."

My heart, my mind, my body aches to be closer to him. To hear him speak more. No one has ever spoken to me like that.

"You flatter me too much, Jake," I say, the heat of the blush on my cheeks tickles my nose. I couldn't think of a better reply.

Creak. Squeak. Creak. Squeak.

The rocking bench groans as we rock back and forth. Birds fly overhead, and the trees move with the wind. I open my senses and listen to nature; it is beautiful. I hear the gentle roaring of the river as it flows downstream, the leaves brushing against each other as the breeze blows past, little insects buzzing about, and the crunching and padding of the forest floor as the animals make their way around. I am amazed by how much I am able to hear. It is truly incredible. I close my eyes and continue listening to the gentle music of wildlife.

Hmm… I wonder. It can't hurt to try the impossible. My eyes fly open, as I get ready to test out something I've never thought of doing. I shift my eyes, looking around for a good landscape that is far away. My eyes focus on a tree about half a mile away. And I let out a shocked breath. I can see every single detail of the tree; it is more than I could ever see before! *Neat. My sight has improved*, I think with a grin.

"What are you thinking?" Jake whispers. His lips are close enough that his breath tickles my right ear. I tense at first; I didn't know he was so close. Then he slips his hand into mine and I relax, breathing out.

"I'm actually trying out my new senses." I say. My face turns to look at him. "It's weird. But it's incredible. I can see perfectly half a mile away, and I can hear everything! I bet I could smell everything too!" I feel my mouth stretch out into a big grin.

"Yes, it's amazing isn't it?" Jake is looking at me, his eyes shining with amusement. "When I 'bloomed' about two years ago, everything changed. I could see, hear, and smell so much better. And for you, your senses are probably twice as good as mine. It must be really interesting."

I turn back to the scenery and nod; too engrossed with my surroundings. I am, however, still aware of his lips so close to my face and his fingers tangled with mine.

"It takes the beauty of nature to a whole other level." I murmur.

"Eh, it's alright." Jake says quietly. "It's nothing compared with the beauty I see next to me." His lips press against my neck. "Maybe the reason I don't feel bad about us dating in such a short time is because I've really known you for years."

I turn my head to face him, our foreheads now pressed together; we share the same breath. My head is clouding, nature forgotten. There is only Jake. He is leaning closer, but doing so slowly; savoring every moment. He shouldn't have, because our peace is about to get interrupted. I sense someone coming closer to the deck door and hear footsteps. I lean away just as the door swings open and out comes Aunt Alicia.

Jake is looking excited and alive, but I can see a hint of annoyance in how his mouth is slightly turned down. Well, that and the fact that I can feel it through my emotion reading ability.

"Hello Jake! Hello Veronica!" Aunt Alicia greets us with enthusiasm. "So I've heard Jake's theory about you from your grandparents, Veronica. And I think he's right. It did seem to make sense; but then this hypothesis got proven as soon as I stepped into this house: my headache disappeared as soon as I got close to you. Your aura is very strong."

"Erm, Hi!" I say back, mouth open from her statement. "And Ya, I guess?" I don't know what to say; what can I say to that? What would be a suitable response to that?

"You need something mom?" Jake pushes in; I think he sensed that she is here for another reason than just to tell me 'my aura is strong'.

"Yes, dear. Do you think you could go into town? I need..." She pauses and gives me a look; but she seems to decide that I can be trusted. "A couple of things done."

I don't understand. What things?

But Jake understands perfectly. He stands up and stretches, then reaches to pull me up and a little too close to his body. He supports most of my weight, even though I don't need it.

"Sure mom. Can I bring Veronica?"

"Of course dear." Aunt Alicia sounds very grave. "You should definitely bring Veronica."

Jake nods seriously as if he can hear what Aunt Alicia is thinking. But it doesn't take long for me to realize why Aunt Alicia is giving me such weird worried looks; and why she wants Jake with me. Because as we walk past her and back into the house, I see her gaze skim my body. The crows' scratches are visible against my pale skin. I didn't bother trying to hide them in the morning, as the scars on my arms and legs are not prominent, and are fading quickly. However, what I didn't realize is that the scars on my neck are more obvious. They were the deepest punctures and they stand out against my skin like blood against snow.

11

Trees and roads pass in a flash as Jake drives down the highway towards the closest town. I had changed into jeans shorts, a white spaghetti strapped shirt with a denim jacket, and boots cover my strangely chilled feet. I need to wear the jacket to cover my neck and shoulders; the scratches are still visible, even after over twelve hours. My arms, from elbow to wrist, are bare.

"So, where are we going?" I ask, breaking the silence.

"You'll see," Jake smiles. "I think you'll like it the place."

"Hmm, ok," A grin is tugging at my lips. "So… while we're in town, can we get a coffee or something?"

His eyes quickly flash to mine then back to the road. Jake's grin turns into a beam, making his dimples very obvious. Even though he is facing away from me, I can see his eyes twinkle with laughter.

"So, like a date thing?" Jake asks, turning to look at me again.

"No, well, no…" Heat rushes to my face; I can't find the right words. "Only if you want it to be… well, no. Whatever you want it to be… Well, it's just coffee." I slip a glance at him; I hope he doesn't think I'm extremely weird.

Jake's chuckle fills the car, one hand reaches out to find mine while the other stays on the wheel.

"Sure, whatever I want it to be." He answers, his face still lit up with humor.

His hand is warm but my fingertips are cold; he will always be my warmth. I stare at our connected hands and smile to myself; I'm lucky to have Jake.

We probably drive for ten more minutes more before the car turns a corner and Jake parks the car, cutting the engine. He lets go of my hand and takes off his seatbelt; I do the same and am out of the car before he is.

A shiver goes through me as I step out; the temperature outside is cooler than in the car. Why is it so cold? It's summer. Weird.

My eyes drift to the board above the front door of the old looking warehouse that we are parked in front of.

"Ancient Souvenirs?" I read out loud. "What is that?"

"It's a store with things that might have some mystical properties. Not exactly magic, but close to that." Jake is by my side before he finishes his sentence, his hand on the small of my back, guiding me forward.

A cold wind blows, ruffling my hair; a shudder goes through me.

"Why is it so cold Jake?" My teeth are starting to chatter. "Isn't it supposed to be summer?"

"Yes it is." Jake looks bothered and alert. "I don't know what weather this is; but it's not natural. Something else is at work here… Let's get what we need and go. Quickly."

I listen to Jake. He looks a little tense, probably a sign that things are not normal. Even though I haven't had my abilities for long, I can sense that this is not normal. There's something bad in the forces that move the wind, something that's not natural.

The bell tinkles as we push through the front door. It is not a lot warmer in the little warehouse than outside; but at least we are out of the biting cold wind.

"You can look around," Jake says, facing me. "I'm just going to talk to the person in charge. Be right back." And he is gone; but I don't mind too much. As my eyes skim the shelves of the store, my curiosity swells. I wonder what they sell here...

I move into the store, looking at everything that they have. All the products appear old and simple. But that doesn't fool me; I sense power radiating from some of the objects. There are vases, mugs, feathers, stuffed animals, pendants, crosses, and many other things. But what stands out to me is a dream catcher. The dream catcher hangs on the back wall and seems to be calling me towards it.

As I move closer, I can actually feel the power that it has; it scares me a little, but dream catchers are meant for good. My fingers reach out to stroke the little feathers connected to it.

"Beautiful isn't it?" The voice is right by my ear, familiar, though I don't think I've ever heard it before.

I turn my head to the sound and jump back. The man whom the voice belongs to is closer than I thought. He has dark brown hair and very striking green eyes; they look like emeralds. His skin is pale but lovely. He possesses a dark kind of beauty.

The man smirks at my reactions.

"Sorry to startle you."

I shake my head, my heartbeat slowing down.

"No, it's ok." I breathe. His eyes are beautiful. They are close. So close. So close. Too close. "Yes, it is beautiful." I look away.

"And it has power."

I turn my eyes back to the stranger, suspicious, and let my senses free. Power, different from all the natural forces, radiates from him. A startled gasp escapes my lips; he's like me, someone with special abilities.

"Yes, it does." I feel a probing in my mind, like something is trying to get past my barrier. "And so do you." I don't know where I got the courage to confront him. I haven't met him before but I feel like I know him from somewhere.

His eyes glint. "You shouldn't be the one to say that. I could say the same for you if you can sense me." He steps closer. Even closer. "You have power, my dear Veronica. But you can't even recognize me. That hurts. After all, I've been in your room."

My stomach churns as adrenaline and fear course through me. Oh, oh, oh.

"Nicholas." I whisper, my voice trembles.

"Oh yes. But you can call me Cole," A smile tugs his lips. It is friendly, but not real. His eyes are so beautiful. His eyes undress my face; they brush the length of my body. "And you really are a natural beauty. Little Jake doesn't even know what he's got."

"Don't call me beautiful. And don't talk about him like that." My voice sounds angry. Where did I get the strength to be angry with someone so evil? "He's greater than you. You can't call him little."

"Oh please." Cole says firmly. "I could get rid of him in a second. But you, on the other hand, wouldn't be so easily dealt with." His hand reaches for my face; I slap it away.

"Don't touch me." The anger I hear in my voice is so clear. It doesn't come naturally for me. I'm not used to this hot red feeling. It is hard to control.

"Hmm, you're even more powerful when angry. I can see it in your eyes; I can feel it from your aura. And what a strong aura it is. I was drawn to you." His eyes turn thoughtful and he almost looks good again. "But there is something about your presence that weakens my power… and I can't get into your mind anymore, even though I could as a crow…"

"Well, too bad for you then." I find myself smirking. I weaken him, but I know it isn't my action that keeps him out of my head because I'm not strong enough even for that. So what's protecting me? My eyes drift to the dream catcher, my mind answering my question for me. *Oh… OH.* The dream catcher!

"I have to get going…"

I try to walk past, but Cole stretches his arm out, his palms hitting the wall, blocking my exit way.

"Not so fast, I would like to talk to you Veronica." His eyes narrow. "And you haven't asked me how I knew your name." He's too close. Way, way too close.

I snap.

"What? You think I don't know how you know my name?" This is really bugging me. I want to get away from him but I can't. He's blocking the way. I want to look away from his strikingly beautiful green eyes. But I can't. I am too mesmerized by their intensity.

I hear the irritation in my raised whispered voice.

"You've been spying on me. In the meadow, that dark presence was you. During my birthday, when I felt like my insides were burning, that was you. And in my bathroom, in my room, the crow, that was you! So don't ask me how I'm not wondering how you know my name."

The whole speech sounds like a hiss to me; I shift my feet, uncomfortable of what I'm feeling. It isn't good or love. It is hate. It is horrible.

"Woah! Feisty aren't you." His eyes widen in mock surprise. "I've never actually seen you mad like this. I can feel your strength. Hmm…" He grins and almost looks like a young mischievous boy, though I'd guess him to be about twenty-five.

My thoughts about him falter as my rage cools. What am I doing? I have to save him. I shouldn't be getting mad and wishing him strangled; I should be showing him care and love.

"Don't call me that." I close my eyes and open them again. Summoning patience. "I really have to get going. Please."

When I say 'Please', Cole leans closer to me, so close that his stunning eyes are all I can see. I can't move back; I can't move at all. I am frozen by confusion. His nose is almost touching mine; his eyes are dark and soft but focused with an expression I do not recognize. I can't think.

"I know. You may not believe it. But you are already mine; I've got you in my hand and you can't do anything about it." He is so close that I can see each eyelash. My breathing accelerates; I can't back up. His eyes are like crystals of ice, beautiful but cold.

"Veronica?" I hear Jake call, and I am released from the spell of Cole's gaze. But I still can't move away.

"I'm here!" I call back; relief coloring my tone.

I face Cole; he has a murderous expression and I can feel rage radiating from him but he doesn't back up. So I do. But not far enough.

"You don't have me. And you never will." I say to him; my voice sounds like knives to me and I don't like it.

"Oh, but I already do." His eyes stare into mine. "You and I are more alike than you think." And before I can stop him, his hands are pulling the side of my shirt up, revealing my crow mark. His stare is meaningful. I feel his silent victory.

"Veronica?" Jake's voice sounds startled. He's at the end of the shelf; staring at Cole with an angry expression, I feel his worry, disbelief and shock. I step further away from Cole, finally able to move. My eyes harden, even as my cheeks burn.

Never. I say in my mind. Cole stares at me in surprise. His smile is cold as he realizes that I can mind-speak.

We'll see. And he looks away; he looks towards Jake.

"Hello Cousin." Cole says to Jake, and Jake's eyes widen.

Before Jake is able to answer, Cole takes his hands away from my hip and steps away, disappearing into shadows. His hand leaves a feeling on my skin, as if it were burned with ice. When Cole goes, the room and the weather outside suddenly become warmer. Sunlight streams through the window. The coldness was Cole.

As I take my first shaky step towards Jake I hear Cole's voice echo over the warehouse.

"I'll see you soon; I'll see you both soon."

And I feel Jake's warm arms around me before I collapse to the ground.

■ ■ ■

"Here, drink this." Jake hands me a cup of steaming dark brown liquid. Though it is warm again outside, I am cold.

"Thanks," I say as I take the coffee.

Jake becomes silent, his eyes watching my every movement.

"Please say something," I mumble against my cup.

"That was Nicholas." He says.

"Yes… But he told me to call him Cole." I reply, wary of his reaction.

"What did he want from you?" His voice sounds hurt. "Why did he have his hands on you? Why was he so close?"

I let out a shaky laugh.
"Is it your turn to ask so many questions now?"

But Jake doesn't laugh, it isn't funny to him; he is serious.

I sigh.
"He didn't want anything, I was just looking at the dream catcher when he appeared. He said something about not being able to get into my head for some reason and that he's drawn but weakened by my presence."

"Well, that makes sense. He's broken and crooked, and you're practically love and light. So when anyone gets close to you, they will feel renewed. He probably felt that. But you probably weren't feeling any love when you were with him, so he wasn't feeling renewed, just weakened of evil." Jake adds.

"And… he had his hands on me because he was showing me…" I can't get the words out at first; but I manage. "My crow mark. And he said that we are the same." I shudder. "He also said that I was his." My voice cracks with fear and uncertainty.

Jake's arms wrap around me in comfort.

"Don't worry… you're not the same as him." He eyes set. "And you're not his. You'll never be his."

I nod, unsure of myself, because I'm not so certain. Why couldn't I move away from Cole in the store? Why could I not look away from his eyes? Why didn't I *want* to?

"We'll talk more later ok?" Jake whispers against my hair. "I don't think that you want to talk about it now, right?"

"Mm…" I exhale in reply.

"Come on," Jake stands and offers me his hand. "Let's get home." His eyes are soft and churning like blue lava; they warm my insides and give me the will power to get up and return to reality.

■ ■ ■

Everyone is shocked when Jake and I tell them what happened with Nicholas. And they are even more shocked when I replay the conversation I had with him. No one can make sense of it.

The fear and anger I felt with Nicholas evaporated as soon as he left. It is like he brought on those dark feelings, like he brought out the dark side in me. He could probably do that for everyone. My head still feels like it's swimming, I can't really think past all the questions I have.

Firstly, I don't trust Nicholas, but I felt connected to him when he was standing so close to me. I can feel that he could use me and bend me to his will. So the solution for that is easy; my will has to get stronger, and I have to learn to fight back.

Secondly, How am I going to help him? He doesn't want help… He probably doesn't even think there's anything wrong. Maybe he wants to be that twisted person that he is. Maybe it's something else. I need to feel love for him in order to save him, but how can I feel love for such a crooked man?

And thirdly, what protected me from his mind powers? I could feel him probing my mind, trying to take control of it like he did the other night in my room, but it didn't work. So what was different today? Was it only the dream catcher?

Since the third question in my head is the easiest to answer, it is to be the one I ask.

Jake, Gran, Gramps, Mr. and Mrs. Blanchard and I are sitting around the dining table, the atmosphere as dim as the silence that fills the room. After Jake had finished his story, no one speaks. Perhaps they are thinking it through in their minds like I did in my own.

"So," I clear my throat. Five pairs of eyes in the room turn to me, making me the center of attention. Great. "I do

have a question… You might not think it's the most important one that could be answered right now, but I do. Plus, it's
been bugging me."

No one moves, no one speaks; no one even blinks. Gosh,
I'm in a room full of zombies. But I know that's not true, because zombies can't feel fear, they can't feel worry; and that's
all I am sensing from my family right now.

"Erm, well… You see, I think when I was talking with
Cole…" I can feel Jake's burning glare on my face as I look
at anyone else's. My slip with the nickname that Nicholas
told me to call him by is not welcome. "… Nicholas, I mean.
Well… Uhh…" Why am I stumbling? *Just get it out.* "Well,
I think he was trying to take control of me, like he did last
night. He was trying to get into my head, but for some reason,
it didn't work. And I think that it is because of the dream
catcher that I was standing next to in that antique store; it
radiated power, and I'm pretty sure that that's what protected
me. But I still don't know…"

"No, you're right." I hear Jake say, I turn to face him. His
voice is hard and I hope he isn't thinking about how close Cole
was to me in the store. I don't know what I would do if I lost
Jake. "It was that dream catcher, that was what I went to the
store to get anyways. It shouldn't surprise me that you found
it first." Jake sighs. "Well, the good thing is, I don't think
Nicholas realized what it was, I think he must have come up
with a theory that you just learned how to block him out."

"Well I think that us adults need to do some memory research." Uncle Tom states; his voice has an edge to it. "Natasha? Paul?" My Grandparents and the Blanchards get up; they head for the study.

Once Jake and I are alone I turn back to him and reply shakily to him. I feel like I could break down right now, just the slightest push will send me over the edge.

"Yes, I think he must think that." I suppress a laugh; Cole isn't smarter than any of us. "He doesn't know anything... He will never use me again." The determination in my voice cannot be mistaken. I am certain that he wouldn't be able to invade my mind again.

"Use you?" Jake's voice sounds angry. "It looked like he was trying to kiss you!" He lets out a frustrated breath. "He was definitely close enough to." His eyes flash.

"You know that's not it! He was showing me my crow mark, trying to make me think that I'm linked to him!" I can feel warm wetness in my eyes. "I can't be linked to him; but for some reason, I think he's telling the truth." I rake my fingers through my hair; hard enough that it hurts, but not enough to pull the hair out. "I don't want to be like him. I *can't* be evil like him, Jake! How can I help him if I can't even help myself!" The tears leak over without any warning and before I know it, I'm gasping for air. I'm burning with the humiliation of crying in front of Jake. But I can't stop. The quiet sobs sound loud in the silence of the room. "Jake please understand; I can't do it! I'm scared."

And that's the push that sends me over the edge. I hug my knees closer to my body and cry into my legs. I should be stronger. I shouldn't cry over this. But I can't help it. Even the anger that I feel can't drown my fear and hopelessness. It scares me.

I feel Jake's hands wrap around my curled up body and feel weightless. He carries me towards the couch and sets me on his lap like I'm a child. Jake strokes my hair as my wet tears seep into the shoulder of his shirt. He kisses my hair and continues to stroke.

"I'm sorry," Jake whispers quietly. "I shouldn't have said that when so many other things matter." He chuckles slightly. "I guess I was just jealous. I'm sorry Rose."

I lift my head up; my cries died down as soon as Jake had me in his arms. He is all I need to feel strong again. His lips find mine and the ache in my heart dulls. I like it when he calls me Rose.

"Don't feel scared, I'll teach you how to fight." Jake murmurs. "I promise."

"Okay," I croak out; and even though my voice is raspy and uneven, it sounds resolute. It's strange how blooming changes a person. "We can go to the meadow to practice. It's a very magical place."

"Sure," I can hear a smile in Jake's voice. And I want to reply, but I am too far-gone. Behind the fogginess and heaviness of sleep, I can still hear him humming, just as he did the other night; and I know that I will sleep without nightmares tonight. And I will learn to fight tomorrow.

12

"No way," I say, my voice sounding clear in the middle of the meadow. Sunlight streams through the trees making the meadow seem as beautiful as it was last time. Jake is facing me, telling me to try throwing a punch at him.

"I am *not* hitting you," I shake my head. "Even if it's not real." Even if I probably could not hurt him, I can't use him as a target.

"Come on Veronica!" Jake's trying very hard not to smile. He appears to find this funny. "You fought me before remember?" He winks.

"Yeah, but that was a joke!"

"And this is just practice," He rolls his eyes. "Trust me. You aren't gonna hurt me."

That makes me think twice. Did he say that because he thinks I am too weak to hurt him? Or because he doesn't think I am able to actually do it? I'm stronger than he thinks. I have to prove it.

"Remember who won last time?" I say.

Without warning I lunge for him and knock him to the ground. I'm on top of him now; my weight pressing him down before he has time to recover, I playfully touch my fist to his face.

"That good enough an attack for ya?"

He blinks a couple of times, then smiles broodily and laughs. Jake rolls over so he's on top of me instead; carefully placing none of his body weight on me before he gets up and rocks on the balls of his feet. He pulls me up with him and brushes off the grass on his pants.

"You're fast!" He says lightly. "That's good. Speed and surprise will always win the fight." He grabs my arm very suddenly and jerks me closer to him. Our bodies are now touching. I gasp.

"But even though you're fast and strong for your size, your physical strength isn't good enough compared to others who have similar abilities." He eases his grip. "But that's probably because of your petite and birdlike body structure."

I pretend to take offence.
"So what? Are you my trainer now?"

Jake seems to find my anger funny. "Nope. But you did ask me to teach you."

I sigh; I shouldn't get impatient. I am usually very patient. I guess I just want to be as strong as everyone thinks I am.

"Ok, shoot." I grin. "Teach me." I say as I extend my hand and motion him forward.

A wicked grin stretches out on his face and before I even process what is happening, he's right in front of me. Gripping my wrists together, not allowing any movement on my part.

"Now, you won't be the only one with speed and the element of surprise." He says very quietly. It's not helping me concentrate. "It's a good thing you know it though, so I won't have to teach you. But the rest of us with abilities have it too."

Jake is so close that I can feel his breath on my face. I twist, bringing my hands over my head in a spin and forcing him to turn as well. Now I am behind him, my hands clasping his behind his back. I lightly kick him behind his knees, making them bend so he kneels on the ground.

I bring my mouth close to his ears and whisper.
"How's that for a beginner?"

I release him with a small feeling of self-triumph.

Jake stands and faces me, gripping both my shoulders lightly. He looks me in the eyes.

"Not bad…" His eyes grow thoughtful. "It seems that you have your own survival instincts which guide you in fights. Whether or not the fight is real."

Jake's gaze burns into my soul and ignites my whole body. I don't want him to release me but he does. His expression turns mischievous and he rubs his hands together playfully.

"It seems that there's not much I can teach you," He says teasingly. "But we can always have fun play fighting each other. Don't you think?"

I start to object, afraid that I could hurt him. But he interrupts.

"And relax; I don't think you will hurt me. Even though I know you can if you wanted to." He looks very natural in a crouch, as if he's done this many times before. "Your instincts seem to tell you to capture a person without inflicting pain. It's like your soul is influencing your actions. It makes sense since you're suppose to bring love instead of pain. And I won't hurt you, so don't be afraid." Another wink.

I shrug.

"Okay then," I swiftly move into a crouch. "Suit yourself." Adrenaline swims through my veins, probably from the excitement I feel. "Prepare to get your butt whooped."

"Ha!" Jake laughs and runs towards me. My body is moving before my mind has time to process. It seems that Jake is right; I work on instinct. But it appears that my instinct runs on a deeper part of my brain, because even though I do not control my actions, my mind is aware of everything that is going on. And I know what to do.

My knees bend and I'm in the air for a split second, jumping over Jake as he charges towards me. I do a flip before my feet touch the ground once more. My body turns to face Jake, prepared for another assault, but he has stopped, and isn't doing anything but staring at me with wide eyes.

I straighten.

"What?"

He shakes his head in disbelief.

"I really should stop underestimating you. I'm not even going to ask how you did that."

"Did what?" I ask, confused. "You mean the flip? Oh, that has nothing to do with special abilities. That's just something I learned in dance."

Amusement fills his eyes and he recovers from his surprise.

"Hmm, I've gotta get me some dance lessons."

It sounds so ridiculous that I burst out laughing. Jake is probably an amazing dancer with or without lessons, but hearing him say that makes me lose it.

While I'm giggling, I don't notice him come closer to me. So when I manage to stop and straighten, I'm stunned as I feel his lips on mine. I don't try to stop him; I don't want him to, even when I feel tree bark pressing against my back. He has pushed me back against a solid tree. Our bodies are touching and on fire. My shirt is rather thin so I feel Jake's warmth. My arms and collarbone are bare and though it's a warm day, I have goose bumps. I shudder as Jake's hands brush my hip under my shirt and wraps around me. His fingers trail my skin, blazing a path wherever he touches. My hands find the back of his neck and stay there. I'm content with just kissing Jake, but I want to get back to work. I have to stop this before I don't want to anymore. Already my mind is starting to haze over. Already am I seeing, feeling, *tasting* nothing but him.

I break away.

"Hey," I try to sound light, but my voice sounds breathless. My grip still hard on his neck. "What was that for?"

"I just can't get over how remarkable you are." Jake's voice is as breathless as mine. "You catch on to everything so fast, and it all seems so natural for you. You give me strength."

I laugh a little at that. It's funny because I don't understand it.

"That's funny, because *you* give me strength, and I think you're the amazing one." I shove him lightly, playfully. "Which is why, Mr. Blanchard, you should get back to teaching me." I lightly give him a peck on the lips and skip to the center of the meadow.

When I turn back I see Jake eyeing me, his face glowing with love. My insides warm but I know that I have to focus. I have to in order to beat anyone.

"Let's get going."

That wakes him up. He struts slowly towards me at first, but then he breaks into a run. I want to try defending myself instead of just running away so I stand my ground; my arms ready. Jake closes the distance in three long strides and knocks me off my feet. I scramble back on my toes and aim a high kick at his face. But before my foot can make contact, he catches my leg and flips it. I probably would have landed on my face if I hadn't drawn my legs together, flipped horizontally with my body straight then pulled my body close together and rolled on the ground. My palms graze the dirt and the grass; it feels nice.

Time seems to slow through all of this, or maybe it is just my brain picking up speed and accessing and making sense of each little movement. It feels good to be moving constantly. It feels like a dance. And even though it isn't a dance, both Jake and me move with grace and quickness far beyond any normal fighter; so from someone watching from the outside, it might look like we are dancing.

I stand up and turn to face Jake again. This time, it is my turn to charge. I run to him and place my hands on his shoulders, prop myself up so that my arms support all my body weight, then flip onto his back and stay there.

"Hey there," I murmur to Jake good-naturedly. I kiss his neck and jump from him onto the ground.

"Yep," He says as he turns around and grips my waist. "No training, but a natural fighter. You don't even use your fists." He then chuckles at something he seems to find funny. "I bet you can't even throw a punch."

Jake's chuckle turns into guffaws and he lets go of me. I swiftly spin around and aim a kick at his stomach but he blocks me once more; I try to punch him, but as he said, I don't know how to punch. My knuckle grazes his chin slightly but I think I hurt myself more than I hurt him.

"Ow," I say as I shake my hand back and forth to ward off the pain.

Jake stops laughing and takes my hand in both of his; his warm palms numb the ache in my hand. Though he is no longer guffawing, I can still see laughter in his eyes and can still feel the humor in his emotions.

"Not funny..." I mumble.

"Sure. Whatever you say." He seems to be trying his best not to laugh. I slap his shoulder hard with my other hand. It makes a soft thud and turns my palm red.

"Ohh, sheesh." Jake lets go of my hand and lifts his sleeve to look at the raw mark I left on him. "You can't punch. But you sure can slap." He rubs his shoulder. "Ow."

This time it's my turn to laugh. I can't help it; at least I have a way of defending myself without having to use my weak wrists and knuckles.

"You gonna just laugh?" Jake says, but it looks like he is trying not to himself. "Or, do you want to continue?"

I stop. All the humor drains from me as determination replaces it.

"Let's continue,"

We start where we left off, with Jake attacking and me defending. But eventually, I'll have to learn to attack.

■ ■ ■

The sun is just setting behind the west trees, surrounding the meadow with a warm glow. The sky, a beautiful shade of orange and yellow, reflects its light onto my skin; making it look like bronze. The grass makes soft bedding under me, supporting and comforting my body. Jake seems as relaxed as me; his eyes are closed. I can see each eyelash that the sun shines on; his eyelashes are perfect, thick and curled. His skin is a nice warm tanned color, glowing as it is highlighted by the sun.

Jake is very beautiful; it's strange to call a boy that. And a lot of times when we say it, we don't mean it. But I mean it for Jake. I'm looking at him now, not looking at the way the leaves around me glow with the light, but looking at how Jake glows with the light. I roll closer to him and place my fingertips on his face. He doesn't react much; the only hint that tells me that he is awake and aware is the slight curl of his lips as I touch him. My fingers trace his features. I marvel at how they are almost perfect. It's funny how he calls me beautiful, because I'm not the beautiful one. He is.

Jake sighs. His eyelids flutter open and his eyes focus on me. He takes hold of my hand and kisses each finger.

"Jake," I start. "You know, you're really quite beautiful. More attractive than any other guy I've seen." My cheeks heat up.

Jake laughs softly, he still has hold of my hand and I feel his breathes on my skin.

"Funny you say that."

Jake sits up and pulls me closer to him. He wraps around me like a jacket, protecting me from any cold.

"We'd better get back soon." I say.

We must have been practicing in the meadow for hours. Jake and I had left the house right after lunch with a swift 'Bye' to my Gran. She's probably getting worried since we've stayed out so long.

"Don't worry, your Grandparents will know you're safe." Jake grins, his dimples flash. "Anyways, you're with me. They trust me." He winks.

I roll my eyes playfully like I've done many times since I met him. Jake is a lot like a child himself: playful, mischievous and funny. But he is also like an adult: Calm, warm, smart, and independent. I always feel safe around him, so I know that he is correct about what Gran and Gramps think.

"But," He says. "You're probably right." Jake gets up and pulls me with him. We walk out and away from the meadow, towards my house. "After all, we don't want to miss dinner. I bet your Grandma has gotten some delicious food ready for us."

My stomach growls and Jake laughs out loud.

"Yep, I'm ready to eat." I say. "Race ya back to the house?" My heart beats faster. I love racing Jake. It's nice being fast.

Jake's eyes twinkle with humor as he says.
"Ready. Set. GO!"

And we both take off towards the house, leaving the sunset behind us.

■ ■ ■

Jake reaches the porch about five seconds before I do. My muscles burn and my lungs fight for air, but I love the feeling of the wind brushing my face as I run. I am fast and smooth,

I cut through air as easily as I breathe it in. But this time, I didn't beat Jake.

"You let me beat you last time, didn't you?" I demand from him as soon as we both can catch our breaths.

"Barely, I just know what to expect from you this time is all." He says, his chest still heaving. "I tried harder. It's actually very difficult to beat you."

I feel fierce pleasure course through me. I am hard to beat. I shouldn't let pride get to me but it feels good.

"Why thank you," I smile at him. "You're not so bad yourself, sir."

Then before I let myself think again, I lunge at him, hoping to catch him by complete surprise. It doesn't work. He catches me. But the force I use as I collide with him sends both of us toppling down the deck and onto the grassy ground. We both stay there laughing and enjoying the moment. Looking up at the sky, it's easy to believe that there could be nothing wrong in the world. But that's not true; there are so many bad things, evil things, on earth. And I can't fix all of them, but at least I can help in whatever small way.

"Come on slow poke." I say as I get up. Jake gets up after me and puts his arm around my shoulder.

"Who you calling slow poke?" Jake says and he kisses the tip of my nose lightly.

We enter the house laughing only to be stopped in our tracks. Jake stops before I do, seeming to notice the problem before me. I don't see anything out of place, but I certainly feel it. The vibe in the room is tense, and the emotion in the room is cold. Not at all like how it usually is in our warm cozy cabin.

There are three figures sitting around the dining table: a light curly brown head for Gran, blonde for Gramps, and a dark brown head for a stranger. But even without looking at his face, I know who this stranger is. It's impossible to not notice his presence, and the way that he seems to suck the life out of everything he's near.

Nicholas.

But seconds after Jake and I walk in, the pressure and coldness in the room seem to be over taken by a little warmth and light, the dark and light now share the area. The darkness seems to be radiating from Cole, and the light from… me?

"Ah, Veronica, Jake. Good for you to finally join us." Gramps says. His eyes are tight. He seems to not know that both Jake and I already know whom our 'mysterious' visitor is, but he is warning us. "Erm, You should meet someone. This is…"

"Nicholas," I say in a tense voice. "What are you doing here?" My voice sounds loud and demanding. I don't mean to explode with anger, but how could I not? The person who tortures and brings pain is in my house.

"*Get. Out.*" My index finger is already pointing towards the door.

Cole turns to face me, his face and eyes hide all the emotions that I can feel radiating from him: Anger, surprise, humor, smugness, victory... and what is that last one... Fear? Cole is at least a bit scared of me. I don't know why. Well, maybe it's not me in particular. It could be that Jake is giving him a death look.

"Now, now. My dear Rose." I stiffen as he calls me Rose. So does Jake. "You can't kick me out just yet. My aunt and uncle are just about to arrive. They want to say... hi, to me. You should do the same." Cole smiles at me cruelly. And I realize that I don't have the authority to kick him out; the power in this room to do so actually belongs to Gran and Gramps.

I look at each of them meaningfully in the eye, trying to indicate what I want. But Gramps just shakes his head and focuses his attention back to Cole. And Gran just gives me a look as if she means to say 'Wait.'

Wait? I think. *Wait for what?*

Well, if Gran wants me to do nothing about Cole right this moment, I'll listen to her. I take a seat next to Cole; maybe if I'm closer to him, I can control him more. Jake sits very close next to me, as if to make sure that Cole doesn't do anything to me. He is eyeing Cole with a stony look, as if it's taking all his willpower not to jump up and punch him. I can feel the tension between the two guys and wonder whether something other than Cole's coldness had caused a breach between the cousins.

"So, Nicholas," Gran starts. "You and Jake are still cousins?"

Cole says, "Yes," the same time that Jake says "No,"

I feel an urge to slap my palm to my face. Obviously this little war between them is more personal than I thought.

Cole clears his throat.
"Yes, we are." He looks at Jake; I can feel his irritation. "But little Jake here refuses to acknowledge it."

"Don't call me little." Jake's says silently, deadly. I've never heard him use that tone and it scares me a bit.

"Now, now," Cole says, as if to a child. I can feel Jake's anger building and I set my hand on his thigh, trying to sooth or distract him. It works; Jake looks at me and takes deep and calming breaths. The anger drains out of him.

Before Jake, Cole, or anyone else could reply, I speak up.

"So, Cole," I mean to be friendly with the use of the nickname. But Jake stiffens and his grip on my hand tightens. But I don't let that get to me. If Cole won't leave my house, I will make the best of him staying. "What, exactly, are you doing here?"

"I actually came here to catch up with my family and get to know them again." He replies. But I think I hear a double meaning in his words.

Cole looks at me and I stare back into his eyes. For a second I think I see some of that ice in his beautiful eyes melt. Like he is losing some of the coldness that surrounds him. This gives me hope; maybe he can be just like any other person who needs help. Love floods through me with my new found knowledge. Maybe I can help him. But as the warmth of my love floods through me and reaches my eyes, I feel his withdrawal; as if he knows what I'm thinking.

I look away, feeling like I've failed, and look back. He is glaring at me with even more ice in his eyes than before. I feel the wall he is building against my help and feel a deep sense of loss. Even though I had not healed him, I was softening him down with compassion. But now, he is even more on guard than before. That will make it harder for me to help him. But through all of that, I feel as if he is split.

There is a fight going on within him, and none of us can do anything about it. Not yet, at least.

The doorbell rings, breaking into the silence. What seemed like minutes to me was less than half of one. Fighting mentally seems to take little time, and I accomplished nothing.

"I'll go get that," Gran says quietly, and she gets up to go to the door. Without a word, Gramps follows her.

Once Gran and Gramps are gone, I feel like I can speak freely to Cole.

"You didn't answer me before." I say heatedly. "What are you doing here?"

Cole looks impatient as he answers.
"I told you the truth, Veronica."

"Not all of it."

"Okay," Jake interrupts. "You're here to catch up." He rubs his hands together, trying to look casual. "So once you're done, you can get up and go."

"That's very hospitable of you Jake," Cole says sarcastically. "But I was actually thinking of staying for dinner." He looks at me again. "That is, if the beautiful Rose here wants me to." I can feel him probing my mind again. The power of the dream catcher that Jake bought for me after our last encounter with Nicholas must not be working. After all, it was all the way in my room. I feel Cole's dark presence in my mind, forcing me to want him to stay, and

I will myself to resist. It is harder than any physical fight that I ever had before. I sense myself weakening under his weight. Maybe he should stay. Do I want him to leave? No. I don't think I do.

I see and feel his triumph. He is smiling amiably at me but I know better.

"Stop it." I hear Jake say, and the will that was crushing my freedom of mind vanishes. I breathe in and out, trying to get my strength back.

"Hmm," Cole looks at me attentively. "You have gotten stronger. You can resist me a little more than you could last time. I could have won though, if Jake didn't interrupt."

"Don't try to take my will away from me, Cole." I say, staring at him with as much boldness that I can master. "It won't work again."

"As I said before..." Cole says quietly to me. "We'll see." He winks.

I look at Jake, wary of his reaction. But he is not reacting to what Cole has just said. Jake is just glowering at him conspicuously. I can sense that his concentration is on Cole and vise versa. If I am to guess, I'm thinking that they are having a mental conversation. I wonder what it's about. Curiosity sparks in me as it always does.

"What are you guys talking about?" I say pleasantly. I am not sure whether it's normal to be able to know whether there is some silent conversation going on, so I try to sound as casual as possible.

They both stare at me in surprise. Jake and Cole have the same expression for that emotion, and for the first time, I can almost see that they are related. Silently I wonder to myself which family member makes them related.

Before either of them can reply, Gramps and Gran walk back into the dining room with Aunt Alicia and Uncle Tom. All their expressions are stony, revealing none of their feelings. But, obviously, though it's still a little weird to me, I can still feel them. Mostly, there is anger and fear. But irritation and curiosity is also there. I guess that's why Gran and Gramps let Cole stay. They are all curious. And sometimes, it seems, that curiosity can lead to dangerous situations.

"Uncle! Auntie!" Cole says cheerily, I'm not sure whether it is heartfelt or fake.

"Hello Nick." Aunt Alicia replies; her posture and voice are stiff as she takes her seat at the table. Gramps and Uncle Tom have gone into the storeroom to get an extra chair. They return, and the table is now full.

"If your family calls you Nick," I begin before anyone else can talk. "Why do you ask me to call you Cole?"

Cole doesn't reply at first, he just looks at me compellingly. But I continue staring at him, forcing him to reply.

He sighs and smirks at me.

"Why don't you figure that out for yourself. Eh, love?"

Jake's already stiff body tenses even more. Without meaning to, I find myself thinking that if Cole weren't so evil, he would be quite attractive; what with his striking eyes, and accent and all. And I realize, with a start, that he has a slightly foreign accent.

"Your accent isn't completely American," I think out loud.

This seems to get Jake's attention.

"Yes, it's changed..." He says thoughtfully, his anger momentarily forgotten. It is replaced with the urge to know more. "Where have you been these past years?"

"Nice of you to finally ask, Cousin." He smiles at Jake, but it looks unreal. "I've been in Europe. All around, searching."

"For what?"

"Why would I tell you?" Cole says unemotionally.

"Because you want to." I say softly and place my hand on Cole's arm. I try to be as compelling as he is, because if he says we are more similar than I know, then maybe I could use that to my advantage. He looks at me and appears to almost want to tell me, but then as my serenity and joy flood through my palm into him, he flinches away.

"You know what," He says as he stands up. "I'm going to use the bathroom."

"Down the hall and to your right," Gran says.

Cole's footsteps don't make a noise, but they are heavy, weighed down by something. I sigh.

"What was that?" Jake says to me. I am surprised by the anger I hear behind his words.

"Huh?"

"What were you doing?" He says. "Why did you touch him like that?"

"Because…" I start. Jake has to control his emotions; I can feel his jealousy and protectiveness for me. "Because he said we are alike. And if we are more alike than I know, then perhaps I could use that. Can't you see? Maybe I can connect with him that way."

Jake looks into my eyes. He seems to believe me, but even more than that, he knows I'm right. He trusts me.

"You're right. You are like him; you share similar abilities. Except his are used for bad, and you use yours for good."

"Thank you for understanding," I look into his eyes. He needs to understand. I need him to. "I'm going to try to make him take down his walls okay? I can feel them blocking any access to his inner self."

I shake my head and add,
"Jake, I don't think he's the one we need to worry about. Sure, he's bad now… but I think I can heal him. He wants it, deep inside. I don't know how, but I can feel it. I don't think he's the broken one that I absolutely need to heal."

"And again, I know you're right." Jake replies. "Because I saw how you had almost helped him just now. A part deep inside him wants to be good. I think someone or something is making him do all this bad; it's not he himself. He used to be good, he use to be my best friend."

I nod, I had guessed that this rivalry was more than it seemed. And I am right; it is personal.

"What happened between you two?" I ask gently.

"I'll tell you later,"

"Okay,"

Jake looks away from me towards the rest of the family around the table. And though they haven't spoken through our whole discussion, they nod their heads now in agreement.

Cole is not the broken heart that I need to heal. Sure, I must help him and make him good again, but he isn't the broken one.

Just then, Cole walks into the room smiling to himself. As if he knows something that we don't. His eyes lock with mine and I know that he has something of mine that I never intended to give. He has the part of me that aches for all those people and anyone who is in pain, the part of me that wants to help even the most foul a person. Cole already has the loving and caring part of my heart.

13

We have finished dinner and I am helping Gran clean up. Gramps is with Mr. and Mrs. Blanchard out on the living room couch and Jake and Cole are outside on the porch. I wonder what they are talking about.

I don't want to talk about this with anyone but I need to let it out. I know I can trust my family, so I will tell Gran before I tell Jake.

"Gran?"

"Yes dear?" Gran replies while loading the dishwasher.

"Well, it's about Cole."

Gran looks at me. Her expression is almost worried, and I can feel her reluctance about the subject. I don't know how to continue. But I do.

"Why do I feel connected to him?"

"Honey, I don't know whether I'm the right person to tell you this."

"Tell me what?" Now I am really feeling scared for the answer. If it's something that Gran doesn't want to tell me, then it must be bad.

"Do you remember that little boy, not Jake, but that other boy who used to take care of you when you were a toddler?"

"No…" I say carefully.

"Well, it's okay if you don't. But the boy I'm talking about, the one that used to play with you as well, that was Cole."

"Oh."

I was not expecting that, for me to know Cole since I was young? Just like how I knew Jake, but even longer than I knew Jake.

"That's why he wants you to call him Cole." Gran says quietly. "Because that's what you always called him… from the time that you could speak."

"And?"

"Well, he's always been attached to you. I think everyone who knew you then and knows you now is attached to you. Just like Jake." Gran sighs. "Cole was very protective over you."

"And how did he become like he is now? And what about Cole and Jake?"

"When Cole was seventeen, he and Jake used to hang out, even though Jake was just nine. Cole was like an older brother, like a best friend to Jake. But then Cole's parents died…"

"That's horrible…" I say, quietly, interrupting her without meaning to.

"Yes, it is. Well, when Cole's parents died, Jake's family accepted Cole as one of their own. They treated him like a son…" Gran voice continues, making me imagine a picture behind the whole story. "When Cole turned eighteen, he bloomed. And he was absolutely amazing. He was good and true as well as powerful We were all proud. Cole finished college and was someone to look up to. Jake was always staring at him with wide amazed eyes. Cole was very close to your father. And when your dad disappeared, something in Cole seemed to change as well. He spent days away, searching maybe. And a few months after your dad disappeared, he vanished. But before he left, he and Jake seemed to fall out over something. I am not sure what it was." Gran sighs. "Even though Cole is different and wicked now, I believe he can be helped. I do not know what happened to him, but it pains my heart to see him so lost." A tear slips from Grans cheek. I think about how dad's disappearance affected not just me but Cole as well. Cole used to *love*. What happened to him that he doesn't feel those things anymore?

"It wasn't just curiosity that got you to let Cole stay for dinner was it?" I say softly. "You love him, don't you?"

"Yes, dear. And so does your Gramps and mom. Your dad loved him a lot too. I think the Blanchards still love him too."

"What else did he do that let them know how bad he is?" I question. "And what happened to him? What happened?" I am starting to feel sad for Cole.

"You should ask them that dear." Gran replies shakily. "And as for what happened to him… I'm not sure. Something evil must have gotten to him. Maybe if you ask him, he'll tell you."

I just nod. I can't speak. Cole is an old friend, someone who used to take care of me. Something terrible happened to him when he was looking for dad. Something *changed* him.

"How did we know him in the first place?" I ask Gran before I walk out of the kitchen.

"His parents were close friend of ours."

I can feel that Gran is hiding something, and I need to know what it is.

"Gran, what aren't you saying? What is it?"

Gran breathes out slowly and heavily before answering me.

"Cole left his mark on you when you were young, my dear. And you left yours on him." She seems to be trying not to shake. "Your fates are intertwined together; a long and dangerous path."

"How do you know this Gran?"

"Because when he became evil, when he was *forced* to become evil, he had to think of something that held his heart, the only love that's left in him." Gran looks at me deeply. "And we think that he thought of you. And this connection that you feel with him just proves that he did."

■ ■ ■

Everything that Gran told me swirls in my head as I creep out onto the porch to find Jake and Cole. I hear deep voices, not raised, but not calm either. They don't notice my approach. I can't go near them or they will sense my presence, so I stay by the door and open my senses to listen.

I have caught them in the middle of an argument.

"And why can't I?" A deep and cold voice says. Coles' voice.

"Because I won't let you!" Jake says back. I can feel the passion he is letting out. "You've taken a lot from me. You can't take her too."

"Of course not." Cole says maliciously. "After all, how can I take something away from you, if you don't have it."

Jake growls.
"I have her more than you do." He says, but his voice trembles like he's unsure.

"Ah, but do you?"

"I don't care if you've known her longer than I have Cole. You haven't been there for her."

"Hell. Have you? And who says I haven't?" Cole hisses. "I've always been there."

"Oh, and I guess torturing her is protecting her." Jake growls back. "And spying counts too."

"I didn't want to do those things!" He spits in frustration. "I need her. And I'm taking her."

"For what?"

"None. Of. Your. Business." Cole answers in an icy voice.

"I know Rose is powerful, Cole. And I know that whomever you serve needs her power or needs her dead in order to fill the world with darkness. But I'm not going to let that happen."

"You don't know what you're talking about." Cole says. I can feel his fear. "You haven't seen her."

"Her?"

"Jake," Cole begins. "I can't tell you this. You've got to figure it out for yourself."

"What?" Jake sounds confused.

"Please." I can hear the urgency in Cole's voice. The once icy tremor of his deep voice is gone, replaced by an unmasked fear. I suddenly remember a blurry kind face that looks like a younger Cole in front of me, laughing with me as I giggle with glee at the paint I had smeared on his face. Cole use to be good, and he can be good again.

"I don't understand." Jake's voice is unsure. All the anger is gone.

"You will, in time."

I peek around the corner to see Cole's hand on Jake's shoulder. I don't know what to make of this conversation but I will find out. Cole needs to come back to us. I suddenly re-member the childish love I felt for him, I remember now how I always thought that he was my older brother. How could I have forgotten him?

The silence on the porch is my cue. I step out from around the corner and start towards Jake and Cole. They both turn as my aura fills the open space.

"Hey guys." I say lightly. It is dark out and the stars are bright in the sky.

"Hey," Jake says as he walks towards me and gives me a light kiss. Cole says nothing. He just stares at me. I think he knows that I have found out about bits of our past. I look back at him and give him a slight nod. His eyebrows lift and he smiles a little. This smile is unlike the others that he has given me. This one looks real.

Tell me? I think silently to Cole.

I'll tell you when I trust you. He replies. *I'll tell all of you when the time is right.*

How do I know whether I can trust you? I say; I'm still suspicious.

Cole just looks at me.
You'll know.

I sigh and lean into Jake. I suddenly feel tired.

I don't get it. I think to Cole.

Get what? He smirks, but his eyes are serious.

Why you are trying to hurt me one day, and then the next, you act like family. I reply stubbornly.

It's complicated. He thinks back, his eyes withdrawn.

It always is. And somehow, I manage to sound sarcastic in thought.

I had no choice Rose. Okay?

What do you mean? I ask.

I mean, that unlike you, I have no free will. And this time, his thought slices through me as if he had cut me through the heart.

I stare at Cole, pity spilling from me. I know he hates it so I look away.

"I'll leave you two alone."

My eyes look up at Cole in surprise. Did he just say that? That must be the nicest thing that he's done. Maybe he is already changing.

Just before he walks back into the house, he faces us.

"Don't think you know who I am." He says, his tone serious. "Because I will keep surprising you whether I want to or not." Then he looks at me, and speaks to me only. "And don't think you can help me. I don't know whether that's possible anymore."

My eyes soften as I feel for my friend. The friend that I know is still in there.

"Don't worry Cole. I will always help you. It's always possible to be helped."

Cole's gaze doesn't waver; he looks like he is in such pain. He was once both Jake's and my best friend. And we have to bring him back.

■ ■ ■

"That is a little strange." Jake says after I tell him everything that Gran had told me. "I never knew that part of the story. I guess I only knew my side."

"That reminds me." I say, hoping that he would answer me. "What happened between you two?"

Cole had left about ten minutes ago, saying a quick bye to all of us and winking to Jake and me. He had put back on his bad boy act in front of the adults, even after we had gotten at least a little of his mask off just now. But now that Cole is gone, it is quite safe to talk.

"After your dad disappeared. Cole went to look for him." Jake sighed. "He came back months later acting all different. He spoke to me different, spoke to my parents different. He... he hurt my mom physically, by mistake or intentionally, I'm not sure. And hurt all of us emotionally real bad. We felt like we had lost a family member. There was a crazed light in his eyes that was not there before. He wouldn't tell us where he's gone or what he had done...

"Today was the first I heard that he's been in Europe all that time. Which makes me wonder where and why."

I sense that Jake is keeping something from me, something that still hurts too much to talk about, or to even think about.

"I guess we'll find out in time." I move closer to Jake. "Just like he said."

"Yep," Jake says. I feel his breath on my hair. "And can I ask you something?"

"Sure,"

"Do you love him?"

"Yes," I reply. Then I add. "But I love him the same way that you do. As a best friend, as a brother."

"I think he loves you," Jake mumbles so quietly that I'm not sure whether he means for me to hear.

"No," I say back anyway. "I don't think he loves me that way. I think he's just drawn to me because he needs me. Plus, he was like an older brother."

Jake doesn't say anything. His silence is a thousand screams in my ear.

"Can't you see?" I say. "He needs me to free him. Free him from the 'Her' that he was referring to."

"So you did hear us." Jake says humorously, conveniently changing the topic. "You little eavesdropper."

"Haha, very funny." Sarcasm drips from my voice. "What I was curious about is how you guys didn't sense me."

"I know why,"

"Well?" I say when he doesn't continue.

"It's because you didn't want us to." Jake says quietly, thoughtfully.

"What?"

"See, you don't even know you're doing it." He says as he rolls his eyes. "You do the same thing when you're fighting. It's unconscious. Your instinct, your body, your mind just does what it needs to do. So when you knew that you didn't want us to sense you, your mind automatically created a shield. None of us can do that. Only you. You're special."

"Hmm," I don't think I'm special. "Maybe it's not that I'm special. Maybe it's just that I'm completely and utterly raw."

"Well, it could be that too,"

I can tell from Jake's tone that he doesn't believe me. But if he thinks I'm extraordinary, time will prove him wrong. So I'm just happy he thinks I'm special now.

"We can help him Jake,"

I look into Jake's eyes and see the sadness and loss that he has tried to hide behind anger whenever in front of Cole. I wrap my arms around Jake, letting my love flow through me and into him. His arms tighten around mine as we both stare up at the sky.

The stars that fill the blue blackness above burn brightly, bringing fire to the sky. But the stars are nothing compared to the moon, which outshines them all. Though the stars are beautiful, the moon is more so; it is much more than beautiful. Stars twinkle, but the moon shines bright, steady and full.

14

I sit at the breakfast table, slowly eating the warm oatmeal that Gran had set in front of me. My brain is not entirely awake; part of it is still in the dream I had last night. A dream that could answer all our questions. Well, questions about Cole, that is.

In my dream, it is snowing. The little flakes float down past me as if I were actually there. I could see Christmas lights in little houses around and hear faint hints of laughter and merriness. It felt so real, but I knew it wasn't. I knew this, because Cole was there. And he looked different. He looked younger, and brighter. More innocent. More good. He was wearing a coat and shivering. But he was walking fast, looking for something. I didn't recognize my surroundings; I had never been to this place. But it was beautiful. Though the light was dim, as the sun was covered by storm clouds, the beach on which I was standing was glowing. Cole had continued walking quickly towards something I could not see. As I looked around, I realized that though I had no memory of this place, it was familiar. The water glimmered, waves making soothing noises. My dream did not follow Cole; instead, it allowed me to take control. I moved towards the water. The water was warm beneath my skin; it caressed my hand and welcomed me. As if it were my home, welcoming me back to where I belonged. I looked up and around once more. I *did* know this place. It was where I was born. It was where I spent the first year of my life. Ithaca, Greece. I stared at the sky in fascination. My dream must be some deeper part of memory for I had no idea what Ithaca looked like before now. It was a magical place, and even in a dream, I could sense the ancient power.

Out of the darkness of my dream, there comes a cry. It is a man. It is Cole. My feet run towards the sound but stop before a cave. There is a flickering light inside but I am not brave enough to go in. I am not brave enough to save Cole. *It's just a dream.* I think. *It's just a dream.* But if it were just a dream, how could I sense evil? How could I sense power? How could I sense danger? I fight my feelings and walk into the cave. After my first step, I feel a heavy weighted oppression. A dark and malicious force threatens to crush my soul. Even in a dream. Even in a nightmare.

It is even colder in the cave than in is outside. From the darkness, I hear a voice; high and wild, but full of depth and dominance.

"I knew you would come," The voice says. "Young, handsome, *powerful* Nicholas."

The voice said Cole's name with greed and eagerness, like someone who has waited a long time to eat a delicious meal. The voice belonged to a female.

"Who are you?" Cole grunts. He seems to have difficulty speaking, as if he's in pain. My soul aches as it tries to fight the forces that are keeping me at bay. I forget that this is a dream. All I know is that I need to help Cole. I must help my friend. Because I am pretty sure that this is the point in time when he turns to the shadows. I can't move fast enough. It is like moving through thick jelly.

"Someone who has control over everything," The voice says with a soft chuckle. "Including you."

"Never," Cole hisses.

"Now, don't be testy. After all, your beloved *Uncle* gave in to me. Like all the rest." The voice says.

I hear Cole growl in anguish and anger. I force my muscles to move closer. I see a large circular chamber, a dome, with a bonfire in the middle. The bonfire is huge and unnatural, almost reaching the top of the dome. At the end of the room, there is a throne with a figure sitting on it. I see Cole slumped close to the fire; nothing is touching him, yet he writhes like he is being tortured. I inch closer but don't get far before the voice speaks again.

"Hmm," It says. "Yes. I can feel your anger. I can feel your hatred. Let it feed you. Let it control you."

"No," Cole says, but he sounds weak.

"You want to, dear Nicholas." The voice says. "Stab me," The figure on the chair moves. "Torture me." The shadow moves closer to Cole. "*Kill me*," It almost seems to command, seeming to want it.

Though there is a huge fire in the chamber, I feel cold as ice.

"What will happen?" Cole demands.

"You'll be mine,"

"Then why would I want to do such a thing?" Cole groans.

"Because you want to, because you want revenge. Because your dear family and your dear *Uncle* and his daughter will endure serious pain if you don't."

"My uncle is dead." Cole replies flatly. I can hear the pain in his voice. He really did love my father.

"Then why are you still looking?" The voice asks viciously.

"I don't know…"

"It is because you know he is not." The stony voice says. "But he should be the least of your concerns. I already have him." I hear a laugh and it feels like knives are scraping the skin off my back. "Ohh, I bet your little adopted family would be nice in my collection of toys. Your attractive 'brother' would be quite the plaything for me. But what I really want, but don't have, is your uncle's young daughter. *Imagine what I can do with her.*" She hisses.

I hear Cole yell and see him launching himself towards the lean figure of a woman. There is a glint of silver as he drives a knife into her body, into her heart. Instead of dropping to the ground, the cloaked woman stands even straighter and seems to look Cole straight in the eyes.

"Now," She says. "You are *mine.*"

The last thing I see in my dream is Cole turning around and looking at me directly in the eyes. But his eyes are not the green that they usually are. They are coal black and merciless. In the dream I see him smirk as he did to me in the shop; his face showing horrible cruel humor. I hear a wicked laugh from the witch that he just stabbed. She should be dead. But she is not.

She got Cole to give into the blackness that is in every man's heart. Cole is the way he is because he tried to kill evil, and in doing so, he sunk to evils level and absorbed the darkness too. Cole went in good, but came out bad. He was defending the Blanchard's, defending me, defending *Dad.* And it cost him; it explains why he has no free will. It also shows that Cole isn't the one that has Dad; it's the dark cloaked figure that has Dad. And though Ithaca Greece could be the source of my, Jake's, Cole's and many others abilities, great evil also dwells there.

Even though this could just be a dream, I feel certain. Darkness cannot be killed with anger, hatred, or revenge. It has to be killed with love. But how can you *kill* something with love? When love is life and not death?

■ ■ ■

My grandparents had invited the Blanchards over for lunch, since Jake was coming anyways. And after I tell them all about my dream, Jake's only comment is: "But it can't be Ithaca, Greece. It almost never snows there."

"I told you," I say, exasperated. "It WAS Greece. The strange weather was probably caused by that woman in the cave! Remember how Cole made it cold that day when we went to town? Well, the same power was at work there. Only... it was stronger... more sinister."

"But we can't be sure that this dream is real, dear." Gramps puts in.

"Come on guys," I plead. "Trust me on this. It WAS real. It actually happened. We have to see what is going on there. We have to find out what happened to Cole."

"Well, I don't know, honey," Aunt Alicia whispers. "After all, it could just be a dream."

"More like a nightmare," Uncle Tom adds quietly.

Aunt Alicia turns her head to glare at her husband.

Grr... I growl in my head, frustrated with their reactions. It is not what I expected. How can they not believe me?

"You've believed me before. Can't you do it again?" I say. "We can ask Cole."

"No," I hear Jake say, his voice soft and calm. "I believe you. You were never wrong before. And I do believe that you may get more dreams like this."

I nod; it feels like it will happen again. I don't want it to. It's selfish. But I don't want to see any more of those night-marish flashbacks, even if it shows me the truth. I am not brave enough to crave being haunted in order to help some-one else. But I accept it.

"Do we talk to Cole?" I ask.

"No," Jake sighs. "It might be too painful for him to re-call. Either that, or he wouldn't be allowed to. After all, your story fits and would explain why he was compelled to hurt you and others. He was forced to. He has no free will."

"Now," Uncle Tom utters. "Don't jump to conclusions."

"Actually," Gramps states. "They could be right. It would explain everything."

I've always known that Gramps is smart. He can see things more clearly than others, but like most adults, his mind usually works in a fixed way. That's why it is the young that are put to the task of saving the world or doing some-thing new. For the young are usually more open minded than their elders. They have seen less of the world, and so they are fresh to new ways and new ideas.

I smile warmly at Gramps, because also unlike most adults, he can sometimes break free and think like a little boy. That is part of what makes him so wise.

"Great," I exclaim. "We all believe my dream." But looking around the room, I'm not too sure.

"Awesome," Jake said as he rubs his palms together. "Who's ready to go to Greece?"

That stops us all short. None of the rest of us had even thought about making our way to that ancient land and finding out who this cloaked figure is. It is illogical and dangerous.

But it makes sense to Jake, and I completely agree with him…

"Woah," The adults exclaim. "You are NOT going to Greece."

… but it doesn't appeal to the adults.

I sigh. It is too risky an idea for our family. They don't want to see us in danger or trouble or hurt.

"Trust us," I interrupt their protests. "We are not like normal teenagers. This is what we were born for. You know that." My hands trace the marks on my wrist, on my neck. I think about the mark on my hip; which is hidden under clothing. "Anyways, Cole will be with us."

Now that stops Jake short, his mouth opens to retort; but I don't let him speak.

"He has to come if I am to help him, Jake,"

My reminder to the adults that this is our destiny seems to make them think. They look thoughtful and worried, but resigned. Because no matter how much they want to protect us, our fates aren't like those of normal children. We are born different, and that can help us make a difference, no matter how small, in the world. It can enable *me* to help others. Something I've always wanted. And the deer from the meadow, so long ago it seems, even said that it is my destiny. I, and I alone, am fated. I am the one that will heal the broken heart to help tip the balance of the world away from the dark.

And I will see that task through.

■ ■ ■

The sun is in the center of the sky, shining down on the grass and trees. The swing I am seated on makes occasional squeaks and creaks as I rock back and forth. It is a nice, cool and sunny day, much like the first day that I spent here this summer. Birds chirp all around and the river whispers on the rocks. Jake and his parents had left right after lunch; they were going to look at plane tickets to Ithaca. We still have to tell Cole what our plan is; he will most likely be coming with us, though we don't know whether we can trust him.

My head shakes as I think of him. I feel a fierce strength in my heart to protect him; he is like my brother, one of the oldest friends that I've got. I have to help him.

My eyelids flutter shut as I think of everything that has happened. It's all been so much. And now, I might even find my father. He could be the prisoner of the woman that changed Cole; he has to be there. No matter how much I try to tell myself not to hope, my heart tells me that I might see my dad soon.

Wow, I'm going to Ithaca; and not for a holiday either, I think. It's not how I imagined my first trip to Europe would be but…

"You sleeping?" I hear a familiar voice say, but much too close, right next to my ear. My eyes fly open quickly only to be blinded by the sun. A dark figure leans over me, close enough that I can feel his breath against my face. My eyes narrow as I recognize who the voice belongs to.

"Cole," I exclaim softly.

"Hey there," Cole grins widely, showing a line of perfect white teeth. His dark brown hair looks bronze in the sunlight; his emerald green eyes are staring at me with a hint of amusement. Of course, he just has to look absolutely flawless.

I exhale slowly, trying to get my thoughts in order. Cole is like Jake in a way, they are both very beautiful; but in that, they are also very different. Jake is like a light kind of handsome, with his dark blonde hair and bright blue eyes. Whereas Cole is dark; but his eyes are bright and shining now, more so than I have ever seen them.

"So," I start. "What are you doing here?" I don't ask how he got in because technically I'm not inside. All Cole had to do to reach me was walk around the side of the house and climb up a couple of steps.

"I came to see you," He says matter-of-factly. "But you don't seem shocked to see me."

"Oh, no." I breathe out shakily. "I am shocked. It's just that I know how to hide it." I think about what he said and add, " Why do you want to see me?"

"You're going to Ithaca."

Cole says it like a fact, not a question. So I guess he already knows. No point in hiding it now. Anyways, we are going to get a ticket for him too.

"Yes," I say. "And so are you."

"Oh, I know," His grin softens into a small smile but his green eyes are thoughtful, not playful.

"I don't understand you," The words come out of my mouth before I could stop them.

"Oh?" His eyebrows shoot up towards his hairline. "And why not?"

"Because one moment you're vicious, and the next you're normal. Like how you are now." I exasperate. "It's like the person who tortured me and pecked me are completely different than the person who is standing in front of me now." My hands move upwards in a movement of frustration. "And I feel like I can trust who you are now, but not who you are when you act all bad and are bent on terrorizing me and others." My eyes meet his meaningfully. "Do you get what I mean? I don't know whether I can trust you fully. How would I know whether you will turn on us until it's too late?"

He thinks about this, his eyes attentive but I feel amusement rolling off of him.

"Well, you seem to already think that I am on your side. When I have done absolutely *nothing* to make you believe that." Cole's eyes narrow, "And I can't tell you myself whether you can trust me or not because I don't know whether you can either. But you can trust me right now; I am not going to hurt you." His voice is low and soft, I hear sadness in it. "But I don't know when I am going to start acting like that person who hurt you. And I am sorry that I did what I did."

"So you really are like two people?" I question. His feelings are true. Nothing indicates that he is lying and I want so much to believe him and tell him everything. But I know that it isn't possible, because the evil is still inside him… moving through his veins like venom that slowly poisons his soul. And that woman, whoever she is, is still controlling that part of him.

"I believe so." His eyes are hard and his face betrays nothing he feels beneath. But I can feel his emotions like they are my own; pain, unhappiness, loss, regret, anger, hope and love. I can feel his love for me radiating from him, but I don't feel uncomfortable, because this must be a tender sort of love. Nothing like what I feel for Jake. What Cole feels for me could be what he would feel for a sister. That is what I conclude, because Cole could never love me in a romantic way.

"Cole…" I whisper sadly. It's like I have lost my best friend, or brother. His hand reaches for my face and rests on my cheek. Shock rolls through me because I see in his eyes nothing that is supposed to show from the tenderness of a brother. My heart does somersaults in my chest. I want it to stop; it's reacting in a way that should not be allowed. Not from this touch.

I lean away from Cole because we are a bit too close together. His hand falls back limply to his knee and his eyes blaze.

"I will free you." My voice trembles with force.

"I know," Cole says firmly. "I believe you. You have always freed me."

Cole bends down to me so that we were eye level. I am still seated on the swing but he is standing. He presses his mouth to my forehead; his lips are warm where they touch my skin. My eyes close automatically, confusion runs through me at this gentleness he is showing. The pressure of his lips disappears and I open my eyes. Cole is staring at me with broken beautiful eyes. He turns and jumps from the deck onto the flat plain of grass below, as graceful as a gazelle. Another trait that people like us have. Cole disappears into the shadows of the trees without a backwards glance, his figure melting into the darkness of the cool shadows of the forest.

15

"I can't believe we're going to Greece!" I say; my voice is high and clear with delight. It has been two weeks since we discussed going and now it is actually happening. I might see my dad soon, and we can help Cole!

The two guys have been getting along rather well; I guess it is more like how it used to be when Cole and Jake were like brothers. Cole has been eating dinner over at my grandparents' house for the past couple of weeks. Over that time, he also seemed to become more natural and not as cold as he had been on our first meeting. He doesn't give off as strong a hostile and evil vibe as he once did. But I still see him tense up occasionally, almost as if he were fending away some unwanted feeling, thought or force.

I can feel him fighting to stay with us.

Jake thinks that Cole's had a change of heart because my presence and touch is affecting him like it affects everyone else, making them feel healthier, brighter, and happier than usual. Blocking the evil that was controlling him. Gramps and Gran calls it my 'Love medicine'. Ha. *I* think it's just that Cole was reminded of everything he lost, and now he wants it back and is fighting for it.

I look out the plane window at the setting sun as Jake and Cole squirm in their seats. Both of them look extremely uncomfortable but that isn't surprising since they are both quite tall and there is very little space in economy class size chairs. The corners of my lips quirk up in a small smile as I watch them fumble around, trying to get comfortable in their seats. Jake looks over and catches my grin before I can pull a straight face. He raises his eyebrows up at me.

"What's so funny?" He asks. His mouth twitches, as if he is trying not to smile himself.

"Oh, nothing," I say casually. Jake's eyebrows inch even further up his forehead but he seems to give up on trying to decipher the reason behind my sudden look.

My eyes catch Cole's before he looks quickly away. He hasn't really made much contact with me since that day on the deck. The most he's done was to smile at me across the dinner table, or pass me something without touching my skin. He seemed to be avoiding me, seems to still be… Maybe that will change once we reach Ithaca.

"What are you staring at?" Jake inquires. My eyes shift away from Cole; I hadn't realized that I was staring at him with so much concentration. Jake follows the line of where my eyes were a moment ago and chuckles. I turn my gaze to glare at Jake instead. What does he find so funny?

"What?" I demand. Maybe a little too harshly; but impatience is growing in me. I should cut its roots before it sinks them in.

Jake reaches his hand out and lightly places it on my shoulder.

"Don't worry about him. He's not avoiding you; I don't think anyone is capable of that. He's just trying to stay close but keep his distance at the same time." He shrugs. "Maybe being too near you makes him feel like he's on enemy territory. Your presence does help. It seems that with you around he can control whether or not that shadow woman can take him over."

"Yeah, sure." My voice sounds more confident than I feel. Deep down inside, I wonder if the reason Cole has been keeping his distance is actually to keep the connection to that woman open. But I can never be sure; might as well not think negatively.

I jump as the plane jerks to life in a sudden movement. Jake takes my hand reassuringly. Within moments, after the bouncing and roughness of the plane wheels on the concrete runway, I feel a sort of lightness as the vehicle defies gravity and lurches into the air. I loosen the hard grip I didn't know I had on Jake's hand. He smiles at me wryly while rubbing his palm and fingers.

"Strong grip you got there," He says with humor. My arm moves and I find myself play punching him lightly. "Ow," He murmurs. Well, I thought it was light… but it probably was not that hard, he's just amusing me. I know that my punch didn't actually hurt him. His muscles are a layer of rock over his bones; it certainly hurt me to punch him. I think I got more pain than he did.

Jake looks past me at the window and beyond; the glare of the setting sun glows on his face.

"Look," He says softly.

I turn my head and focus on something other than Jake. Air wheezes past my mouth and throat as I suck in a breath. It is breathtakingly beautiful. We are high enough now that the buildings in the city look like little small dots; the green of land is a patchwork of parks and fields. I look above the scenery of humanity to the sky. Clouds surround us, looking like white and pink pillows of soft cotton candy. The sun is blazing orange as it hides briefly behind clouds and emerges from them again. My eyes don't flinch away even as the light hits my face. Even through the thick glass of the plane window, I feel the heat of the sun. I turn to Jake, planning to express my wonder at the amazing sunset only to see that he is already looking at me. His eyes are wide and incredulous and I reach to pat my hair and face, wondering whether there is something wrong with me.

"What is it?" I demand. "Is there something in my hair? On my face?"

Jake shakes his head silently; his hand reaches across the tiny space that separates us but stops just before his fingers touch my skin. It's as if he's afraid to touch me, afraid that I might shatter or disappear or something.

"What's wrong?" I ask, because I do not understand why wonder, amazement and awe are radiating from him as he looks at me.

"Nothing's wrong," Jake whispers. "It's exactly the opposite! You're so... so..." He fumbles for the right word and seems to be failing.

I frown at him; my mind flies across many possible words: Weird, messy haired, tired looking, haggard? What's he thinking?

"… Bright!" He says after a pause. "No, not like that!" He puts in when he sees my expression. "I mean; you're kind of shining Rose."

"What?" Shining? How can I be shining? What does 'shining' even mean?

Jake grins widely at my confusion, and then replies to me very softly.

"I mean, that you look so happy and wonderstruck that you're shining. You must have really liked that view." His eyes twinkle. "And the sun on your face and hair makes them look more radiant." Jake sees the look I give him and holds his hands up in a gesture of surrender. "Hey, that's just what I think."

Out of the corner of my eyes I see Cole nod slowly, I look over at him and see that he is smiling at Jake, as if he agrees with him. Cole meets my curious stare and winks. I feel my lips part in surprise; this is the most he's ever done to indicate that we used to be, and still might be, good friends. Cole smiles at me and looks away as I turn back to face Jake.

"See," Jake says. "Cole agrees with me. But he's been rather silent." He says it lightly enough, but I can feel a twinge of jealousy seeping into his emotions, which is still filled with love and wonder. I lean forward and give him a light peck of a kiss on his cheek. Jake looks at me in surprise; he wasn't expecting that. But he looks pleased enough.

"Don't worry," I say reassuringly. "I don't know whether he agrees with you. You flatter me too much. There are so many more pretty girls that are a better match for you." I wink at him. "I don't know why you chose me."

And this is the truth. Because I really have no idea whether Jake likes me for me. Or whether it's my ability that draws him towards me, just like how it draws everyone else. I'm afraid that I'm *making* him like me. That if I were just a normal girl, he wouldn't feel the same.

"Oh," He looks at me with serious eyes. "I'm not worried about that… and haha,"

I give him the hardest glare I can manage and am rewarded by a little twitch in his lips.

"And don't you think, even for a minute, that I would want anyone else but you." Jake mumbles so quietly, that if I didn't have enhanced hearing, I don't think I would have understood him.

Instead of replying, I gently lay my head against his shoulder and shut my eyes. The flight is about eleven hours. I plan to get some sleep during the flight so that I can be wide-awake in Greece.

With closed eyes, I cannot see Jake's reaction to my gesture. But I feel his hand move in motions lightly through my hair, as if he were caressing me. Then he shifts his body as if he were moving over me to reach something. I smile a little as I feel the heat of the sun through the window next to my seat once more before I hear the sliding of the window covering come down to shield me from the sun's glare with a soft *thud*.

■ ■ ■

I am trapped. There is no sun, no wind, no light. There is not a single sound except for my low, shallow breathing. I see nothing in the darkness of the black emptiness. I cannot move, cannot get out of this black hole. It's like I'm in a cage with no end. A cage of shadows. I am not usually afraid of the dark, but this darkness threatens to seep into my soul. It threatens to undo me. Fear courses through my veins as blood flows through my body with each pump of my heart.

Something changes in the darkness. It isn't soundless anymore; I hear a rumbling piercing noise in the blankness of my solitude. It gets louder and more shrill by the second. A few moments pass before I realize what it is. Laughter. Wicked female laughter. The sound grates my ears and with each hitch of breath, it feels like knives and nails are scraping down my back, leaving raw skin and scratches. I exclaim in pain but my scream is soundless. I cannot hear anything but that laugh. The laugh ceases, replaced by a piercing strong voice.

"My dear Roza. Coming straight to me. Come at me if you will, little Rose, I'll be waiting." The voice is soft and euphonious, like a sleeping ghost. But it slashes through me with a force as hard as water crashing against a rocky shore. "You can never beat me. I will just consume you

and your powers and hold you in my collection." I hear a chuckle. "You will not win. No one can beat me! I am Tenebris Daemon! Demon of the darkness and shadows! You will shatter beneath me."

I can't think. My brain pounds with icy heat. I feel the sinking, falling action of my body, but I do not feel the hard texture of the ground as I faint. It's like I'm numb to everything but the pain that the voice instills. There is the laughter again; surrounding me and suffocating me like an airless space. My lungs burn with the effort of trying to get in some oxygen, but nothing is working. Layers of hot tears fill my eyes as my heart rate slows and I feel myself sinking into the vacuum of space.

I'm dying, I think.

Though life seeps away from me, I do not fear death. My muscles relax with the conviction of my thoughts. I will not be brought down by the fear of death. I will live on in heaven and life everlasting.

A low growl fills the bareness of the dark as the woman whom the voice belongs to realizes my serenity and joy. She cannot control me because I am not afraid of death. Nothing she can do will hurt me.

"I win," I whisper in thought, and I hear a hiss before I am swallowed up by darkness.

"Veronica…" I hear a deep beautiful voice call me; a voice as soft as feathers. Not female this time, but male and familiar. I drift even further into the blank space expecting the burning to be over. I am floating in calm waters. My mind goes dark, only to be blinded, a moment *later, by a bright white light as warm and comforting as the fireplace, welcoming me home...*

"Veronica," I hear the same deep beautiful and familiar voice calls me. "Veronica, wake up! We're here!" Something soft and warm brushes my face; my eyelids force themselves open. Jake's face appears in front of me, bright and luminous. My heartbeat slows as I process reality and separate it from my dream.

"Veronica?" Jake says, his voice full of concern. "Rose, are you all right? What's wrong?"

I look at him in surprise and realize that tears have spilled over my eyes and dampened my cheeks. I wipe my hands carelessly over my face and smile up at Jake.

"Nothing, nothing." I say with as much conviction as possible. But as I say it, I recognize my lie. My hands shake delicately. Jakes' eyes show his disbelief as he reaches out to push a lock of hair away from my face.

"Rose," He murmurs. His mouth opens as if he's about to say something but I cut him off with a wave of my hand.

"I'll tell you later." I reply. "When we reach wherever we're going..." If not for the fact that I am still haunted by my dream, I might be annoyed that Jake still hasn't told me where we're going to be staying. A shudder goes through my body as I recall the dream. "I can't say it now." *Not without breaking down…*

"Ok," Jake says very gently, seeming to catch on to my mood and wanting to comfort me.

The speakers of the plane *ding* and we look up as a flight stewardess starts announcing our arrival.

"Ladies and Gentlemen. We are about to land in Kefalonia, Greece. Please fasten your seat belts, put your chairs upright and open your window covers. It is eight thirty two in the evening in Greece and the land temperature is seventy-four degrees, Fahrenheit, and twenty-three degrees, Celsius. The weather is nice, warm and breezy. There will be a guide to bring you to the terminal for flight changes or to collect your luggage and to check out. Thank you for flying with us and we hope you enjoy your stay." A Pause. "It might be a bit of a bumpy landing so hold onto your seats and get ready to enjoy the beauty that Greece has to offer. Fly with us again!" *Ding.*

■ ■ ■

The ocean breeze blows past my face into the car that is driving us to the house where we will be staying. The sky is already dark and stars are coming out to illuminate the sky like little diamonds.

I can hear the crash of the waves as it hit the beach. The smell of salt water mixed with fresh clean air makes my lungs sing with pleasure. Ithaca has both the sea and the mountains, so it is what I would call a perfect place. Cole is in the front seat next to the driver and Jake is next to me. He is looking out the window, as I am, so I don't bother to make conversation.

Ithaca is truly beautiful, though it is small and we've hardly seen any of it. Ithaca is too small to have an airport, so we landed in Kefalonia and took a ferry to Ithaca. The ferry ride from the mainland to this island was amazing. Though I was half asleep through most of it, I can still remember the awesome feeling of flying while the boat moved agilely through the white-capped waves. But beneath the beauty of Ithaca, there is a force too subtle for normal humans to sense. There is ancient power in this land, and a great evil. But along with that, I sense the good power of the people like me, 'the gifted' as I have come to call them. I feel the joy of nature all around me, vibrating in my bones, fighting against the shadow that consumed Cole and captured my dad. *When I leave this place*, I think, *I hope that it will not be so dark.* I don't want to let darkness powerful enough to change a good person to stay in this beautiful serene land, or any other land on earth. But right now, I have to work on taking it away from here. Though anger is an uncommon emotion for me, I feel anger against Tenebris Daemon, the so-called demon of the shadows.

We've driven for quite awhile with more to go; I drop my head against the window of the car, allowing me to look at the view. The trees and scenery go by in a blur and I find myself fading into another reality, away from the cab, away from Cole, away from Jake, away from myself.

I open my eyes only to be blinded by a bright white light. I see nothing in front of me, nothing behind me, and nothing of me. I am there, but not there. Wherever I am, I am alone. I walk unseeing, unfeeling, until my legs give way. With my knees on the flat ground, I breathe. With each breath, a figure materializes out of the blank whiteness.

I've always thought that darkness was nothing but a vast emptiness, but too much light can be nothing as well. The figure is black, and getting even blacker by the second: a shadow in the brightness, polluting the white. This shadow, though smaller than the light, fills it, and darkens the bright light. The light is dying, being sucked by the shadow… but I am finally able to see, I can finally feel.

My legs push my body upright until I am standing. I am not alone in the brightness anymore; there is darkness with me. As the light fades into a bearable sight, and the dark melds into the white, I can finally make out something of the figure. The figure has brown wavy hair, brown eyes, pale skin, and rosy cheeks. The figure is me. Darkness radiates from the other me.

Pure horror fills me before I can make sense of the situation. Everyone has a dark side and light side; no one can function with just good, or with just bad. There has to be a balance. The darkness is not around me; it is in *me. The goodness that fills me could eventually consume me. Some might not think it a bad thing, but perhaps the bad have some good qualities about them. And maybe the good have some bad qualities about them. Perfection will only come when they both work together. I must not be afraid of the darkness, or of Tenebris Daemon, a demon in the flesh of a woman, who haunts my dreams and fills Cole's heart. I must be brave, I must be equal, and I must be the balance in between, in order to tip the balance of the world towards the light. I must open up to both sides of me in order to be my strongest, in order to see my clearest, in order to love the greatest. I must love both dark and light creatures of the earth in order to heal them, in order to help them.*

As this realization dawns on me, I see that the brightness and darkness have merged into one, creating a beautiful scene, a world containing both light and dark. Both sunlight and shadow. A sunrise followed by a sunset.

The darkness of night creeps up or fades away into the brightness of day. Those times are the most amazing, where light and dark share a natural and equal place. They are both innocent, and that is what I have to make the dark and light in people: innocent. For those who have turned evil may not have wished to be so, they may have been wronged or they may not have known better. But we share this earth anyways, just like the moon and the sun share the sky. You need both dark and light to survive, both good and bad. But it has to be innocent. That's my job. I have to return the broken hearts to how it was when they had their first breath on this land; like the sunrise, a beginning of a new day. Or I have to bring it to an end if it refuses to be reborn; like the sunset as darkness takes over. I have to be able to do both, save or destroy.

Right now, I've only experienced what I can do as I save. But in order to be 'The One' I have to learn to destroy any threat or great evil. That must be what the crow on my hip means, and what the dove on my neck means. I can be both good and bad; I am. I have both the powers of dark and light, it's what makes me different from the rest. And both sides can trust me, to bring them together and to get rid of the greater evil that makes the natural darkness and light not innocent.

Because before any of this, there was already darkness, there was already light. But human nature corrupted the darkness and turned it into something it was not. Darkness is not evil, it was originally pure and innocent as light, giving a chance for stars to shine. But as people have grown wicked, the sins of the heart spoiled the dark and made it foul. Now it's my job to change that. It's my job to help darkness pass into the light. To try to aid anyone. To sacrifice myself.

But when I finish my job, will I be the same?

16

I'm burning. That's the first thing that comes to mind when I wake up. My muscles are sore when I move my hands to touch my skin. Warm sticky sweat comes away with my hands; damp hair sticks to my face. Sweaty hair is annoying, so I tie it up into a bun.

I am in a dark room; there is a veil around my bed, flowing like soft solid streams. Below me are soft sheets of cotton and silk. The bed bounces slightly with every movement I make; like a waterbed. It's hot in the room so I guess that there is no Air-conditioning. And since there is no movement in the air to cool the room, I'm guessing that there isn't a fan either.

This must be the house we will stay in while we're here in Greece. I don't remember walking into the house, but I'm so slight that Jake had probably managed to carry me all the way from the car to this bed.

Wow, what a great impression I must have made on our hosts. Looking like a child isn't something I enjoy very much, and my dad used to carry me from the car to the house whenever I fell asleep. Now Jake is doing that.

My head screams in protest as I move into a sitting position. My dream comes back to me in fragments. My eyes are wide open. Fear courses through me as the realization of what I have to do hits me.

I am scared.

The house is silent. Not a creak in the wooden floors, no faint sound of crickets or the stream, no sound of the leaves rustling with the wind that tells me I'm back home with Gran and Gramps.

But there is noise. There's noise coming from outside. I get up from bed and look for my boots. Instead of the jeans and t-shirt that I had on for the journey, I am in PJ shorts and a linen thin hoodie.

The door creaks as I open it. The sound I had heard from the bedroom gets louder as I make my way into what appears to be the living room. Gentle moonlight seeps through the window, lighting the room with its pale glimmer. I can see the moon and stars in the sky, and the beach and ocean from the house.

That must have been the sound I heard: waves crashing onto the rocks. To the east, I see the sky coloring up a bit. It must be close to dawn. There is no sign of life in the house; it is that silent. My fingers find their way to the door that leads outside. It leads to the beach and the crashing waves, the moon with the stars and the coming sunrise. My first sunrise in another part of the world.

I have to cross a platform of rocks and pebbles; they move and give way beneath my feet. But thanks to my ability, and my normal agile movements and gracefulness, I manage to not fall flat on my face. Thank God.

The sea breeze hits me right after the smell of salt water. I love it; it feels like what I would like to call home when I'm older.

Rocks and pebbles turn into soft sand, my shoes slide and sink into the sand, but my feet can't feel it. Very carefully, I take off my boots one by one and put them to the side. Then I am running, running fast, the sand getting kicked up behind me as my heels drive into the soft surface. A bubble of gleeful laughter rips through me and springs from my mouth.

The sound is loud compared to the silence before, but soft compared to the booming waves. My feet take me towards the water, towards the east, towards the rising sun. With the fading moon to my right side and the rising sun to my left, I look down at my arm and am reminded once again of my dream.

The yin-yang symbol etched onto my skin finally makes sense. I am both dark and light, the night and the day, the sunrise and sunset, the sun and the moon.

Both are needed to create a balance in life. Many things depend on both. There would be no tides without the moon, no life without the sun. And though the sun is more important than the moon, they both have a part to play. Neither one of them could cease to exist, or else we would all cease to exist. Many people are both good and bad, but no one is truly and fully good or bad. I have to open up to the darkness within me in order to be my fullest good.

I only pray that I can control the darkness.

But I do not know whether I am strong enough.

The brightness in the east is getting more and more prominent, soon the moon will have go back to sleep and the sun will take the day. Beads of color rip through the sky, light pink, bright orange, gold and silver from both sides; it is beautiful. The sunlight reflects on the ocean, making the water glitter. I look directly towards the light, wishing I could see past the center of our universe. Happiness, serenity, peace and longing fill me as I stare at the start of a new day. The innocence of the natural light and dark engulfs me with strong relief. That's how we all have to be. Innocent. Just like nature.

The streams of sunlight warms my skin, I lift my face up to let the heat bring color to my cheeks.

"Enjoying the sunrise?" A soft voice says warmly by my ear.

I turn to see Jake standing by my side. Close enough that I am able to feel his body heat against my own. His face is inches from mine. It's funny that I didn't sense him or notice him coming. Perhaps I was too overwhelmed by the sunrise.

He grins. "Good Morning," Jake murmurs with a twinkle in his eyes.

"Hi," I say softly. Not taking my eyes away from the sun, I reach out to hold his hands.

I feel the soft skin of his palms against mine and breathe in contently.
"It's beautiful, isn't it?" I sigh. "This whole place is beautiful and I've hardly seen any of it yet."

"Yes, it is beautiful." Jake goes silent for a few moments. He looks thoughtful, maybe a little bit brooding. When he speaks up and breaks the silence, I jump a little. "It's beautiful, but can you feel the darkness? And not the innocent darkness either, it feels like coldness."

"Yes..." I mumble. "I do feel it."

And I do.

I feel it all around me. The coldness of evil mixed with the warmth of natural goodness. Evil here is cold. But it isn't dark; it could be as bright as day, but it would be a freezing, unnatural, and evil brightness.

I can feel it everywhere. I can feel it in me, just waiting for me to touch that side of my nature, waiting for me to come to the full strength of my ability. I need to be both dark and light. But how will I keep the darkness from turning into cold evil?

I shiver involuntarily at the thought of losing control, of losing who I am. Jake looks at me with concern and puts his arm around me, assuming that I am cold. But as soon as my eyes meet his, I see comprehension in his eyes and know that he knows that something isn't right. He opens his mouth to speak but closes it before getting any words out, for I shook my head in a silent plea.

He understands and gathers me in his arms instead of asking me 'What's wrong?', which I appreciate.

Gratefully, I let my body melt into his and let his warmth seep through our clothes and skin, down to my very bones. Some of the coldness that I was feeling leaves me and I sigh in relief. We stay like that for quite awhile. The sun is up and shining on us both.

I would have been happy to stay like that forever. It is so peaceful, so serene. With the waves crashing on rocks and the beach, the feel of the warm water on our feet, the warmth of the sun and the coolness of the breeze, with Jake's chin on my head and his arms around me, and no human-made noises. Well, until I hear someone shout Jake's name.

We both turn our heads to the sound; I see the silhouette of a female, and thanks to my heightened sense of sight, I manage to make out her features.

She is extremely beautiful; she has dark glossy curly short hair that just goes over her chin, the color almost raven black. Beautiful night-sky-blue eyes that shine. Her skin is tanned from the sun and she has light brown freckles on her cheeks. Her nose and chin are sharp, and her lips are full.She looks about my height, though maybe a little more broad; no surprise there, I am rather slight. As I assess her, I feel rather aware of my own rather plain looks, for she is a thousand times more beautiful.

Jake pulls me towards where the beautiful girl stands and we hold hands while strolling towards the house. She waits for us near where I had put my boots. When I get near, I see her mouth widen into a big smile, and her eyes brighten as she looks me over. I open my senses to feel her emotions; I sensed admiration, happiness, welcoming love and something else, maybe a sudden peace or calm shock? I don't know.

"Hello," She says. Her voice is gentle, clear and melodious. Very pleasant, something you can fall asleep to because it's so soothing. "You must be Veronica," She extends her hand out to me and I shake it with a smile. "I'm Angelica, but everyone calls me Angel, so you may do the same if you want." Angel winks. Her smile softens into a slight grin as her eyes drift to Jake.

"Hey Jakie," She adds quickly. She goes over to hug him but he picks her up in a big bear hug then drops her but she lands, like a cat, on her feet and punches him playfully on the arm. I watch this all feeling very warm inside; so much love and friendliness is radiating from them that it is affecting me. They act like family.

"Come on in and meet everyone!" Angel shouts as she runs into the house.

Jake pulls me towards where Angel had taken off.

"Come on, Rose." He murmurs softly. "Don't be shy."

"Right," I reply with firmness that isn't very heartfelt. "I'm not shy. Not at all."

But my face must have been scrunched up or something because Jake knows I am lying. He lets out a big guffaw, picks me up and swings me over his shoulder so fast that I don't really notice anything until I am dangling over his shoulders.

"Hey!" I scream and laugh. "Put me down! And don't you dare drop me or I swear you'll..." But I don't get to finish my sentence because he sets me down gently and as quickly as he had picked me up.

We make our way towards the house laughing and holding hands. When we are just outside the door I stop and take a deep breath. Time to meet some more new people. Not something I really liked to do. Oh, well.

Jake smiles down at me and opens the door. The scene before me is the most normal and welcoming thing that I have ever seen in my life. It makes me feel comfortable, not awkward in the slightest.

There are four people in the room; the oldest is probably less than twenty years. Angel is by the stove cooking some pancakes, there are two boys, one of whom looks twenty and the other looks ten, and a little girl standing by Angel. No one but Angel seems to be expecting us; the only thing that gave away the fact that they know we are coming in are the small smiles on all their faces. They probably heard me screaming when Jake had picked me up.

I look around the room and frown. Cole isn't here.

"Hello," I hear a small quiet but high voice exclaim from below me.

I look down and see the beautiful little girl that had been standing next to Angel. She is maybe six years old, though I could be wrong because she looks much smarter than a six year old. I guess that she is Angel's sister because even though this little girl has light brown hair that curls around her face and light brown eyes, her face and features are just the same.

"Hey there," I reply gently. I love kids; they always manage to make me smile.

"I'm Katherine!" she giggles, "But you can call me Kate! I'm eight but I'm short and small looking." She reaches out to take my free hand; I look at her small palm in my delicate hand. "You are very pretty, like a flower, your cheeks are nice and pink and your eyes are strange because they are brown but not exactly brown. I want to be your friend. What's your name?"

I look over at Jake to express my amusement. Kate has a very advanced vocabulary for her age, and is rather forward. I see that Jake is smiling down at Kate with affection in his eyes. But as soon as my head turns, his gaze shifts to me, and he winks. What Kate just stated is very similar to what

Jake had said to me the first time we met. He had said my cheeks were rosy pink, and that's why he had first called me Rose.

I return my attention back to Kate and kneel so I am able to look at her face to face.

"My name is Veronica Rose, little Kate." I smile at her and her round eyes twinkle. "But you may call me Rose. Most people do nowadays, thanks to Jake." I wink at her. "And you are the beautiful flower here. Are you Angel's sister?"

"Yep! I'm many people's sister! I'm Thomas's sister, and Simon's sister and Angel's sister. Will you be my sister too?"

A little giggle escapes my lips and Kate giggles with me. Without reflection, I pick her up and balance her on my hips. As I get up from the floor, I see that everyone in the room is watching me. The two boys that were on the couch are now making their way towards Jake and me. Jake goes forward to greet them and they hug and laugh and smile and bump each other like brothers. I stay where I am with Kate and she makes no indications to want to move so I just contently keep her in my arms as Angel directs me towards the boys.

"Thomas, Simon," Angel calls for their attention, which they immediately give, "This is Veronica, or Rose." She smiles at me, and so do the two boys. "Rose, this is Thomas," She indicates towards the older looking boy. "And this is Simon," She points to the younger one.

"Hey guys," I say with as much enthusiasm as I can manage.

"Hey Rose," Thomas says and comes forward and hugs me as if we were old friends. I smile at him as he releases me. Thomas looks just like Angel, same features and coloring too, but paler skin with no freckles.

Angel walks forward and hooks her arm around mine.

"Thomas is eighteen, he treats everyone as if they are his buddies. Though he doesn't know that no one thinks he's *their* buddy. But don't tell him that." Angel winks, and I smile, recognizing a joke. "He is also rather blunt and good at easing tension. Some people find the familiarity and bluntness annoying, but others like it."

I nod to show that I think it is nice but am not able to reply further because Simon comes up to me.

"Hello," Simon says quietly. He looks very shy. But he is just like his sisters, same features but different coloring. He has white blond hair and hazel green eyes with glasses that look too big for his face.

"Hey Sime," I say to boost his confidence.

It must have worked because he looks me full in the face and smiles widely with a one-dimpled cheek.

"I like that nickname, I hope everyone calls me that now. I like you, you are very nice and pretty and Kate liked you immediately so you must be true." Simon says matter-of-factly. "Can you pick me up too?" He adds last minute.

I look at Angel in confusion.

She rolls her eyes and pats Simon on the head.

"Simon…" She pauses because Simon looks at her with narrowed eyes. "Or Sime," And Simon smiles again. Angel lets out a small laugh and continues. "Is eleven and like most of us, has special abilities. His own unique specialness has not been revealed yet but some people like us only have better senses and nothing else. Little Kate here is a very early bloomer. She has quickened learning abilities and a sense of trust, meaning she knows who is trustworthy and who is lying, but not really any super strength or speed. And if she trusts you now, it means you are 'true' and we can all trust you. And they both really like you so you must be pretty different because usually they are very shy around other people."

Angel must have known what I was thinking because she answered the questions about the children that I was asking myself in my head. And now that I could hear her speak continuously, I notice that her accent is faintly Greek but not fully.

Thomas breaks my chain of thought as he continues after Angel.

"Angel bloomed when she was twelve, and she's sixteen now. That's your age right? Right. And she has heightened senses, though maybe not as heightened as yours, and can vaguely sense what a person might be thinking. She is stronger and faster than an average person but probably slower and weaker than all of us here." Thomas winks and is rewarded with a punch in the gut by Angel. But they both laugh and continue with the 'briefing'. "I have heightened senses and better reflexes, strength and speed." Thomas adds; Angel mumbles something that sounded like 'show off' under her breath but Thomas ignores her and speaks to me. "You probably have all that including other specialties of your own. I know Jake does, and from what he has been telling us, you're a lot more powerful than he is, so you must be pretty good."

I can feel the heat rushing through me, the blush showing on my face as Thomas finishes talking. The words rush out my mouth in a hurry because I really think that whatever Jake had said had been exaggeration.

"Well, I'm really not that great… really. Jake is just being himself and making me seem like a superhero when I'm actually pretty normal. All of you guys sound much more awesome to me! I mean a truth teller like Kate? That's amazing! And being super strong and fast sounds really cool to me. And being able to read someone's mind is truly extravagant and useful! I mean, that's probably why you brought this whole subject up right Angel? Because you heard my mind wondering about it?" Angel smiles and nods, "That's amazing! And Jake, I think he has a similar ability to yours, Thomas."

"That's true," Thomas replies. "But you can sense emotions, and do everything that Jake and I can do. That alone is already very good."

"But it's not only that," Angel begins. " I could feel you. I felt your aura radiating through this place as soon as your car was a mile away from this house. I didn't know it was you at the time, but suddenly I felt happier and healthier!"

"Ya!" Kate interrupts. "And my tooth stopped hurting!" She pulls her lip back to show me a growing tooth. I smile at her again.

"There is that!" Thomas adds. "You bring joy and serenity and healing wherever you go. And it's unconscious. And we siblings will probably never have another fight while you're here so you are welcome to stay as long as you like!"

"Well, thank you Thomas." Jake says sarcastically.

Thomas fakes a bow and grins at Jake.

I feel very overwhelmed by all this, and am saved by my stomach. It growls loudly and everyone laughs, including me.

We make our way to the dining table to have the delicious pancakes with sausage that Angel had cooked up.

"I can feel your stomach shouting Rose!" Kate exclaims happily as she settles into the chair next to mine. Jake sits across from me, but that is probably because Simon had sat down on the chair on the other side of me before anyone else could take it. Thomas sits on one side of Jake, leaving the other seat for Angel as she brings in the pan full of yummy smelling food.

"Bon appetite guys!" Angel exclaims as we fill our plates with food. For the first time since getting off the plane, I actually forget about the dream and everything that I have to do. I even forget about Cole for a second. All I remember and feel is the love of new friends around me. This could possibly be another family for me for I am already starting to love Kate in the little time that I have known her, and feel affection for Simon and Thomas. And I know that Angel and I are going to be great friends.

17

"Where's Cole?" I question as I help Angel clean up. Jake is helping stack the plates, which Angel hands him, into the dishwasher. He looks up as I ask. He glances around but there is no sign of Cole. Simon is on the floor tying his shoelaces and Thomas is on the couch watching some movie with lots of guns. Kate is skipping around the room but comes to stop in front of us to answer my question.

"He went out very early this morning." Kate says cheerily. "Big Cole said he'd be back but that he had to do something very important. He was telling the truth so I know he is going to be back soon. You don't need to worry Rose, and you don't need to worry either Jakie."

"Big Cole?" My eyebrows rise at their own accord.

"Hmmph," Jake clears his throat. "Ya, we used to come here a lot. Cole, Mom, Dad and I. Kate knows him as Big Cole and I'm known as Jakie. I wonder who came up with those nicknames." He looks over pointedly at Angel, who looks like she is trying not to laugh.

"That's because I'm much bigger and awesomer than you Jake. Of course you know that." A familiar voice says softly from the front door.

I look around and see Cole standing near the television couch where Thomas was. My heart lurches as I see him, probably because I really was worried. I think. Little Simon looks up in surprise, and then runs with untied shoelaces towards Cole. Cole bends down to hug him and then picks him up in a swing.

I have never seen this side of Cole before, the caring, children loving side. I like it; it shows just how much compassion he has.

"Hey Cole," Thomas says casually from his spot on the couch. Cole goes over and fist bumps Thomas.

"Cole?" Jake asks. "Where did you go?"

"Oh, sight seeing. Down the beach, here and there." He replies very vaguely. I frown in confusion and see that Angel and Kate are doing the same. Well, if Kate's confused then it must mean that he is telling the truth, just not the whole of it. And if Angel is frowning it probably means he's blocking her from seeing his thoughts. "Hey little Kathy," Cole adds warmly and Kate's frown is replaced by a toothy grin as she runs into his arms.

"Big Cole!" She exclaims, giggling.

Cole laughs and bounces Kate up and down in his arms.

"So," Jake says by the kitchen counter. "Where did you go?" He insists.

"I'll tell you later, Jake."

"But I want to know too," I put in.

"Fine," Cole says in a very irritated voice. His expression darkens as he sets Kate down and makes his way to me.

Cole stops a little less than an arms length from me then reaches in his pocket. "You want to know where I've been? I've been searching, for something, for anything." He takes my hand and places something in it. "And since you want to know, you had better be able to deal with it."

Speechless, I look down at what Cole had placed in my hand.

It is an open pocket-watch with a picture of my mom and a young me smiling in it. It is my dad's watch.

I look up at Cole, but I can't get the words out. He is closer than I had previously thought, close enough that I am able to feel his body heat. His eyes are soft and guarded as they stare into mine intently. He radiates worry, conviction, anger, fear and relief.

"I found something," He whispers softly. His breath moves my hair, our faces so close that our noses are almost touching. "And I'm going to deal with it."

With that, he steps away and moves towards Angel, gives her a sisterly peck on the cheek, and moves past Jake without any physical contact, but their eyes lock. Cole stops right in front of his bedroom door and turns around, making eye contact with the four of us who are old enough to understand.

"We will start searching for more when you're all ready." His eyes hold mine for so long that they start to feel sore, but I can't look away. Cole seems to be trying to tell me something, but I don't know what it is. Just then, he breaks the stare and disappears into his room.

The silence lasts for about a minute before Simon gets fidgety and asks "What's going on?" quite loudly.

Jake walks over to him and helps him finish tying his shoelaces before ruffling his hair.

"Nothing Simon. Big Cole just got Rose a gift that means a lot to her." Jake looks over at me but I look down at the watch as he mentions it. I feel Angel looking at me as well, and then looking at Jake. I see her shake her head slightly.

"Are we still going to the beach to play?" Simon asks.

I meet Jake's eyes and see him looking uncertain.

"Oh please, oh please!" Kate pleads. "I can come too right?"

Seeing that Jake will not be any help in replying, I answer for him.
"Of course you can, dear Kate!"

"Yay!" She screams and runs to put on her shoes.

"I think we should all go," Angel suggests kindly. I nod in agreement and see Jake smile. Thomas looks at all of us and cocks an eyebrow when his eyes land on me.

"Well, maybe we can," He says wryly. "But perhaps Rose should put on something that doesn't look like PJ's first."

I look down at myself and burst out laughing; I hadn't realized that I still had my bedclothes on. The kids laugh with me. Angel was right; Thomas is very good at easing the tension.

"Let's get you changed, I'll help you pick what to wear." Angel says as she pulls me towards the room where I slept. "You guys go on ahead with Simon and Kate. And make sure they don't fight, though I doubt they will. We'll meet you there."

Jake pulls Simon by the arm out the front door and Thomas follows a running Kate towards the beach. I smile with fondness for this family and feel the love I already felt for them grow and spread through me, leaving me completely aglow.

"Wow," Angel remarks as we reach my door. I look at her curiously. "Oh it's nothing," She replies, "It's just... I can really, really feel your power; you must be feeling love or happiness very strongly now because however good I was feeling just doubled." She smiles as I blush. "Don't worry, they are all very easy to love aren't they?" Angel gives my hand a little squeeze.

"I'm really glad you're here Rose."

■ ■ ■

The sand sinks as Angel and I walk on it towards the three boys and Kate. They all are laughing so loudly I was able to hear them all the way from the house.

I am now wearing black ripped jeans, a white crop top and an army camouflaged printed jacket. Angel suggested my wearing of just the top and jeans as it was hot, but I felt a little too exposed so I added the jacket. Angel herself is wearing a short summer dress without sleeves, which just perfectly reveals her bronze tanned skin.

As we make our way down the beach I study Angel again. When I look more closely at the side of her neck, I notice a mark much like mine. It is a swan. I ponder on this but have no idea what it could mean.

"Angel," I start. "What does the swan mean?"

Angel looks confused at first, but then seeing where my gaze is lingering, she immediately understands and her eyes spark.

"Oh, it means: love, empathy, dream, balance, and innocence mostly. The empathy and dreamer part could show that I can see your dreams and feel for them. So I can partly read your mind, I guess? I'm actually not too sure, but none of us are sure of much when it comes to the marks. And I really don't see how I'm swan-like. They are soft and I've always been rather hard."

I keep silent, wondering what Thomas's mark is, and whether Simon and Kate have marks.

"Well, Thomas's mark is a phoenix. Phoenixes have strength, energy, and they overcome impossible odds. So that also suits him, he's strong and he can break tensions when no one else can." I look at her with wide eyes and she winks. "Yep, I heard you wondering in that head of yours. And Simon doesn't have a mark because he hasn't bloomed yet. But Kate has a mark; it's an owl. Owls can see behind masks, they have wisdom, they are true, and they are patient. Kate is all of those things. She learns fast which implies wisdom, and she knows when a person isn't telling the truth, which suits because she can see behind masks, in this case, lies. Simon might never have a mark, that happens to some of us… but he would still be different from normal people."

"Well, all your marks truly do fit you." I say with awe.

"Yours do too, if I'm correct." Angel replies and I look at her because the tone in her voice wasn't normal. "You have three or four, right?"

"Yes…" I mumble. "I have four…"

"They are?"

"A rose, a tiny a yin-yang symbol, a dove…" I pause.

"And?"

"A crow."

"Oh," Angel breathes. "That really is very different. The rose and dove represent, peace, love, beauty, harmony and strength. And the ying yang sign sort of speaks for itself. But what could the crow mean with all of that? Crows aren't exactly bad, they kind of belong to both the light and the dark."

I suck in my breath; fear ripples through me. Angel must have sensed my discomfort because she drops the topic.

"Never mind," She says in her soft melodious voice. "Come on, look. They are waiting for us. I think Kate misses you already."

Angel and I have almost reached the shallows where Thomas, Jake, Simon and Kate are picking seashells. As soon as Kate spots us, she drops all her seashells in Jake's hand and runs towards me.

I have just enough time to open my arms as she comes flying into them with a force that almost knocks me over. Angel laughs and ruffles Kate's hair before she continues walking the last few steps towards Jake and Thomas. I pick Kate up and carry her to where everyone is standing. It is bright and windy, but the sun is partly behind clouds so it isn't blazing hot.

Kate starts talking about the different colored seashells that Jake had helped her find, and then Simon is there interrupting her and saying that he found a blue crab and a red crab but that Thomas wouldn't let him keep it.

I am laughing and listening to them both, but they are talking over each other.

"Come on now," Angel scolds. "You don't wanna' give Rose a brain attack do you?"

Thomas roars with laughter and shoves Angel lightly. She looks at him in question.

"Brain attack? Angel, really?" Thomas buckles with laughter again. Angel rolls her eyes as the kids join him. "Where did you hear that one little sister? Learning for the dim-witted?"

Jake smiles widely at this.

"Now, now Tote, no need to live up to be the idiot we all know you to be." Angel answers back to him and slaps him lightly on the shoulder.

A laugh escapes my lips at Angel's comeback because even though it wasn't the best comeback, the name 'Tote' does make up for it.

"You find that funny? Eh Rose?" Thomas mouth stretches into a grin, making him look much younger than eighteen. "I'll show you funny!" And he splashes me with so much water, so fast, that I only have time to react by shielding Kate and Simon. Thomas is quite a big guy, broad but gracefully so, with muscle that ripple throughout his body. So the wall of water he sends towards us is pretty big. When it is done, all three of us are drenched, and Kate's hair and mine seem to stick together.

"Hey!" Simon shouts and charges at Thomas. Thomas makes no movement, probably expecting no force behind Simon, but force there is. Simon's charge has enough power to knock the big strong Thomas into the water. Angel and Jake laugh, and so do Kate and I, but I think we are all surprised. I guess Simon is now the strongest fellow in the house.

"Yay! Go Simon!" Kate shouts to her brother. She struggles out of my arms and towards where Simon is lying on top of a very stunned Thomas. Both Kate and Simon are now splashing and dumping water on Thomas, but to be honest, I don't think he could have gotten any more soaked. Angel leaves Jake's side to help Thomas to his feet, but he just pulls her into the water and she falls with a splash into the sea. I laugh. I am doing that a lot more now.

I see Jake make his way towards me.

"Amazing, aren't they?" Jake says.

"Yes," I reply with a smile. "They truly are."

"So much love and care and playfulness with siblings. I've always wanted that. I miss that."

My eyes move away from the happy scene of the four siblings towards Jake's bittersweet gaze. I guess that he's thinking about Cole. They used to be close like brothers.

"I'm sorry Jake," I say, but I don't know how to ease his pain. My hands reach out to touch his and he grips mine tightly.

"It's okay…" He mumbles. "At least I have them. I have my parents, I have friends, and I have you." He leans in and gives me a quick kiss on the lips. "Thanks,"

I return the pressure to his hand and ask him what I've been wondering for the whole day.
"How do you know them?"

"Well, they are actually family." Jake says matter-of-factly.

I look at him, astounded.

"Yep, well, I probably should have told you, right?"

"Well, ya!" I add in a shouted whisper.

"Ha, eh, well, yep. They are my cousins, or second cousins. Or something… I'm not sure, but we are related."

"Well, then. Good thing they like me!"

"Everyone will like you. No one can hate you."

"Har, Har, Ha." I laugh sarcastically. "Very funny."

"What's very funny?" Angel asks. Thomas, Simon, Kate and Angel are in front of Jake and me. I must have been so caught up with the conversation that I didn't hear them.

"Oh, it's just Jake that is funny." I answer.

"Well that's true!" Kate squeals. "Jake is funny! That's right!"

Thomas snorts.

Jake rolls his eyes.
"Well, if Kate says it, then it must be true." Jake declares humorously. "After all, I do have a witty kind of charm," A wink.

Thomas's snorts turn into laughs but he pretends that they are coughs. Jake raises one eyebrow at him and laughs himself. Angel and I put a hand to our heads at the same time, look at each other, and start laughing ourselves. Then

Simon and Kate join in the laughter just because everyone else is laughing. Everything seems perfect; I think at that moment that nothing could go bad. I couldn't be more wrong.

■ ■ ■

After a day spent at the beach and around the trees near the house, we are all tired as we sit down on the chairs on the porch. Streaks of sunlight are pushing past the low clouds as the sun sets behind the horizon. I stare at it contently, feeling warm with Jake's arm around me, and Kate sitting on my lap. I close my eyes.

"Feeling sleepy?"

My eyes open slowly at the sound of Angel's voice.
"I'm feeling serene," I mumble softly as I close my eyes once more.

I feel Angel's amusement and I imagine her rolling her eyes as she sighs.

"Well I won't bother you then," She says. My eyes snap open at her tone and she smirks. "If you won't help me, I'll just have to ask Little Katherine to help me prepare the table and cook dinner." Angel winks. I am about to object and say that I would love to help, but Jake beats me to it, saying the exact opposite of what I intended.

"You do that, Angel," Jake puts in suddenly. "I would like to sit out here awhile with Rose because you've stolen her for most of the past day."

Angel sticks her tongue out at him then beams boldly.

"Fine," Her voice drools with mock defeat. "Come on Kate, you have to help your sister with some food."

"Okay!" Kate shrieks ever so enthusiastically as she slips down from my lap onto the wooden floor to take Angel's hand. Kate loves to cook; she doesn't even mind the heat of the oven. Plus, she adores Angel so I'd guess that she does not mind getting up.

Kate turns to me, smiling; showing her little baby teeth. "I'll be right back! I'm going to cook you yummy food!"

She runs off into the house, probably heading for the kitchen as we all stare after her. Simon and Thomas, who had been playing with cards on the deck, look up as Kate's foot-steps make tremors on the floor. Jake, Angel and I stare after her with smiles on our faces. Angel shakes her head.

"No matter how smart she is, she always reminds us that she is, in fact, still just a little eight year old." There is a lot of love in Angel's voice. It is coming off her and affecting me. Now I can't be sure whether it is my love for Kate that I am feeling, or Angel's love. Probably both. And even though

I've only known this family for about a day, I love them all dearly.

Angel goes into the house after Kate and after a minute or two, I hear the sizzling of food being cooked and Angel's laughter and Kate's giggles. The environment around this house and the feel about this family is so positive that I am sure that I will never want to leave them.

Ten minutes pass and the cooking and playing is still going on. All my attention is on the sounds around me for there is a lot to listen to: the trees, the waves, the birds, Angel's voice, and Kate's laughter. Everyone else is going about their own business and I am just listening in.

I don't know what Jake is doing but he is rather silent. Perhaps it is luck, or maybe fate; but it is fortunate that I am listening so intently to Angel and Kate because if I were not, I wouldn't have heard the *thump*, as if something or someone had fallen on the floor. And I wouldn't have heard the quiet whimper.

With those two sounds, I am already on my feet in a flash and at the door before I hear Angel scream. At that point, the guys leap to their feet but I am already through the door, looking at the horrifying scene before my eyes.

Kate is on the floor, her body bent over her straight rigid legs. Her neck is bent over her body and everything is shaking.

Twitching. Trembling. Jerking.

Little Kate's eyes are rolling to the back of her head, only showing white. She has bubbles, foam, escaping from her mouth. Though she is shaking, she is not conscious.

I rush forward and kneel next to her where Angel is crying, clearly not knowing what to do. I don't know what to do either. What do I do? What is this? Did she hurt her neck? Is she dying? No. She can't. I can't cry. No tears escape my eyes. My throat feels swollen as I feel the panic rise from inside of me. It is all blurry, as if it isn't real, as if it were part of a very bad dream.

"Kate, Oh my God. No. Kate! Wake up!" I scream. Angel is sobbing hysterically and mumbling. I catch a couple of words. Angel is praying silently.

"Oh Jesus, please don't. Don't take away the one I love so much. God no." Angel repeats on and on, seeming unable to stop.

"Please! Don't take her away! Help! Save her. Kate, please wake up," I say, my voice trembling but clear. My heart fills with fear and a deep throbbing pain that I've felt before. Two years before.

I don't dare touch her, if she had broken anything, I would just hurt her more.

"Jake! Jake!" I scream. "Help!"

But he is already there with Thomas and Simon. Simon is looking on the scene with wide eyes and an open mouth. Thomas is already on the phone speaking into it, asking for an ambulance.

By this time, Kate has stopped shaking. She has stopped everything. She is completely still.

She isn't breathing.

Angel has one of Kate's hands and is rubbing it. But I go over and feel her heart.

It is still beating.

But a few minutes of not breathing and she would be gone.

Oh God.

Please no.

Jake raises Kate so she is sitting in his arms, limp as a doll. After a few seconds, her chest lifts.

"Oh, oh God." Angel breathes out in relief. Kate is breathing. But she is still not awake.

All the love, all the fear, all the worry, the anger, and the relief, all the good and bad feelings I feel, I let them flow through me as I take Kate back into my arms.

"Please Kate. Please" I whisper to her. "Wake up." A single tear slips from my cheek and drops on her face. Very suddenly, startling all of us, she takes a sharp breath and jerks awake, her eyes flying open.

"Oh God." Angel says. "Thank you."

"The ambulance will be here soon." Thomas says, his voice rough. He has tears on his cheeks. So do Angel and Simon.

Jake is patting Kate's legs with tears in his eyes, but they do not spill over. I, however, can't speak, and am still holding Kate, crying in relief and gratitude.

Kate looks around in confusion.
"What's going on?" She asks very weakly.

"Nothing, dear baby." I say to her. Not wanting to frighten her. "You're fine. You're going to be fine."

She still looks very confused as her eyes wander around and threaten to close and bring her deep sleep, from which I fear she would not awaken.

"No, Katherine. No. Don't sleep. Don't sleep." I whisper and pat her cheeks.

Thomas comes over to pick her up; I let him pull her out of my arms. My hands drop to my sides limply.

"Will she be okay?" I ask with a closed throat.

"She's going to be just fine. Thanks to you."

"Thomas, I didn't do anything." I whisper.

"You may not have stopped her seizure… Yes, that's what it looks like now," He puts in when my eyes widen. "But you helped wake her up. "

"How?"

"Your love. Your tear." Jake tells me. "I felt your power radiating off of you and moving through her. Your love brought her back to consciousness."

That is not possible. I could not have done that. Could I? I didn't even know what I was doing.

My mouth will not let any words pass through. I have letters, words and sentences all stuck on the tip of my tongue. But I can't reply.

"I don't think Katie will need the ambulance." Comes a quiet childish voice.

We all turn to Simon. He had spoken. But he doesn't make any sense.

"Why do you say that Simon?" Angel questions.

"Well..." He hesitates, looking smaller than ever. "She feels alright. There's nothing strange about her."

"What do you mean?" Jake asks.

"I don't..." His face scrunches up as he searches for the right words. Simon's glasses are working their way up his nose. "Well, her energy is healthy. It is actually brighter than it was this morning or yesterday. She's more alive than ever."

"Wait, Simon," Thomas cuts in. "You can feel her energy? Can you feel mine?"

"Yes, and yes." Simon replies in a shy voice. "I've always been able to do it. I guess. I just didn't know what it was."

"That could be your ability, dear Sime." I tell him.

"Oh,"

"Well, I agree with Simon." Says Jake. Seeing our look, he adds. "Rose definitely did something. Can't you guys feel it, or see it? Look, she's kind of glowing, radiating light. And Kate is too."

He is right. I hadn't noticed it before, but Kate certainly is glowing or shimmering in Thomas's arms. She is awake but silent, watching all of us. Occasionally, Thomas bounces his arms whenever Kate's eyes become heavy and threatened to close.

"I'm okay." She says. She smiles at us, as if to reassure us.

"Okay," Thomas says as he puts her down. "I'll tell the ambulance to leave once they arrive." And he goes out the door.

As soon as Thomas sets Kate down, she comes bouncing towards Angel and me. Literally bouncing, like a happy excited little girl. As if nothing had just happened to her.

I let Angel hold her, since Kate is her sister. But when Kate holds her hand out for me, I immediately take it with both of mine.

"Come here Simon," I say. He walks towards us. "You're a very special little boy." I tell him.

"And you are a very special person." He says, shocking me. "Thank you for helping my sister."

"No worries," I reply, and kiss him lightly on the cheek. "I will help any one of you anytime, until forever is over."

A smile grows on his face as I speak.
"You promise?"

"Pinky promise. Cross my heart."

"You are nice. I am glad you came Rose." His glasses
don't hide how clear his eyes are when he says this.

"I'm glad too, dear Sime."

I let him climb onto my lap, but my hand is still occupied
by Kate's. I hold onto them both tightly and Angel puts her
arm around me. Thomas comes in and sits on the floor in
front of us. Jake throws a blanket over Angel, the kids and I
and settles down next to Thomas.

Sitting there, facing everyone, our hearts close together;
it is almost as if we are all family.

The only thing we have forgotten is that there is another
person who was as much a part of this family as I am now. A
young man who has been through a lot of pain, a lot of love,
and a lot of loss. A man who needs to be saved more than any
other. Cole.

18

"Waakkkeeee uuupppppp!!!" High pitched shouting and the bouncing of my bed is what pulls me out of sleep. My eyes open slowly but close immediately because it's too bright and I'm not used to it. I groan loudly and bring my hands up to cover my face while turning over and pulling the sheets up over my body. I hear laughter of all different pitches, all dripping with uncontrolled humor.

"Don't worry, we'll let this little sloth sleep her way through of the day. Doing absolutely nothing of any use." I hear Jake say. It is definitely Jake, I cannot mistake that voice anywhere.

"Go away, Jake. I'm not a sloth." I mumble into the sheets and am rewarded with laughter again.

The bouncing of my bed erupts into shakes and laughter that sounds like someone small is jumping over me. I turn and open my eyes fully to see Kate and Simon jumping around me on the bed. Jake, Angel and Thomas are staring at me with huge smirks on their faces. I throw a pillow at them; not bothering to see who it hits, and pull myself up groggily. As I look around, I notice that Cole is still nowhere to be seen, but I push that thought away because it is way too early for me to be doing heavy thinking.

"What time is it?" I ask.

"It's almost ten, sleeping beauty." Thomas answers humorously.

I stare at him with annoyance before smiling my good morning.

"Morning Kate, morning Sime." I say to the kids as I get out of bed. Jake is there to greet me immediately. He hugs me from behind as I gather my sheets to make my bed. Angel is already on the other side of the bed, grabbing the other end of the sheets, ready to help me make my bed. I smile at her.

"Thanks Angel."

Angel and I finish making the bed and we turn to Thomas and Jake.

"Hey guys. Sorry for being such a sleeper." My voice sounds quiet and sheepish.

"Don't worry Rose!" Thomas says happily. "I got to eat all of your pancakes!" He bursts into laughter.

I roll my eyes at him, like I would do to a brother if I had a one.

"Don't worry," Angel whispers in my ear. "I saved you some." She winks.

"Thanks," I whisper back. My eyes shift to look outside my bedroom door; Kate and Simon are already out there in front of the TV laughing at what looks like an episode of SpongeBob. I smile to myself because the kids are just so cute and innocent.

"Why don't you get cleaned up and I'll warm up your food?" Angel suggests.

I nod my agreement and everyone leaves my room except Jake. He watches me as I get my clothes out and go to the bathroom to turn on the heater for my shower. The reflection of myself in the bathroom mirror is atrocious. Ha. I look away; painfully aware of how horrible I must look next to Angel. My hair, though in a bun, is a mess, and my eyes have bags and I look awfully sleepy. I groan in irritation.

Jake is behind me as soon as I groan and he wraps his arms around my torso.

"What's up sleepy head?" He says in my ear.

"I look horrible!" I say matter-of-factly.

"Don't you ever say that," Jake growls at me playfully. "'Cause it's not true."

"Ya, right," my reply is dripping with sarcasm as I nudge him. "You're an awful liar."

"Why thanks," He mumbles. I turn around to face him so that I am hugging him too. But after a minute I shove him away lightly.

"Now go away!" I playfully demand. "I need to shower and you can't be in here."

"Can't I shower with you?" Jake asks teasingly. I laugh at him because I know he is joking and he walks out of the bathroom with a short 'see you in a bit' wink. I smile to myself as I realize how lucky I am to have such a great guy like Jake.

I turn the tap on and let the warm water wash over my body. I sigh in contentment, the morning daze slipping away. I find myself humming and then I'm jumping and singing my lungs out. Through my loudness I hear laughter coming from outside and I know that they are all listening in on me. But I don't care; let them think what they want. So I continue with my singing until I'm done with my shower.

I dry myself and put my hair up in the towel and get changed. I look at what I had laid out previously and sigh. Without actually thinking about it, I had laid out a dress that went just below my mid-thighs in length and had a tighter section around my waist where I would put a belt. The dress is light blue, had a halter-top section, and the skirt part of it could swing around my body when I turn. It is a comfortable summer dress. It allows movement. I wonder whether it will be suitable.

After pulling the dress on I go to the bathroom to see what I can do with my hair and face. My hair is a mess this morning so I decide to tie it up into a ponytail. Strands of baby hair escape from my neat hairdo, but I can't be bothered to pull them back.

I look at myself once more in the mirror and decide to put on mascara. After I'm all done, I pull on my boots and walk out of the room feeling awake and ready to start a new day.

I walk to the kitchen and see that Angel has put out a plate full of warm food for me to eat. Angel must be in her own room, probably dressing Kate up, because I don't see her. It's like yesterday's scary turn of events never happened. Everyone is completely happy and normal, as if they trust that it'll never happen again and that Kate will be okay. Thomas is minding his own business watching TV. Well, he did say good morning to me. Jake and Simon are nowhere in sight, which makes me wonder, but my stomach offers me a distraction by growling.

Thomas's chuckle fills my ears as I take my seat on the table. I'm munching on my breakfast when I look out of the window and see the dark figure of a man standing near the waves on the beach.

"Hey Thomas?"

"Yep, Rosie?" He replies.

"Where is everyone?" I question.

"Angel is in the bathroom with Kate doing 'girl stuff'" Thomas emphasizes on the last two words. I roll my eyes and he winks. "Jake took Simon out the back to help him fix his bike." A pause. "And Cole went out a while ago. But I'm not exactly sure where he is."

"Mm," I contemplate. It is as much as I had guessed. Not the Cole part though, because I already knew where he was before asking. "I'm going to go for a walk, okay?"

"Sure," Thomas says with a smile in my direction. His eyes don't leave the screen of the TV; this time he's watching a show about war.

As I reach the door, Thomas calls out to me.

"Rose," He suddenly puts in.

"Yes?"

"Don't go out for too long." He turns his eyes away from the screen and looks at me squarely. "And be careful. I'll tell Jake where you are, but I'll make him stay here."

"Thanks," I reply in surprise. Thomas could tell immediately where I planned on going, and what I planned to do.

The door opens willingly as I push it and make my way out onto the deck, then across the pebbles, and onto the sand. My shoes are left inside the house because the feel of sand on my feet is nice. The sand sinks a little as I make contact with its surface and the wind blows my hair and my dress. The sun is bright in the sky today; hardly any clouds fill the blueness above. It is cool but bright; just the kind of weather that I enjoy.

Cole doesn't turn around to acknowledge me even when I know I'm close enough for him to hear my footsteps and breathing. He is facing out into the ocean, standing ankle deep in the water. I walk to join him and find that the water is surprisingly cold. My feet break the surface of the water with each step until I plant myself firmly in the sand, and sea, next to Cole. He doesn't even look my way; he just keeps his eyes wide open, staring ahead of him. I am just about to say something to announce that I am there when he speaks.

"Rose,"

He says just that single word, just that nick name, and I feel as if it were my soul name, the name I am supposed to have. I wait for him to continue, but he doesn't.

"What is it Cole?" I urge him to tell me.

He breathes in and out a couple of times before replying. "I know what you have to do." Cole says flatly.

Shock rolls over me before it gradually disappears.

"Well, of course you do." I reply in defeat. "You're the one that told me that we are alike. And we are."

"Not like that Rose." His voice is so icy that I look over to him, only to see that he is glaring at me. "Not like that."

"What do you mean? I don't understand."

"You're stronger than me. Sure, both of us have a link to the dark and light side. And I know that you have to open up to the dark side to yourself, but Rose, we are not alike. You cannot be as weak willed as me to give in so easily." He sighs; his eyes hold such old sadness that it is impossible to believe that he is only twenty-five. I can feel his emotions, they fill me with such grief and such love that I am pretty sure those are the most dominant emotions that he is feeling right now.

"Cole," I murmur to him, my voice revealing the sadness and love that I feel for him. I reach out to touch him on the shoulder but he flinches as soon as I make contact. I try to hide the hurt from my face but judging from his expression, it doesn't work. How could this be what's become of him? He was my best friend, my protector when I was younger… how could he be this scared? It's not right. Not right at all.

"You can't…" he takes a ragged breathe. "You can't do that. You can't trust me. Not here. Not when we're so close to *her.*" He doesn't elaborate any further.

"Don't worry Cole," My voice is soothing as I try to reassure him, though I am just as scared of *her* as he seems to be. "I trust you. And I know who you're talking about. I've seen her and felt her." The last sentence I speak is almost a whisper. Just thinking about Tenebris Daemon makes me shiver.

"What?" Cole hisses. He grabs my wrist and forces me to look at him. No longer is he flinching from my touch, instead, I now cringe from his. His eyes burn with such intensity that I find myself unable to look away.

"Yeah, it's no big deal." I rethink what I just said. "Okay, actually it is. I've still never told Jake about any of it. But I'm too afraid to." I frown.

"What is she doing to you?" He growls. The anger radiating from him makes me afraid, but it is not anger towards me, it's anger towards Tenebris Daemon.

"Nothing," I tell him. "She can't do anything but give me nightmares."

Cole is silent but I can sense his control slipping. I quickly touch his arm and squeeze it.

"Don't worry." I say. "She can't touch me."

"She doesn't have to touch you to hurt you, Rose." He replies unhappily.

"Well then I'll just have to be stronger." I look him in the eyes meaningfully.

Cole doesn't answer. I don't know whether it is because he thinks that even at my strongest I won't be able to defeat the shadows, or because he has guessed and doesn't approve of my method of getting strong.

"I saw you." I suddenly blurt out.

Cole looks at me curiously, his anger momentarily forgotten. I blush but continue.

"I had a dream." I start. "It was of you, and it was here. There was a cave and there was snow. I don't know whether this dream was real or not, but it seemed real. And with every ounce of my body I believed that it was real while actually having the dream. It was the most realistic nightmare I've ever had, and so I was thinking, maybe it was actually real."

"Stop." Cole whispers. "I know what you're going to say. I think I know what you dreamed about. You're talking about the time that I…" He gulps. "When I…"

"It's okay, Cole," My voice is filled with sympathy. I can't keep it out. "You don't have to tell me. Yes, it's that. I already know exactly what happened."

"So you know what happened to me?"

"Yes," I mumble.

"Okay, then you know how sorry I am." His emotions are raw; grief and melancholy mixed with hope and love. "You know how sorry I am Rose."

I nod my assent because I feel like if I open my mouth to speak, I won't be able to control my tears.

His fingers are still clasped around my wrist; they are warm and gentle but firm. I could not break hold even if I wanted to. Before I know it, he has pulled me into his arms. I wrap my own arms around his body to give him comfort and he pulls me closer. I sense happiness and calmness radiating from him for the first time.

"I'll help you," I mumble into his shoulder. "I'll help you no matter what."

Cole pulls away at that. His expression is unreadable but his emotions suddenly are cold and hard.

"No, Rose." He tells me firmly. "You will not help me no matter what. I will not let you get hurt because of me."

"Fine," My answer is brief.

I can tell that he doesn't believe my lie, but he doesn't push it. Cole just stares at me with lingering emerald eyes that pierce my heart. I'm left speechless, my mind fogs up but it isn't because of anything unnatural. *Focus*, I tell myself. But it isn't easy; Cole has charm, as well as a certain masculine dark attractiveness, along with his good looks.

"Come on," He finally says, breaking me away from my thoughts. Thank God. "Let's get back before everyone wonders where you are."

Even though he said 'everyone' I can't help but think that he meant Jake.

We walk side to side on the beach back to the house. Leaving the waves behind, the sun beating on our skin. The edge of our arms are brushing and sending shivers up my spine. It is only then that I realize that maybe Cole means more to me that I let on. And though I do not love Cole like I love Jake. I wonder if that could change. I can't let it change. I will not let it change.

■ ■ ■

Cole and I walk into the house without speaking. We were silent the entire walk back but I could sense Coles' changing emotions. This could be because he was going through many thoughts in his head; but since anger was the most dominant emotion, I guess that he was thinking about Tenebris Daemon and how she was giving me nightmares.

As soon as we step into the house, Kate runs up to me and jumps into my arms with a big grin on her face. Simon follows quickly behind and jumps into Cole's arms. I smile at Simon in greeting and my eyes drift to Cole to see him doing the same. Our eyes meet and, for some reason, I blush. But I have no reason to, so I drop my eyes and look around.

Angel is fiddling around the room, looking like she is trying to find something whilst Thomas is eating Oreos at the table. My heart skips a beat as I see Jake coming out of one of the rooms with a wallet and a phone in his hand.

I smile broadly at him and start towards him. At first he seems a little wary of Cole, but he gets over it because he takes Kate out of my arms, sets her down, pulls me into his arms and kisses me swiftly but fully on the mouth.

I don't object but as soon as he lets me go, I feel rather shy. My eyes do another skim around the room to see Angel smiling happily at us, Thomas smirking mischievously, as if he has found something else to tease me for. And Cole, well, he is turned away but I can feel loss and jealousy radiating from him.

I don't feel bad, but I feel sad for him because I don't fully understand why he might be jealous and his loss pains me. Kate is looking at Jake and me with wide eyes and Simon has his tongue out in disgust. A small giggle escapes my lips and I feel light headed.

"Hey there," Jake speaks to me privately and quietly.

"Hey," I reply with a small smile of my own.

"Hey Cole," Jake raises his voice to Cole in greeting.

"Hey Jake," Cole answers quite warmly. Judging by the look on Jake's face, Cole's friendliness must have caught him by surprise. But then he recovers and beams. Cole sets Simon down and walks towards Jake and me. I stand my place, not knowing exactly what to do. But though I know Cole wouldn't do anything to hurt any of us right now, I'm still wondering what his actions are.

But this time, he takes me by surprise. Cole sticks his hand out towards Jake and waits. Jake looks at the hand then looks back into Cole's eyes, takes the hand and shakes it. Then very brotherly, they pull on each other's hands and end up in a one armed hug. I watch this all with a smile on my face, I can feel the love for them both coming off of me.

"Alright guys! Now that we have all made up and what not," Thomas practically shouts. "How 'bout we get going? I'm bored!"

"Woah, wait, wait, wait," I cut in. "Going where?"

"To look for stuff; more clues and such like the one that Cole found yesterday." Angel answers.

"You mean things that may belong to my dad?" I ask.

"Yep," she replies softly; her eyes are sad.

"Well then…" I mumble, not able to get more out. I'm being reduced to speechlessness a lot recently.

"Here's your bag," Jake says as he hands over a small sling-over bag with my phone, wallet and snack in it.

"Thanks," I take the bag and snap out of my loss for words. "So, where are we leaving Simon and Kate?" I inquire. "We certainly aren't bringing them with us. It probably won't be safe."

"You're right," Jake says. "And that's why we are currently waiting for some more family friends who live near here to come and pay us a visit and babysit these two trouble makers." He finishes by going over and picking up both Kate and Simon and swinging them over his shoulders playfully. They giggle and laugh with glee and I smile at their happy childlike gladness.

"Oh, when will they be here?" I think that I'd like to meet more of Jake's friends, since all his friends turn out so well.

The doorbell rings.

"Right about now." Jake replies jokily. He puts the two kids down, and with an extremely cute goofy grin, he walks over to answer the door.

I roll my eyes, because I find this really ironic.

Jake opens the door to five girls and two guys.

"How many people do we need to take care of two little kids?" I whisper to Angel.

She doesn't reply but she laughs quietly by my side.

"Hey guys!" Jake says.

They reply with enthusiastic 'HEY's and 'HI's. Angel goes over and greets them with Thomas, and Jake comes over to me to pull me into the group.

"Come on and meet more people," He tells me quietly. I nod my agreement and put on my best smile.

Among the group is a girl with long dark brown hair and big light happy blue eyes with white skin and pink cheeks, a girl with blonde hair, hazel eyes and pale skin, and another girl with almost black hair and big dark brown eyes and brown skin. Behind them were the other two girls, one of whom has brown hair and eyes, tanned skin and pink cheeks, like me, though her skin is a little darker, and a blonde haired blue eyed girl who is rather tall. Both the guys are talking to Cole and one is taller than the other. The taller one has hair so blonde it is almost white, with dark amber looking eyes, and the other has black hair and ice blue eyes; but aside from the coloring, they are completely identical, so I guess that they are twins.

I don't know why I'm so fixed on the eyes… perhaps it is because eyes have beautiful colors that are unique to each person? Or maybe it's because eyes usually are windows to a person's soul…

"Hey guys!" I greet them as warmly as I can manage, I don't feel anything different about them so I guess that they aren't like Jake, Thomas, Cole or Angel, or me.

The girl with dark brown hair and big blue eyes steps forward.

"Hey," She replies. "You must be Rose."

"Yep," I say with a smile. "That's me,"

"Hi, I'm Nat, " she says with a friendly grin. "This is Alice," she gestures to the blonde with hazel eyes, she waves. "This is Sasha," she gestures to the girl with brown skin, who must be Indian. Sasha nods with a smile. "And that's Sage," she gestures to the girls with the same coloring as me. Sage beams at me. "And that's Melissa," She gestures to the other blonde with blue eyes.

The girl whose name is Sage steps forward and pulls the two guys with her.

"These two morons are my brothers. They are twins, if you can't tell, and they are absolute idiots, especially together." She says this with a smile so I know she doesn't mean any offence.

"I'm Charles," says the white blonde one.

"And I'm Dylan," says the one with darker hair.

"Hey guys," I greet all of them.

"Hey pretty lady," Dylan says with a wink. Charles shoves him and leans forward in front of me.

"Don't mind him, Rose," Charles says. "You don't want him anyways. I'm way better!"

That draws a laugh from me; I love it when twins act this way. I find it quite adorable especially since these boys look about seventeen.

"Too bad for you guys," Jake says as he steps towards me and puts his arm over my shoulder. "She's already taken."

"Come on, Jake," Dylan winks.

"Share a little," Charles adds.

"Haha," Nat says. "You guys are such drips."

"Drips?" I question.

"It's an English term," Nat replies with a wink. "Stands for irritating person,"

"Ah,"

"Well, Hi!" Alice says and comes forward and hugs me. "I'm Alice! Obviously," She adds with a smile. I smile back, not minding the warm physical contact one bit; it makes me feel like I belong.

The girl with darker skin addresses me.
"Yep, and I'm Sasha, as you've been told." She starts, "And don't mind Alice. As you can tell, she's the real idiot here."

"HEY!" Alice replies. "Haha, well, that's true." And they both start laughing like there's some inside joke.

"Hey," Melissa says shortly. Her accent is faintly Scottish and I like it.

"Hi," I reply. I guess she is a quiet kind of girl. I like that too.

"Melissa doesn't talk a lot with strangers." Sage says. "But once you get to know her, oh boy, she's a bomb."

"Very funny, Sage," Melissa says.

"Ha, I know I am." Sage replies smartly, and flips her hair over her shoulder.

I smile at all of them; they are all like best friends.

"So Nat," Angel asks. "Why all of you? Seven people? Just to take care of two kids? Really?"

"Well, you see…" Nat starts, and then sighs. "… Maybe I should let Sage answer."

Angel turns to Sage.

"Well," Sage begins; it all comes out in a rush. "I haven't been to Ithaca in forever! And Nat has never been here before, and neither has Sasha or Alice or Melissa! And my brothers haven't been here either. So we kinda just called each other up and decided: what the heck." Pause. "Sorry for any inconvenience."

Angel looks really serious for a second, as if she is really mad and is about to blow. But then a grin stretches across her face and she starts laughing.

"Of course it's okay guys! You're practically family to us! Come on in!"

"Aw ya!" Charles says.

"Awesome!" Dylan exclaims.

"You guys are weird." Cole tells them.

"Why thanks, Cole!" They say simultaneously.

Cole rolls his eyes at them and settles on the couch. The two brothers look at each other, shrug, and then join him. I feel Cole's annoyance and curiosity and I have to hold in a laugh. Jake has left my side and is greeting and taking Nat's and Alice's bags and bringing them into one of the guest rooms. Thomas has Sasha's, and Sage's bag in his hands and Angel has Melissa's.

"Hey Rose," Angel addressed me. "Do you mind staying in my room? We need to give the other room to Sasha, Sage and Melissa. It's the biggest one we've got. And I'm not sure how long they're staying."

"Sure!" I reply. I had the biggest room? Why? "No problem at all!"

"Great," Angel says enthusiastically. "Come on people, let's get moving."

I watch them leave the room before I remember that I have two hands. So I follow Angel and help her with the bags. Apparently the twins are going to stay with Thomas, Simon is moving in with Jake, and Kate is moving in with Angel and me. This house is bigger than I had previously thought. Once we have everyone settled, it is about two thirty in the afternoon. That's when I remember the whole point of the seven newcomers; they are babysitters for Kate and Simon. Which means that Jake, Thomas, Cole, Angel and I are suppose to be going out.

"Angel," I stop her from leaving the room. "When are we leaving?"

"Soon," She says with a smile. "Don't worry, we've got lots of time." And with that she leaves the room to see whether everyone is comfortable. They are; all seven of them are on the couch watching some weird show about zombies, and Kate and Simon are playing on the floor.

Jake and Cole seem to be packing some things into bags while Thomas is on the phone ordering food. As soon as we walk in, everyone looks up from what they were doing. Their eyes shift between Angel and me, but then eventually, all eyes rest on me. I'm starting to get awkward with the weight of the eyes that I could almost feel on my shoulders.

"So, Rose," Sasha starts. "Are you like Angel, Thomas, Jake, Cole, etc.?"

"Um, Yes?" I reply, "I guess."

Sasha nods.

"But you have a different feeling to you. When they are around, I don't feel any different, or you know, I can't tell that they are different. But with you, I can really, well this will sound weird and all, but I can really feel you. Your vibe, or something."

"I agree," Melissa adds.

"Same," Nat and Alice say at the same time, look at each other, and start giggling.

"Oh," is all I can reply.

"It's not a bad thing." Sasha tells me quickly. "It actually feels pretty awesome! I feel completely happier and healthier. But from what Jake has been telling me, that's like your thing right?"

"Ya, I guess,"

"Stop guessing!" Dylan puts in. "You gotta accept who you are. Like start hugging yourself or something."

"Ya!" Charles says. "You're really something special." Then he winks. "If I were you, I'd totally hug myself."

"Back off boys," Sage says sounding very bored. This earns a smile from me; having siblings must be great.

"Sure," Dylan says. Pause. "Mom."

He gets a glare from Sage and sticks a tongue out at her; all she does is roll her eyes and goes back to talking to Thomas, who had settled next to her after hanging up the phone.

"Yes, and just to tell you guys," Thomas says with a smirk. "Apparently Rose is a badass who can beat Jake at wrestling,"

"That is not true!" I exclaim.

Thomas just smiles broadly at me and turns his attention to the television.

"Hey Sasha," Angel says. "Can I talk to you for a second?"

"Sure," Sasha replies. They both go off to the other room. I'm curious on what Angel is saying but I decide not to eavesdrop with my acute hearing because I know it's rude.

"Ya, Rose." Angel's muffled voice says from behind the door of the other room. "No eavesdropping."

This makes me blush from embarrassment and a huge stupid smile creeps up onto my face. I feel someone coming up behind me and I turn just as Jake puts his arms around my waist.

"Don't worry," He tells me. "She's just filling her in on everything that's happened with Kate. And what she should do if anything happens again."

"Oh."

"Yep, Sasha is probably the most sensible, other than Sage, of course. But Angel knows Sasha better so she feels more comfortable talking to her."

"Okay," I reply with a smile. It's good to know we are leaving the kids in good hands.

"Get a room guys," Nat says from the couch.

"Don't worry Nat," Jake says humorously. "I know you're jealous. But don't worry, you've got the twins." He winks at me when I look at him in confusion.

"Ugh," Nat says and slumps back down on the couch with crossed arms. Alice looks like she's trying very hard not to snicker and Melissa is already turning red with laughter. Sage rolls her eyes, but I guess she has the right to do that since we are talking about her brothers and her best friend. By this point, Angel and Sasha have already come out of the room, Sasha looking serious and Angel looking ready.

"Okay guys!" Angel addresses Thomas, Jake, Cole and me. "I've got everything taken care of. Ready for some treasure hunting?"

19

The car is just starting up when Thomas lets out a long sigh.

"Thank God we're out of there! It was a little chaotic."

"Yes, I know Thomas," Angel replies. "I only asked Sasha to come, but since she was on a trip to Crete with the rest of them, they all came." She nods to Jake as he eyes her. "Plus, they are going to be gone by tonight or tomorrow, I've called a new babysitter. Someone I've known my whole life, and I trust her."

I wonder who this is, but I decide not to ask. Anyways, I'm too busy looking out the window at the gorgeous view; there are mountains and beaches and greenery everywhere. It is amazing. There is so much beauty here.

The car is nice and big, but I am still wedged between Jake and Cole. Angel and Thomas are in the front two seats, they are the only ones who know how to navigate through this place. Cole is looking out the window seemingly lost in thought, and Jake has my hand in his and is absently rubbing his thumb against the back of my hand, causing shivers of pleasure to run up my arm.

"I didn't get to say goodbye." I mumble.

Jake turns to me and looks like he's about to start a long sentence. But Angel, being Angel, interrupts him.

"Don't feel bad, Rose. You can call them. Plus, you've got more important things to worry about."

"Worry?" Thomas asks gruffly.

"Well, not exactly worry." Angel says defensively. "More like think. You have more important things to think about." She amends.

Cole nods his head, giving his agreement and the whole car falls silent. After about five minutes or so, I'm about to lean my head against Jake's shoulders and take a nap when someone starts humming. It's a female's voice, and it's beautiful.

It's Angel.

I look up and listen more attentively. Thomas looks at her and smiles; then he joins in. They are still humming a tune I am not familiar with, but between Thomas and Angel, they are able to break their voices into different harmonies and make it sound so beautiful and magical. I can feel myself smiling as pleasure of music fills me.

I look over at Jake and see that he's looking at me with a smile on his face. My eyes must be filled with wonder. Then Jake joins in as well, he hums a different harmony than Thomas and Angel, Angel looks to the back at Jake, lets out a big clap and a "Whoop" then starts singing some lyrics. Between these three, no instruments are needed; all they need are their voices.

It's a beautiful song, something about how the world is a big place but through all of that, you'll always be able to find that one person you love. I look over at Jake and see him staring intently at me.

I smile at him and decide that I want to try to join in. I listen to a few more of the notes and lyrics of the song and when the next chorus comes, I sing along with Angel. My voice is higher then hers, but I'm doing the harmony anyways. Within seconds, the car is filled with what seems like a symphony. With all the different voices melding in together, it really is very pretty. We are all enjoying ourselves. And as Angel comes to what seems like the last chorus, I break into runs and high notes that help the music come to an end. When the song finishes we all break into laughs and claps and comments of glee.

"Angel, you're amazing at singing!" I tell her. "You voice is just so beautiful it makes me want to cry from joy!"

"Haha, you're one to talk Rose." She replies with a wink. "You're just as good, but thank you."

"Angel, I don't think anyone can beat you when it comes to an awesome voice," I laugh. "And Thomas! You're great! You should sing more instead of watching gruesome movies."

"I like gruesome movies, gentle Rose." He replies. "But yes, that's probably the one thing that all of us with special abilities have. We all love music, and as a result, we all love to sing."

"Is that so?" I question.

"Yep," Jake tells me.

"Interesting,"

"Haha," Angel laughs sarcastically at my comment. I smile at her, feeling as if I've known her my whole life. Already, I am starting to love her like a sister.

Now I turn to face Cole, ready to demand why he didn't join in, and find him already looking at me.
"Cole, why didn't you join in?"

"Didn't feel like it." He comments. "Plus, I didn't know the song."

"Well, I didn't either." I answer back to him.

"Well, I wouldn't expect anyone but Jake and Thomas to know it. Since I wrote it myself." Angel puts in.

"You did?" I gasp. "It's so good Angel! You are so amazingly talented!"

"Oh yes, Rose?" She asks. "How many songs have you written?" Her tone implying that she has won a argument that had not even started.

I mumble something unintelligible and stick my tongue out at her.

"Well, it's good to know that you ladies have a lot in common." Cole remarks.

"Kinda like how you and I use to be, right Cole?" Jake adds.

"Right." Cole replies shortly.

I look over at Jake and see that he looks sad, and I know that though Cole seems to have returned to us a lot, he still isn't fully with us.

"Well guys, if you're all done jibber-jabbering, I need to know where we're going." Thomas says to us in a very bored tone.

We all look at Cole for an answer, but he just shrugs and looks at me. His eyes give a clear message that only I would be able to understand. I sigh and answer Thomas, telling him the description of the place that I think should be our first area of search.

We are going back to the cave where Cole lost his freedom to the women in the shadows.

■ ■ ■

It's very different here, without the snow, without the cold and the darkness. It looks very harmless in daylight. But there it is, the cave entrance that Cole entered a few years ago, when his life changed forever. Except it isn't the same. There is no overwhelming evil presence in this cave. It looks abandoned. But it is just like in the dream; the cave is by the beach and looks dark and foreboding.

"I don't think Tenebris Daemon is here anymore." I whisper as I reach the mouth of the cave. My hands press against the hard stonewalls. When I remove my hands, I see that cave sand has stuck to my palms.

No one says a word as we venture deeper into the cave. There is no sound except for our breathing. As usual, my footfalls make no noise, but neither do the others, so I guess that is an advantage.

I keep my hand on the right wall at all times, because even though it's broad daylight outside, it is dark as night in here, maybe even darker. It is a heavier kind of darker. Oppressive.

"You feel that, guys?" I mumble quietly, afraid to wake any sleeping monster that may be roaming these caves.

"Yeah," Thomas says. "We should have brought flashlights."

I hear Angel scoff and I swear if it were bright, I'd be able to see every single one of my companions, except for Thomas, roll their eyes.

"I've got something," Jake tells all of us. I see some movement in the darkness, then the soft glow from something in Jake's hand. "It's one of those glow stick things, except this is more of a glow stick ball, and much brighter."

"Do you have more?" I question.

"No,"

"Then you had better take the lead." I suggest and hear no objections.

"No," Jake suddenly says. "I think Cole should lead. He's the only one that has actually been in this place."

I smile at Jake through the darkness, glad that he trusts Cole enough for this. Jake shines the glow ball in front of Cole's face and that's when I notice how pale he looks.

"Cole?" I ask. "Are you okay?" I place a hand on his arm, and his blank eyes and pale face turn placid. He clears his throat.

"Yes," He says and takes the glow ball from Jakes' hand. "Okay, I'll lead."

We follow him through some tunnels that I don't remember from the dream, but that's probably because I was filled with fear and adrenaline as I ran through the cave to reach Cole. Now I'm calm and quiet, and I notice everything. No one speaks as we walk through the cave, but as we get deeper I notice that the air gets colder. And before long, my breath comes out in puffs of white.

"Is this normal?" Angel asks, breaking the silence. "For it to be this cold?"

"No," Jake tells her. "This is the effect of an evil presence. It's definitely not natural."

"But why should it be cold?" Thomas interrupts. "I feel no dark presence."

"Neither do I," I say.

"I second that." Angel adds. "Or thirds that. Or whatever."

And through the darkness and cold, Jake manages to laugh.

"Oh Angel," He whispers in humor. "You can never find the right words, can you?"

I smile at his attempt to set us at ease. It's almost as if he's done this before. Cole certainly has. I take in how Angel and Thomas are both very calm and collected and how they don't question where we're going and seem prepared for anything. And as I'm contemplating this, I realize that all four of them have been on adventures such as these before.

"Yes, Rose." Angel says to me. "We all have been in similar situations. After all, what else is there to do with our gifts?" Her hand reaches out to me and I feel her squeeze my arm.

"Ha, you heard my confused thoughts." I answer back.

"Yes," she says. "But they weren't very confused at all, they were… smart. Very organized"

"Well, at least I know I'm in good hands." I tell all of them.

"We could say the same about you, Rose," Angel says.

I keep silent because I do not agree with her. My hands are probably the worst anyone could encounter. I'd probably accidently get all of them lost or hurt. The last time someone else's life was in my hands; I failed them. I saved myself and let them die. So I will not trust myself so much again.

And if I were the one leading this expedition, I'd probably break down. Already I'm starting to feel scared; this cold dark place is no place for someone like me; for someone who loves warmth and light. But there is something in me that is urging my body and mind forward, towards the cold and the dark.

Since the illumination of the glow ball is in the front with Cole, I don't see Jake reaching out to me but I feel his touch on my hand, and I clutch him gratefully, happy that there's something I can hold on to.

"Okay," Cole finally stops. "I think we should be close. But I don't see anything." He starts touching the walls and the floor, looking for something. But there is nothing there.

"Maybe I can help," I tell him. Because the urge to go towards the darkness is growing, and I have a feeling this tug will bring us to our destination. I walk forward, pass Cole, and onwards. I don't have to look behind me to know that the others are following, because I can sense their tension.

I feel hope; maybe my dad is here, trapped. Perhaps that's why I have this tugging in my gut, leading me to the unknown. A longing feeling now joins the tugging urge; I have never felt it before. But I know the sensation of power when I encounter it, and I know this is what it is. I feel the power that I need, and its source is calling to me, dark and compelling.

I break into a run and can hear the others following me, feel their confusion.

"What are you doing?" Angel halfway shrieks, halfway whispers at me from behind. But I don't answer because I'm so close, so close. And that's when I hit a dead end. Nothing. Nothing. Just a hard jagged rock wall. My hands scale every surface of the solid dead end, finding no opening. I feel the others run up behind me; hear their ragged breaths from running. Was I really running that fast?

"I... I don't understand." I murmur, partly to myself, partly to the others. "I could feel it, it was right here, somewhere. But there's nothing." My hands are still frantically searching every inch of the walls. The hope of finding the power, and possibly finding my dad is fading away. "There must be something. I must be missing something."

"Rose," Jakes' voice is right by my ear. "What's going on?" I feel his hand on my shoulder and I turn to him, half crazed for a reason I can't explain.

"I need to get it, Jake." I tell him urgently. "I need it. I need to find it. It was here. It is here. I can still feel it." And that is true. I still feel the tugging urge that sent me running through the cave. It is like gravity, pulling me to something that I can't see, pulling me to the core of what I need. It is similar to what I felt on my birthday, that tugging in my gut that led me to the meadow where I learned about my destiny. That tugging was light and strong pulling me forward. This tugging is different; it's heavy and forceful, pulling me…

"Down!" I exclaim. I drop to the floor and search the ground frantically, for anything. I can feel the other's concern and their uncertainty. Surely they think I'm possessed now. But I'm not, I have a purpose and I must complete it.

Dust. Dust is all my hands encounter and I finally give up. I just sit there, thinking. What is wrong? What am I doing wrong? My gut led me here, and I have learnt to trust my gut. But it seems that my gut has two sides, just like my soul does, a good side, and a bad unreliable side.

"Maybe we should search somewhere else." I hear Thomas tell Jake. It must have been more than ten minutes since I dropped to the floor and sat down. Jake agrees and I can hear the worry in his voice. He kneels down next to me and cradles my face in his hands, forcing me to look him in the eye.

"What did you feel, Rose?" He whispers very quietly. "Why did you run and bring us here?"

"I don't know." I answer. And it's the truth. I don't know what led me here or why it did, only that it had to be the darkness. "I need to do something Jake, I need to. And I felt like this would help me. Finding whatever was supposed to be here."

"She was led," Angel says. I don't look up at her because I know she is right. Something is leading me, and I don't know whether that something is good or evil.

"We have to go, Rose." Jake tells me, his fingers push away the little hairs that had fallen in front of my face. "We can't stay here. It's not safe."

I nod my agreement because I know that Jake is worried, and I don't want him to worry. So I let him slowly help me to my feet but once I stand up, a sudden weakness overwhelms me and I fall to the ground again. Jake is just fast enough to catch my shoulder and head before they hit the ground.

"Rose?" He says frantically. "Are you okay?"

I wave off the others as their hands reach out to pull me upright.

"I'm fine." I tell them weakly and put my hands to my head. "I don't know what's wrong." I use my hands to push myself up into a sitting position and suddenly a sharp slicing pain shoots through my left palm, the hand closest to the cave wall. My head is towards the dead end with my feet towards my friends. I lift my hand up and find a long gash across my palm with blood oozing out of it. I probably cut it on a rock.

"Damn," I say.

Jake sees my wound and immediately takes my hand and gets ready to perform first aid on it. I'm about to let him put a bandage on me when I have a thought. Yes, why not? This is, after all, an evil place filled with magic.

"Wait, Jake, hold on." I tell him and pull my hand away. He starts to object. "Trust me." I add earnestly. He nods and releases my hand. I can feel all four pairs of eyes watching me as I walk over to the dead end.

"Evil loves death." I explain to them. "Evil wants blood." I place my palm against the wall and push hard, forcing more fresh blood, my blood, to pour out of the wound. "So you give evil death and blood, to let evil accept you." My blood trickles down the stone wall, dark against the already black rocks. As the first drops of blood fall to the ground, the cave starts to rumble.

"This is it." Thomas says and he clutches Angel's hand, who then clutches Jake's hand, who clutches Cole. I can't hold Jake's hand because his are both occupied, so I take hold of Cole's. As his hand encloses around my right hand, he looks into my eyes.

"Good job," Cole says so quietly that only I can hear him. The rumbling in the cave is so strong now that it feels like an earthquake. Then the ground starts to break open, but too perfectly. Finally, the rumbling stops, and what I find in front of me is something that I did not expect: a perfectly symmetrical circular hole in the ground, leading deep into the earth.

There is no sound; no one dares make a noise until Thomas whistles in wonder.

"So, who's going first?"

"I think Rose should go first." Jake says. His eyes sparkle with wonder and I feel his confidence in me. "She knows what she's doing." Any doubt he or the others had felt has vanished. Now, however, along with the longing and hope, I feel doubt myself. Doubt that what I find will not be what I wanted.

I smile at Jake and take the glow ball from Cole. Before I know exactly what I am doing, I cup the ball and blow on it. The ball begins to glow brighter and warmer until it becomes a small shining sun. Some older instinct in me must have taken over and told me to do that.

"Okay," I say. "That's better. Now I can actually see all of you." And I can. Very clearly. All their faces are lit up in wonder. I take one last look at the ball and throw it into the hole. I can feel the others' brief surprise, then their understanding. As the ball falls, it tells us how deep the hole is. It turns out that this hole isn't that deep at all.

"Okay!" Thomas breathes. "Ladies first!"

■ ■ ■

The ride down the hole isn't even scary. It is actually quite fun, like a roller coaster ride or a slide at a playground, but a really long one. But, in the end, we all make it to the bottom. There is a long tunnel, leading deeper into the caves.

"Whoo!" Thomas yells in excitement as we all get to our feet. "Lets' go again!"

I allow myself to laugh.

"Wow, a secret passage way…" I say in amazement. The tugging in my gut is pulling me further into the tunnel. The air is even colder down here. I know that we are close.

"Yes," Jake says. "And you unlocked the door with a key that no one else could think of." He shakes his head and smiles at me. "How did you know?"

I just give him a small shrug.

"Lucky guess?"

But I am not so sure that it was luck.

"Great that we have a lucky guesser then!" Angel says. "Should we move on?"

"Yes," Cole murmurs in a hushed voice, his tone so serious that the laughter dies in all of us. With that, we march further into the darkness, possibly to my dad, but definitely towards a dark captivating power. A power that I will soon have to acknowledge.

20

The hissing starts as soon as the air turns to what seems like below freezing-level. We put on our jackets; the cold is really quite uncomfortable. It is strange how cold the air is down here since it was quite warm outside.

"We're close," Cole murmurs. I can feel that we are getting to our destination, but it seems that the closer we get, the colder it is.

We follow Cole, our breaths coming out in puffs of smoke. Angel is shivering in the back so I stay behind and put my hand on her. She stops shaking as soon as we touch; I guess my warmth can still reach others through this freezing dark coldness. That's good.

"It's not safe here," I whisper to Jake.

"I know," He answers back. "I think that without you here, we would already be frozen statues."

"I agree," Angel puts in.

"Hey Rose," Thomas calls to me from the front. "Wanna warm my lips up for me? They are turning blue!"

"No, thank you." I tell him. And since I know he's joking, I am unable to keep the smile from my face.

"Sorry Thomas," Jake says. "She's all mine." He takes a hold of my hands; it steadies me.

All of a sudden, Cole stops walking.

"What is it?" I ask him, and come forward to stand next to him. Jake, who is still holding my hand, walks with me to Cole. We three stand in front, with Angel and Thomas at our flanks. All five of us are looking in amazement at the sight before us.

The corridor, or tunnel, has now opened and reveals a little room covered in ice and snow. Icicles hang down from the ceiling, and the floor is a mixture of solid ice and frozen snow.

The room is bare, except for a long rectangular object at the far wall.

It looks like a coffin made of ice.

A coffin.

Coffins are used to hold bodies, usually of the dead. But there's nothing usual or normal about this one. Maybe this coffin holds someone who is trapped. Maybe it holds someone who is cursed to stay alive but imprisoned. Dread fills me, along with hope.

I walk into the room. Not wanting to leave my side, Jake and Cole follow me just a little behind. I stop just a centimeter away from the coffin, filled with a mixture of dread and hope.

I look up at Cole to see in his eyes the reflection of my own emotions. Then my eyes shift to Jake to find that he too is staring at me intently. He looks hopeful, concerned, and very scared. We all don't know what we would find.

"What do you think is inside?" Angel asks.

"Someone we've been looking for, for a very long time." Cole replies tightly.

"Hold on," Thomas intrudes. "Did you say someone?"

"Yes," I reply nervously. "We think that it might be my dad. He's been missing for almost two years."

"Yes," Cole says darkly. "I went looking for him, but instead, I found Daemon." If it weren't such a dark moment, I probably would have chuckled. They had all started calling Tenebris Daemon by her last name. It means demon in the old Latin language, and I guess they all think she is one hell of a demon, so that stuck.

"Can you open it Cole?" Jake asks. "I sense dark magic at work here. Whatever is sealing this coffin shut is foreign to us."

"I'm not sure," Cole replies. "I'll see."

Cole steps forward and places both his hands on the top section of the coffin. He concentrates briefly before he starts glowing. I guess this is what dark powers look like, instead of a bright shine, it's just a harsh glow. But since Cole is sort of in the middle of the dark and the light, his glow is soft and somewhat bright. A low humming of power fills the room; the sound vibrates to my very bones. Cole squeezes his eyes shut and the air shimmers around him. After what seems like a long time, he opens his eyes. The sound dies.

"I can't do it." He says weakly. "Something is blocking me. And I'm not strong enough in the dark side. My dark powers have weakened the longer I've stayed with you," He pauses before he adds: "It's rather painful actually, when the dark power fades. It's like it gets cut away. Maybe that pain of giving up the darkness is what makes people want to keep it." He mumbles, almost to himself.

"What are we going to do?" I ask dejectedly.

"You should do it, Rose," Cole says suddenly and calmly; but I hear an edge in his voice, almost like he really doesn't want me to do it because he's afraid of the outcome.

I don't reply because I'm scared. But I know that I am right. My dad is most probably in this coffin, and the only way to open it is through the use of dark power. Could it be that I need to unlock my dark side to unlock the coffin?

Angel and Thomas are silent; I can almost sense Angel peeping into my thoughts, trying to figure things out. Thomas just stands and watches without saying anything, probably waiting for something to happen, not knowing that it could put everyone in here in danger.

I don't know what revealing my dark side will do, I already have such a powerful light side, such a powerful good side. So what would my dark side be capable of? Would it reverse my abilities somehow so that instead of making everyone happy and healthy and positive again I would be bringing them pain, and sadness and suffering?

Isn't that what Cole did in the beginning? He and I aren't so different from each other, it seems. But no, my gift of happiness, health and positivity is an unconscious thing. It just comes with my aura. Perhaps I will be able to control the negative things. Or maybe I won't even have them. There is no telling what could happen. But that's what makes it so perilous.

Finally, I look at Jake. His is the reaction that I am most concerned with, because he is the one that I care about the most. His eyes hold confusion, and then swiftly it changes to embrace understanding as he searches my face for answers.

I can tell that he knows what I have to do and why. I will be more powerful if I have the light and the dark on my side. If I can control the darkness and keep it innocent of evil, then I could get rid of the darkness in Tenebris and maybe help more people. But the problem is: there is no guarantee that I can control this darkness and stop it from making me become the very thing I am trying to destroy.

He steps closer to me until our noses are almost touching and puts his hands on my shoulders.

"Are you sure about this?" Jake murmurs to me softly, his breath moving the hair that has fallen over my face.

"Yes," I tell him, my voice high and unsteady. But I am determined to get this done.

Without a clear idea of what exactly I am doing, I walk up to the coffin until the toes of my shoes bump against it.

It isn't a particularly big coffin. The whole thing comes up to around my waist, supported by a raised platform.

Without warning, tears slip down my face. I didn't even know I was crying. The tears fall from my chin onto the coffin. Where the tears fall, it glows a little.

I stare at it, curious for a second but then sadness hits me again, overpowering. More tears slip down.

"Please, Daddy," I cry softly. "Don't be dead. Please," And I set my palms on the coffin. I don't know exactly what I'm supposed to do, so I just bring forth my love for my father, the longing and loss I felt when he was gone, the quiet sudden hope that we could find him.

I can sense myself growing brighter, shining fiercely but not strong enough. I'm not strong enough.

But since I know that I will need my dark side, I unlock the box in my heart that has all the horrible feelings. Hatred for the Tenebris pours forth; anger at everything fills me, anger that I have been so weak, anger at the evil that exists in the world, anger at all the pain that everyone, including me, has to feel.

The dark joins the light in my heart. The good emotions and the bad come together, both trying to conquer that muscle in my chest that keeps me alive. It seems for a second that there are more bad things in life than there are good; a war rages in my heart as the darkness strives for full control. I would have let it, for I really do hate Tenebris Daemon, the person who caused my mom such grief, and gave me such a sense of loss. But then I think about what my dad would tell me "Stay strong, fight against all the horrible pain that's in you, fight against whatever is the cause of it. And know that no matter how lonely you feel, someone is always there for you." My dad's voice in my head helps me.

I feel as if I have control now, I am not driven by the need to take revenge on Daemon. Not driven by the hatred of so many things.

Now I am driven by all the good and bad things put together; and I feel strong.

Stronger than I ever have, but I know that if I ever have a moment of doubt, I will lose control. If I, even for a second, let the darkness seep through and take more than half of what I feel in my heart, then I would have failed.

But I don't think about that now.

I focus on putting all my power into opening the coffin and to release my dad from the cold oblivion. In the corner of my mind, I'm aware of someone gasping; I'm not sure exactly at what though.

Am I shining too bright?

Then I see what the gasp was directed at. From where my hands touch the ice coffin, a deep orange glowing light is spreading over the whole box.

A fire burns from my soul and pours over all the ice, taking away the freeze and replacing it with warmth. The ice melts, but not like normal ice; it evaporates as it melts.

It's quite amazing actually. But concentration is essential; I have to concentrate on getting rid of the ice that has imprisoned my dad in his frozen cell, and concentrate on the positive things and not let the negative take control of my heart and mind.

The fire that is melting the ice touches the skin on my hands, but it does not burn. I don't feel anything. I am numb. My thoughts are completely focused on spreading the fire.

I feel a hand on my shoulders, and vaguely hear someone screaming for me to stop the fire, that it is scorching me.

But I can't move. I can't stop. I don't want to.

My eyes are on the flickering flames that engulf my dad's coffin, melting his cage away. The ice is almost fully melted and I can't stop. I won't stop, though the flames are licking up my arms. My eyes stare, dazzled at its strange beauty. Now the heat is growing, and I finally feel the blazing pain. It is intense and controlled, and extremely unbearable.

But I will bear it; I have to get my dad out first.

Burning myself is nothing compared to freeing my dad from his icy prison; so I push more power through me, and the fire burns brighter, higher, and hotter; melting whatever is left of the ice.

Someone tries to grab me to pull me away from the fire, but I'm not going anywhere. I have to stay to control the fire. I am compelled to.

Through my daze, I'm aware of a noise. It sounds like screaming.

I think it's me.

"Veronica!" Jake's voice reaches me through everything, though nothing else could at this moment. "Rose! It's done! Stop! You're going to burn yourself and your dad to death!"

I look down and realize he's right. There is no more ice and my dad is lying on a block, unconscious but breathing.

Now I have to stop the fire. But I don't know how to. It seems like I can only move it, not extinguish it. If I don't move it now, it'll burn my dad.

So I do the only thing that I can. I draw it into me.

The flames move past my elbows, down my body, and to my legs, burning my clothes. I can hear Cole shouting at me to stop, and Jake shouting at someone to get water, a rag, anything, to put me out of fire. I can feel the pain, it's horrible, but I'm too busy concentrating on removing the fire to really do much about it. It's all over my body, the heat most intense over my heart.

I yell in pain and frustration because I can't control this fire; it is of darkness as well as light. I can feel myself slipping; this heat, this pain is too much.

So I try once more, thinking about everyone I love, thinking about my family, thinking and dreaming about how much I love the beach, and water, and the breeze and gentle touch of wind. Suddenly there's coolness, and then the flames die.

As the flames go, so does the rest of my strength.

I drop to the floor. If Jake hadn't been there to catch me, I would have hit it hard. The fire burned me badly from my hands to my forearm. The burns on the rest of my body aren't as major as I thought, though it felt like my whole body was on fire.

I fight for consciousness in Jake's arms, wanting to be there for my dad, wanting to be strong. But I hardly have enough strength left to speak. I notice everyone else crowding around me, Cole included, my dad momentarily forgotten.

This annoys me because I risked myself for my dad and they don't even go help him now.

"My dad," I mumble. "Go help my dad."

I can barely get the words out of my mouth, but I think everyone understands. Cole pushes the hair away from my face and touches my cheek gently before rising to check my father. This is good; Cole has always loved my dad like he was his own. Angel and Thomas go with Cole after looking me over with concerned eyes. I use all my remaining will power to turn my head towards where my dad now lies, with Cole, Angel and Thomas bending over him.

Even through the haze of weakness and pain, I can see that all the ice has melted, and can see the rise and falls of his chest as he breathes. His eyes aren't open, so he looks like he could be asleep. Watching him makes me want to sleep too.

"It worked," I whisper as consciousness slips away.

The last thing I'm aware of is Jake planting a feather light kiss on my lips; giving me some life and helping to push me into a sleep with undisturbed dreams.

21

The pain in my stomach, accompanied by a growl, is what really drags me from unconsciousness. I must have been asleep for the whole day, because the soreness in my muscles and the ache in my bones tell me that I haven't used them in a while. The discomfort in my empty abdomen also tells me that I haven't eaten in a while; I am hungry.

I try to lift myself up from the bed, but just trying to sit up makes my body shake with exertion and causes sweat and dizziness. What's wrong with me? I groan aloud because I find it annoying to be confined by my own flesh and bones.

Immediately, a head pops into my room. But it is not a head I was expecting. This head has long black hair instead of the short blond of Jake's head, and deep pretty dark brown eyes, instead of the beautiful dazzling blue. Her face is small and her figure petite; I know her as soon as I see her.

There is no mistaking who this is, even though I think I must be hallucinating.

"Mom?" I exclaim in disbelief. Surely, this isn't real. How can my mom be in Greece? The last time I saw her, she was in New York, trying to do the best to get on with life without Dad, but to no end. But now she's here, and though I am surprised, I am happy. Because now I can finally be a child and not be embarrassed when being taken care of.

"What are you doing here? Where are the others?" I don't ask her where Dad is, for I don't even know whether she knows that we've found him. And I wasn't awake to see whether we got him out, but counting on Cole, I'm sure we did.

"Hi honey," She says in her usual way, full of concern, love and a small amount of strictness as if she were saying 'this is why I am so protective'. I smile at her because I have missed her in many ways. But I can't move to give her a hug, so I just wait until she comes over and touches my cheek. "I will tell you what I know before asking questions, okay?" She tells me. I nod.

"So Angel called me. She had needed someone to take care of her two younger siblings; someone responsible who she knew and trusted, and who was free. I told her I would come, because I wanted to keep my eye on you anyways. When I got here, the previous visitors were leaving and a very smart young lady named Sasha told me all about what had happened to Kate, and what to be careful of. I stayed with them for the rest of the afternoon. Then you five older kids came back in the evening, right before dinner. And boy! Was I surprised! Jake had you in his arms, and baby, you looked terrible. Your arms were all burned, your clothes were black and horrible and some skin was already blistering on your legs! But Jake got you in here real quickly and applied some special medicine. It helped a lot, the burns are already starting to fade." She sees my expression and moves on. Probably guessing that I don't want to hear about what happened to me.

"Okay, anyways, obviously I followed Jake into this room and watched carefully while he was putting medicine on you. So I wasn't there when Thomas, Angel and Cole brought your dad in. I only saw him when I went out of your room; and boy, it was a shock. I didn't know whether it was real, but there he was, breathing and alive. And I knew that it was thanks to you. But Ronnie, I think he's in a sort of coma. He's not waking up so we can't feed him or anything. So we were going to get a personal nurse and doctor to help him get the nutrients he needs through the tubes. I had suggested the hospital, but it was too dangerous. After a few days, however, we realized that nothing was happening to him even though he wasn't eating. His body stayed perfectly healthy, "

I stay silent through the whole story, processing what I am hearing, and trying to figure out how to help my dad's coma problem. Did my mom say a few days?

"All the others are out somewhere. They are all rested and well again." My mom adds. She knows me so well that I don't even have to tell her what I want to know next.

"Okay." Is all I reply. It hurts to speak since my throat and mouth feels like sandpaper. "I'm thirsty, mom, and hungry. Why am I so weak and sore?"

"Well honey," My mother says hesitantly. "It's because you been asleep for a little over a week."

■ ■ ■

It turns out that a little over a week was an understatement, it was actually close to two weeks, but my mom just didn't want to scare me. I can't even sit up on my bed, so my food has to be brought to me. Even though I've been asleep for two weeks, with no food or water, my body has not fallen apart. None of us know exactly why. But my mind and body have been weakened. I will have to start with the simple task of walking to the kitchen, but my mom is certain that I will get my strength back very quickly.

While eating, my mom tells me what happened in the two weeks that I was asleep: My family, as in Jake, Cole, Angel and

Thomas had tried everything to wake my father up, but to no avail. And even though he wasn't eating anything, his body stayed as healthy as mine did. My mom has this theory. She thinks that somehow I'm keeping him from dying, and that if someone tried to starve me to death, or something like that, it wouldn't work. My mom thinks that I can only be killed a certain way, so I am rather safe from any threat. But, that's only a theory. And of course she thinks this. Every mother would like her child to be safe forever.

I don't know what could have kept me alive without eating and drinking for two weeks, or what could be keeping my dad alive now. One thing's for sure. Whatever enchantment that had been put on my dad to keep him alive while in his icy prison is still at work. So there is no way to wake him up without a counter spell or something.

Except for my dad, everything is fine, great even. Kate and Simon love my mom; they helped her get the meals ready while Angel was out with Thomas, Jake and Cole, trying to figure some things out. Cole is a lot better too; apparently whatever evil presence that had been with him had been burned away by my fire when I freed dad. So Cole now belonged to the light, again.

My mom says nothing about my presence, or anything about the fact that I have accepted the darkness into me; so I decide not to bring it up. Jake had sat by me as much as he could, and Angel had helped change me whenever my clothes got too old. Cole always watched me sleeping from outside the room, so Jake would be next to me and Cole would be on the couch looking into my room.

Thomas was the most optimistic; he kept on telling everyone that I was fine and would wake up soon and that instead of brooding over me, someone should go make him a sandwich.

Well, someone had to ease the tension… even if it was in a rather lazy way.

Anyways, when I first woke up and saw my mom. Jake, Thomas, Cole and Angel were out getting more food supplies and any extra stuff that they needed. Well, that's what they told my mom. But I have a feeling that they went to do some research on whatever preserved my dad's body in his sleeping state.

By the time they get back, I already finished my lunch and, with the help of my mother, took a bath. After the bath, I feel tons better, and am able to walk all the way to a kitchen stool before I collapse from exhaustion. Using dark powers really drained me, or maybe it is my injuries from using the powers, or perhaps just accepting that darkness in me had changed the whole way that my body and mind works. But I doubt that, because it seems that my good powers still work unconsciously; at least this is good. So I can use the light consciously and unconsciously, and only use the dark consciously. Because accessing the darkness is easy, it's keeping it reigned that's hard. Maybe that's what caused me to pass out for two weeks: the mere effort of chaining up the cold darkness back deep within me.

Now I am sitting on a stool at the kitchen counter, watching my mom fuss with the food. Kate and Simon sit on either side of me talking to me and filling me in on whatever they think is important. I listen attentively to the kids' every word while watching my mom clean up around the house.

An hour later, they come back home.

When they come through the door, surprise is on all their faces. But I can also sense worry, admiration, happiness and relief. But since surprise is the strongest of all those feelings at that moment, it is the emotion that escapes onto their faces.

I smile broadly at them to show them that I really am okay. At first they just stare at me, probably trying to figure out whether I am faking it. Then Angel smiles and lets out a huge squeal as she runs towards me. She slows down enough to not crush me, but the contact still hurts after being practically immobilized for half a month. Angel pulls back and reveals a whole row of naturally perfect teeth. Her beautiful blue eyes sparkle with glee; her dark brown hair is in gentle waves that frame her small tanned face.

After weeks of not seeing her, it is literally like looking at a face of an angel. So I guess her name does suit her; it is almost as if I had forgotten how beautiful she is. But I can see her more clearly. Every single detail. Even the small imperfection of a scar near her lip, makes her look more perfect.

It is as if my sight had gotten even sharper. Huh, weird.

"Hey Rose!" She says excitedly to me; her voice doesn't conceal any emotion.

I smile at her, touched that she's happy to see me.
"Hey Angel."

I think she would have jumped on me again if Thomas hadn't pushed her aside, quite roughly actually. But Angel slides away from him right before he manages to use his full force. She rolls her eyes, gives me another huge smile, and goes to help my mom.

Now I fix my attention on Thomas, and boy, he looks bigger than ever! It is like his muscles tripled in size. His brown hair seems to shine, and his blue eyes, so similar to Angels', have the same sparkle. It almost looks like they are glowing. Even his pale skin isn't very pale anymore. He's smiling at me, his smile even bigger than Angels. Then very suddenly, he reaches out and picks me up in a big bear hug. Lifting me off the ground and practically crushing my bones.

"Can't breathe!" I croak out.

He lets out a big laugh and sets me down. With the amusement and mischievousness of a youngster on Thomas's face, he looks very handsome. More than he did before. I really wonder why both he and Angel seem to look clearer to me now, and I can read their expressions even better and feel their emotions almost as if they are my own.

Thomas moves away chuckling. I feel the smile on my lips, which is already huge, growing.

Then Cole steps forward. His beautiful green eyes communicating all the words that he doesn't ever need to say. He puts his hands on my shoulders and leans in; I feel his lips touch my cheek, the sudden warmth that flows from that spot, and a weird suddenly empty feeling in my heart as he pulls away. But he doesn't pull away fully; he brings his lips close to my ear.

"Good job, Rose," Cole whispers. "I'm glad you're okay." And as he pulls away, I feel a sudden sadness fill me for I know that the empty feeling is there because I can never have him. I cannot allow it. And I really hope that Cole doesn't love me, because that would just hurt us both. Because I know I love Jake, and loving two guys at once isn't right.

Unable to speak, I just nod and smile at him, pushing away the tears that threaten to spill over. But I'm not successful; a single teardrop manages to escape and make its way halfway down my cheek before I manage wipe it away. I try to keep the rest from escaping; I don't want to cause my friends worry.

Cole frowns unhappily, probably wondering why I would start crying. I look him in the eyes and see his expression darken even further; perhaps he's guessed. Or maybe he thinks it's something else.

Then, thankfully, I'm distracted. For the most amazing and handsome face appears in front of me, taking up my whole field of vision. I can see every single feature perfectly, see the shine in his eyes as he takes me in, see his lips pull up in a gorgeous smile as he comes even closer to me. Then we're holding each other, his hands gently but urgently cupping my face, tracing my skin. My own hands clutch at the back of his neck, pulling him closer. Not kissing, but somehow managing to make it more intimate and sweet than that.

"Jake," I say, my heart threatening to explode with the love I'm feeling.

"Hey there," Jake replies softly as his fingers trace the features on my face, his touch sending little tingles of warmth through my skin. He touches my hair and then he's cupping my face again. "I thought you were going to die," He whispers hoarsely. I let my fingers wipe away the tears that escape from his own eyes.

"I'm right here," I whisper back to him; putting force into my words. "And I'll never leave you."

Then he's kissing me. His lips crushing mine with so much force that I'm taken aback at first. After my surprise I kiss him back, my arms gripping the back of his neck tightly, not wanting to release his body from mine, wanting us to become one. His hands find the small of my back and he pulls me closer to him; and since I'm still not strong enough to stand so long on my own, he practically holds me up. The heat from his lips spreads through me and over my whole body, igniting me just like the fire did, burning me. But instead of hurting me and bringing me pain, this fire gives me life and strength. The fire spreads through me, all over my body, down to my toes. I'm tingling all over, and I realize that I'm standing by myself now, no longer needing to be supported by Jake. I'm strong again; Jake made me strong again.

I feel awake all over again.

Technically, I have already bloomed, but this feels like a second blooming, a blooming with both my light and dark side.

Jake pulls away and smiles at me, and picks me up and swings me around contentedly. I'm laughing and yelling for him to put me down and when he does, I see that Kate and Simon are running towards us. Kate jumps into my arms and gives me a little kiss on the cheek and Simon jumps into Jakes' arms.

"Swing me around Jake!!! Like you did with Rose!" Simon yells. And Jake laughs and does as Simon requested. The room is filled with Simons squeals, and then Kate wants to be swung around too. I'm about to pick her up when I hear a high pitched music, no one else seems aware of it; so I must look weird as I stand up and look towards the direction of sound. It's coming from outside.

"Do you guys hear that?" I ask them. Everyone in the room shakes their heads, but none of them are looking at me bizarrely. That makes me feel a little better.

"What is it, Rose?" Cole says, he looks intense, and almost shut off, his eyes unreadable. But then he smiles at me, and kindness fills his eyes; he understands. I don't know how; but he knows what I hear, without having to ask or even hear what I'm hearing.

I smile back at him and say.
"I don't know."

And I make my way to the door – towards the beach, towards the music, and towards my first sunset after my second awakening.

22

"Roza," That single word, no, single name is being repeated over and over again in song. The pure voices that had pulled me out the door continue with their beautiful melody. I notice that no one else can hear anything. They don't seem as entranced as I am, and I feel no wonder in their emotion and see no amazement in their eyes. But I do feel curiosity from all except Cole. He seems to be the only one who can guess what I might be hearing. But I don't know how that is possible.

With my legs ankle deep in the water, I can still feel the warm heat of the setting sun on my skin. Jake comes up behind me, probably wondering what I'm staring at. I don't know what I'm so enchanted with either. All I know is everything looks so clear, so much more pure and beautiful than it ever did before; more so than when I first bloomed. It is truly amazing.

"The voices," I whisper quietly to Jake, not wanting to disrupt their music. "Do you hear them?"

"No, Rose," He replies, clearly worried. "I don't…"

"It's like singing." I explain to him, not wanting him to think that I'm crazy. "A high pitched beautiful melody that carries on, always repeating the same words over and over in the song."

"Roza," I hear Cole's voice say from a distance. But it shouldn't be from a distance, for he is standing right next to me. Everything seems quieter, only the music carries on loudly, almost ringing in my ears.

"Yes," I answer Cole softly. "How did you know?"

"I can hear it."

I turn to him in question. He can hear it too?

"How?"

"It started off as a soft ringing; slightly annoying, but wholesome. I figured that the ringing that I could hear, had to be the music to you. That it was so pure and natural that only you would be able to pick it up." He explains. "It's louder now, now that I'm so close to you, and now that we're outside."

"Yes," Angel says. "It's definitely louder. I heard the ringing too. But now I can also pick up a bit of song. And that word you said Cole. Roza." She pauses. "Do you think that Roza could be meant for Rose?"

"Yes," Jake tells her. "Roza is Rose. But probably her soul name."

I let their conversation carry on, my mind no longer listening to their words. But they are right. The music is getting louder, and now I can understand all the words perfectly.

"Through time we've waited, as the world corrupted.
With evil and bad, it makes us so sad.
Please help us dear Roza, you are the one.
We've called you through centuries; through you evil will be done.
Take up the sword, of black and of white.
But don't let the light escape from your sight.
Dear Roza, pure Roza, through you we'll be free.
You'll help us regain our mighty supreme.
Your heart will be whole, even with darkness inside.
Only you can hold such horrible might.
Others will perish but your soul will not break.

Roza, Rose, Roza, you are the one,
To bring us justice by killing the evil one.
Not the evil in hell but the one that escaped.
It's the evil that humans have sadly embraced.
Through Roza, cursed hearts will be pure again.

But make sure that you yourself come to end.
For it is said that once killed,
Evil moves to the next free heart, no matter how consumed.
Yours will be the closest and so bad will dwell,
In you for the longest, after evils' been dealt.
But no worries, dear Roza, you can fix this plight.
For your heart will always belong to the light."

Those words plant themselves in my brain. Over and over again, I keep thinking about the line: *But make sure that you yourself come to end.* I keep thinking that I knew – I know that I have to die, to help save everyone else; I have to die, or to sacrifice. It's what I expected. But to hear it, in actual words, just makes it seem more realistic and frightening.

To hear it in this song as if it were prophesied makes fear creep deep into my bones, right down to my heart and soul.

The voices are angelic voices, voices of the pure, the young and the sweet. They shouldn't be the voices that tell me that I have to die. But even as I think this, I know it's the dark side of me thinking. The side that would fight for survival no matter what, the side that would rather sacrifice millions of people, sacrifice my loved ones than to sacrifice myself. I know this is bad, and so I fight those feelings. It is my job to help people, to sacrifice myself for the greater good. And as I think this, my heart lightens, and the fear I felt earlier, the fear that was so dominant, disappears.

"Rose," I hear someone say my name. But I don't answer, I can't. Not yet. "Rose," Someone's calling me again. But I can't bring myself to speak. It's as if I have lost my voice. "*Roza*" The voice comes again, but this time, with my name, but not my name. It's my name in another language, but it is my true name.

I snap out of my reverie and focus my eyes to see Jake staring down at me, right into the depth of my eyes. And as I look into his, I realize that the saying 'the eyes are the windows to the soul' is right. Because I can see Jake's every thought in that moment, feel his every fear, his every emotion, see my eyes and my soul in his. And at that moment, I realize that I cannot keep my promise to him, my promise of always being here, and never leaving him.

I look away because I can feel my eyes burning.

I can't keep my promise in the physical sense, but perhaps I can keep it in the heart.

I look up at him again, through my tears, and see what I know in his eyes. We don't need words to express our thoughts and feelings. We just need this: to look into each other's eyes and know that we can never be together forever.

"Did you guys just hear what I heard?" Thomas speaks up through the dead silence. The voices are gone. The enchanting music is gone. The song had lived out its purpose:

to tell me what I had to do. To tell me exactly what I had to do. There is no more music to fill my ears, no more beauty, except a silent everlasting ringing note.

"Oh yes, we heard." Angel said, her voice breaking. "Oh, Jake. What are we going to do?"

But Jake doesn't reply. He is still staring into my eyes intently, and I, as usual, am still unable to look away from him.

Then he speaks, and I don't feel as if I'm lost.

"We take every step and turn as it comes our way." He says hoarsely. It sounds as if he's holding back a scream.

I smile at him to show him that I agree but he breaks his gaze.

No longer am I trapped by the power of his blue fire eyes. But Jake isn't smiling. And I can't bring myself to say anything. What can I say to comfort him?

"Well," Thomas suddenly says. "If we're taking every step and turn as it comes, then the next step should be making some dinner."

He bursts out laughing as we all stare at him with shocked and probably bemused expressions on our faces. Angel looks like she's trying very hard not to slap him and that just makes me laugh along with Thomas.

"What?" He says. "I'm hungry!"

I turn to Jake to suggest that we should make pasta for dinner, but he has already turned away and is walking back to the house, his footsteps making prints in the sand. I stare after him; my heart hurting as if every step he takes away from me is a knife driving deeper and deeper into my core.

"It's okay," says a voice near my ear. "He'll come around. He's just processing the idea of possibly losing you."

I turn to see Cole looking down at me, his expression closed off, his tone neutral.

"What do you think about this?" I ask him even though I already know the answer. Cole is a lot like me, and he understands.

But when he replies, his eyes are hard but glistening.

"I think that when the time comes, you'll do what you believe is right."

■ ■ ■

My eyes open, and I stare into the darkness of my room. Sleep evades me as I remember, yet again, the prophecy, and Jake walking away from me. He had been silent throughout dinner, and had quickly kissed me goodnight and closed the door to my room without giving me a backwards glance. No one told my mom about what we heard.

No one wanted to.

But I know that I will have to, in time.

Very quietly, I get out of bed; not wanting to wake my mom up for she now sleeps next to me. I'm wearing nothing but a tank top and boxer shorts that I use as pajamas; it's just too hot.

I slip out the door and make my way towards Jake's room, not knowing exactly why. The moonlight streams through the many windows of the house, and I can see my shadow. I close my hands around the doorknob of Jake's room and take a deep breath.

The door creaks open and I make Jake out in the dark. He's still lying on his bed, but is staring at the ceiling, wakeful and alert. Jake pulls himself up on his elbow; he is wearing nothing but pajama pants. Even in the dark, I can see the shadows on his abdomen, highlighting the strong muscles. His eyes follow me as I make my way across the room and sit on the edge of his bed.

I stay silent, not daring to look him in the eye. Why did I come here? What is there to do here? Maybe he doesn't want me here. I'll go back. I'm just about to get up from the bed when his hand grabs my wrist. I look at him now and see that he's staring at me very intently. I can feel that he's worried, and anxious, and that he's nervous but happy that I'm here.

"What's wrong?" Jake asks me, his voice no louder than a whisper.

"Does something have to be wrong for me to come to your room to see you?" I answer back just as quietly.

"Well, it is kind of three in the morning, Rose." He tells me, sounding rather amused.

I sigh. "Yeah, you're right."

Silence.

"So is something wrong?" Jake repeats again, his voice sounding a bit shakier this time.

"No," I mumble. "I just... I wanted to... I couldn't..." I curse myself mentally for not being able to find the right words.

"Come here," Jake says softly and he pats the bedside beside him, lifting up the sheets so that I can climb in. I do, I am cold anyways. I sit cross-legged next to him, thinking of something to say.

"I'm sorry," He tells me. Jake still holds my hand and I can feel how warm they are. "I'm sorry for walking away and not comforting you. You should have been the one that needed comfort but I walked away to comfort myself, and I'm sorry."

"No, Jake. No." I start even before he finished speaking. "I don't mind that. I was fine. And that's not why I came here." I let out a long breath. "I guess I just couldn't go to sleep, and this was the first place I could think of to come to."

His hand had been tracing my arm and had stopped when I finish my sentence. The next thing I know is that his arms are around me, not like a cage, but like a haven. I bury my face into the crook of his shoulders; his skin is soft and warm and I smile against his bare chest. He pulls me onto him so that I sit on his lap and his hands are stroking my hair, like I'm a child.

"I was thinking about you too," He murmurs. "And I would have come to you, but you share a room with your mom and I didn't want to wake either of you up."

"Well, here I am," I say in an attempt of wit.

"Yes," He says. "Here you are." He chuckles. "Was the whole point of you coming here to tell me that I was a terrible person for not being there to console you?"

I pretend to consider this.

"Erm, Nah." I trace my fingers on his chest, his breath quickens but he doesn't comment. I can't see very clearly in the dark, but I can feel lean, hard muscle. "And you aren't a terrible person."

His breath moves my hair, I can feel it against my neck; a shiver runs down my spine even though I am no longer cold. He moves his hand up and down my arm, probably trying to warm me up.

"You cold?" He asks quietly, his voice husky.

"No," I tell him as I shut my eyes, a smile forms on my lips. "I'm perfectly perfect."

I feel him move, his hand reaches to touch and lift my chin up. I feel his lips brush mine very lightly, touching but without pressure. My heart skips a beat.

"Is this okay?" He mumbles against my lips. I'm breathing quicker, suddenly no longer drowsy.

I smile against his lips.
"It's perfectly perfect," I repeat.

Jake chuckles, then I feel the pressure of his lips against mine, his mouth opening mine, making our lips move together. His hands are still on my chin, tilting my face up. He moves his hand to my back and my head, supporting me. My arms move to wrap around the back of his neck. His breathing picks up and he moves, carrying me on top of him. My knees straddle his hips, his hands on my waist. Unable to control my actions, I move my hands across his stomach, feeling his muscular abdomen, his warm skin. He is perfect. I can feel his emotions changing as he responds to my touch.

Or maybe those are my emotions.

"This is bad of us," He whispers as he moves his kisses down to my chin and my neck.

"Mhmm," I mumble, unable to think straight enough in order to form words.

"Rose…" Jake says, his voice very rough. I pull his face up so that our lips touch again.

"Just one more," I say, my lips brushing against his as I say the words. And I get one more, but a hard one, though his lips are soft, they are forceful. Jake pulls me even closer to him, as if he wants to merge our bodies to make one. It starts to hurt but I don't care. It's Jake, and I love him. *I love you, Jake.* I say it in my head, but am too scared to say it out loud because I don't think I will be able to bear it if he doesn't feel the same way.

"Rose," Jake whispers again as he breaks away. His cheeks are flushed and his hair a mess, but it is cute. Then I realized with a jolt that I can see his face and its color, and I can see some gold of his hair.

"What time is it?" I ask.

"I think it's just about dawn," He murmurs and bends to kiss my cheek. "The sun's coming up." He adds with a smile.

"And that's my cue," I say. After placing a peck on his lips, I move myself off him and make my way to the door.

"Nice shorts," He calls out to me, I turn to look at him with raised eyebrows and he winks.

"Thanks," I say. "It's Paul Frank," I add with a laugh but instead of turning back to the door, I run back to his bed, pick a pillow up and start hitting him with it. He's too shocked to do anything about it at first, but then he starts laughing and trying to grab the pillow away from me. "No, no," I say between fits of giggles but he still manages to pull the pillow from my grip, but he's so strong that he drags me down as well. I'm lying across his stomach, laughing hysterically and Jake's chuckling and looking down at me with an amused and tender expression on his face. But then he pulls a serious face and pulls his eyebrows together.

"The male gender," He starts sternly. "Does not play with pillows and they do not hit each other with pillows; we are too manly for that. If you want to fight a man, I suggest a rock, or a stick, or a club..." He isn't finished but I burst out laughing again and tell him to stop. He smiles at me, and bends down to kiss me, once again, on the lips. It sparks something; I can feel the fire blazing again.

"Okay," I tell him reluctantly. "Now I'm really leaving."

"Sure," He says, a huge grin still plays on his lips and I fight the urge to stay. I reach the door and open it quietly, not wanting to wake anyone up. The last sight of Jake I see is his smile disappearing, and a troubled frown taking its place. But before I can think about this to let it start bothering me, there is the sound of someone clearing his or her throat from behind me. I spin fast on my heals, my heart racing, and realize that my hands had gone up to the sides of my head, as if I'm surrendering.

"Well," Angel says, clearing amused. "I don't know why you're so surprised I'm up and awake. Your laughing and talking could wake up the whole house." I must have looked really sheepish because Angel laughs and waves her hand. "It's okay, I'm a light sleeper. You weren't that loud. I'd change into something else if I were you though, you don't want anyone but Jake seeing your Paul Frank boxer shorts, now do you?"

"Very funny," I snort as I make my way to my room. "Good Morning, by the way." I add.

"Morning," Angel's face brightens up then turns into a somewhat curious expression. "Did you stay with Jake all night?"

"Err, no." I tell her, slightly awkward. "I only went there when I woke up and couldn't go back to sleep."

"Oh, okay," Angel shrugs, but the curious expression still lingers on her face.

"Nothing happened," I tell her. For some reason I feel the need to back up my purity.

"Oh, I know." Angel replies with a smile. "You're kind of that type of person. The type that saves themselves for someone special."

"I *am* saving myself, I just don't know when that special someone will come. Maybe he has come. But I still hope to wait for marriage." I say, matter-of-factly. I had decided that since I was young. I don't think I'll change my mind.

"That's what I meant." Angel amends with a sigh. "Me too. By the way, do you want breakfast? I'm making myself a mini omelet. Want one?"

"Sure," I say with a smile. "I'll be right back."

I slip into my room and shut the door quietly. My mom is still asleep. I tip toe over to the closet and pull out a short white lace spaghetti strapped dress that flares out around the waist, and my denim jacket to use as a cover up. I grab my combat boots from the floor and make my way to the bathroom.

It only takes a short time to change, I decide not to shower because I already showered the night before and hadn't done anything to make myself unclean. I leave my hair down and apply a little mascara before going to the kitchen.

Angel has put the omelets put out on a plate, but she is nowhere to be seen. She probably went to change or went to the bathroom. Sitting on a chair in front of the plate of omelets with a fork in his hand is Thomas. I run forward and smack him on the head, taking him by surprise, and using his frozen shocked moment to take the plate of omelets away from him.

"Those are mine," I say and grin at him mischievously as he looks at me with a stunned expression on his face. The expression swiftly changes to one of annoyance, and humor, then of pride.

"You're getting good at this," He says to me with a huge smirk.

"I learned from the best," I reply with a wink, pluck his fork out of his hand and use it to take a bite from the omelet.

"Oh, I know you mean me," Thomas says while rolling his eyes.

"Actually," Angel cuts in suddenly, seemingly appearing out of nowhere. "She meant me." And with that, Angel takes the fork from my hand, and takes a bite from the omelet in the plate that I hold.

"Hey!" I yell at her playfully and move to put the plate back down before chasing her around the room. Thomas looks at us with an incredulous expression on his face before picking up the plate and eating the omelet again. I catch Angel but she's still holding the fork away from me. We laugh and laugh and somehow end up on the floor.

"Well, I see this is already a very exciting morning," says a voice from above us. I open my eyes fully to see Jake grinning down at us. He holds out both his hands for Angel and me, and pulls us up.

"Oh, strong man," Angel says with mock flirtatiousness. She squeezes Jake's biceps playfully then walks over to where Thomas is sitting, patting his stomach with a cheerful expression on his face. "And you," Angel says to Thomas, her voice colored with irritation. "Ate all my omelets." And she smacks him across the head with her hand.

"And I'm not going to apologize," Thomas says, a huge smirk growing on his face.

"Jerk," Angel mumbles under her breath.

"That's why you love me," Thomas replies to her.

"I only love you because you're my brother," Angel says with affection. "It's kind of required."

"Haha,"

"Anyways," Angel turns to Jake and me. "Would you two like some omelets?" Her eyebrows shoot up. "Or would you just like to stand there holding each others' hands for breakfast?"

I look down at our intertwined hands, only realizing then that I am holding on to Jake tightly.

"An omelet would be good," Jake tells Angel with dry humor.

"Two omelets coming right up!" She says with merriment.

I smile to myself; Angel always seems to be happy.

Jake pulls me towards the table and we take our seats across from Thomas. Only then do I realize how thirsty I am.

"I'm going to get some water. Want some?" I say as I get up and walk to the sink. Thomas and Jake reply shortly, already seemingly involved in a conversation. I sigh inwardly; men get distracted so easily, only able to focus on one thing at a time. Whatever happened to multitasking?

I grab four cups from the cupboard and am about to turn on the tap to wash them when I look out of the small oval shaped window and see a dark figure walking up the driveway.

"I'll be right back, guys," I tell them as I quickly fill the glasses with water, place them in front of Jake and Thomas and walk hurriedly out of the door.

It is cool outside, too cool for summer. The clouds make a ceiling of grey in the sky, not a ray of sunlight can be seen. The day is grey and dull. I quicken my pace, wanting to get to Cole quickly so that I can return inside.

"Cole!" I shout for him. He doesn't seem to see me yet. "Cole!" I yell again. He looks up the second time I yell, and that's when I see how drained and lifeless he looks. My heart starts drumming in my chest and I can feel the blood pounding in my head. "Cole?" I ask, this time not certain about whether it is a good idea to call him. Cole doesn't answer; he stops moving completely and falls to his knees. I take off on a sprint, running to get to him before he falls any further. I catch him just as he sags to the ground.

"Cole," I whisper, shaking him slightly, urging him to answer. "Cole, what's wrong? What are you doing outside so early? Are you okay? What happened?"

"Rose," He croaks out. His voice is so quiet I have to lean in to understand. He grips my hand, and shoves weakly, as if trying to push me away. "Rose, run."

"Run?" I ask bewildered. "Run from what?"

He mumbles something unintelligible. His grip on me tightens.

"Ow," I say. "Cole, you're hurting me." But his grip doesn't loosen. Instead, he pulls me closer, his lips pressing against my ear. A chill runs down my spine. He's too strong. I am unable to break away.

"I said run." He repeats viciously. Cole pushes me away so hard that I fall on my back. His eyes are filled with fear; fear colors his emotions. But that is not what makes a scream rise up in my throat. Cole's eyes are not green anymore; they are red, bright red and glowing.

I gasp and startle backwards, not able to shout for help. No sound escapes from my throat, there is pressure there. As if someone is choking me.

"Run from me," Cole finally answers. But it isn't Cole speaking. It is his voice, his face. But it isn't him. Cole has green eyes so rich that they shine, and a sharp but kind face. He would never hurt me. But this Cole is different. His eyes are ruby red and they glow with a dark power. His expression is one of a hunter looming over his prey.

And right now, I am the prey.

I try again to get a sound out, to scream at him, but no sound comes out. I gag and slump forward, trying hard to release the pressure in my throat. It is starting to burn.

Cole moves forward then, his hands catching me, and pulling me up back on my knees. His fingers cradle my chin, so much like the real Cole had. It could have been him if the grip wasn't iron hard and rock solid; demanding that I pay him full attention.

"No, no, no, no," He says and clicks his tongue together as if I'm a child who has done something wrong. "Don't try to speak, Roza. I have blocked your throat. The more you try to get out, the less you'll be able to get in."

His eyes burn holes in me. I can't look away from them, they are not Cole's; so whose are they? I stop trying to scream and just stare at him, as if my gaze could force him to tell me what happened to my Cole, the Cole that is my friend.

"Ah," 'Cole' says. "Good." He releases me and steps back a couple of paces. His gaze seems to be analyzing and taking in everything about me. "I've never actually seen you in person, only in thought." He tells me, his tone unreadable. "You really are as beautiful as a rose," He reaches out to touch my face but I snap my teeth at him.

He flinches away with distaste. "But you've got thorns. Feisty little thing. No one told me," He smirks down at me.

Who are you! What have you done with Cole? I scream at him with my mind. The anger and confusion momentarily blocks out my fear, stopping the panic from getting the best of me.

"Hmmm," he contemplates with interest. "You have gotten better at that. The mind-speaking thing, that is; I heard you very loudly there." He gives me a bored look. "Cole is still very much here, darling. He's trying his best to get back to you, but my will is just too strong." The person in Cole's body kneels down until we're eye to eye again. "Oh yes, I'm possessing him. It must be excruciatingly painful to fight me. But nevertheless, I had to use him to come here. If I had come here as my true self you would have sensed me from a mile away." He sighs. "Technically, I'm not the one you're looking for. I merely work with *Her*. She's stronger, but I am still strong enough."

The demon woman? This thing works for her? I struggle again to scream at him, but again, it's like I'm choking. Trying to get air in my throat burns and I have to support myself on the ground.

"Remember what I said Veronica," Cole's voice says. "More out, less in. So if you want to breathe, I suggest not even fighting." He brushes aside the hair that has fallen across my face. "My, my." He whistles. "You really are a pretty thing." He winks. "And I like that dress. Very feminine." His fingers go down from my face onto my neck, to my collarbone, stroking and brushing the skin as he goes.

I choke down the bile that is rising within me for I can't move and can't do anything to flick his hand away. I decide that the best I can do is stare him down with my hatred. I glare at him as his hands reach the neck of my dress. "But you shouldn't have worn that jacket. No," His hands move to the jacket, tugging it off slightly. "I would like to see some more *skin*," He sneers.

With all my might I break free of whatever spell is holding me in my place, and slap him across the face with a yell. I try to move away. But that effort is too much. I stumble backwards and fall. I hear him growl and see that he's walking towards me with big heavy strides, he bends down before me and picks up a sharp looking rock. But what he does next surprises me. I expect him to hit me in the head. But instead, he cuts himself on the arm and forces his arm against my mouth, opening it and pushing his blood into my mouth. It is bitter and disgusting and feels hot and boiling as it goes down my throat. Then he releases me and I choke and try to spit out the vile stuff. But I know that most of it has already gotten into my system. The monster in Cole's body grabs my face and pulls me closer.

"Now, you have my blood in you. Not Cole's blood; *my* blood. I'll be able to find you anywhere." His eyes glow even redder, as if he were burning on the inside. "I have many names. But you may call me James." He brings me closer; his finger nails digging into my skin. "*I'll be back for you*," He whispers viciously into my ear.

Then the pressure on my face, on my throat and on my body disappears, and it's all I can do not to fall to the ground.

My hands move to my mouth and come away bloody; whether it is James's blood or my blood, I do not know. I look to where James's had been in Cole's body and see nothing. Where is Cole?

"Rose!" I hear a voice shout from next to me. I turn to see Cole reaching out to me, his face a mask of anxiousness, horror and grief.

"Cole," I strain to say. Relief floods through me as I see that his eyes have returned to their normal mysterious green. This is Cole.

"Rose, I am so sorry," He croaks out. "So, so sorry."

"It's okay, Cole," I whisper, and push myself up. But that is a bad idea because as soon as I get up, everything spins around and around. I wonder why the world is turning. I can't focus. Dizziness sweeps through me and I fall, but Cole catches me and pulls me closer to him.

"Rose!" He sounds frantic. "Are you okay?"

I wave away his worries.
"I'm fine…" I think. "How 'bout you, Cole? Are *you* okay?"

"I'm okay," Cole says, sounding a bit astonished. "I am the one that attacked you Rose."

"I wouldn't count that as attacking," I tell him, trying to smile and to be a little funny. But he doesn't smile back; he looks dreadful.

"I'm fine," He says curtly

"But you got cut!" I exclaim, my hands brushing lightly against the wound on his arm.

"Well, I did that to myself," He says, his eyes looking disgusted. I grab his arm tightly and force him to look into my eyes.

"No," I tell him fiercely. "You didn't. That wasn't you. That was James."

"James," He breathes out, regret and anger mixed with his emotions.

"Do you know who he is?" I ask, genuinely curious.

"Yes,"

"Well?" I urge impatiently. But what the answer is, I never know; for at that moment, running footsteps are all that I hear.

"Cole!" I hear Jake shout nervously. Of course he is nervous, Cole and I are both on the ground. Jake reaches us in the next second, and I realize that only as he's standing above us that he sees me. "Rose?" He says in disbelief. "What's going on? What just happened?"

"Jake," I start in relief. "It's not Cole's fault. I came out because I saw him walking up the driveway. He was staggering and fell and I caught him. He told me to run but I didn't because there wasn't anything to run from. Then his eyes started glowing bright red, and then he wasn't Cole anymore. It was still his body and voice but it wasn't Cole. It was someone named James." When I say James's name, Jake's eyes snap away from mine to meet Coles'. They hold each other's gaze intently and I can tell that they are having a private conversation. Then Jake looks away.

"It can't be," Jake says distantly. "James is dead."

"But he isn't," I insist.

"Well this is bad," Jake replies, and then he notices the blood on the ground and on my face. His expression changes from disbelief to concern as he kneels down and touches my face. "Why is there blood? Are you hurt?"

"No," I say shortly; somehow not wanting to tell him that James had forced blood into my mouth. "But Cole is. James made him cut himself. Who is James anyways? And why do you say he's dead? He's definitely the opposite of dead. He possessed Cole."

Jake looks over at Cole's still bleeding arm and then at his pale face, completely ignoring my question, everyone seems to be ignoring that question. Then almost as if it were an afterthought, he pulls off his shirt and wraps it around Cole's arm, using it to staunch the bleeding. The muscles on Jake's back and shoulders work as he ties and tightens his shirt around Cole's arm. I fight back the urge to want to feel them. I shouldn't be thinking about that sort of thing right now. Not after what just happened.

"There you go,"

"Thanks, brother," Cole says with a smile. But when he looks back at me, his smile disappears and I know that no matter what I or anyone else says to comfort him, he will never stop blaming himself for hurting me a second time after promising not to.

"Cole," I reach for him, wanting to ease his pain, wanting to heal him, but he flinches away. I pull my hand back, trying to hide my hurt.

"I'm sorry Rose," Cole whispers quietly. "I don't think I deserve your touch."

"Don't be silly," I tell him gently and reach out once more to place my hand on his face. "You didn't do anything wrong, there's nothing to apologize for." As soon as my skin touches his, I can feel a tingle run through me and over to him. He closes his eyes and sighs, when his eyes open I see that the self-hate and the anger have disappeared.

"Let's get you inside," Jake says and reaches to pull me up but I wave him away.

"I'm fine," I say. "Not hurt at all. See?" I stand up to prove my point; the dizziness has passed, a sense of blankness replacing it. "Help Cole. He lost some blood."

"Okay," Is all Jake says as he reaches for Cole. I turn away and walk towards the house on my own. As soon as I walk through the door, I wave away Thomas and Angels' questions and run towards the bathroom. Closing the door behind me I quickly move towards the sink.

Gagging and coughing, I try to get rid of the bitter blood that went into me but to no avail. Cold sweat breaks out on my forehead and a blinding pain starts between my eyes. I look in the mirror and see that red veins protrude a little bit all over my face but go away as quickly as they come. Then a searing pain begins on my chest and I look down in the mirror to see that a bright red 'X' has appeared on my skin, right above my heart. It is glowing. Just like James's eyes.

Very unbidden and unwelcome, his voice comes back to me.

"Now, you have my blood in you. Not Cole's blood; my blood. I'll be able to find you anywhere. I'll be back for you."

I sink to the ground, my hands and knees shaking; pressing the heel of my palms against my temple, trying the best I can to block out the voices.

"No, no, no," I moan quietly as my world turns black and all that I see is James's glowing blood red eyes in Tenebris Daemon's' hooded face.

23

"And that's when I said 'Oh no you didn't!'" Angel just keeps on going on about her argument with a classmate. She is trying to lighten the mood, I suspect. We all sit around the table picking at our lunches; none of us are really up to talking after Cole told everyone that James is still alive.

No one has answered my question either, so I'm still left in the dark on who he is and why everyone thought he was dead. I tune Angel out because I'm having my own arguments in my head. The sting of the red X is still very present. I let my hair fall down my shoulders even more, covering my face.

"You okay there Rose?" Angel's voice interrupts my thoughts. I snap out of it and smile at her.

"Yes," I say. "Just fine."

She eyes me suspiciously then shrugs her shoulders. I feel Jake's gaze on my face, but I can't look up at him because I know that he'll know that I'm not 'just fine'.

"Where are Kate and Simon?" I ask, mostly just to change the subject.

"They're with your mom, walking somewhere down on the beach," Thomas tells me through a full mouth.

"Alright," I mumble. "I think I might go look for them."

"But you've hardly eaten anything!" Angel exclaims.

"I'm not very hungry," I tell her with a smile.

"Alright then,"

I keep my eyes down as I take my plate to the sink, then make my way out the door. I'm barely down the porch steps when I hear the door open behind me and turn around.

"What are you doing?" I say to Jake.

"I'm following you," He says back, his eyes are full of disquiet. "You don't seem alright."

"I'm fine," I tell him, but my voice breaks.

"Rose," He says as he walks down to me and puts his hands on my shoulder and forces me to look him in the eye. "Please. Talk to me. What's wrong?"

I don't answer because I can't bring myself to say it. Jake seems to sense my reluctance but he doesn't get angry.

"You know what?" He says as he takes my hand and leads me towards the sand.

"What?" I ask and manage to bring a smile to my face. Jake always makes me smile, even when he's not trying to.

"I think we should go for a walk," He says. "Alone."

"Okay," I say and tip toe to kiss him on the cheek. "Let's do that."

■ ■ ■

"Please," I whisper. "Say something."

Jake sits silently by my side. The ocean breeze is blowing, making our hair fly all around us. The waves are crashing into the beach and the smell of the sea is in the air. The clouds are still covering the sun, making the day seem rather dull.

I have just told Jake about what James did to me, and about what he said. Anger, confusion, worry, and disbelief are radiating from Jake; and I want him to say something. To tell me that it's all right.

"Jake," I start.

"Rose," He says. "This isn't good."

"I know," I mumble.

"Why didn't you tell me before?" He demands.

"I was too scared."

He lets out an exasperated breath.
"This is seriously bad."

"Jake," I say again. "Who is he?" I shake my head. "I thought our big problem was Tenebris Daemon. But now there's James too. And I really don't understand anything, except for the fact that James works for her."

"James," Jake starts. "James is…" He pauses as if he said something wrong. "James was my friend. He was a friend to all of us. He was Angels' friend, Thomas's' friend, Coles' friend and my friend." He sighs.

"Okay," I say gently, suddenly not wanting Jake to explain to me who James is as much as I had wanted before. "He was a friend. What happened to him?"

"He was a friend," Jake says. "And he was also an orphan. We went to school together, but he missed a couple of grades. He was about two years older than me. This was about three years ago, and I was fourteen. Since he was an orphan, my parents and your parents took special interest in him. We all liked him, and our parents treated him as if he were their own, my parents especially."

"You were not with us that summer. I remember looking forward to meeting you again for the first time in so many years, but you were in some sort of camp with your friends, and could not join us. So you've never met him…"

"We were all coming here, to Ithaca, for our summer trip that year. That was actually the year that I met Angel and Thomas, though our families have known each other for years. It was very exciting, my first time in Europe. It was also James's first time. Not Cole though, he's been here before, him being a lot older than us. Back then, none of us but Cole knew about the Gifted people. Cole, in a way, was completely alone, until James bloomed, and we all found out that he was Gifted too. That's when I first learned about it. Even though we were all really confused about James being Gifted because that would mean that his bloodline would be from the ancient Greek times, and usually would have been known, our parents accepted it willingly. It was a magical night. All of us were sitting by the fire, and your dad was telling stories about his Granddad who fought in the World War Two, and how he was one of the Gifted.

"I remember being in awe of the whole thing. And I remember James sitting through it in silence. I thought he was too overwhelmed to speak. None of us guessed that he actually felt out of place and uncomfortable. There was just no reason that he should feel that way. That night us kids went to bed, while the adults stayed up talking. James and I couldn't sleep, so we decided to creep out and listen to the grown-up conversation. It was James's idea, he seemed very eager to go outside to the porch to listen. I wasn't as willing but he got me to do it. Neither of us knew that we were walking right into an assault."

Jake takes a deep shaky breath and closes his eyes, as if the memory tortured him.

"Jake, it's okay if you don't want to continue." I tell him soothingly.

"No," He replies firmly and opens his eyes. They are a bright almost electric sky blue; filled with pain. "You need to know.

"There was a woman on the porch steps. She was dressed in black; a dark cloak shadowed her face. But that couldn't hide her glowing red eyes. My parents and your parents were standing, forming a line in front of her. Your dad stepped forward and demanded what she wanted. I think they knew who she was. But our parents aren't Gifted like we are; they are more extraordinary than normal humans, but they are not as powerful as us. The woman with the red eyes just laughed and called him a 'petty creature'. She said that she wasn't here for them. She said that she was here for the boy who had just bloomed. She said that he was her long lost heir, that he was special, and that he was hers. I turned to look at James, because obviously, she was talking about him. But he wasn't looking at me; he was staring very intently at her. His brown eyes were unblinking. I was scared for him.

"My dad stepped up with yours, and shouted at the woman to go away, for he loved James already. I think that they were actually planning to adopt him. But she wouldn't go away. The woman just started laughing crazily. Her laughter was the most horrible thing I've ever heard. I wanted to run away, but I knew I couldn't. She seemed to find our parents amusing. She said that they couldn't stop her; that he was already here, and had already made up his mind about whom he belonged to. This shocked me, of course, because I thought that James loved my family as well. After everything we had done for him. I turned again to look at him, but he wasn't there anymore. I looked around and I saw him walking away from our hiding place, towards *her*.

"I wanted to run to him, to pull him back, but my muscles were frozen. I don't know whether it was because I was in shock, or because he was doing that to me. Immobilizing me as he did you. I couldn't even scream. He was already in the adults' line of sight, but none of them were moving as well; the woman just smiled at him and opened her arms, he went straight into her embrace. The woman then turned back to our families, saying that she could blast them into dust, but she still needed something more from them, something more powerful than anything, even more powerful than her. She said that she needed that final piece when the time came, and that she would let them live so that your parents could deliver that final piece. I think they knew that the final piece she was talking about was you.

"Then James spoke. He said 'can we please bring Jake along?', the woman's eyes twinkled red as she smiled. 'He will come on his own, chasing the one he loves most.' Her voice was like hissing snakes; it felt as if all the warmth had been sucked away. James just nodded and took her hand. I thought they were going to disappear the way that bad guys disappeared in movies, you know. Like in a puff of black smoke. But all she did was tap the ground, and a hole appeared, big enough for the two of them to go through. 'You first', she had said to James. But before he could go through, Cole was suddenly there. Something flashed in his hand before it was in the air, sailing towards the woman. She didn't make an effort to move away from it but James did moved, he moved in front of her and shielded her from the knife. It struck hard and sunk deep into his chest, blood gushed out, soaking his shirt. He collapsed."

"Still, the woman didn't move, she just stared at Cole with unblinking eyes. It looked as if a smile was forming on her lips; as if she had just found and chosen her new favorite toy. Then she gathered James in her arms and brought him through the hole too fast for any of us to do anything. And by the time that Cole got to the spot where they were standing, the hole had disappeared. This happened the same summer that your dad disappeared. So you see, Cole and I had a tough time through that period because it was just one bad thing after another."

"Oh," Is the only answer I can come up with. I look over at Jake to see that he's staring at me. His eyes are wet; it looks like he is on the brink of breaking down. "Oh, Jake," I say sadly.

Then he is in my arms. His face buried in my shoulder and neck, Jake is shaking violently. He is not crying, but tremors of dread rack his body. I put my arms around him and kiss his hair, my heart breaking for him because he has had so much pain in his life.

"Jake," I say. "Everything will be fine."

"No, it won't be." His voice is ragged.

"But it will." I insist.

"Then tell me you're not going to leave me." He demands as he pulls away so that he can look me in the eye. He eyes are a brilliant blue as he stares me down, forcing me to say the truth.

"You know I can't say that," I murmur, suddenly not wanting to face him. But he doesn't allow me to break gaze. His eyes keep me imprisoned.

"Then everything definitely won't be okay,"

"But Jake, it will be." I sigh. "It's possible to move on once I'm gone. Because you know that there is no other way. I have to destroy the evil in me when the time is right. And the only way to do that is to destroy the whole of me. You heard the prophecy, Jake. You know it's inevitable. You'll move on."

As soon as I say it, he starts shaking his head.

"No," He says hoarsely. "I'll never be able to move on from you."

My heart contracts and starts beating so rapidly that I'm surprised that I haven't fainted.

"I love you Rose," He says firmly. His hands reach to brush my hair. We are very close together; I can feel each breath on my face. "Please don't leave me."

I love you. Jake had said those three words to me. Those three words that I have been dreaming for the man I love to say to me. And now he has, and he is the perfect man, everything I could ever ask for. And now I can't even do the one thing that he's ever asked of me.

The soreness in my throat is unbearable, my eyes start aching and I feel the tears spill over. Jake's expression softens and the love and pain radiating from him fills me with such despair. *I am going to bring him so much more pain*, I think. He wipes the tears away and kisses my cheeks. He's holding my face in his hands, I could not move away even if I wanted to.

"Jake, Jake, Jake," I whimper silently as his fingers explore my face. "I love you too. I love you so much Jake. So much." I gasp for air. "I'm sorry. I'm so, so sorry."

But no more can be said because his mouth crushes mine, making it impossible to form words. His lips move viciously against my mouth, as if he would devour me. His arms wrap around me and press me against him, keeping me locked to him. He rolls over on the sand. Now Jake is on top of me, his elbows are on either side of me; keeping his weight off me so he won't crush me. But I don't want that. I hook my fingers around the belt holders of his jeans and pull him closer to me. Jake groans against my mouth. My hands reach up and under his shirt, feeling his lean firm muscles. Then as if he can't take it, Jake reaches for the hem of his shirt and pulls his shirt off. I stare for a second, mesmerized by the perfection of his body before he starts kissing me again.

Breathless, I pull away to get air, but his lips don't leave my skin, they move on to my neck and collarbone. Then suddenly, my jacket is off, leaving me in just my sleeveless white dress. Jake kisses my bare shoulders and moves up. He kisses the skin on my neck and jaw and my cheek. His fingers trail my thighs, making my skin tingle. I'm breathing hard, the feeling of love soaking through me. His body heat leaks from him to me, as he brings his face up to mine and looks at me with bright eyes, I see that both our faces are flushed with heat and passion.

"You might want to stop me now, Rose." He says, his voice no louder than a rough whisper.

My head hums with confusion and indecision; I don't know what I want. I know what is right, and I have a feeling

Jake knows it too. I even told Angel what I have in mind for my virtue. But right now, I can't quite remember why I said it. Both Jake and I want it.

The sand beneath me suddenly feels like a soft bed, cradling me from the back as Jake cradles me from the front. With a groan of what seems like defeat, Jake sits up and pulls me with him. The wet sand sticks to my back as Jake lifts me up so that I end up on his lap, with my legs wrapped around his waist. We stay there looking at each other for what seems like forever, our eyes never wavering, even as he reaches up to trace my face with his fingers.

"You're a good guy Jake," I tell him, my voice shaking with love and desire.

"Or so they tell me," He says with humor, his eyes lighting up.

"I bet many people have,"

He just shrugs.

I lower my eyes, suddenly shy.
"That was the first time you said it."

"Said what?"

I look up to see him looking at me curiously with his head tilted sideways.

"Said that you love me."

His gaze softens, with the ocean reflecting against his eyes, the color looks like a sea blue green instead of an electric blue now.

"And I will say it again," He murmurs. "Because I mean it. I love you, forever and always. There will be no other, I swear to you. It's the truth. I don't think I can ever love another girl again, not after you. You're beautiful, intelligent, athletic, talented, kind, loving, and just amazing. No one can compare to you."

I stare at him, mesmerized by his every word. My cheeks warm along with the rest of my body as I take in his words. I am flattered that he would even think that of me.

"Well Jake, I love you too," I manage to get out. I feel a smile growing on my lips. "No one can compare to you either,"

But he doesn't smile back, and the light in his eyes dulls a bit.

"Except Cole."

Shock rolls through me with sadness trailing just behind it.

"No, Jake," Putting on my most convincing tone. "Honestly, no. I don't love him like I love you."

"But you love him."

"As a brother," I say desperately. "As a friend." I sigh. "I promise you."

Jake doesn't say anything. He just looks me squarely in the eye.
"Okay,"

"Good," I say and move to plant a quick but firm kiss on his mouth. As I move away he grabs me by the shoulders.

"You know he loves you right?" Jake says matter-of-factly.

I try to swallow but my throat feels dry.
"No," I say. "He can't. He never said so. He doesn't."

"But he does," Jake says, his voice still hard.

I shake my head furiously because I don't want Cole to love me. Because if he does, then that means that I would be bringing him a lot of pain and I don't want that for him. Jake probably reads my expression because his voice softens as he says, "It's okay Rose; I don't blame him or you. Anyone who knows you would fall in love with you. I'm surprised that Thomas hasn't,"

Now the tears break free, even as I laugh.
"And hopefully he never will," I gulp in a breath of air. "I'm hurting Cole, Jake. I'm causing him pain." I tell him weakly.

"It's not your fault," Jake says as he pulls me closer to him. I rest against his chest and bury my face against the curve of his neck.

"I love you so much," I whisper.

"I love you too," He whispers back. His voice is surprisingly gentle and firm. "You have no idea how much I do. I'd follow you anywhere and do anything for you. Because I love you."

24

The rest of the day passes pretty fast. No one brings up James and what he did to me, though I guess that Jake has told them everything. Everything is pretty normal; no more tears are shed. We all decide that we will search for James and the she demon again, partly because Dad isn't waking up.

Mom has this theory that only the person who put the curse on will be able to take it off; too bad for us. I don't think anyone told mom about James or what he did.

Perhaps they are too scared to; I don't blame them. Mom can get pretty scary once she switches on her protective mode. Cole still hasn't come out of his room, not even for meals, and as the sun sets over another day without progress, my heart feels heavy with remorse.

"Do you think he'll ever come out?" I ask Angel as she comes out of Kate and Simons' bedroom.

"I don't think so, not anytime soon anyways," She says. "Not unless you go in there and drag him out by his ears."

I laugh unwillingly; the thought is just so funny. But the laughter dies as quickly as it came.

"I wonder what's wrong…"

"Well, Rose," Angel exasperates. "He did just get possessed. I bet you would be feeling a little down after that."

"He didn't mean to kill him,"

"I know," Angel mumbles.

"Were you there?" I ask.

"No," She sighs. "Not really. I was in the house, sleeping."

"Did you know James well?"

"Nope, I just met him that summer,"

"What was he like?" I question, genuinely curious.

"He was very quiet." Angels' brows draw together, as if remembering is hard. "He was very sweet and polite." She smiles. "Very charming too; I was quite taken with him. But of course, he was three years older than me, and he looked at me as if I were his younger sister."

"I was fourteen, Jake was almost fifteen and James almost seventeen." Angel tells me before I ask, probably sensing my question.

"Oh," is all I can think of to say. They were all so young.

"Rose," Angel says softly. I look back at her. "Do you think you can help him?"

"I'm not sure Angel," I mumble. "I'm sorry,"

"Well, that's okay." She replies with a smile. "If only I knew whether —"

But the sound of laughter breaks her off, and I never learn what she wanted to know.

I tense for a moment, because the laughter is so loud that it startles me. But it is only Thomas and Jake laughing as they come through the door.

"Back so soon boys?" Angel asks humorously. "Not much of a run,"

"Are you kidding?" Thomas's eyebrows shoot up. "We ran all the way from one end of the beach to the other, which, by the way, is a very long run."

"Yep," Jake adds, his eyes twinkling with laughter. "We ran for an hour straight, no breaks; up and down the beach." He pauses. "Well I ran up and down the beach, Thomas ran up and didn't bother running back down. In fact, I think he crawled it!"

"Did not!" Thomas roars, looking annoyed but also embarrassed. I smile at them; they are like two best friends, arguing over something that has no importance.

"Did too," Jake grins. "In fact, I think even little Kate could have beaten you."

"Well of course Jake," I say. "Kate's a strong little one. I bet she could beat you as well!" I laugh and tackle him. We both tumble to the ground, me not caring whether he is sweaty or not.

"No," Jake manages to say between chuckles. "Not I. No one can ever beat the great and extremely handsome Jake Blanchard." His voice sounds so superior and dramatic that it is impossible not to notice the humor and sarcasm.

I laugh against his chest and sit up. Thomas helps both of us up, looking as if he were trying very hard not to throw us back down.

"Okay guys," Angel says, sounding very motherly. "The kids are sleeping and Rose's mom is in the guest bedroom with her still-sleeping-in-a-coma husband so try not to make too much noise."

"But doesn't Rose stay in the guest bedroom? Where will she sleep now that it's full?" Thomas inquires.

"She's welcome to sleep in my room, and I'll sleep on the couch of course," Angel offers.

"Oh, no," I put in. "I wouldn't want to take your bedroom from you." I move to the couch and jump on it, making my point. "The couch is just fine."

"Or," Thomas says with a wink. "You may sleep in my room,"

I giggle at that, Thomas is always trying to make everything funny.

"Thank you, but no thank you." I say. "I don't think I can survive your snoring." I add just to be witty.

"I do not snore." Thomas says defensively.

"Oh yes, you do," says a smooth voice from the shadows. "I can hear it from all the way in my room." I turn to see Cole closing the door of his bedroom and walking towards us. His hair is all tousled, so he must have been sleeping.

"Cole," Jake says, his voice sounding slightly worried. "How are you?"

"Extremely sore," Is all he answers.

"Well that's understandable," I say before I can help myself.

Coles' eyes narrow in on me, his emotions are a mix of relief, love, hurt, pain, and anger.

"And what about you? Are you okay?" He asks.

"I'm fine," I tell him, meeting his gaze with my own. Cole looks away from me, towards Jake.

"We have to find him," Cole says angrily. "We have to, it's not safe for her if we don't."

"I know," Jake mumbles quietly.

"So what are we waiting for? He could find her anywhere because he put his mark on her."

"Can we not talk about me like I'm not here?" I retort.

Of course, Cole completely ignores me.

"A clue," Angel says quite impatiently answering Coles' question. "We can't dive into a mission that we know nothing about." She throws her hands in the air. "We don't know where he is, or what he'll do. For all we know, he could just be shadows and dust, only taking form through other people."

"No," I finally say. "He's solid."

"How do you know?" Thomas asks, his voice sharp. He must really dislike this James.

"I can feel it," I tell them. "In here," I tap the red cross on my chest. It isn't until then that I realize what the weird pulsing feeling is, I had thought that it was my pulse, but as the conversation led to James, its beating grew stronger and I now know that he is *aware*. "For some reason, I can feel him. He knows we're talking about him. I know this because it started throbbing as soon as we began speaking of him. He's a real person; he has blood and flesh. That's how he gave me his blood, you can't be shadows and still have blood. And even though it was Cole's body, James possessed his being, which probably made the heart and blood black,"

"Rose is right," Thomas says.

"Of course she's right," Jake adds. "When is she wrong?"

"You'd be surprised," I mumble quietly, but so that no one could hear; however, since they all have super hearing, they still heard me. They all turn their heads to smile at me reassuringly.

"Don't worry Rose," Angel says compassionately. "Humans beings are hardly ever correct, they're actually mostly a destructive race, building and inventing, but taking life away as they do so, their actions both wrong and right.

Let's just say that our wrongs and our rights have a more extreme impact, given who we are."

■ ■ ■

"You ready?" Jake asks as I pack all I need into my bag.

"As ready as I'll ever be," I say.

"Great," He smiles lightly, and then his eyes harden. "You know you don't have to do this right? It's your risk more than ours,"

"Oh, I know,"

"You're so brave." He murmurs. Jake is so close to me that I can feel the warmth of his breath.

"So are you," I tell him. "So are all of you." I lean up to kiss him on the cheek. "Don't worry about me," I say with a smile. "I'll be fine."

Jake doesn't reply; he just nods.

The night before was a blur as we planned how we were going to find Tenebris Daemon and James.

I think it will not be so hard.

James wants to be found.

As we get into the car, and wave goodbye to my mom, Kate, and Simon, a foreboding feeling fills my heart.

"Jake," I whisper as Thomas starts driving, with Cole riding shotgun and Angel to my left on the back seat, and Jake on my right. "This doesn't feel right."

"What do you mean?" He asks, his lips pulling into a frown.

"I mean," I try to explain. "This feels wrong. I feel it in here." I say, and point to my chest, my heart. "I can't describe it. All I know is that as soon as we started driving in this direction, a darkness has been creeping over us."

Jakes' eyes darken as he thinks hard, trying to understand what I mean. I can hear the others breathing evenly and I know that they heard what I said, and that they are trying to make sense of it as well.

Suddenly, too suddenly for me to do anything about it, my vision turns black. I feel as if I am no longer in the car. I must have slumped down on my seat because I can hear Jake shouting at me, and Angel screaming to stop the car.

What's going on? I think, even as reality dawns on me.

I'm being taken away spiritually, my soul is being dragged somewhere else.

I feel wind and coldness brush by me. But as quick as it happened, it stops and I find myself in an open space, with nothing near me except a young man who stands in front of me, staring at me with strange brown eyes. His features are sharp, angular, but also very elegant. And I'd be lying if I said he wasn't good looking. But as I stare at him longer, his brown eyes get brighter and brighter until they turn into a glowing red color. He smiles a harsh smile.

"Well, hello again, Rose." He greets me, his voice delicate if not for the fact that it grates against my mind.

I press my fingers up to my temple, my head thrumming as if I have something in there that wants to break free.

"James," I hiss through gritted teeth.

"Ah," He says. "Good. I was afraid that you would not recognize me."

"What am I doing here?" I demand. "Send me back."

"Tsk, tsk," He clucks, as if I am a complaining child. "She needs you here, so I brought you here." He smiles again, revealing a row of white teeth. "You were right you know.

When you said that something was wrong. You were very right indeed." He chuckles a bit. "In fact, the dark feeling you felt in your heart, that was me. You guys drove right into my territory."

"How is it yours?" I question, partly because I want to stall for time, and partly because I am actually curious.

"Well, I made it so," James tells me, his eyes lighting up. "But that is too long an explanation. And we don't have time." He puts his hand on my shoulder, and it feels like my whole body has turned into stone. "Don't worry. Stay still. She'll be here any second and she wouldn't want you to struggle."

"I'm not really here." I spit through my frozen mouth. "You can't do anything to hurt me."

"Silly, silly girl," James says. "If you were not really here, would I be able to do this?" He grabs my throat and digs his nails into my skin.

I scream in pure agony as I feel my flesh ripping open. Blood trickles down my neck, tickling my collarbone and coloring my cream jacket. He lets go of me and I slump to the ground, breathing hard. James kneels down with me.

"It actually feels a little bit regretful hurting you." His eyes turn thoughtful. "I wonder why. Maybe it's that pretty face." His fingers reach to cup my chin, but I jerk away. He just shrugs casually. "It's alright if you don't want me touching you now. After Tenebris is done with you, you won't mind one bit. In fact," He sneers. "I think you'll like it."

"No," I say hoarsely. My throat still hurts and my lungs still burn as if his hands are still around my neck, cutting off my airway.

"Well of course!" He says, his voice rising and his eyes igniting. "Forgive me for I have forgotten." James sounds very gentleman like all of a sudden. "You already have two men waiting for you at home. Why would you want another?"

I grimace at what he is implying.
"You have no idea what you're talking about,"

"Oh but I do, love," James grins down at me. "I want you for myself. My master has already promised me the most extraordinary girl, and I'll get her. But of course, there's trouble where you're concerned, what with your two lovers and all. I'll just have to get rid of both of them."

"No," I beg and struggle to sit up.

"But I see," His voice lowered. "Oh I see. They both love you, but you love Jake more. And where Cole is concerned, you are confused." He smiles sweetly at me. "Personally, I would choose Jake. He's much more pleasant than Cole." He shrugs. "After all, Cole did put a dagger in my chest."

"Stop it," I whisper. "Stop."

"You're going to break them apart you know." James says matter-of-factly. "Might as well give your heart to me so you spare theirs."

"You don't even know me!" I shout. "I'll never give my heart to you."

"But you will change your mind,"

"No," I hiss.

"Well," He shrugs. The gesture making him seem like an ordinary boy for a moment. "We'll see about that. Your stubbornness is to be admired, Roza."

I flinch as he uses that name, for in his mouth it sends a thousand blades through my skin. James notices this and smiles at me cruelly. Then he looks up suddenly.

"She's here," He murmurs into my ear. His voice sounding so seductive that a shiver of disgust runs down my spine.

"That's enough James," A cold voice drawls. "Leave the girl alone. For now,"

James releases me, and smiles at me; his face looks charming if not for the eyes.

"I will have you," He whispers one last time before walking away from me, towards the woman.

I look up and see a figure of a woman walking towards me, but unlike before, she is not hooded. What had always been beneath the hood is revealed to be an inhumanly cold but beautiful face. Not what I had expected. Black hair pours forth in waves, framing a marble white face. Glowing red eyes behind thick lashes stare down at me. Lips red as blood pull into a smile.

She could be Snow White; since Snow White is always described as "Lips as red as blood, hair as black as night, and skin as white as snow". But this *thing* is not Snow White, for Snow White is good, and what's before me is wicked. And though she is beautiful, she is a frightening sort of beauty, a wicked sort of beauty.

"Well now, Rose," She says, her voice bottomless and strangely still. "We meet at last. Face to face."

I can't answer, struck down by the power. I struggle to form insulting and hateful words but to no avail.

"Why? Why bring me here now?" I finally manage to croak out.

"Well, I needed to be sure first!" Her fingertips brush my cheek. "I needed to make sure that you're fully in power."

She smiles. "You're not your strongest now, but I'll make sure of that."

I stare at her, not understanding.
"What do you mean?"

"Well, don't worry, darling. You're not really here now, only your essence is. But when I really bring you to me, your beautiful boy will follow, and you'll do whatever I want, just to keep him safe." She chuckles cruelly.

"Jake won't come after me, he's too smart for that." I retort, even as my heart freezes in my chest because I know that Jake will do exactly as she says if it comes to me being in danger.

"In that you're wrong, Rose," Her eyes glow even brighter. "He *loves* you," She sneers. "And love, especially his, is very powerful, for it is the love for you." She strokes her chin, as if thinking deeply. "You two have got something special, dear girl."

My eyes close as I try to block her out. The hatred and anger that I feel in my chest threatens to consume me.

"Ahh," She breathes. "I can feel your anger, your hatred. You and Cole are so alike." I open my eyes to see her smiling at me. The emotions that I feel in my heart flash red in my eyes.

"The only difference is," I order my voice to stay firm and strong though what I'm really feeling is the exact opposite. "I am not Cole." My lips pull up into a grin as I realize that the paralysis of my muscles is fading as I became stronger with both the dark and the light as emotions of love for my family and hate for this woman join together in my chest. "And when I attempt to kill you, you will perish." I pull myself up into a standing position, no longer feeling weak.

James's gaze of astonishment and fury burns holes through my skin, but I do not break my eyes away from Tenebris Daemon. "You will not touch my family. And you cannot use them against me, or me against them."

Tenebris Daemon's deadly beautiful face becomes one of a monster as she absorbs in my threats. Her eyes, which were red and glowing, now blaze with cold poisonous fire. Her skin, which had been marble white and flawless, now pulses with black veins that cover every inch of her face and neck. Her lips turn dark blood red and her teeth now become razor sharp and bare. This is her true self, not that illusion of a beautiful woman.

I gasp, unable to help myself, and take a few steps back.

"Now you're afraid of me?" She hisses. "Huh? *Beautiful, pure, innocent* Roza." She says those words like a curse. "This is what I am! You will never defeat me! I will rip out the throats of all who you love, as you watch, then I'll torture you until you die."

When she says my name, it feels like I am being pierced with a thousand needles. I realize that I am at a horrible disadvantage for I don't know her true name, so I can't use that against her. Though panic and horror courses through me, I stand firm and still and will myself to control my emotions.

"Touch one hair on any of their heads, and I'll end you." I say, trying to put as much courage into my voice as I can, even though I feel my heart weakening with dread.

Now James takes a step forward, his arms raised. But Tenebris Daemon puts out her hand to stop him.

"No James," She says. "The time will come when her blood will either be spilled or be joined with mine." Her hideous face morphs and changes back into how it had been, the beautiful pale woman. "But it is not the right time, or the right place." Her eyes, red and glowing, never leave my face as she speaks to James. "Deal with her, but don't kill her."

I glare at them both and will all of my remaining strength of power into keeping them away. A strong wind starts from where I stand, and I stare around me in thrilled surprise as what seems like a tornado forms around me, keeping both James and Tenebris from touching me. I laugh with triumph as the winds pick up and the two fall to the ground. I guess nature will always be on my side; it will always be against something so unnatural

"I'm not that easy to deal with," I say, my voice echoing loud. "Or that easy to kill."

Tenebris Daemon screams out something unintelligible, and even though I feel myself pulling away, her scream still causes me pain.

"How is this possible?" She is shouting through the howling of the wind. "You will regret this!" She screams as she fades away. "I will have you and that strong heart of yours." She disappears.

I let the winds die down. My strength gone. All that's left is utter silence.

25

"Rose!" A voice reaches me in my daze. "Rose! Wake up! Please!"

Other voices blur over me as I struggle to open my eyes. Bright light hits me and I squint in discomfort. Shadows of people loom over me as my eyes adjust.

"Jake," I hear a girl's voice. "She's waking up. Don't freak out on us."

"Freak out on you?" I hear Jake respond. "She has fingernail marks on her neck. And she's bleeding. Now how could she have gotten that? She's been here the whole time, physically I mean." He grunts. "And do I have to mention the fact that she was screaming and now is unconscious? And she's as pale as a corpse."

"Well, I think we can guess what happened." Another male voice says. I try to fully open my eyes, but the light hurts and focusing just makes my head ache. "Rose did say that she felt something wrong. And I think that we all felt it too, after she slumped. She was summoned and had her essence taken away somewhere. Probably by James and maybe even Daemon." Judging by the seriousness of the voice, it's probably Cole.

I groan as he mentions Tenebris Daemon and James, the cuts on my neck throb as I move.

"Look!" A deep joking voice says. "She moved! I guess she's not dead then." A pat on my cheek forces my eyes to open further. "Hey Rose. You gotta' wake up now. You're getting drool all over my car." A chuckle.

I slap away the hand that had patted my cheek, knowing that it is Thomas; only he would make a joke at a time like this.

"Don't make me wish that I could punch you in the gut right now, Thomas," I mumble, trying to sound funny. But even to my ears I don't sound funny, because my voice comes out as a croaky whisper, barely even strong enough to be heard.

"Oh, Thank God." Someone breathes.

"Rose," I hear Jake whisper, and open my eyes to see his blue ones staring down at me with worry. "What happened?"

I quickly tell them about everything that happened, wincing a little as I recall the true face of Tenebris Daemon.

"It's incredible that you can do what you did!" Angel exclaims.

"Ya, it's real great." I move into a more comfortable position since we are all still in the car. "I just managed to get the most evil woman on earth really mad with me, and I'll probably really regret what I did. As she said." The sarcasm in my voice cannot be mistaken. Angel rolls her eyes.

"Don't worry," Cole murmurs steadily. "We won't let anything happen to you."

"It's not me I'm worried about." I say. "It's you. It's all of you." I blush because as I stare at Jake and Cole, I realize that I had, unintentionally, left out the part where James had been taunting me about Jake and Cole.

"Well, we can take care of ourselves." Jake says in a hard voice. I place a hand on his cheek to show him that I understand. His blue eyes look almost stormy as they stare into mine. He reaches to touch the marks on my neck.

"Let's go home." He says. "I think we've found enough for today."

"But we've barely found anything!" I argue.

"No, we're going home." He switches his attention to Thomas. "Drive. Please,"

"Very well, Mr. Bossy-pants." Thomas retorts.

"Jake," Angel starts, her voice revealing all her worry. "What's wrong?"

"Well you heard what Rose said," Jake answers somewhat impatiently. "Daemon wants her, and for what, we don't know. So we have to keep her safe." He pauses, as if recalling the prophecy. "Even if it's just for a little while."

"Alright,"

"I'm not a child that needs to be protected," I say, for the first time feeling annoyed. "I can take care of myself."

"Of course you can!" Jake retaliates a bit. "But you still have to be careful,"

"I think we all have to be careful," I say softly.

"Jake's right." Cole suddenly interjects. " But Rose is right too. Daemon said she'll regret it, and we don't know yet what she'll do. And since Rose is the way she is, I'd think that the way that Daemon could make her regret it would be to hurt someone she loves. So I'd probably guess that none of us are exactly 'safe' right now."

I glance at Cole with a smile, because Tenebris Daemon was right about one thing: Cole and I are alike. And that's partly why he is more like a brother to me; we are peas in a pod. As if reading my thoughts through my face, Cole looks away from me in disappointment.

I frown slightly, but the frown is immediately replaced by a smile as I feel Jake's hand slip into mine offering warmth, reassurance and protection.

Even from far I can see the house drawing nearer and nearer as we close the distance. And even from the distance can I sense something not quite right.

As if sensing it too, the others sit up straighter on their seats, and in the matter of seconds, Thomas pulls the car up onto the driveway. As soon as we've gotten out of the car, the front door opens and reveals my mother, shock and anguish painted clearly on her face as she runs towards us in desperation.

"They're gone!" She screams, her voice holding such pain that my own heart threatens to burst with what I can feel from her own emotions. "She's taken them! I couldn't stop her!" She shouts through gasping sobs. "She's taken them!"

"Mom!" I yell as I run to meet her, I can feel the others following behind me. I sense their shock and anxiety. "What's happened? Who's gone? Who's taken who?!" I ask, even though I know in my heart and mind the answer to my questions.

"The children!" My mom's voice trembles. "Tenebris Daemon has taken them. She's taken little Simon and Kate."

■ ■ ■

Everything goes still. It is like the world has become frozen. My mind doesn't process what my mom has just said even as Angel lets out a cry and runs into the house, with Thomas following just behind her. I'm aware of Jake asking my mom questions, demanding to know exactly what had happened. But I can't join in, I don't feel anything; all that I'm aware of is a numbness in my heart, and two little holes in my chest that had been filled with Kate and Simon.

"No..." I manage to get out in a hoarse whisper.

"What about Alec?" I hear Cole ask mom rather harshly. "What about my uncle? Is he still here? Is he okay?"

"He's just fine, Cole," Mom answers, her voice cracking with tears. "But he's the least of our problems now. The children... Oh, what ever would she want with them?" My mom hugs her chest. Her pain is like a sword through my soul, all I want is to end her pain, and to find Kate and Simon.

I snap out of my daze and pull my mom into a tight hug. She clings to me like her life depends on it.

"It's okay Mom," I say, fighting for my own calm. I have to stay strong for my mom, with Angel probably losing it, and Thomas having his hands full with Angel; I have to stay strong in order to get the children back. "I'll find them. We'll find them. We'll bring them back safe and sound. Don't you worry," I stroke my mom's hair and her sobs lessen.

Jake looks at us, his eyes shining with tears that have not yet spilled over. I hold out a hand to him, because I know how much the kids mean to him. He takes my hand and kisses the palm.

"We'll find them, Mrs. Prædixi." Jake's voice holds a determination that is so strong that I feel myself believing him. If I wasn't so shocked, I might be surprised that Jake used my last name. I've never heard it come from him before.

"And we'll bring them home." Jake adds.

I nod at Jakes' words and pull myself away from my mom. Taking her hands, I lead her into the house and bring her into the room. She settles down next to my dad.

"Mom," I say. "Will you stay here with Dad? We'll look for the children, okay?"

She nods her head in agreement.
"You be careful, Ronnie." She orders. "Don't you dare get hurt or I'll give you a piece of my mind."

I don't tell her that I'm already hurt. I don't tell her that the marks on my neck, which are currently covered by thick waves of brown hair, are probably only the first of the many more injuries to come.

I smile at her sternness and bend down to kiss her on her head.

"Of course, mom." I smile with love. "I'll be careful. I'm always careful."

"Yes, you are always the most careful. So how is it that you're always the one to get hurt?"

"I don't know…" I frown a little.

"I know the answer to that, my little flower." She whispers as her voice fills with tenderness. "It's because you're always the one sacrificing yourself for the sake of others."

■ ■ ■

I close the door of my mom and dad's guest bedroom quietly, not wanting to disturb her after she finally fell asleep.

Arms wrap around me as soon as I turn around. The familiar smell of mint, lavender and masculine cologne surrounds me and fills me with ease. I wrap my arms around Jake and we stay in the embrace for a long time.

"I can't believe she took the children." I say in anger. My face still stays buried in the crook of his neck and shoulders.

"She's evil. She said you were going to regret it." Jake murmurs, sadness drips from him onto me.

"And I do." I say bitterly. "Oh, I do regret it. I regret it with every ounce of my being!" My fists ball up on his shoulder blades. "Why do I always save myself? Even if it might cause others harm?" I ask, almost begging for the answer.

"What do you mean?" Jake demands rather harshly. He pushes me away to get a full look at my face, but always keeping his hands firmly on my shoulders. "How could you possibly say that?"

"I have every right to say that." I answer resentfully. "I've done it before, now I did it again."

"There's nothing wrong with saving yourself!"

"No," I smile sadly. "There's nothing wrong with saving yourself unless it puts others at risk."

"This is not your fault." He tells me fiercely.

"Oh yes, it is." I answer. "And it's also my fault, that there's a little girl somewhere in New York without a father."

"What are you talking about?" He stresses, his eyes showing confusion.

"I'm talking about the accident Jake!" I almost yell in frustration. "The accident that caused me to be in the hospital for a month! The accident that haunts me when I sleep and makes me regret my living! The accident in which I could have saved a man and his daughter, but instead, I saved the daughter alone and gave up on the man because I wanted to save my own stupid skin!" Tears escape my eyes without my permission; I wipe them away hotly. "It's the accident that has left me feeling as if I owe the world my life because I let someone die, right in front of me, so that I could live."

I gasp in breaths; unable to help the sobs that have broken free from all the pain and hurt that has been buried in my chest. "Oh Jake. It's the accident that left me wondering whether I should have regretted saving my own life, or whether it was the right thing to do, because now, I'm glad I live, because I've met you. And if I had died to save that man, then I would never know you as I do now; and so deep inside, I feel relieved that I live instead of him. And to be as selfish as that makes me feel horrible! This accident has set everything in motion and has made me question who I am and what I have to do in this world."

Then I break down completely. The sobs racking my chest cause me to feel weak. I am vaguely aware that Jake has picked me up and is carrying me to the sofa. He sits down with me on his lap and cradles me tenderly.

"It's my fault…" I continue to cry. "It's my fault… my fault, my fault."

"Shh," He whispers as he strokes my hair. "It isn't in any way your fault. Anyone would have done what you did."

"But I'm not anyone," I cry stubbornly. "I'm *me*. And I should have done differently."

"Will you please stop putting yourself down?" He exasperates. "In all my life, I have never met anyone as kind, caring and thoughtful as you. Even if you didn't manage to save the man, you still risked your life to save his daughter. And it's not your fault that Daemon witch took Kate and Simon."

"But it is," I croak out. "I made her mad, and she wants to do something to hurt me. And so she took them. She took them to get back at me. That makes it my fault."

"It's not." Jake insists as he strokes my hair. "And we had better find them hadn't we?"

I nod.

"Gosh, Rose," He laughs lightly; the slight shaking of his chest against my head settles me. "You're almost as bad as Angel. The only difference is, you don't have snot running out your nose. Plus, you still look beautiful when you cry."

"Stop lying," I say and smile through my tears the same time that the door opens and Angel walks in with Thomas.

"Well thanks Jake." Angel grunts, and throws herself onto the couch. The puffiness of her eyes and tremble of her lips give away how fragile she now is. This saddens me because Angel has always been strong.

"No problem," Jake replies with a grim grin. Thomas settles in next to Angel and pats Jake on the shoulder and me on the head.

"I guess we're all a little broken, huh?" Thomas grumbles.

"Yep," I say, and try to laugh. It comes out sounding strangled and fragmented.

"We have to find them." Angel says. She stares off into space as if her mind isn't really with us.

"Yes," I say in agreement.

"I'm going to kill her." Angel mumbles forcefully.

"No," I tell her. "I have to. Remember? Prophecy? Blah, blah, blah," I sigh and hiccup. "Plus, I think I earned the right to kill her. She's mine."

"Fine," Angel says and smiles at me resignedly and in appreciation. "Then I get to kill James."

"Girls, girls," Thomas interjects; he seems to like doing that. "Now why are we choosing who to kill? Rather barbaric isn't it?" He smirks. "Why don't you leave all that bloody stuff to the men. Plus, why do you get to choose who you want to kill? Jake and I should have a say as well."

"We're more man than you are," Angel mumbles under her breath.

Thomas opens his mouth to defend himself when I add, "Plus, it's proven that women actually fight more viciously than men, because they don't really keep the sense of honor. We'll fight fair or unfair, we don't really care. You, boys, will still want to test who is stronger and you'll fight strength against strength. But girls fight with wit and strength." I smirk. "So if you were to fight against a female, you'd probably lose."

Jake chuckles at that and bends down to give me a quick kiss on the cheek, Angel actually giggles despite the awful situation, and Thomas, though my remark is aimed at him, actually smiles at me.

"You're good," Thomas says whilst pointing a finger at me. I wink at him in reply.

Angel sighs once she's done with her giggling.

"Thanks Rose." She says. "I actually thought that I would never smile or laugh again." Her bottom lip trembles. "Kate and Simon are my responsibilities. I wasn't supposed to let anything happen to them. Now look at the situation." She puts her hand to her face. "If Mom were here she'd kill me."

"And me," Thomas adds. "They're my responsibility too."

"And you all are my responsibility. Since I'm the oldest." I hear Cole say. I turn my head to find him at the front door, his jacket, and hair, dripping wet. "It's raining like crazy outside, by the way." He adds as he slips off his jacket and shakes his hair dry.

"You know, Cole?" I tell him tiredly. "You're very mysterious. You always seem to come in and join the conversation at just the right time so you say just the right thing that makes you sound very smart. Even if you actually aren't," I blush at the last part; I didn't mean to say it.

Jake's chest vibrates and I look up to see him smiling down at me and shaking his head. He seems to be trying to hold his laughter. Cole walks over and settles down on the sofa across from us, a grin is brightening up his face. His eyes are soft as he looks at me.

"Well, mysterious is charming and attractive." He says with his old humor. It makes me smile to know that he's more comfortable around me now. "I'll have all the ladies running to me, wanting some of this masterpiece." He gestures down to his whole body.

"And I bet you do get some. In fact, I bet you get a lot by the looks of you." I say, trying to be humorous, and to hide the fact that even though I love Jake, the mere thought of Cole having other girls makes me feel sad and angry inside. I think that's jealousy. *"Stop it,"* I chide myself mentally. *"You can't have both of them. You love Jake more and should love Jake only. That is that."*

"Why of course," Cole replies, his eyes glinting with humor and something else, something darker. Curiously, I feel his emotions to find out what that deeper darker glint in his eyes was.

Desire.

Desire rolls off of him like storms and a love that can never be beats in his heart. It is desire and love directed towards me.

"Now you're just being snobby," I say childishly, wanting desperately to rid myself of the ache that has begun in my chest. I'm not sure whether it is because I want to protect him, or because I think he is just using those girls, or because

I think that none of them will ever be good enough for him. *Or because you want him for yourself*, a soft hypnotizing voice says in my brain.

I shake my head, confused at what the voice implied, but as I feel Jake's arms tighten around me, the ache in my chest vanishes, and the voices disappear. I trace my fingers across Jake's shirt, making swirly motions. As Jake's hands move up and down my arm and warm my bones, I know that I will want no other. Even if I feel something for Cole, nothing can or will ever be as strong as the love that I feel for Jake.

26

The sun peeps through the clouds as the wind blows them across the sky. Jake sits next to me on the sand. Angel and Thomas are in the house discussing possible places to look for Tenebris Daemon and James, since where they are, the kids will probably be. Jake came up with something for us to do. He called it "Debriefing the fresh-bloom about the root of what we do."

The day is beautiful; it's rather cool, but with the sun out, it isn't cold. The sound of the waves is soothing, only adding to the effect of Jake's melodious voice. His eyes sparkle as he looks at me whilst explaining.

"What we do is not magic. We take the power of nature and the deeper power of the brain and the heart, and we use that. Everything that makes us different and stronger is natural and from the core of our very being. It seems that what Tenebris Daemon does is magic, but a very black magic that is unnatural and unhealthy for everything." Jake's voice seems to echo through my head; it lingers on in every fiber of my body. "Our power is basically everything that normal people have, but for us it's enhanced. That's what gives us our so-called 'powers'," He winks. "So basically, the normal human uses about ten to fifteen percent of their brain; we use way more. That's what gives Angel the ability to sense thoughts, or yours and Cole's ability to speak in the mind. Yes I know you can do that. What else? Oh ya," He snaps his fingers together. "Your ability to sense emotions! A normal human can tell, vaguely, when someone is feeling a particular emotion because of the way that they act or the expression of the face or voice. Your ability comes from that being enhanced. So not only can you sense emotions, but also you can influence them by making the person feel happy and calm. Not to mention the healing abilities and positive energy. Everything else is stronger too, your senses, your strength, everything." He smiles at me. "You're special Rose."

"No more than you are," I tell him with a smile of my own. I normally don't feel very special, but sitting here with Jake, he's starting to make me believe it. He makes me feel extraordinary. And that makes him more special than anyone.

"Yeah, well to an extent anyways," He flashes me the grin that I love. The one where one side of his lips pull up just slightly before the other, relaxes, then repeats the action and becomes a big smile. My heart contracts as I look at him. He is beautiful, and he is mine.

"Well, keep going!" I urge playfully. I feel my grin expanding as he rolls his eyes.

"Alright," He says and takes my hand in his. His hands are warm and big compared to mine. "Are you cold?" He asks, frowning. "Your hands are freezing,"

"I'm fine," I say softly. "You'll just have to hold my hands to keep them warm, is all."

His smile returns, "I'm perfectly okay with that,"

"Great," I curl my fingers until they're tangled in his.

"Okay, so where were we?" He asks quizzically, one of his eyebrows shoots up, abandoning the other as his eyes reveal challenge me to answer.

"Everything is enhanced, our brain, our senses and our strength, and that makes us different from normal people though we are still human." I say in my most serious voice just to prove that I was listening and that I wasn't distracted. "And something about you being special," I grin at him teasingly.

"I'm pretty sure I specifically said that you were the one that is special," He winks. "And you just had to go against me and say just the opposite." He pouts jokingly.

I roll my eyes to show fake annoyance as my smile grows, and his grin widens.

"I just love when you do that," He says.

"Do what?"

"Smile and look at me with those beautiful doe-brown eyes of yours," He says softly. The wind blows then and ruffles his hair. I reach up to touch it and smooth it back down. His hair is soft and a lovely golden color.

Jake catches my wrist and pulls me towards him gently but quickly so that I am unprepared when my body falls against his and his lips meet mine. They are soft and have a faint taste of mint. I fight the urge to keep kissing him. I want to learn more about what we do. Pulling away, I see that his eyes have darkened tremendously; the pupils fill most of the blue. We're still very close together, our noses touching.

"Now, Jake," I retort good-naturedly. Being pressed against him, I can feel his heart beat rapidly in his chest. I bet he can feel mine. "You're supposed to be teaching me, not doing this. I have to learn."

"Who says I'm not teaching?" He asks with a small smile. "And who says you're not learning."

"I do," I reply with mock seriousness even though my head is spinning. I lean in to give him a small peck on the lips, but he holds me there longer before letting go. "Now come on, don't go off topic again. Plus, we have to find Kate and Simon."

This brings him back in check. He immediately becomes serious, and his pupils narrow, shocking me again with the brilliance of his bright blue eyes. He releases me, only keeping me captured with my hand in his.

"Okay, right." He seems to say to himself.

I smile at him to show that I'm ready for more learning.

"So everything we do is perfectly natural." He says, slowly, as if collecting his thoughts. "But not only is our physical and mental ability enhanced. Our emotions are enhanced too, so we feel everything more strongly and more clearly."

"That makes sense," I mumble.

"So when we feel anger, heart-break, pain, grief, happiness, longing or anything; it's stronger and more deeply rooted." He says softly. "And when we love, it's so much more than that. It's stronger and more ever-lasting than anything there is." As he speaks, his hands travel up my arm and up to my face. I put my hand over his, holding it there. "So what I'm feeling for you is incredible, I can barely –"

"Guys!" Jake and I turn around as Angel screams for us. She interrupts him so that I can never hear what he could barely do. Jake is up even before I realize what Angel is shouting. "Get in here!" She continues to shout. "We think we know where to start searching!"

■ ■ ■

"No way," I say again, not wanting to believe my ears. "No way,"

"Rose," Angel says, not for the first time. "You can't just keep denying it. It's the most obvious place."

"No way," I whisper again, unable to quit saying it. Angel rolls her eyes and walks over to Jake. Jake bows his head a little as Angel tells him frantically about what she thinks. The life seems to be draining from him as dread takes it's place.

"You're right," I hear him answer Angel. "It seems the most obvious choice. Too obvious, almost as if she's taunting us to return."

"But back to the cave?" I put in sharply. "To the place where we found Dad? Where she had hidden in the past?" I shake my head. "Why would she go back there? It would be stupid for her to go back there because we know how to get in. There's no more security there at all."

"It's because she's devious." Cole adds in a low voice. "She knows that we would not think she would go back there, and so she did, giving her time. It also makes it easy for us to find her, and easy for us to penetrate the place. It's what she wants." He looks me seriously in the eye. "Rose, think about it. She *wants* you to find her. That's why she took the children and brought them to a place where we've already been. Taking them ensures that you would go to her."

"Well, then I'll go to her!" I say. "If she has me, then she has to let the children go."

"Don't even think about it." Jake says harshly. I look at him in surprise; I've never heard him use that hard a tone. He stares back at me with force, his eyes burn with their blue fire.

"But—" I start.

"Don't be stupid, Rose," Cole interrupts. "We would never let you go."

I look at Angel and Thomas because they have been silent as soon as I gave the idea of trading me for their two siblings. It would make sense for them to agree with me. Right?

"Thomas," I say. "Angel. You know I'm right! Why make the little ones go through that fear? Tenebris Daemon wants me, so she will try to get me no matter what." I sigh. "It's inevitable." I add. No one is smiling now. The mood in the room is so depressing that I feel the weight of it threaten to crush me. Everyone is confused about what to do. Anger radiates from all of them, especially Jake.

Angel and Thomas have hope, along with all the bad feelings. I can tell that they aren't sure what to do, that they would never ask me to sacrifice myself for the kids, but that they want me to try if it means getting their brother and sister back. "Angel," I urge. "That's your little sister, and your little brother. How can you not let me go?"

Angel looks up at me then, her eyes wet with tears. The grief in them breaks my heart, but fills me with a new sense of purpose. No one can stop me now.

"You guys can't stop me. None of you can. I'm going."

"Well then, I guess we'll just have to tie you to a post and lock you in a room." Cole says firmly.

"You wouldn't dare." I say, my voice trembling with frustration.

"Try me," Is all he replies. I glare at him and he glares back, somehow able to make his eyes the coldest that I've ever seen them.

"Well Angel and Thomas wouldn't let you," I retort and lift my chin. "They agree with me. I can feel it." I turn to face Jake. "And seeing that you're so silent, I'm guessing you agree with me."

"Of course I agree with you," Jake says. "But you're still not going!"

"But you just said——."

"Yes, I agree that something has to be done. And that someone has to go get the kids. But I don't agree that you or anyone should go and play right into her hands! Why should we give her what she wants?" His tone is incredibly exasperated.

"She won't be able to do anything to me!" I fold my arms. "I'm stronger than she thinks."

"Yes, we all know you're strong. I know more than anybody else," He says, making me blush. "But you still can't go, because you'll be risking your life and all of our lives if we go."

"Well," I say firmly. "I never said anyone had to go with me. I'm planning to go alone."

This causes everyone to break their silence. I catch some words through the mass of messy voices. Some of the words sounded like things that aren't exactly polite, especially in front of kids, mostly coming from Cole. I meet Jake's eyes as everyone continues to argue with me. He silently stares at me.

"How can you possibly think we won't go with you?" Angel asks after shushing everyone.

"Ya, Rose." Thomas speaks up for the first time. "If you or any of those two kids get hurt, I'm going to punch that witch's nose right into her skull." He grins wickedly. "In fact, I think I'm going to do that anyway."

"If you're going, we're going. Kate and Simon are our responsibility anyways." Angel says powerfully.

"But all she wants is me." I try to reason with them. "There's no point if you all come with me. She will spare me; she won't kill me. But she'll probably kill you if you go."

"There are things worse than death." Cole says quietly. I don't know whether he intended for all of us to hear, but I hear it and a shiver runs down my spine.

"We can't just let you go alone." Thomas adds.

"That's probably the smartest thing that I've heard you say," Jake says with a smile but it doesn't reach his eyes. Thomas smiles back naturally, but then gives a small serious nod.

I growl in frustration. My eyes feel hot as tears of irritation gather.

"So I take it that we all agree that Rose won't go alone?" Jake asks; a hint of victory in his voice.

"Yep," Angel says for everyone. "It's all of us or none."

"Wasn't there some sort of musketeer saying?" Thomas says light-heartedly. "All for one and one for all."

"I don't know whether that could be used for this situation." Cole tells him.

"Sure it can," Jake says, and when he smiles this time, it reaches his eyes. It's clear that his mood has improved as soon as everyone agreed on not letting me hand myself over.

"I'm going to my room." I say as I stand up hastily.

"You don't have one yet," Jake says. "Unless you want to stay with me." He gives me a small smile of victory, which just makes me even more exasperated.

"Or me and Cole." Thomas adds with a slight wink.

"Sorry guys," Angel says. "She's mine."

"I think I'd rather sleep in the bathroom tonight, since I can't seem to agree with any of you at the moment." I say shortly. As much as I try to stop it, hot anger has managed to seep through the cage in my heart.

Jake frowns, as if realizing that this is the first time that I've gotten really mad. He knows that it isn't natural behavior for me.

"I'm sorry if you disagree with us on you walking right into your certain death and, or, torture." Cole says sarcastically.

"I don't think you should have any say." I tell him icily. "You did exactly what I want to do. You and I are too alike for you to not understand me now." His eyes darken as my meaning sinks in.

"Well, if you guys would excuse me." I walk quickly to the bathroom, closing the door and locking it. With my back pressed against the door, I reach up to touch the red X that James placed on me. It throbs as my fingers brush it, as if it is aware of what I want.

I walk towards the mirror and stare at myself. My eyes harden with my resolve. I will go to Tenebris Daemon and no one can stop me. I will force her to trade the children for me and I will see them back safely. Nothing will keep me from doing this; because there is no way that I'm leaving little Simon and little Kate in her hands.

"Come get me," I whisper firmly but quietly while touching the X. It pulses strongly as I send my message. In the back of my mind I vaguely hear laughter of a man and a silent whisper that sends chills down my spine before it brings blackness.

I'll be there for you, do not think you will be able to avoid us. She will have your heart yet. Put up a fight, and the little ones will not be spared. It'll be a fair trade, no need for worry. More laughter. *And after my master is done with you, you are mine.*

27

I silently slip into my mom and dad's room, grabbing jeggings and a light shirt that enable me to move. I guess that I'll need to be able to fight. After changing I move to stand right in front of my sleeping parents.

"I love you guys," I whisper, my heart aching because I already miss them. "I'm sorry I won't be here for you when you wake up, Dad. But hey, I'm doing what I'm supposed to. Take care of each other. I love you both so much and I don't want to leave you, but I need to do this."

A single tear escapes from my eyes, and I don't bother try to wipe it away. The tear lands on my parents' joined hands.

I move silently towards the door and open it. Everyone is asleep by now. After giving up on trying to get me out of the bathroom, they all went to bed. The moonlight shines brightly through the windows and illuminates my whole body. I don't bother leaving a note, because I know that if I do, Jake would come immediately, even if I tell him not to. So I just make my way to the door and open it slightly.

"Planning to leave without a goodbye, were you?" A husky voice says from the shadows.

I spin around in surprise and have to cover my mouth to keep from giving a little squeal. Jake stands half in the shadows, and half in the moonlight. Looking so beautiful and so familiar that it's almost impossible to leave him. I stay silent because I know that if I speak, my voice will crack and he would use my weakness to make me stay. "Were you planning on breaking my heart?" He whispers. "Because if you leave, then you're going to be doing just that."

"Jake," I get out, unable to stop myself. "I'm so sorry. I have to do this."

"No you don't." He seems to plead. "We can find another way to fix this."

"This is the only way."

He shakes his head violently.
"I don't believe that." He says. "I—"

"Oh Roza," calls a dark hypnotic voice. "Come on out."

I close my eyes slowly, knowing that there can't have possibly been a worse time for James to appear. My eyes fly open as I feel Jake grab me by the arm and force me behind his body.

"You aren't going to take her." He growls at James.

"Oh, hey Jake." James says a little too casually. "Been a long time. Nice to see you here; with her."

"Oh James," Jake says, his voice turning almost placating. "Don't make me want to kill you right there, right now."

"You're welcome to try." James replies. "I think that you would find that it is quite impossible."

As my eyes adjust to the darkness I start to make out where James is. He stands right in front of the porch, just an inch before the first step. He carries two sacks over each shoulder. The sacks are squirming.

"Oh my God." I breathe out and try to break free of Jake's iron grip. "Jake. It's the kids. They're in the sacks." Jake doesn't let go of me, he just stares James down as if he could kill him that way. "Jake. Let go of me." I beg. "Please,"

He looks down at me, his eyes full of anguish.

"Please," I say again. He takes a deep breath in, and then slowly releases me. As soon as I'm free, I run towards James.

James's eyes are full of amusement as I reach him and stand right in front of him.

"Let them go." I demand as forcefully as I can. James just shrugs and says "Okay," and drops them.

I hear little voices cry out as the sacks hit the ground. I fall to the rocky dirt floor and begin untying the knotted sacks frantically. I get through the first one and force it down. A small head with blond hair and big scared eyes peep at me. "Oh Simon." I sigh in relief. "Oh my God. You're okay." I give him a quick tight hug, completely unaware that James has moved away from where he was standing next to me. "Help me get Kate out." I say. With both of us working, and Simon's small little nimble fingers, getting Kate out is easy. With a little small exclamation of my name, Kate scrambles out, and reaches up to hug me. "Oh Kate. You're okay too." I pull both of them into a big hug and hold them there.

"Rose," I hear Jake call out. "Are they okay?"

"Yes!" I respond in relief. "They are."

"Good," He says. "Now bring them into the house quickly. Now."

"Come on," I tell them as I carry them up. They walk on either side of me, taking longer little steps in order to keep up with me so that they can follow Jake's instructions.

I'm just walking past James and pushing them along in front of me when a firm stony grip catches my upper arm and jerks me backwards. The kids stop just as they reach where Jake stands on the porch, realizing that I am not with them anymore.

"Not you," James says candidly as he holds on to my arm with a grasp as strong as steel. I stay by his side obediently, because for all I know, he could blow the children and Jake to bits if I move.

I look up at Jake and see his eye blaze with rage. But he doesn't move to take me back, and doesn't move as the kids open the door of the house and run in. He just stands there, perfectly still, as if he were a statue.

"Now this is easy," James says, smiling happily. "You'll just stay there and I'll take Rose with me."

Jake's face is turning pale, then horribly red, his veins popping out. James grins at Jake, appearing to enjoy his discomfort. The bigger his smirk gets, the more Jake seems to be in pain.

"What are you doing to him?" I shout, my heart creeping with fear.

"Well, I've paralyzed him." James says. "But remember what I said, the more you try to get out, the less you'll get in.

And he's trying *very* hard to break away from my paralysis. So I'm guessing that he's getting very little oxygen. And he probably can't breath right now anyways." He smiles at Jake without any mercy.

"Stop it." I say. "Stop it!" My voice rises. "I'm coming with you. Just please don't hurt him."

James just shrugs again.

"I can't, baby. He's the one that's making it hard for himself."

"Then un-paralyze him!" I plead; scared of the color of Jake's skin and of the sweat that coats his body. "Please. He's not strong enough anymore. Please."

"Alright," James says with another shrug. His shrugs are getting on my nerves.

Jake sags to the floor as James's power leaves him. He lies there shivering and breathing hard. I start to move towards him but am stopped by James's strong grip.

"Let me go to him. I give you my word that I'll return with you."

"And why would your word mean anything to me?" James asks, looking honestly curious.

"Because you know that I know that you would hurt the person I love most in the world if I do not follow you."

James's eyes narrow at my simple declaration of love for Jake, but he lets go of me. I rush towards where Jake lies and pull him into my arms.

"Oh Jake," I murmur sadly. "You can't stop him. He's just too powerful, that's what you get when you join the dark."

"I'm sorry," He whispers so weakly that I have to strain to hear him. "I love you."

The tears break free, my composure no longer strong enough.

"I love you too. I'm sorry." I stroke his face. "I'll come back to you. I promise." I can't come back to him physically, but I'll always come back to him spiritually. That's what I'm promising.

I smile at him and lean down to give him a kiss. He moves up and pulls me towards him, his strength surprising me. He kisses me with force and desperation, the heat radiating between us makes my skin tingle with longed for pleasure. He drags me up until we're standing and finally pulls away.

He's no longer weak and dying as he had been. His skin glows and his eyes burn.

"You're not going." He says firmly.

"You can't stop me." I mumble. "James will do everything in his power to make sure that I follow him."

"I can't let you go," Jake says desperately.

"Well you're going to have to." I reach up to give him a peck on the lips.

I force all my love and all my desperation and heartbreak into that kiss, using all my ability to influence him and to make that kiss something that will keep him from stopping me.

"I'm so sorry, but when you wake up, I'll be gone. And I want you to know that you're the one I love most in this whole world. And I'm doing this to keep you and everyone else that I love safe." I move away just in time to see his eyes narrow in confusion and then widen in comprehension, and then he sags as the effect of my kiss takes place. As his body goes to sleep, I lie him down gently onto the ground and kiss him one last time.

I stand up and walk towards James, letting all the hate and the rage flow through me, forcing James to sense that once all the people I love are safe, there is no way that he or Tenebris Daemon will be safe. But he just smiles at me as I come to stand by his side.

"Interesting, that," He says as he jerks his chin towards Jake. "What did you do?"

"I have learned that if I want something strongly enough and if I put all that I've got into making something happen, it'll happen. Especially if it's something easy and small." I frown. "I just really wanted him to sleep, so I made him sleep."

"Brilliant," James says, almost sincerely. But I know that he feels nothing of sincerity. "So why can't you make me go away?" He asks sounding genuinely interested.

"Because I can't concentrate enough on my good emotions to let me use innocent powers when it comes to you." I smile sweetly. "So if I force you to go away, you would probably go away and kill yourself. Because all I feel when I think about you is hate, and that hate would turn my ability into darkness and cause me to want something bad. And I want you to know that the only reason that I'm here with you is because I *want* to be. Because this will save those I love."

"Nice to know." He says with an easy smile that sets my nerves on fire. "Ready to go?"

"Do I have a choice?" I reply.

"I'm afraid you've already made it." He says. "Grab onto me."

"Do I have to?" I say just to make trouble for him.

"Yep, unless you want to die an excruciatingly painful death."

Instead of answering his smart remark, I put my arms around him and shut my eyes.

"Oops, there's your little girl friend. We've got to go now." James mumbles. "I hope you like falling."

I open my eyes in question just in time to see him step into a black bottomless pit. As the wind rushes past, and the sound of whispering in the darkness gathers around me, it's all I can do to not hold on to James tighter and scream.

■ ■ ■

"Wakie wakie, sleeping beauty," A quiet voice taunts the darkness of my mind. I force my eyelids open. And blink, because instead of the bright morning light that I was expecting, there are only shadows. Then I remember. And everything that has happened since this morning hits me like a wave. Melancholy crushes my chest. It's hard to breath through my fear and my rage. But how did I end up sleeping?

"James." I say with dread. "What happened?"

"Well, you kinda blacked out, sweetheart." He replies with a smirk. "Yes, as soon as we stopped falling, you slumped to the floor like a sack." He clicks his tongue together. "Guess you're not used to falling. But you will be." He smirks at me, his eyes glinting with cruelty. "Because you're going to be falling a lot."

I glare at him with as much force as I can master, not trying at all to hide my disgust or hate.

"Am I supposed to be scared?" I question, putting as much bravery and calm wrath into my voice as I can.

He eyes me with an almost amused expression and shrugs.

"No, I guess." He says. "You're never scared for yourself. Sometimes I wonder if you even value your own life at all." His lips curl up in a harsh smile. "But," He sneers almost elegantly. "You are always scared for the ones you love. You can't help but try your best to ease their pain." He emphasizes on the word help.

I look away then, because what he said is true; and I don't want him to know it because my eyes can't lie.

"Look at me." He says in a quiet voice, without tone or emotion. It would have been less scary if he shouted. I look up at him with tears of anger in my eyes; my heart beats wildly in my chest. He stares into my eyes for a couple of seconds before a nasty looking grin sets on his face. "I was right." He tells me with triumph. "I guess we know how to get you to comply to our needs."

"I won't do anything for you." I spit at him. "Especially not anything you need or want."

"Ooh," He says in mocking fear. He puts his hands palms out to me, like a gesture of restraint. "Scary. Tough. I like that."

"I couldn't care less what you like."

"Oh I know," He replies. "Too bad really. Because it would be much easier for you, and for your dear loved ones, if you do everything we ask you to… willingly."

"Don't you dare hurt anyone," I shout, taking a step towards him without thinking. But I don't get more than a step, because my muscles freeze instantly. I look down at my feet and at my body with disgust. Why can't I fight his paralysis? I look up at him, hoping that my stony glare full of hate will somehow burn holes in his chest.

"You know," He says while picking at his cuticle casually. His casualness makes me want to punch him in the face. "Glaring at me won't help you. It certainly won't hurt me."

"Lucky for you," I say through gritted teeth. For some reason, my anger has made me braver. I'm not scared of what he'll do to me, as long as he keeps his hands away from my family. He walks towards me slowly, as if cautious of the fact that even in a paralyzed state, my muscles are still coiled up tightly as if I were going to spring at him as soon as I break his spell.

He stops a foot away from me, his eyes moving up and down my body predatorily. I shiver with revulsion. He smiles maliciously at my discomfort. James moves his hands, his fingers graze my collarbone, my neck, my mouth, and back down to my neck; his hand circles my neck, not digging his nails into my skin, but rubbing the surface of it. His eyes darken. I look away before I do something that I will regret. I'd much rather he dug his nails into the skin of my neck rather than touch it like a caress. It would be much less disturbing.

"Now, now," A dark wispy woman's says from the darkness. "Don't play with her James. We don't want her to be disgusted with us."

"Too late for that," I snap at Tenebris Daemon, unable to help myself. My rage trumps over my fear of her. That's good. Dauntless is good.

Her hood is off so I can see her face, still beautiful and pale in the darkness. In fact, her white skin stands out, making her look like a ghost. She smiles at my retort and walks to stand a couple meters in front of me.

"Oh?" She chuckles. "And why would you say that?"

"Hmm," I say sardonically. "Let me think. You kidnapped my father and turned him into a block of ice. Not to mention put him in a coma. You turned Cole evil and controlled him to hurt me. You tried to kill me, and the ones I love; multiple times. And you took the children so that you could drive me into coming to you." I pretend to pause. "Did I get everything?"

"I believe so," She replies with a glint in her eye, which just makes her look even harsher. Then she puts her hand to her chin like she's thinking. "Hold on... No, I don't think that's all."

"What?" I say, not liking how she's taunting me. I've never associated taunting with her, but maybe that is just something else that is a mystery to me about this woman.

"I think there is one more thing that you've forgotten to mention." She smiles nastily.

"And what is that?" I ask sarcastically.

She smiles viciously, making my heart freeze painfully."The accident."

28

"What?" I manage to choke out after the shock fades a little.

"Oh you know," She replies vaguely. "The accident where you managed to save the little girl but the dad still died? Yes, that one. I actually didn't mean for you to save either of them. You were just supposed to see it and fail in opening the doors and watch them both die as the car exploded. But it never occurred to me that you would be strong or brave enough to break the window." She frowns. "So you still managed to get the daughter out. But nonetheless, the father still died. And it created just the effect I wanted it to." She grins sharply, showing a row of white teeth. "You've not been able to get away from the guilt have you?"

I shake my head, not wanting to believe what I'm hearing. I can't give her another thing to use against me. I can't. I can't let her know that not saving that man has been tearing me apart.

"Have you ever wondered," She begins. "What kind of life the little girl is having now? And what kind of life she could have had if her dad was still with her?"

"Stop," I mutter weakly. My head starts to spin with fury and pain.

"I would have thought," She continues, ignoring me. "That you, of all people, would understand."

"Stop!" I scream at her, wanting to shut her out. Tenebris Daemon doesn't even flinch, but James moves forward as if afraid that I am going to break away from his powers. But I can't, because the guilt and the pain have overwhelmed my anger; and I am not strong enough.

"I bet," She keeps going as if I didn't make a sound. "That the little girl is crying in her bed right now. Wondering what kind of life she would have if that selfish girl who saved her, could have saved her father too, instead of just saving herself."

"No," A sob breaks from within my chest and I feel tears running down my face.

"I bet she doesn't get a single night of sleep because nightmares plague her dreams." Tenebris Daemon approaches me, continuing to speak in that low persuasive voice. "And I bet that she is broken inside, whenever she is reminded, once again, that she has no father to call her 'my little Princessa',"

"Stop it," I feel pain in my heart, too powerful to push away. Because my dad called me 'my little Princessa'. And I feel, once again, that pain I felt when I had to go through the years without my dad.

I feel more pain when I imagine that the little girl is going through the same thing that I went through before I found my dad. Except my dad was lost and could be found.

Her dad can never return to her because he's dead.

He's dead and it's all my fault. My fault.

"It's your fault you know," She murmurs in my ear, sending needles of sharp pain through my entire body. I have no more will to fight; the pain is too much. "Take her away, lock her up for now." Tenebris Daemon tells James. "She won't be much use now because of what she's feeling. But she'll be angry later and we'll use that."

"Why bother making her feel that guilt again if we want her strong?" James asks as he lifts me up from where I am curled up in a ball on the floor. I don't even remember falling.

"Because I need her to be broken first. Well, re-broken." Tenebris Daemon replies. "She will mend herself. But when she does that, her heart will heal with hate for me, and anger at what I have done and what I am planning to do. It will heal with darkness."

I'm only half listening to her, and too busy fighting the pain in my being to fight her words.

"And how to you plan to do that?" James grunts.

"We have to wait for him to arrive. I plan to use her love, which is, possibly, the most powerful thing now." She sighs as if sad. "Even more powerful than me. I plan to use her love to make her do something that she hates."

I groan in confusion and fear as James carries me to the unknown. What Daemon said scares me because she has a plan, and I don't. And even though I don't know what she plans to do, I have a feeling that I will not like it.

■ ■ ■

In the dark emptiness of my mind I hear a deep calming voice; a voice that I've missed more than anything.

Rose. Rose, do not feel this pain. It was not your fault. Do not feel guilt. You saved someone already, and tried your best to save another. You can't do everything. It is not your job to help and watch over everyone. That is God's job. Don't feel like the weight of the world is on your shoulders, because it is not. Share the burden sweetheart. Two hearts are stronger than one. Always remember that.

I try my best to reach the voice, because it lessens the ache in my chest and it makes me believe that I am not to blame. But the emptiness engulfs me once more, and I am, once again, drowning in my pain and in all the pain of the world. But it is different, because now hope has reached into the black water with strong hands, and slowly I feel myself being dragged out of my waking nightmares.

■ ■ ■

Hard rock presses against my right cheek, sending a sharp pain through my face. A groan escapes my lips as I struggle to sit up.

My hands rub against cool uneven ground, and the breath that escapes my mouth comes out in a puff of visible mist.

It's cold.

I stand and look around. It looks as if I'm in a small solid cave. There is an opening before me. But as I walk towards the opening, my hands, which I hold out in front of me, collide with what feels like a wall. I move my hands over that space; it's flat and smooth, like glass. But it is colder than ice. I jerk my hand back, my fingertips burning with cold.

"What in the world?" I murmur. I examine the tips of my fingers curiously, forgetting completely where I am as I contemplate this burning ice. Either it is so cold that just holding my hand there for a second meant that I was getting frostbite, or it is enchanted. But the rest of me is not that cold, so it's probably enchanted to act like super dried ice. "Huh." I grumble. Looks like I'm stuck in here. But I need to get out. Why are they keeping me in here?

"Well, hey there." I jerk out of my thoughts as I hear James speak to me; appearing out of nowhere. "Finally awake are you? How nice."

"What's going on?" I demand. "What is this? Why am I in here?"

"It's just some cage that my master thought of." His eyes glint. "Since you are full of warmth, aren't you? So we decided to construct a cell just for you." He smirks. "I wouldn't touch the ice wall if I were you. It can... burn."

If I didn't know better, I would have charged at him. Instead, I just glare at him and sit down on the spot right in front of the wall. Seeing this, James just shrugs and disappears in the shadows. With him gone, I can finally think. My muscles relax as I look around me.

It's too quiet, almost eerie.

My breath comes out in puffs, but I'm not cold. I focus on thinking. What happened right before I woke up? I can't remember anything from my sleep other than the fact that something important happened. As I dig deeper inside of me I realize a couple of things. The first thing is that my heart no longer aches with the pain of guilt. And after that dawns on me, I realize a second thing. I DO remember what happened in the dimness of my unconsciousness.

"Oh!" I exclaim softly. That deep calming voice; I know it. It was always a voice, and still is a voice, that can bring me peace and make me feels better. A voice that can make me believe in anything, even if I didn't once believe it myself. "Dad…" I murmur with awe.

I feel a warm smile growing on my face even as the coldness of this cave creeps into my body. My dad spoke to me! He's okay. He told me to forget my guilt and to let it go. And unconsciously, my heart does just that, because I know in my core, that it *is*, it is God's job to be able to help everyone, and to be able to save everyone. Not mine. And as I realize that, it feels as if the weight of everything that I've been unintentionally worrying about lifts off my shoulders. "Oh, thank you…" I breathe out as I press my clasped hands against my forehead. "Thank you," Now Tenebris Daemon won't be able to use my guilt, or my pain against me.

But there are still other ways.

Worse ways.

Ways that I can't let her use to get me to do what she wants.

I open my eyes and look up at the ice wall, suddenly filled with new purpose. Pushing myself up, I glare at the walls as if I could burn holes in them. A sizzling noise starts and little bits of steam appear from the section of the wall I am glaring at.

I blink in shock, and the steaming and sizzling stops as my concentration wavers. *What?* I think. That's strange. I let go of my shock and put all of my concentration into the ice wall. I glare at it with unwavering eyes. I want it to melt, so that I can get out. I imagine the ice melting and turning into water, creating an exit for me. I imagine fire starting at the spots where I stare.

Hot fire.

I place a palm on the wall, the ice no longer stings. The melting and sizzling starts up again at the point where my hand make contact with the ice wall, I can see the ice melt, water drips through my fingers; warm water. I feel a grin on my face. I can get out of here. I place my other palm right next to my first, and the ice melts further. But the wall is thick, so it will take more power. I need more power…

"What," says a low feminine voice. "Do you think you're doing?"

I jerk my hand away from the wall. I don't reply.

"Do you really think," she walks closer, eyes glowing, her hood covering her face. "That you could even *manage* to get out." She stands right in front of me.

Nothing but the ice wall stands between us. She places her hand on the two spots next to each other where I had started to melt the ice.

"I, myself, constructed this cage. You are not powerful enough to break it." The spot where her hands touch the ice starts to freeze over again, whatever ice I had managed to melt just reappears. She smiles at me cruelly.

"You don't scare me." I say to her. "And you can't use me. You can't use the guilt or the pain against me anymore. I've realized it's not my job to save the world. I'm only a pawn. Just a small piece. And I only need to do one thing." I glare at her. "And that is to get rid of you. To get rid of your evil presence." Her smile fades as I finish.

"Foolish child," She hisses. "You're nothing. Nothing compared to me. And I will crush you."

"We'll see about that." I answer back, folding my arms. Even though my heart pounds in my chest, pounding so hard I swear that it's trying to escape the cage made of bone, I know that I have to put on a brave front. And it's not really hard to do that when there's someone in front of you making you raging mad.

"Oh, yes you will." Her smile returns as she steps away. Tenebris Daemon turns around and seems to drift away; both she and James leave by disappearing into the shadows at the end of the room. So I have no idea how to get out, even if I manage to break out of this ice cage.

As she vanishes, all the tension and adrenaline caused by anger and fear leave my body, leaving me with a feeling of foreboding. As I sit down and put my head between my knees to stop my body from shaking, I know that I will not like what comes next.

29

The screaming starts as soon as I put my head down. There is no time for me to find it in myself to stay calm. But as I listen further, I realize that it's shouting instead of screaming. And the shouting belongs to a tenor male voice; one that I could never forget, even if I wanted to.

"Release me!" Says the shouting voice. "Where is she?" Thumps and heavy breathing follow. "Bring it on, you bastard." The voice lowers. More thumps and wheezes of the breath.

Oh no.

The shouting ceases, obviously the struggle has finished.

I jump to my feet and almost run into the ice wall as three figures enter the little cave. One of the figures is slumped, his body practically dragged by James, his blond hair matted with dark liquid.

"Oh no…" I can hear my pulse in my head. "Oh Jake…"

He lifts his head up at my voice and looks at me. His eyes are filled with relief, but deeper than that is worry. I place my hand on the ice wall, unable to help myself, and jerk back. A hiss escapes my lips, as my fingers burn with cold.

Jake's eyes turn angry as he watches me, and he begins to struggle again. But I can tell that he's weak because it seems as if even breathing is difficult for him. James places his hand on Jake's back and Jake lurches to the floor in a series of spasms.

"Stop!" I yell. "What are you doing?"

James looks up and smiles at me. Jake stills. I stare at his body on the floor, my heart dripping with dread. I know how Tenebris Daemon plans on forcing me to do her will. It's just as it was foretold.

"Oh, Jake," I cry. "I told you not to come!" He lifts his head and looks at me again. Even his eyes seem to have lost their fire. It's as if the life is going out of him. My voice rises as I practically scream at him. "I told you not to come!" I bang my fists against the walls. "Why didn't you listen to me?! Why?" My breath hitches, as the sobs break free. But I do not cry, the crying is done inside. On the outside, I'm bent on staying strong, letting my anger fill me.

At the corner of my eyes I can see Tenebris Daemon smiling at me triumphantly, but I pay no attention to her. I am completely focused on Jake.

"I couldn't, Rose." He gets out, his eyes still glued to mine. "I couldn't let you go."

"Jake," I cry, half in anger and half in desperation. "It was my choice! I did this to save you! And now I practically did it for nothing! Jake, you're so smart. But why do you have to be so stupid now?"

His eyes spark. "Because love makes us fools, Rose." He smiles at me sadly. "And I will not, no, I cannot live without you."

I put my palms on the wall as if I could reach him. I will my palms to be warm, hot as fire, so that I will not be burned.
"Oh Jake. Jake, Jake, Jake, Jake…" I whisper. "I love you so much. But I am giving my life for you… why do you waste that gift?"

"Because that's not a gift," He says back. "I don't want your life, your life is yours to live, not to give away! And I want you to live it with me!" He pushes himself up and looks me squarely in the eyes. "There is no world for me without you. So it's you and me together. For everything." James grabs Jake's shoulders and forces him up.

"How sweet," James jeers, rolling his eyes.

"Indeed," Tenebris Daemon says, her eyes glinting. She turns her face to James but keeps her eyes on me. "Secure him. And make sure you put him somewhere she can see him."

I stare helplessly as I watch James drag Jake up and throw him against the wall. The stone in the wall wraps around Jake's arms and legs, creating shackles out of solid rock. All the while, Jake keeps his eyes on me.

I throw my palms against the barrier of a wall, trying to escape my prison in order to get him out of his. But the ice doesn't melt like it did before. Nothing happens. Tears blur in my eyes. I am not concentrated enough to make the ice to melt; I can't think about anything except Jake being chained up.

"Why?" I croak out; silent but insistent tears break free and run down my face. "Why, Jake? Why?"

He doesn't reply. Jake just continues staring at me. James is smiling at us cruelly; he seems to find our torment amusing.

Tenebris Daemon watches me, her red eyes glowing. I turn my attention to her.

"Let him go. You don't need him. Let him go." I say to her.

"I will." She smiles, showing a full row of white teeth. "If you give me what I want."

"I—" I start.

"No, Rose!" Jake yells. "Don't you dare do anything for her!" James looks at Jake with bored eyes and places a hand on his body. Jake starts twitching like he's in pain, blood starts running down his nose; but he doesn't cry out.

"But she won't be doing anything for me." Tenebris Daemon says. "She'll be doing it for you…" She steps past James and he lets go of Jake. Jake stops convulsing and just hangs there, panting.

Tenebris Daemon runs her fingers across his stomach; Jake glares at her with hate filled eyes even as the rest of his body sags with torture. "You should have seen the fight he put up." Tenebris Daemon smiles at Jake, then turns her head and fixes her attention on me. "He actually managed to get past our first defenses. We only found him in the lower tunnels. And it was very hard to get him to obey." She takes her hand off his body. He relaxes but still breathes hard. I stare at the part of his abdominal section where Tenebris Daemon had placed her hand, the shirt is ripped and on his skin there are burn marks. The marks are the shape of her hand.

"You'll do what I want Rose." She growls as she walks towards me. "You'll do what I want. Or else I'll torture him, and then kill him. And if that doesn't work; I'll continue on to everyone else that you love." Her eyebrows go up as she grins viciously, her face contorting into that monster. "But I think dear Jake here will do well enough."

I shake my head a couple of times, denial washing through me. This can't be happening. The tears come faster now and the weight in my chest increases. I already feel myself weakening. And I sense that Jake can feel it too.

"Rose! I didn't come here to be the reason for you helping her. So don't," He says quietly, staring intently at me.

"You shouldn't have come here at all!" I nearly scream at him. My hysteria's rising, I should control myself better. I should, but I can't. Not when the person I love is being used against me.

"I know." Jake groans. "I know, Rose! I couldn't think about anything but finding you." His eyes glisten. "I'm sorry."

"Now," Tenebris Daemon says, reclaiming my attention. "Should I start torturing him? Or will you comply?"

"I don't even know what you want!" I shout at her, the anger and hate filling my heart. I can feel the darkness over-taking the light, but I fight against it; I still have love and hope. Though they are diminishing, they are still there.

"I want you to give into the darkness. And once your heart is filled with it, it will be mine. And you will help me." She says.

"Why would I do that?"

"Because if you don't, he dies."

"Well, it wouldn't make a difference, now would it? Because as long as I have love for him and for anyone in my heart, I can never be truly dark." I stand up straighter. "But if I do give into the darkness, then I won't really care whether he's dead or not. Isn't that how it is? Right now, I'm half and half."

"You are not half and half!" Her voice rises. "Your light is still forcing the vile darkness away. *You* are still forcing the darkness away. The darkness that enables you to have might is the most powerful thing, because you won't care what you do to get what you want!"

"And that's what makes it evil." I murmur, my voice getting quieter with realization. "Many things will stand in the way, but cold darkness doesn't care. I already have the innocent darkness, the natural darkness that is uncorrupted by the world. But I have not accepted the darkness that will turn me into a monster that craves blood. That type of vile darkness will just devour. It's evil."

"Well," She says dangerously. "There are other ways to make you do what I want. Maybe if I actually act, rather than just speak, then you will comply."

My eyes grow wider with fear as Jake eyes close, preparing for the worst.

But something makes me stay quiet. It is like wings wrapping around me, keeping me comforted, letting me know that nothing will happen.

Trust me. I hear a voice in my mind say, and my eyes flicker to Jakes'. He smiles at me weakly. *I didn't come here to die, Rose. It's all planned. Others are coming. But I needed to be here in order for them to find us. Stay strong. Don't worry about me. Do not give in.*

Just as he finishes his sentence in my mind, Tenebris Daemon places a hand on Jakes' head. Jake starts writhing uncontrollably, his eyes roll to the back of his head, but he stays silent as I watch in horror. Blood trickles down his nose and finally, he screams. He screams as if his worst nightmares are being brought to life. He screams as if he is no longer conscious of what is happening, as if he can't control his own actions.

He screams as if he wants to die.

And I, unable to help myself, scream along with him.

■ ■ ■

"Stop!" I finally shriek. "Stop!" I don't know how long it's been since his first scream, but I finally break when his screams quiet down into whimpers because he doesn't have strength enough to scream. I forget what Jake told me about not worrying and about not giving in. I just can't stand him getting tortured like that. "Please. Stop." Tenebris Daemon takes her hands off Jake and looks at me.

"Will you give me your power?" She questions.

"I don't know how," I sob. She places her hand on Jake again, and his scream fills the cave once more. Blood drips from his nose and ears and splatters on the floor, creating a dark red puddle.

"What are you doing to him? What's happening?" I ask, sobbing, because I've never seen torture like this. It is like she's torturing him inside his head, she doesn't do anything physical; it seems mental. Every time he cries out, it is like he is seeing or hearing something that hurt him more than any wound could.

And it's the worst type of pain I've ever seen.

"You have to submit to me. Then whatever you have is mine." She says smoothly, casually. It ignites my anger and sets my nerves on fire. My vision turns red and I press myself against the ice wall, surging forward, wanting to break free.

"I wouldn't do that if I were you." She growls, but I keep beating and throwing myself against the wall, unable to stop. Cracks appear from the force that I use. Strength will have to do because melting requires concentration and I have none of that.

But anger has given me strength.

I cry out as my arms and body start to ache horribly with each impact, but I continue. I feel it jar through my whole body, vibrating my bones and jolting my guts.

Tenebris Daemon glares at me when the crack widens, as if shocked that I have enough strength. Pain laces up my arm, partly because of the impact and partly because of the cold, but I can't think of anything except getting out.

Jake groans and lifts his head. When his eyes focus on me and registers what I'm doing, he struggles against his restraints. His movement only fuels me, and I throw myself against the wall with twice the strength I had before, with no other thought except to get out.

"Rose!" Jake yells at me weakly. "What are you doing? You're going to get yourself killed!" I fling myself against the wall, my heart pumping when more cracks appear.

I can already feel it weakening.

I can do this. I have to. I have to get out.

It appears as if my anger and hate and the will for freedom has given me more strength than I've ever had before.

My body hurts but I continue to fight.

"Why aren't you stopping her?" James hisses the question at Tenebris Daemon. She just holds her hand up to shush him silently; I can feel that her eyes never leave me. In the back of my mind, I feel amusement and revelation rolling off her, as well as a dark sort of curiosity. I know that it's bad that she's not stopping me, but I don't care.

With a yell, I slam my body harshly against the wall and feel it crumble.

But the power that I used to break the ice drives me forward, and I fall hard on the floor outside of my cage. The ice that I fall on cuts my bare skin, blood trickles down my arm. I groan as I push myself up, but then smile when I realize that I escaped that ice prison.

"Interesting…" I hear Tenebris Daemon exclaim softly. I look her way to see her red eyes gazing at me intently. I stand up unsteadily and run to Jake.

"What are you doing?" He mumbles; his eyes are wide with amazement and fear. "Why did you do that?" I reach to touch his face, his eyes close when my fingers meet his cheek. Then they open, blazing with a blue fire that was not there a second ago. Even as I watch, his nose stops bleeding and his eyes clear. His breathing steadies and I breathe out a sigh of relief.

"I had to." I tell him, even as I feel James come up behind me. "I couldn't stand it. I just had to."

James grips the back of my neck and I feel darkness creep around me. The spot where his fingers touch my skin burns coldly, and I find myself gasping for air. Then suddenly I'm in the air, it feels like flying, then my body hits something hard and I cry out in pain as I slide to the floor. I hear Jake roar in anger.

I struggle to blink the stars out of my eyes.

James threw me… He *threw* me! My back got the worst of it; it feels heavy. I cough to try to relieve the pressure, and when I take my hand away from my mouth, it's red with fresh blood. I spit the blood out of my mouth in disgust and growl as I look up at James. He walks towards me.

"Not a very smart thing to do, Roza." He murmurs as his hands go around my throat and pulls me up. I claw at his hands, trying to break his hold. My lungs burn for air. With what feels like the last of my strength, I swing my leg and kick him in the crotch. He releases me and falls to the floor, hugging himself. I guess evil dudes still feel pain in that area. My legs were always the strongest part of my body; it pays off now.

"Really?" I say to him shortly, heaving a little because of the air I lost. "I thought it was smart. I thought it was very smart." I kick him in the stomach. "Don't ever throw me again." I growl at him, decide that I like kicking him, and do it again.

When I'm satisfied, I turn to face the stare that I've been feeling throughout the whole commotion.

She is just standing there.

Standing and watching with those eyes of hers and a smile that curls on her lips. My body screams at me as I force myself to stand up straighter and face her.

I will not look weak in front of her. But I already feel my adrenaline fueled strength dying.

"That was very good, Rose." She seems to purr. Her face changes even as I watch, even as she speaks. "But that will not be enough to beat me." She lunges for me; her glowing red eyes fill my vision. Faster than I thought possible, I feel her claws around my neck as she forces me against the wall. Jagged stone presses against my back. "I'm impressed actually," She hisses through her sharp teeth. I can hear Jake struggling against his restraint; I feel his fear. Of course. He's never seen Tenebris Daemon's true face before. Even as I'm aware of Jake, I can't bring myself to look away from the eyes of the monster in front of me. "You used simple physical strength. No powers at all. You were probably desperate. Can't concentrate enough to use your influences, can you?" She nods towards James, who has recovered slightly. It seems as if all my kicks were very hard. "I'm a little disappointed in him."

"Really?" I spit out. "I wonder why; he only got beat up by a girl half his weight."

"Don't act smart." She says. "I can feel your fear. I can feel your anger and your hate." She smiles at me. "They make you stronger. That's good. Let them consume you."

"No," I gasp. She tightens her grip, her nails digging into the skin on my neck. My mind blurs as the agony consumes me. Black spots darken my vision. Then she releases me, and the blood flows from my neck. I fall to the ground for there is no longer anything to support me. And this time, I stay there.

"Rose!" Jake shouts. "Rose! Get up!" I look at him to see his eyes tear filled. His muscles become strained as he pulls against his manacles. He's angry. I can feel it. The tears in his eyes disappear as he turns his gaze towards Daemon. Now they are filled with hate.

"A pity you can't heal yourself like you can heal other people." She says as she walks away from me, as she walks towards Jake. "I wonder…" She purrs as she reaches Jake. "… If there are wounds too deep for you to heal." She tears away Jake's shirt, revealing his naked chest. The horrible ice burn left by her earlier is gone. "See how you healed him?" She continues talking as she traces his stomach with her clawed fingers, leaving bloodied scratch marks on him. Whether it hurts, I don't know. Because Jake doesn't do anything, he just glares at her, his chest heaving.

"Don't touch him," I say, but my voice sounds wrong. The wounds on my neck are still bleeding, though I no longer feel the pain. I must be losing a lot of blood.

"But why?" She says, her ugly face moving as she smiles cruelly at me. "He's perfect. Beautiful face, beautiful body." Her hands move to his chest. Right over his… "But does he have a beautiful heart?" and she digs her clawed nails into his chest as if she could take out his heart. Jake jerks, but his jaw stays locked as if he's trying not to scream. This pain is different, perhaps not as unbearable as the pain she performed before. But this pain will kill him.

I scream at her. I scream in anger at my own weakness, at my own disability. The hate I feel grows and clogs out even the remaining hope. But I still feel my love and that's how I know I can control it. I am doing this because I love Jake, and even as the hate fills my heart, the love still holds some space. I push myself up and to my feet. I no longer feel weak from loss of blood, but I feel strong because I know what I have to do. I stand straight and meet her eyes.

"Don't touch him." I repeat, but more coldly than before.

She takes her claws out with a sharp jerk, and Jake jerks along with her. Blood pours out of his wound. Though she hadn't touched his heart, the wound is deep. It's mortal.

"Much better." She hisses through a victorious smile.

Blood pumps through me as my anger increases. But worry clears my head and gets rid of some of my bloodlust. I don't know what else to do. So I run towards her and jump over her, planning to touch Jake to help heal him. But before I reach him, someone grabs my hair and pulls me back.

"Not so fast," Tenebris Daemon hisses, her teeth only centimeters away from my face. "Agree to come with me, and follow me. And I'll let you heal him." She inches closer. "Don't agree, and I'll make you watch as he dies, knowing that even though you could have healed him, you were unable to."

I look to Jake with dread. Even though he's as weak as he can be, he shakes his head at me. But I don't heed him, because I cannot live with that kind of guilt again.

"Okay, Yes. I'll—" I start but am interrupted when Jake yells and pulls his arms and feet from his rock shackles, rolls on the ground, gets up right in front of Tenebris Daemon and heaves her hard against the wall. Her body flies through the stone and continues to be thrown through more walls by some invisible force. When she becomes impossible to see through all the rock rubble and dust, Jake slumps to the ground, weak.

I grab him quickly and support him.

"How did you do that?" I ask him as I kiss his face many times in relief.

"I used the element of surprise," He replies, his voice already seeming to grow stronger. The love I feel for him fills me as I take him into my arms and kiss him on the lips. He holds my face to his with his fingers on my chin as he kisses me back.

"Not that!" I laugh, when I can finally break free. "I mean how did you throw her through so many walls when you were so weak?"

"I couldn't stand the thought of you going with her. And that made me stronger." He explains softly. I move my hand over the wound on his chest, the bleeding stops and it looks a lot better, but it isn't healing fully.

"It's not healing." I mumble, fear creeping into my chest.

"No," He says. "And it probably won't. I think she cursed me. I won't heal until she dies."

"Then she must die." I say firmly. "And now." I stand up and look at the rubble.

"She's gone," He says softly.

"Yep." I say, silently cursing myself for being so unobservant. "And so is James."

30

The sound of running footsteps pulls me up short. I stop creeping along the never-ending cave and listen.

"Jake," I whisper. "You hear that?"

He stops walking and listens. "Yep,"

"Well, don't you think we should go check what that is?" I urge, wondering why he is so indifferent.

"I already know who it is." He turns to me with a smile.

"Oh. Who?" I look at him with raised eyebrows.

He looks past me and focuses on something. Then his smile widens and his eyes fill with relief.

"I thought you'd never make it." He says to someone behind me. I turn to see who he could be talking to. I suck in a breath of delight when I see three figures walking towards us.

"We got lost." Thomas replies with a shrug. Jake looks past Thomas at the other two with a look that said 'someone serious tell me what happened'.

"Some sort of earthquake made the part of the cave that we were in crumble. It sent us running for dear life and forced us to figure out another way to you guys." Cole says; his green eyes look at Jake in question.

"No earthquake," Jake says with a wry smile, he places his hand on the back of his head and starts rubbing as if he were shy or unsure. In spite of everything, I can't help thinking that this is extraordinarily cute. "That was me; I threw Daemon through a couple of walls."

There is a twinkle of laughter in Coles' eyes, but his lips only pull up slightly. "Good for you."

Cole then looks down at me and his expression darkens. "What happened to you?"

I look down at myself and wonder why Cole didn't ask Jake that question, because I think Jake is more hurt than me.

A sharp breath wheezes past my lips as I take in my condition.

My shirt is ripped in many places and can no longer be called anything but a bloody rag. There is a long gash on my left side rib from my back to the side, which is rough with dry blood; probably an injury I acquired when I hit and slid down the wall. I touch my face and feel a sharp pain on my right cheek, so I'm guessing there's a bruise or a cut. And my head still pounds from hitting the wall after James threw me.

I look at Jake and see that though his wound is worse than mine, it probably looks better for most of it is healed because of my touch. Plus, it's only in one spot. But he's the one that's poisoned. He's the one that's cursed. And he is looking at me with a pained expression. As if I'm the one who is in danger.

"Nothing," I tell Cole.

"Nothing?" His eyes flash. He glances at Jake. "How can you even look at her and continue?"

Jake's eyes flicker back to mine briefly before returning to Cole. "I haven't been looking at her." He says hoarsely, and I realize that he's right; I noticed that every time he looked at me, he quickly looked away. As if he couldn't take the sight of me. "Plus, it wouldn't do any good. I would never have been able to stop her from carrying on."

"And you know why." I say to Jake, my eyes harden. "Now for one more reason than before." He looks at me again and I'm suddenly scared that I might lose him.

I hear someone suck in a breath.

"No," Angel groans, her eyes fill with tears as she looks between Jake and me. I now remember that Angel can sense thoughts.

"What?" Thomas demands; his face turns serious. Angel shakes her head and looks at me.

"Jake's been—" I gulp, unable to finish. "He's been…"

"I've been cursed." Jake says matter-of-factly. He takes my hand to steady me. "My wound won't heal, and I think that it will never heal until Tenebris Daemon dies."

Thomas and Cole look angry. But I can feel worry as well as hate rolling off of them.

I try to reassure them as much as possible.

"I've healed him some. But it won't fully heal. The wound used to be mortal. Now it's healed a little and it's stopped bleeding. But I think that there may be poison in Tenebris Daemon that she passed onto Jake." I feel Jake glance at me, I haven't told anyone my thoughts, and now I spill them all out. "Anything that evil has a black heart and cold blood. What flows in her veins might as well be poison." I take a breath. "She dug her nails into Jake and almost clawed his heart out. She didn't finish, but I can't heal him. She is the only one

with that poison and if she's gone, the curse will vanish."
Unconsciously, I reach for my neck where there are four open
wounds on one side, and one on the other side.

It has never occurred to me until now that I could be
poisoned too.

"What's that you're touching?" Angel asks, her eyes reflect her worry.

"Rose is poisoned as well." Cole says; his eyes fill with
comprehension and pain.

Jake cusses under his breath.
"Why did that never occur to me before?" He comes to
me and takes my face in his hands and turns it to the side to
reveal my neck more clearly. "You were clawed too. I never
thought that it didn't heal."

My eyes water. "Don't you remember Jake? Tenebris
Daemon said it herself. You know I can't heal myself."

He forces me to look him in the eye, his hands still cupping my face. His grip is rather strong. The blueness of his
eyes fills my vision.
"Where else are you hurt like this? I asked you just now
where you had been hurt. And you said the obvious. Your
head and your side; your skull is probably cracked from the
impact and you got scratched while sliding down the wall.

But has she or James touched you anywhere else where you could have been poisoned?"

"No," I croak out. His grip loosens.

"I can't lose you." He says quietly.

"Then I guess we understand each other."

He looks at me with a soft expression and I feel a smile creeping on my lips.

"Well then," Thomas clears his throat, bringing all attention to him. "We had better get going if we don't want the two of you to drop dead in front of us."

I know he means this lightly, but the tension in the cave corridor increases. As we start down the cave, the gnawing feeling that I'm missing something keeps popping up.

It's something about what Thomas said. He immediately thinks that this curse, this poison that is in Jake and my veins will eventually kill us.

Isn't that what everyone and anyone would think?

But I'm not anyone, and I think differently.

And what I think is too horrible to even bring up for there are things worse than death.

What if this poison could be used to bring sickness on us, or even worse? What if it could be used to torture or control us?

■ ■ ■

I know that we're getting closer because it is getting colder. That and the fact that the five cuts in my neck are getting so icy that it feels warm.

"We're almost there," Cole whispers, his breath coming out in a puff of mist before him. I get a strange sense of dejavu.

"And where exactly is 'there'?" Angel asks softly, her voice holds no fear but there is dread.

"The evil witches lair of course!" Thomas says sarcastically.

"I'm serious," she murmurs.

I look at her curiously, wondering why she has suddenly turned all quiet and glum; but she avoids my eye contact.

I open myself up to sense her feelings and am almost crushed with the intensity of her emotions; she's extremely worried, sad and angry. Angel is also scared, but not for herself or Jake, who's hurt; she's scared for me.

"What's wrong Angel?" I ask, concerned for her.

Everyone stops and looks at me, then at her when I ask. It's probably funny to be asking such a question when we're in a place like this, but there is something else bothering her, and I want to know what it is.

When Angel doesn't answer me, I push even more. "I can feel your emotions. You can't hide what you're feeling; and by knowing your emotions I can also guess the directions your thoughts. So, tell me what's troubling you? What are you so scared for?"

"I'm scared for you," Angel says, her eyes glinting.

"I know; I can feel that," I reply, my mouth pulling down in a confused frown. "Why are you scared for me?"

"Other than the obvious?" Angel says. "Well, I think we're getting a lot closer. Because I can kind of sense Tenebris Daemon's thoughts."

This shocks me. And judging from the expressions of the three boys next to me, it shocks them too.

"What?" Jake exclaims. "That's kind of great! What is she thinking? What's her strategy? If we know this, then we can't get caught easily."

"It's not like I get a full stream. Only bits and pieces." Angel explains. "But I can hear and picture one thing really clearly, almost as if she wants me to hear it."

"Well what is it?" Cole asks; his face is a mask of impatience.

"It's Rose." She says; her lips quivering as she looks at me. "Tenebris Daemon wants her to come; almost like she's inviting her." She sighs. "We won't have any problem finding her. She's making it easy, this passage that we're walking in leads us straight to where she is."

"That's great." I say, shutting out my feelings of fear. "Let's go and kill her. We have to." I look at Jake and see his chest wound; my eyes harden. "There's no choice. If we don't kill her then Jake's wound will remain open and poisoned; it'll probably also get infected." I look away from Jake when he looks towards me; his eyes hold a worry for me that I have no concern for.

"Don't forget; you're also poisoned by her. So you need it too, Rose." Cole says gravely.

"Sure," I say, even though I know that it won't matter.

If my plan works and if the prophecy is true, then it won't matter whether I'm still poisoned because I will be dead anyways. For after I kill Tenebris Daemon, the darkness will be passed on to the closest being, which will be me. And to slay that darkness, I will have to destroy myself.

Jake looks at me sharply, his mouth hardening into a grim line; he knows the prophesy as well. Angel glances at me too, her mouth parting in a gasp of alarm.

I avoid eye contact with them and Cole. Because I know that if I look at Cole, he'd know my thoughts. He just knows me that well. I won't be able to hide anything from him.

"Let's go," I start walking before I get any answers. I have to keep going or else I might give into my fear and run the other way. And if I do that, I know that I would be serving the very darkness that I am trying to destroy.

31

The tunnel opens up to a huge circular room. The walls are jagged with old rocks; the only source of light in the room is a bonfire in the middle. I step out into the room. Where I stand, it is freezing, but I can feel the slight heat of the flickering fire. I feel the others come up behind me, guarded and aware.

Wicked female laughter fills the cave, so unbearable that I actually cover my ears with my hands, unable to help myself. This continues for what seems like a long time. By the time the laughter stops, I am crouched on the ground, my palms pressing against my skull. When I recover, I realize that the others are gathered around me. Their worried expressions fill my vision. Did none of them have the same reaction? I stand up straighter and look around.

"What was that, Rose?" Cole asks.

"Nothing," I murmur. I am unsure of what to answer, unsure of why I am suddenly so weak, and not wanting them to realize that I might be losing my control.

Jake comes up next to me and takes my hand. I feel the pressure that he applies; it anchors me to warmth, to hope.

"It didn't look like nothing." He whispers. "We all heard her laughter. But you were the only one who reacted with pain." His eyes search my face, trying to find answers. But I have none.

"I don't know." I say and let my eyes scan the room again.

This time, I see a shaded figure at the far end of the room. The figure stands behind the fire, so I can't see clearly. I take a step forward for a better view, and the figure looks up at me. I see a pair of bright red eyes, the glint of white sharp teeth, then nothing. The figure seems to have disappeared into thin air.

"Did you guys see that?" I ask; fear creeps into my heart and voice, even as I try to ward it away.

"See what?" Angel asks.

"There was a person. A thing." I point a shaky hand. "Over there. Behind that fire." I look back around at their confused faces. My hysteria is rising. "Didn't you guys see that? It had red eyes and white sharp teeth."

"Rose," Cole says steadily. I look at him to see him returning my gaze with a queer look in his eyes, his eyes flicker anxiously when he sees the escalating panic in mine. "There was nothing there."

I look back at the fire and flinch. The figure is back. But this time, standing in the fire. I take a shaky step back, unable to help myself. The figure just stands there as the fire burns it. I don't know whether it is Tenebris Daemon or not. I can't make out anything but white skin, white sharp teeth, and red glowing eyes.

Against the marble skin, the fire scorches look gruesome. But the figure doesn't show pain; it just looks at me, and smiles horribly. I can't help but look into its eyes. In them I see visions of my family dying; almost as if this figure is telling me what's going to happen, what it is going to do.

My heart pounds painfully and I let out a small scared sound. I step back further when the figure seems to break apart into ash, bits and pieces peeling off its face and floating to the ground.

Jake grabs my elbows from behind as I bump into him. I turn to him. His expression changes from confusion to shock as he sees the terror on my face.

"Don't you see it?" I whisper. I clutch his shirt in my fists.

"No, Rose," He replies, worried. His eyes flash, alarmed and aware. "I don't see it. I don't know what you're seeing. I can't see it."

I turn my head around to look at the fire. The figure has reappeared. This time, it's less than five feet away from me. Its face marked with hideous lines, blood runs down its lip and covers its teeth. In its hands there are hearts. I know whose hearts they are as if it were written. I know from the look on the figure's face. They are my parents' hearts. I choke on a sob and press my face in Jake's chest.

"Make it go away," I plead desperately. I hate feeling weak and scared. But it seems that I have no choice. These feelings dominate, leaving no space for anything else. I feel Jake's arms wrap around me, his breath on my hair.

"Rose," He whispers. "It's okay. Whatever you're seeing. It's not real. It can't be real."

I shake my head.

"We don't see anything, Rose," Cole says. "It's all in your head. It must be. You're hallucinating. Tenebris Daemon is making you hallucinate."

"It's real! It's real… Or else I wouldn't feel like this." I feel myself trembling against Jake and I hug him tighter. But it feels wrong. *He* feels wrong. I look up and scream, pushing myself as far away from him as possible. Because it's no longer Jake, it's that figure that was by the bonfire. Its face and hands still bloody. I stumble back, my heart pounds so hard that it hurts. The figure steps towards me.

"Rose," It says. "What's wrong? It's me! Jake."

"No, no, no," I mumble brokenly. "You're not Jake. You're that evil devil thing. You had my parents' hearts in your hands. You're a *killer*." I hiss the last word through my panicked gasps.

The figure raises its bloody hands and I step back, terrified. It hesitates as it sees my retreat.

"Jake," I hear a voice say and look over to where Angel used to stand. But in her place is another figure, almost as horrible as the one with the bloody hands. "This won't work. I can sense her thoughts. She doesn't see you or any of us. She only sees monsters." The figure that just spoke has her grip on another monster, almost as if it were keeping the other from coming towards me.

I don't listen to what the second figure says. It's just trying to trick me into thinking that I'm imagining things. It's trying to make me think that they aren't exactly what she says I see. Monsters.

"Rose," The first monster says. Its bloody lips move, it has Jake's voice. "You're hallucinating. Please. I'm not a monster; I'm Jake. Try to see that."

"No," I say. "You're trying to trick me. You're not Jake. You're not." I take another step back. "Though you have his voice, you don't have his face or heart. You're just making yourself sound like him to trick me."

The monster that says that it's Jake walks towards me. I move back and feel the hard wall of the cave against my back. I can't move away any more. But the figure still moves towards me. I press myself harder to the wall, wanting to escape. The sharpness of the jagged wall cuts my skin, small beads of blood appear.

The monster stops.

"Don't hurt yourself." It says. I look at it with cold eyes, some of my fear disappearing as my anger rises. How dare it tell me to do something as if it were actually concerned? It takes a closer step towards me, so close now.

And I snap.

I throw myself at the ugly figure, tackling it and forcing it to the ground. I roll on the ground and kneel by the bonfire. Then I take up a burning log and hold it in front of me. I hear movement behind me, but I don't look up.

"No!" The figure I had just tackled shouts, probably at the thing behind me that moved. "You'll just provoke her. Let me handle it. I'll take care of it."

Some voice in my head tells me that this means that the figure is going to take care of me, as in, kill me. My muscles tense up in preparation. Then I charge with the log above my head, swinging, ready to make a fatal blow to the head. But the figure catches the log right above its head. Its too strong, I can't crush its skull with the log. But I don't let go of it. I keep applying force. Maybe if I can't give a killing blow I could still set it on fire.

"Rose," It says. "Stop!"

But I don't. It's evil, and must die. Or else it will kill everyone I love.

The log inches closer to his head, I push with all my might, but the figure is stronger. I can feel my strength waning, so I kick the figure in the stomach and hit it on the side with the log. It kicks at the log in my hand, and I lose grip. After that, I don't know how else to fight, so I just throw a fist at its face. It catches my wrist. I throw my second fist, but it catches that wrist too. I try to struggle, but the thing spins me around until my back hits the wall painfully.

I let out a gasp of agony. The rock cuts through the skin of my back, but the figure presses me against the wall, its body is right up against mine; keeping me from being able to move. I close my eyes because I don't want to see the cracked bloody face, or the glowing red eyes and what's behind them. Tears stream down my face.

"Rose," I hear the figure plead. "Please see me." Its voice is a mask of pain. This confuses me. I open my eyes and for a second I see Jake's face and relax. Then the ugly face of the monster returns and I cringe and shut my eyes again. "Rose." It says again. "It's me," I hear again. "Please, Rose. Don't think I'm evil. It's me, Jake. I love you. Oh God… I love you so much." I feel a slight soft pressure on my lips and my eyes fly open in surprise and mild disgust because I think that the monster is kissing me.

When I see Jake's smooth golden skin and his dark blonde hair, I stop fighting.

He opens his eyes, and the piercing blueness brings me fully out of my hallucination.

Jake's eyes fill with relief, then he kisses me again. And I don't resist, I kiss him back, clinging to him. When he breaks away, I would have fallen to the ground if he had not caught and supported me.

"What happened?" I ask weakly. I see Angel, Cole, and Thomas running around the bonfire, towards us. Their faces are no longer scary.

"You were hallucinating…" Jake replies quietly. "Quite badly actually."

I nod, because I know exactly how bad it was.

"I'm sorry," I cry softly, horrified that I had tried to kill him. And ashamed that I had and could actually think that Angel and Jake and all the rest could actually be evil. "I'm sorry I tried to hurt you. I'm sorry I thought you were monsters. You aren't, you never could be."

"Shh," Jake whispers and pulls me close. He strokes my hair tenderly, and I immediately feel better. "It's okay. It wasn't your fault."

I shiver against him.
"What's happening to me? Why did I hallucinate?"

"I don't know," Jake says in a hoarse voice.

"What if it happens again?" I look up at him. "What if I try to kill you again?" My lips tremble. "I should go to her on my own Jake."

"No," He whispers and kisses my brow. "We're sticking together."

"Plus," I hear Thomas say and turn towards him. "We could totally take you on." He gives a reassuring grin. "You are one vicious fighter, Rose. But you ain't got these guns." And he shows his muscles. Amazing how Thomas can still try to be funny at a time like this.

I smile at him, my heart swelling with compassion for my friend.

"You won't last long if she actually uses her powers." Cole says with a smirk. "Even with your guns." He punches Thomas playfully in the stomach.

Funny. I've never seen Cole be playful before. Then he looks at me, his expression serious, and my smile fades away.

"Which brings me to this question. Why didn't you use your powers to kill Jake? Especially if you thought he was an evil monster." Cole's eyebrows furrow.

"Gee thanks," Jake mumbles.

"I…" I start, trying to figure out how to put it in words. "I guess I panicked. I had no control over anything, especially my emotion, which are part of my power. The closest thing I had control of was my physical strength. My fighting skills, and even that was very chaotic. I had no control over my mind or emotions, at all. And those are the most important part for me."

"And what if you 'panic' when you're fighting Tenebris Daemon?" Cole asks, his eyes hardening with anger. "If you can't use your powers, she'd kill you in seconds." He moves towards me and grabs my shoulder, pulling me away from Jake and forcing me to look at him in the eye. "And what if she makes you hallucinate? Makes you think that she is a friend and we are the enemy. Because that's what she just did, and we can't afford that to happen again." His face is so close to mine that our noses almost touch. "You can't defend yourself if she makes you lose control. And I can't lose you." He whispers.

I touch his cheek, my eyes softening with understanding. I know his fear. I feel it for all of them.

"You won't," I whisper back. For a brief second I think that he might kiss me. But then the room darkens and the bonfire turns blue.

"Well, well," A chilling voice from the shadow says. "What do we have here?"

Cole glances up sharply; his emotions are so intense that I actually take a step away from *him* instead of the source of the voice. His eyes burn with murderous rage. I look to where Cole has his eyes fixed and my breath catches. Tenebris Daemon doesn't even look hurt, doesn't even look like she just went through ten walls.

I see James beside her and let myself smile a little in victory. For though he doesn't look injured, he eyes me with a hate that lets me know that I may have damaged him forever.

I am suddenly very proud of my kick. Wanting to ignore my churning stomach, I decide to act witty. Though I feel far from being brave.

"How it going down there, James?" I ask him with a smirk. I catch a brief feeling of surprise from him before it is replaced by anger. "What?" I say. "Shocked that I would even talk to you after kicking your butt? I'm not scared of you."

"Oh," He sneers. "You have no idea what I have in mind for you. If you did, you'd be terrified." His eyes glint. "In fact, I'm sure you would rather have me kill or torture you than what I'm thinking of doing."

Dread fills me, along with disgust. But before I could answer back, I hear a growl behind me. I turn to see Jake walking forward slowly, dangerously, his eyes focused on James.

"You'd lose your head before you could even touch her." Jake says. He walks to stand next to me, touching Cole's shoulder lightly as he passed.

Now I have them on either side of me, like my bodyguards. And though I am glad they are there, I wish that I were alone. I dismiss James with a last repulsive look and fix my attention on Tenebris Daemon. She is looking at us with a bored yet amused expression. I could almost read her thoughts as clearly as I can feel her emotions. She found this taunting childish but interesting. It's as if everything were a game to her, a game that she will always win at because it is a game that she controls.

Tenebris Daemon finally looks at me after glancing at everyone else and scorning them with a look. Her gaze does linger on Jake a little longer; her emotions are a mix of interest, hunger, and irritation. I do not like those emotions in her or anyone when it is directed towards Jake.

Then she does something that makes my stomach turn.

She smiles.

"How nice of you all to join us!" She exclaims, as if she means it. "Of course, all I really need is Rose. But since you're all here, I've got something planned for each of you." She tilts her head, assessing. "You see, only Rose needs to give into me or die. The rest of you don't."

"'The rest of you don't' my ass," Thomas mumbles beneath his breath.

"Join me," Tenebris Daemon continues as if Thomas hadn't said anything. "You'll have power you can never imagine. All you have to do is change sides, and there are many ways to do that. James here did, and look how powerful he is now. Cole did," She glanced towards him. "But then something took him away from me, and see how weak he is now."

"What do you mean when you said Rose needs to give into you?" Angel asks, her voice trembling.

"Well, I want her power. The only way I can get that is if I absorb it by killing her, or just take it from her; leaving her with nothing except her beating heart." Tenebris Daemon purses her lips. "The second option only works if she is willing. So technically, she has to give it to me."

"How can you think I would do that? Especially if it makes me a vegetable." I say, angry with myself for putting my friends in such a position.

"Oh, dear Roza," She sighs. "Still so naïve after all this time?" She flicks her finger and my body starts walking forward. No matter how hard I try, I can't stop my legs from moving. I'm close enough to her that she just has to lean her face towards me to speak into my ear. "If you do what I want," She whispers viciously. "I'll let your friends *go*. I won't make them join me, or kill them. And I know that you think that you have to kill me to get rid of that poison that flows in your dear sweetheart's blood, but that's not the only way. I can take it away, with a wave of my hand." With that, she flicks her hand in a gesture of dismissal and I fall to the floor. Pathetic.

"I'm sure you've guessed, being the clever girl that you are, what that poison in your blood can do." Tenebris Daemon says as she walks around my friends, towards the fire. "It's not the usual form of torture, but for honorable and free people like you, it's torture of the worst kind."

I close my eyes; horror fills my heart because I know that my previous assumption is right.

"And it's not just the physical kind of control. I can also manipulate your thoughts, make you see what I want you to see." She continues slowly. Her fingers dance in the fire; they are getting burned but she doesn't seem to care.

"The hallucinations…" Jake murmurs in realization.

I glance at him with tear filled eyes, because if I am poisoned and she can control me, then that means that Jake is also a victim. Daemon can control him too.

"Now you see what I can do," Tenebris Daemon says perilously soft. Someone grabs me from behind and pulls me up roughly. I feel warm breathing down my neck, and a hard grip on my wrist as my captor forces my hands behind my back. I try to break free, but for some reason, I'm not strong anymore.

"Don't struggle, beautiful," A deep voice says in my ear.

Shivers run down my spine as I feel James press my body closer to his, refraining me from moving. I look at Jake and see that he's looking at James and me, and though his face is tight with boiling emotions, he doesn't move towards me.

Neither does anyone else.

And I don't realize why until Cole takes a small step to me as if unable to help himself, and I feel the bite of sharp cold metal against my chest. I look down to see that James has a dagger in one hand.

The tip of it pointing at my heart.

32

I stop struggling. No one makes any move towards me.

"Of course," Tenebris Daemon says. "I don't need a dagger to kill her," She's addressing Jake and Cole. "But I thought that it might be more entertaining to watch."

"Why do you have to torture her," Jake says. Though his voice is steady, I can feel his fear. "Shouldn't you be torturing us instead? If you want her to do your will, we would be the key."

"Jake, what are you doing?" I yell and try to push forward, but James only grips me harder. I don't even know how he can have the strength to use one hand to hold both of mine behind my back and hold a dagger to my heart at the same time. Or maybe I'm just so much weaker than before that it's insanely easy to keep my captive.

"Just let her go," Jake is saying. "And we'll do whatever you want."

"Unfortunately," Tenebris Daemon says as she walks and stands in front of Jake. "I can hear your heartbeat." She raises her hand. "And I know you're lying." Her index finger touches the skin on Jake's temple and he falls to the ground.

Completely shocked, I don't do anything but stand there with James's grip on my wrist and an open mouth. A choked sound escapes my throat, but nothing else.

Cole rushes forward and puts his ear to Jake's mouth, then to his chest. Then he feels Jake's neck and wrist for a pulse. Cole looks up at Angel and Thomas, then at me.

"He's alive." Cole says. I let out a breath I didn't know I was holding.

"Of course, and he'll wake up in a bit," Tenebris Daemon beams. "I have great plans for that one, even greater than you Cole. There's much potential." She puts out her hand towards where Jake lies, crumpled, and lifts her hand. Jake's body rises from the ground and moves towards the wall. She is levitating him. Then, just like it had when I was in my ice prison, the stone wrapped itself around his arms and legs, creating shackles.

I glare at her with as much force as I can master. Cole steps away from Tenebris Daemon, moving closer to Angel and Thomas. She advances on them, and I can't do anything but watch.

"You're going to make wonderful toys," She says. "Decide now. What do you choose?"

"Hey lady, if you think that we'll actually switch to your side whilst you're threatening our friend, you've really got to fix your brain 'cause obviously you're a bit coo coo." Thomas says, eyes flashing; his voice is firm and slightly angry. Though he's completely serious, it seems that nothing can come out of his mouth without being funny. Yet, though it's funny, nothing can make me laugh right now.

"I see," Tenebris Daemon murmurs. Even though Thomas has insulted her, she doesn't look angry. She looks amused. The expression on her face changes to interest, as she looks Thomas over, as if rethinking her previous analysis.

"That's a no," Thomas says again, making sure his point got across.

"Very well," She says, and with a flick of her hand, Thomas is thrown against the wall as well. But instead of making shackles, the rocks devour his whole body; covering every single part but his face. Though dazed from the impact, Thomas struggles. But no matter how he tries, he can't move.

"Let him go!" Angel screams. Her eyes look at Thomas in horror; I feel her fear of losing her brother, as well as her friends, creeping back into her heart.

"Unfortunately," Tenebris Daemon says. "I can't do that." She starts walking around Cole and Angel. Her hungry eyes take them in as a lioness about to pounce on her prey would. "You see, I *know* about all your abilities. I know what sort of power you all have. Thomas is super strong, even stronger than Jake or Cole. However, Jake and Cole have other properties, not just super strength like Thomas does. That's why I already dismissed him. But, I could reconsider. Another enhancement that Thomas seems to have is his extra cockiness. And if that were used against my enemies, I would be very entertained." She says this cruelly, it's as if she were talking about Thomas like he is a dog.

She looks at Angel with a glint in her eyes. "And you. The mind reader. But you can only sense smidges of thoughts, not the whole stream. Not very strong. But if it were developed, you could be very useful to me." Her eyes measure Angel with distaste. "However, I can see that you would rather die than turn to me. So I'll give you just that. But first," She turns to Cole and walks up to him.

I try to break free again but just feel James's knife against my skin. I suck in ragged breaths because even though I'm in love with Jake, I love Cole too. And I don't want Tenebris Daemon to touch him.

But she does.

She tips his chin and kisses his cheek. "Come back to me, Cole." Her finger is still on his face. Cole doesn't move, but he looks like he's trying to. His gaze is murderous.

"Never," He hisses at her.

"Pfft," Tenebris Daemon replies. "It's all because of pretty little Rose. She's so sweet. So kind. So *pure*. Everyone falls in love with her. And that's what happened. Isn't it Cole?"

Coles' eyes shift to mine and linger. Tears form in my own and spill; I shake my head and whisper his name brokenly because I can feel that I'm causing him pain. And it hurts me.

"Yes," Cole says, moving his gaze back to Tenebris Daemon. "I've loved her from the first time I met her. And I love her now." Tenebris looks annoyed.

"Cole?" I hear a broken groan and look up to see that Jake has awoken. Just speaking looks like it takes effort. The veins stand out on his face and arms. I can hear his heart beating, trying its best to pump blood through his veins. To keep him alive.

"I'm sorry, Jake," Cole whispers back, and he looks like he means it.

"No…" Jake says, his face darkening. "No, Cole. *I'm* sorry. If I'd known… I would never intentionally cause you pain. "

At that moment, I feel such horrible anger at myself that I think I could be crushed by it. How could I do this? I'm causing them both pain. It's not Jake that's causing Cole pain.

It's me.

And Jake is acting like it's his fault and this just makes me irritated.

With a strangled cry, I use the fighting techniques that I had learned from Jake when we first met.

I move my body closer to James's, surprising him and giving me just enough room to jump without slicing my abdomen with the knife. I jump up and over James, ending up behind him.

Since he's still gripping my wrists tightly, I try to use that to my advantage. James's shoulder ball wouldn't turn that far, so I end up being able to bring him to his knees, free my hands because his arms no longer have much strength because they are in the wrong angle, and kick him to the ground.

I back up, and gather all my emotions.

All my feelings of pain, anger, and fear. All the slight relief that I felt when Jake woke up, and that little bit of happiness when I actually heard Cole say he loved me. But most of all, I hone the anger I feel at Tenebris Daemon.

How *dare* she threaten the people I love?

I feel the hate that I have against her increase. The dark feelings hold most of my heart, and though they are strong,

I think I can control them. I feel myself growing in strength and notice a slight glow around me. No. It's not slight. I'm shining with the intensity of my power. It almost blinds me, but I can still see my target.

With a scream, I release everything.

The blast goes all around me; I can almost see the gust of wind, light, and power blow in a three hundred and sixty degree angle around me. Right before the blast reaches Tenebris Daemon, I catch a glimpse of her eyes.

They are full of fear.

Then my flare hits her.

She doesn't fall to the ground to keep from being blown away like Cole and Angel do.

Tenebris Daemon has planted her feet in the ground, and the blast blows over her, ripping away the beautiful marble white skin. Peeling away her fake full red lips and the beautiful cruel sharp eyes.

It is horrible to watch. Horrible to see.

As if my power is blowing away her face.

But when the light dies down and the wind calms, I see the truth of what my blast did.

It undid her.

It undid her mask. Now, we all see her for what she truly is, and not just the mask she has worn.

We see her as a monster, with black veins sticking out on her face, with glowing red eyes and sharp teeth. Her claws are out, and I notice that there are black veins on every part of her skin, not just her face. She looks at me in shock first, her red eyes showing nothing else. Then she sneers and that splits her lip and causes fresh blood to run down her chin. I now know that this is her true self.

This is absolute evil.

■ ■ ■

For a second, no one moves. No one reacts.

They just stare at me.

Stare at her.

Cole and Angel are the first to react. They stand up slowly, wide eyes staring with fear at the repulsive creature in front of them. I look towards where Jake and Thomas had hung and am not very shocked to find that they are getting up from the floor. My blast released them from their prison. It blew away whatever dark enchantment held them captive. Jake looks at me. I know because that's where I'm staring now. I can see his blue eyes fill with amazement, then something else.

He's scared for me.

I try to give him a reassuring look. I check to make sure he's okay, and then I turn my attention to Thomas to make sure that he's not damaged either. He's not. Thomas is grinning crazily as he brushes himself off, as if he has just witnessed the most awesome thing ever. I guess that's what all those freaky action movies do to you. Nothing ever really surprises him. He has seen it all before on screen.

But this isn't a movie. This is real.

For a moment, I'm confused because there is no one dragging me. No one forcing me to the ground.

Then I see James on the floor clutching his head. His nose bleeds, the blood staining the cave floor like black ink. He must not be as strong as Tenebris Daemon.

Obviously not.

For instead of stripping him of all defenses, the flare that I sent out seems to have stripped him of everything. I'm not sure whether he still has his paralysis power. But for now, that power is paralyzed itself.

The split second morphs into a moment filled with screeching laughter from Tenebris Daemon. It seems that not only have I stripped her of her mask, but probably also of whatever sanity she had left. Daemon is clapping her hands slowly and laughing, her eyes lighting up with a dark glee that I don't understand.

"Very good!" She hisses. Her voice is no longer that dark low beautiful sound; it's a screeching voice. Even her vocals were fake. "Now what did that do exactly?" She cocks one ugly eyebrow. She's showing me that I can't beat her; all I can do is reveal her.

But I can beat her.

Or I will die trying.

"I've undone you," I say with as much courage as I can master. I feel a wave of gratification when my voice stays steady, fighting against the true terror I feel. "You can't fool us anymore. You can never take another form to hide what you are. Because now, we know exactly what you are."

"And what am I?" She says with deadly chill, her voice so low that I barely hear her.

I am standing on the edge of a cliff. One slight shove and I'll go over the edge.

Her eyes blaze with anger, glowing red with the intensity of it.

"You're a monster," Jake says from behind her. His eyes sparking as he stands up straighter. To me, at that moment, he looks stronger than he ever has. In fact, so do Thomas, Cole and Angel.

As if realizing what I've just realized, Jake looks at me, he smiles so brightly that I truly believe that everything is going to work out.

But Tenebris Daemon grasps it too. She *knows*.

Her eyes whip from Jake to me, and then she lets out a growl so deep and fierce that I feel it in my bones.

I don't step back for that would show her that I'm scared. But I can't help but feel rocked by the dark feelings that I sense from her. They overwhelm me, and I try to fight them, but there is darkness everywhere, even in the brightest of places. When it is light and the Sun shines, there is always a shadow. This is what this dark feels like. Except that her Shadow is creeping up, putting out my light; making me want to give in to all those dark feelings that I have been feeling lately.

But I can't lose.

I won't.

But my heart doesn't listen to me. It aches. Oh, it aches so much from all the pain and hurt. It feels like I'm drowning on dry land. It feels like I'm sinking into the depression that had hit me when Dad went missing.

It hurts…

Tenebris Daemon stares at me, and smiles.

"No one can escape the darkness," She hisses, then out of nowhere. She lunges for me.

I can't react, not that fast. I wasn't expecting an attack like that. She's on top of me in less than a second. I don't see anyone react; I don't see anything but her bloody eyes. As she pushes me to the ground, my skull cracks against the rock floor. I don't feel the impact, I'm in too much of a shock, but I hear it. I seem to be paralyzed with fear or something else.

My head is starting to get fuzzy and everything is starting to move in slow motion. I see a flash of something silver as it glints in her hand. I see it coming towards me, driving towards my chest, ready to sink into my heart. This is the last thing that I am aware of.

Then I black out. And I don't remember anything.

33

I'm floating in an ocean of crystal clear water.

The feel of my hair drifting and flowing in the surrounding liquid calms me. The only thing my eyes see is pure blue sky and nothing else. This stretches around everywhere.

It's so peaceful.

So beautiful.

I want to stay here forever. I don't want to go back to where I was before. Even though I don't remember it, I know that it was not peaceful like this.

I listen to the water splashing gently around me, as I stay afloat. I start to feel alone.

But that's okay; I can just fall asleep.

I want to sleep.

It will be nice to have a rest, especially here, where it's so serene.

I close my eyes slowly, wanting to save a piece of that clear blue sky for my dreams. My eyes shut and I see blackness.

Then I hear a sound that doesn't belong to this place but it does belong in my dreams. Except, if it's my dream… then why does this voice sound heartbroken? Why does it sound desperate and terrified? This voice breaks through my restful state; it's forcing me to think, to question.

"Rose!" I can hear the voice saying. It seems to echo through the walls of my skull.

This isn't right.

"Get up!" The voice says brokenly. *"You're not dead."* It whispers. *"You can't be dead…"*

What does that mean? I'm not dead. Mostly certainly not. I'm just taking a rest. Floating and sinking into my dreams. Sinking…

"Cole," Another voice comes in, soft and feminine. *"I'll take care of her. You have to help Jake. He can't hold Daemon off for much longer."*

Cole. Cole is the one that broke into my mind.

But Jake... Jake... Jake... Jake... Jake is fighting Tenebris? No. No. No. That's my job. But I don't want to move. I just want to continue floating. If only the water would stop absorbing me. It's harder to stay above the surface now.

I hear a monstrous scream and through my dream state, I feel a dark power gathering. Then there is a crash that sounds awfully a lot like a body hitting hard surface.

Whose body? Who... Who... Who...

"*Cole! Go help Jake now!*" I hear the soft girl voice say. It's so familiar. So nice to listen to. But I don't like what she said. Why would Jake need help? He can't be the one that was thrown. No, no, no. Jake.

I try to resurface, but the clear water is pulling me under, deeper and deeper.

It's so nice and cool against my skin. If only I could *breathe*. I gasp. Fighting to get air.

"*She's breathing!*" The girl's voice says. What does she mean? She's wrong. I was breathing before and they didn't say anything. Now I'm not breathing. I am not breathing. Not breathing. I *can't* breathe. I need air. Need air.

I keep gasping.

"*Oh no,*" The voice says, it quivers with fear. "*What's happening? Rose! Stop it!*" I can't stop. I need air. I need it. Need it.

"*What's happening, Angel?*" I hear a voice. Oh that voice. It's so beautiful. So perfectly toned. This is the voice that I wouldn't mind hearing everyday for the rest of my life. If only this voice doesn't sound so scared and weak. It sounds like just those three words were hard to get out.

That's wrong. This voice belongs to someone who should always be strong. Always.

"*Jake! Oh. You're okay!*"
"*Yes, I'm okay. But Daemon threw me. Then Cole started fighting her. I'm messed up but I just had to get here.*" A sharp intake of breath as I gasp again. Jake's messed up? What exactly is messed up? He's not supposed to be messed up.

I have to help him. I can help him. I can help to heal him. I need to get out of this water.

But first I need air.

I struggle to open my eyes but the intensity of the water forces them to close. I gasp. Gasp. Gasp. But I still can't breathe. My heart pounds in my head. I don't have any more strength to gasp. It's too hard. I just sink. It's easier.

"*Jake…*" I hear Angel say brokenly. Because the voice belongs to Angel. I know that now. "*I don't know what's happening.*"

"*Rose*," Jake says. I think he whispers it right by my ear because I can feel it. I can feel his breathing against my ear. Even though I'm under the water and he's not. "*Please open your eyes. Please breathe. Fight. Please. I'm here. You're going to be okay.*"

He's right. I am going to be okay. He's here with me, and though my lungs are burning, my head is pounding, and my body is aching, my heart is floating.

Floating up, up, up. I feel like telling him that I can't breathe; that I think I'm going to die, but I'm too tired to open my mouth. Too scared to. Maybe he knows that, maybe he guesses, because the next thing I feel are his lips against mine as he whispers, "*Come back to me,*"

Then he's kissing me.

Gentle at first, then harder and more urgent. I want to tell him that this is nice, that I want to go back to him. But then he does something that is very, very strange. He stops moving his lips, and he just tilts my chin back, opens my mouth, and covers my nose. What is he doing? I don't want him to do this. I want him to keep kissing me. That's when I feel him blowing. I feel my lungs expanding; they are sighing with relief. Jake blows again. My lungs sigh again. And he keeps blowing. My lungs fall in love with him, just like the rest of me.

Jake is helping me breathe.

I am no longer sinking in the crystal clear water. I am swimming, moving up. Up towards the surface, towards where I can see Jake's face and kiss it many, many times. I don't want to leave him. I don't want to leave them. My fingertips break the surface. Then my head. Then my body.

My eyes flash open and I breathe.

I breathe in the mucky air of the cave. I breathe in Jake's air. I inhale his face with my eyes. I take many deep breaths. I am no longer in the peaceful place. But I am where I'm supposed to be.

Jake lets out a breath of relief and places his forehead against mine. Angel looks like she's trying very hard not to cry.

"You almost died." Jake says. "Again."

I smile a little at this, because it's kind of becoming a routine.

"And you brought me back from the edge of death," I answer. "Again."

"Thank you," I mouth, and give him a light peck. He whispers 'You're welcome' against my lips and my heart inflates. Jake doesn't look too bad, he has some blood in his hair, and a cut on his cheek, but his face looks fine. But I know that it's his body that is hurt. I want to check it, to feel it, to heal it.

I am brought back to reality when Cole hits the floor next to me. He looks horrible. I can't see anything but blood. He isn't even conscious. It's like all the rocks in this place got thrown against him. I look up, and see why.

Many rocks of all different sizes are in the air, circling Tenebris Daemon as she raises her hands in the air. Jake wheezes in a sharp breath and must have seen my eyes, because he helps me up without a word. Thomas is on the ground, unconscious but breathing. Angel rushes over to him and drags him to where Cole lies.

I stand up straighter, feeling a new sense of power. If anything, almost dying hasn't made me weaker, it has made me stronger. I have a new purpose now that I know what it's like to not be able to breathe, to almost leave without doing what I came here to do. No. I will finish this before I take my last breath.

"Ah!" Tenebris Daemon says wickedly. "Look who decided to wake up! The beautiful and pure Roza," She sneers. "Good thing you didn't die. I need your beating heart in my hand." The rocks circle her more viciously; some of them bump into each other and split, creating more tiny pieces of debris. Then all together, they come towards me.

Time slows down. I see every single rock; I see their shape, their size, and their speed. I welcome them, opening my arms wide. Planning to embrace them as they come towards me. My power waits in my heart, in my mind; ready to do what I tell it to. After a near death experience, it seems to want to listen to me because if I die, so does it. I let go of my power; I let it shield me. But at the same time, I want it to gather the rocks. To stop them before they make contact with my flesh. The rocks move and move and move; slowly, so slowly. Then they stop. They stop right in front of me; right where I want them to. Then with a push, I force them away from me. I force them towards the demon's face. Tenebris Daemon's eyes manage to change just in time for me to look. Just before she becomes nothing but shadow. They are filled with hate and disbelief. Then she disappears, and the rocks fly through where she was, missing their target.

I know better than to think she's gone.

I walk slowly, warily, to where she had stood just a moment before. Something glints on the floor; I lean forward to take a closer look before flinching back. It's the dagger. It's the dagger that she had tried to drive into my heart before Jake stopped her.

It is still clean; there is no blood on the glossy silver blade. She must have not managed to puncture my flesh. I guess I blacked out because of the impact of my head against the rock floor.

I reach forward to pick it up. I hear a weird growling sound from behind me. I turn to see Angel leaning over Cole and Thomas, but she's frozen. Jake is frozen too. He looks like he's straining to tell me something, the veins on his neck stand out. The growling came from deep within his throat; his eyes dart to something behind me, then back to my eyes.

I only realize too late.

I take in a shocked breath as warm fingers clasp around my wrist to spin me around, and then something hits my throat. Hits it hard, and I'm on my knees on the ground, gasping for air. For a panicked moment, I don't do anything but try to breathe; I don't want to drown again. I don't want to be short of breath. I hear Jake yell, but he still can't move.

"How does that feel, love?" James says, his face is just inches away from mine. Of course it's James. That's why Jake and Angel can't move. Why didn't I notice that he wasn't where he fell after my blast? Stupid. Stupid. Stupid.

I struggle to focus on anything but the pain; I can't let him render me useless like this. James smiles at me viciously, gets up and walks towards the dagger. He picks it up and examines it.

"I'm guessing that this is what will be used to kill you and take your power," He says as he twirls the dagger around and around. James walks back to me and places the tip of the dagger beneath my chin. He uses this to force me to look up at him. I try to master the angriest glare, but my eyes are watery from tears. "Never got punched in the throat before, have you?" He cocks his eyebrows. "It hurts, a lot," A chuckle. "As you now know." James's eyes spark. "But oh my… You are lovely. Even after getting punched. It's too bad really," He says matter-of-factly. "Too bad she has to kill you." He smirks. "I have a feeling you would have been fun to keep for company." He leans down closer to me, dagger still touching my skin.

But that's not what's cutting me; it's his eyes that are cutting me. They are cutting into my soul and I want to look away but I know I can't. If I do, it will show that he affects me. I don't speak, I don't think I can; but I can breathe now. Good.

"Excellent." I hear a voice from the shadows. And sure enough, Tenebris Daemon appears next to James, appearing right out of the dark air. James nods towards Daemon and slowly pulls the dagger away from my chin, only to hand it to her. With the sharp coldness gone from my skin, I feel better. Only a little. Fear still courses through me. Fear and Anger.

"Well, well…" Tenebris Daemon looks at me with wrath, and a new sense of dark interest. "That was quite a stunt you pulled back there." Her eyes blaze. "It seems that nearly dying hasn't weakened you. It has strengthened you."

I struggle to get to my feet, but none of my body parts will obey. The more I try, the worse I feel. My eyes seek James to give him a hateful glare; he smiles ruthlessly in return.

"You've got spirit." Daemon remarks. "But it won't save you. Spirit doesn't save anyone. It didn't even save me."

"Save you?" I practically hiss at her; my hatred blinds me. It makes me into something that isn't good, isn't pure. I usually try to avoid it, but right now, I can't help myself. I might be more powerful after almost dying, but I am also unstable. Almost like I've become bipolar. "I don't think anything can save you."

"No matter. I do not need to be saved anymore."

'Anymore' She had said. What does that mean?

"Why would you ever have needed to be saved?" I ask, curiosity diminishing my anger. As always.

The rage passes as swiftly as it came; my emotions are all over the place.

"You'd be surprised." Tenebris Daemon whispers softly. I hear something in her voice. Something that wasn't there before. It's faint but it's there. I feel a pain so old, so rusted, buried underneath all the fresh and continuous hatred for the world.

My need to believe and understand that there is good in everything takes over. Her eyes change for a moment, softening and dulling their usual red glow.

This confuses me. She's supposed to be unfeeling; nothing but a monster. She's not supposed to have any problems other than deciding who she should kill or take power from in order to make herself just that much stronger. But what she said is strange. Even stranger still that she seems to mean it. I don't want to be blinded by hatred; if I were, I would be no better than her. I try to reach her.

"You have a chance to be saved." I whisper back desperately, trying to delay my possible death through sacrifice by her, at the same time as trying to actually help her. "Stop killing. Stop causing other people pain, please."

"I am only doing what had been done to me." She hisses, that vulnerable side disappearing like it was never there. I wonder if I imagined it. No. I can't have. I have to believe that something good lives in the monster, no matter how dim the light may be. For if I think that, I feel as if it is my duty to free her from the darkness. To salvage whatever light she may have deep inside her. To save her from herself. The thought passes my mind, and something clicks.

"To heal the broken heart..." I whisper to myself in wonder. Of course! Tenebris's heart is obviously broken. It's twisted beyond imagining. Hell, it's probably shattered into a million pieces, making her unfeeling and uncaring.

Part of me is excited because I have actually figured out the prophecy... Even though it took a turn that I would never have been able to predict. The other part of me is curious. Curious about what happened to this demon lady who is so evil, yet so complex. I had originally thought that she was nothing but darkness and that was the end of it. But then something about what she said makes me think. Tenebris said she wasn't doing anything but what had been done to her. That means something terrible had been done to her that made her this way.

This proves what I had always thought. I've always been sure that nothing, and no one, is born evil. It is not possible. In fact, everyone is born pure; a child has no evil, children are vulnerable and innocent. Completely and utterly innocent. It's the world that changes a child into something other than innocent. I wonder what the world did to Daemon.

"What did you say?" Tenebris Daemon spits.

Instead of answering her question, I ask one of my own. "What happened to you?"

Her reaction is immediate. Her expression turns confused and the iron grip on the dagger loosens. If only just a bit. Then she hardens; I can feel her withdrawal, her fear of me being able to look into her. That coldness returns and she brings the dagger up to my face. The tip of it traces the skin on my cheek lightly, sending shivers of dread down my spine.

"Nothing that will not give you nightmares for the rest of your short life." She says. But though she tries to hide it, I can sense it clearly, her fear and agony. That's how much stronger my sixth sense has become. I can feel an emotion so small; it's clearly one she is trying to suppress. I can feel her grief, her fear, her loss. It's not possible for anyone to hide those feelings for long, even if they are as old as time. And it seems to be ageless when it comes to her.

"I can feel it." I tell her, trying to keep my voice steady. The intensity of the emotions that she's suppressing is strong; even though it is weaker than her hate and anger. Now I understand; she uses her hate and anger to cover up those other feelings. She uses them to cover up the emotions that will eventually end up destroying her. The emotions that almost destroyed me. I suddenly feel like I understand her. "I can feel your grief, and your loss and pain." I say. "I know how you feel. I've been like that too. Please let me help you. You don't have to do this."

"No one knows what I've been through or what I feel. You might experience my emotions right now, Roza, because of your gift. But you will never *feel* them." She tells me.

"No," I say. "I don't know what happened to you that caused all that pain; but I've felt pain before too." *Pain that was caused mostly by you* "But you can be saved. I *believe* you can be saved. Please, let me help."

I can feel Jake's gaze burning holes in my head. I can feel his confusion and fear. He has no idea what I'm doing. Of course he wouldn't. He can't feel what I can. He doesn't know that there might be something else in Daemon. Something else other than just pure evil.

"Do you take me for a fool?" She murmurs dangerously. "I know what you're doing!" She screeches; her horrible face crumpling with anger and humiliation. Whatever sanity and light I might have sensed a moment ago is gone; replaced by a blinding painful hate.

The blade of the dagger slices through the skin on my cheek. White-hot pain lances through me, it feels like the skin, which was broken, has been burned with ice.

I feel a trickle of blood run down my face, not much. It is a shallow cut. I refuse to blink or show my pain, so I continue to stare up at Tenebris daringly.

Jake moves then. I don't even know how he broke through James's paralysis, but suddenly, there he is. Judging by the position he was in, he had planned to throw himself at Tenebris Daemon. Now, however, he is in a fistfight with James. James must have gotten in between them fast enough. I know this is the cue.

This is it.

James won't last long against Jake. Not when Jake is determined to get to me. His will power proved beyond strong when he managed to break through the paralysis. And now he's mad. No. James definitely will not last long at all.

I look away from them, I don't have any fear for Jake; I have full confidence in him. My own fear for myself has also disappeared. Adrenaline courses through me because I know that it's now or never.

Summoning up all my strength and power, I move. But I don't just move physically; that's easy now that James is too preoccupied with Jake to keep me frozen. No, I move with my heart and my soul. Physically, I get up; slap the dagger away from my face, kick her hand to send the dagger flying, and catch it. Her shock from watching Jake and James fight helps me a little. She can't react. Yet.

With my heart, I move towards her. I reach out to her; I can feel it. As soon as I wanted to merge with her, my power obeys me; it stretches out. I feel all her emotions as if they are my own, and for a moment, I am overwhelmed by the intensity. It almost takes me over, but I keep my will strong, staying with myself. With my soul, I throw her darkness out. I will my ability to help me push away the blackness within her. I don't know how I know that my power could do this. I just feel that this is right; my power can do anything I want it to. I won't push the boundaries right now but later...

She resists.

The darkness within her fights me, not wanting my light to brighten the dark. With the dagger in hand, I move towards her. Tenebris has recovered from her initial shock; she knows what I'm trying to do. She is already weak, and my will is too strong, stronger than it has ever been, but she still fights. I can feel her dark power attacking me from the sides; I'm not even sure what she is doing except that I can feel the occasional bouts of pain on the bare skin of my neck and arms. I still advance towards her, not letting anything drive me away.

I push towards her, push with my power and will. I fight with my love, pity and anguish. Love for my family, pity and anguish for her. I no longer hate her; I want to free her, not to destroy her. I don't know why I have the dagger in hard grip; I just know that some instinct is telling me to drive it into her heart. Just like she was going to drive it into mine.

I'm so close to her now.

So close.

I can see her eyes clearly. Her blacked veined face grimaces in an ugly way that would have made me cringe if I wasn't so intense on the task at hand. I move towards her again. Who knew that a short distance would take forever to cover when unseen forces are moving against you?

From the corner of my eye I see Jake on top of James. It looks like Jake is punching him unconscious, as if he were out of control. Then I see Angel touch Jake's shoulder, and Jake stops and breathes heavily.

Daemon notices where my attention is at, I feel her force moving towards them. Quicker than I thought possible, I intercepted her blast directed at Jake and Angel with my own. It is black and white combining together, creating a deadly firework.

Daemon shrieks with fury. She attacks again. This time aiming at me.

Many dark forces come towards me like a veil of bullets, but like before, I shield them by throwing out my own power. They collide and send sparks in between us.

Tenebris Daemon glares at me, then with an insanely dreadful sneer, she waves her hand in front of her. Everywhere her hand moves, fire appears. Caging her. Cutting her off. Protecting her. Now what stands between us is a wall of fire. It's thick and high, not possible to jump over.

She smiles triumphantly.

I take a few steps back, away from the heat. This isn't normal fire. If it were, I would have been able to put it out. I will the fire to go away, but the more I use my power on the flickering flames, the blacker and harsher the fire became. Almost as if it were taking my light and turning it dark.

I stop adding my power into it. I'm just making it worse. I shouldn't add my light into it; I should *take* the darkness away.

I stick my hands in the flame.

Black white-hot pain shoots up my hands and all over my body. The fire doesn't catch onto my clothes and spread over me, another sign that it isn't natural. But it burns my hand. I hear screaming. It takes me a second to realize that it's me screaming. I don't pull away though, because I can feel the blackness seeping away from the fire and going into me. The fire is turning white and red orange; becoming natural. But as the blackness from the fire seeps into me, I can feel the effect it has, not physically but internally. I can feel the anger and the hate building up inside of me. My screaming turns into an animal like howling. Sounding dangerous and frightening.

Daemon stops smiling.

I feel like laughing.

The black fire that I consumed is making me crazy. Crazy with power and evil. I know that, but I can't help but like it. It feels amazing. I feel strong.

But I also feel blood-thirsty. I feel like killing Tenebris Daemon, to quench my thirst, not to rid the world of her evil. I feel like killing her for the fun of it. But I fight down all the blood thirst and the maddeningly vicious thoughts and I focus on taking and diverting the darkness.

This is what it feels like to take away the darkness from something. Since there is dark and light in everything, taking away the darkness would leave only light. I will do that for Tenebris Daemon.

I pull my hands away from the fire, and unsurprisingly the blisters on my hands are angry and red and bloody.

Then I do something unthinkable.

I lunge for Tenebris Daemon. Across the fire, my body hits hers. I sense that the fire goes out, but I can't see anything except Daemon and the dagger. The world stops.

I don't.

As I drive the dagger towards her chest, right where the heart is, I look into her eyes and I am no longer me.

34

I blink. Blink, blink, blink.

Stare.

There is a mirror in front of me. It takes all my willpower to not cry out in terror. The face that stares back at me is not my own. But I would know it anywhere.

The face I am staring at belongs to Tenebris Daemon.

I am her.

But I am not her.

I can't control her body. It is as if I am watching through her eyes.

Tenebris lifts her hands to tie her hair up modestly behind her head. That's weird. She's not a monster. That much is obvious. Her skin is still pale, but it's not marble. Her hair is a glossy healthy looking raven black, not the perfectly cropped hair the color of darkness.

And her eyes. Her eyes. They are a beautiful light brown. They are not red.

She looks like Snow White.

Oh. Oh. Oh. I mentally gasp. This is what Tenebris looked like before she was the demon. She was a beautiful young girl.

But there is something strange about everything. The bathroom looks weird, different; the mirror looks old. Everything is different.

"Hild!" I hear a lovely feminine voice call. Tenebris Daemon turns her head. "Hild! Come here, darling."

"Coming Mother!" She says sweetly. So sweetly. I am not prepared for that. She walks out the bathroom and I see what she sees. Home.

There are over twenty people crowded in the room with mattresses on the ground. Half of them look younger than ten years of age. They are thin and poor looking. All of them have olive or pale skin and brown eyes, some have brown curly hair, and others have their hair up in cloth so it isn't visible.

A beautiful blond haired, blue-eyed woman stands up as Tenebris enters.

"Hild, darling." She smiles warmly. "Can you please help me get some water for Mrs. Hyatt here?"

"Of course mother," Tenebris Daemon/Hild replies. I feel the lips of Tenebris pull up in a warm smile; I feel the love she has for her mother.

I realize in that moment that she is good. There is no evil in this young, beautiful girl.

I/she walks to the kitchen and fills up a cup of water.

This is strange. All the furniture, the house setting, looks like something out of a book or movie. Everything looks like it belongs in the 1940s.

The kitchen door opens.

A man with brown wavy hair and a beard walks in. He looks weary. The hands I don't control put the cup down.

"Hello papa," My mouth moves. Technically, it isn't my mouth. It belongs to Tenebris.

The man's brown eyes twinkle and he smiles.

"Hild," He rumbles, his voice is kind. "Come here, my dear." He opens his arms.

Hild walks into them and embraces her father.

Now I have an idea what is going on. This is a flashback. Somehow, when I looked into Tenebris Daemons' eyes, I walked into her past. This is her past, and her name was Hild. I am not her. I am only seeing through her.

But it's strange. She seems so normal. So human. But that also makes sense because this is probably before she became evil.

"How has your day been?" Hild asks the man who is her father.

"Tiring," He replies. Sadness fills his eyes. "Things are getting worse. There was another movement. The propaganda is horrible. Now not only are the Jewish Germans not considered Germans, but anyone without blond hair and blue eyes is considered non-Aryan and will be treated as such. Nazi soldiers are becoming ruthless, killing Jews and non-Nazis for fun."

"But papa," I say. "We are Germans. Aren't we?"

"Yes, sweetie," He murmurs, touching her cheek. "But we do not possess the qualities that, Hitler, the Führer, wants. Only your mother does."

This stuns me. Is this what I think it is? Was Tenebris Daemon this old? Was she from this time? This is the time of World War II. A time of great death. And Tenebris Daemon was right in the middle of it. From the looks of it, her mother was the typical German, and her dad may have been half German because judging from his looks, he may be half Jewish too. And all those people in the living room. They must be Jewish or non-Nazi people too.

Oh, no.

I know enough history to know that this is dangerous.

Jews were starting to be slaughtered left and right. If they found them here, everyone living here would be killed, or worse. Including Tenebris.

Before Hild/Tenebris can reply to her dad, her mother calls her again.

"Go help you mother," Her father says. "We'll talk later, *ja*?"

"*Ja*, papa." Hild says.

Hild takes the glass of water and returns to the living room. She hands it to her mother, who then gives it to a woman.

"Thank you, Hild," Her mother says.

"You're welcome Mama," Hild smiles.

Her mother stands up to give Hild a hug.
"My darling," She murmurs. "Your sixteenth birthday is in three days,"

"Yes, Mama,"

"I'm sorry we can't afford for it to be more special."

"It's okay Mama," Hild replies and kisses her mother on the cheek. "I've got you and papa. That's all I need."

"My sweet, sweet child." Her mother places a hand on her face. "What would I do without you?"

Hild kisses her mother's hands.
A woman on the other side of the wall calls for her mother's help, so she lets go.

Hild starts walking away but stops when she hears someone whimper.

A little boy is crying. In pain or because of fear, she doesn't know. She goes to him and kneels before him.

"Hey there," She says softly. The crying stops and he looks up. "What's wrong?"

"I hurt," He says, sniffling. I freeze in her head; afraid that I might disrupt this scene and be sent back not knowing what would happen next.

"Where?"

He holds out his arm. There is a long jagged cut there, it looks old, but because of infection, it has inflamed.

Hild takes his arm gently and places a hand on top of the cut. I feel it before I realize what she is doing. The power surges through her and into the little boy. A power that I am so familiar with, I have a hard time processing the fact that it isn't coming from me.

A second later Hild lets go of the little boy's hand. The little boy stares at his arm in amazement. So do I, through her eyes. The cut is gone, completely healed, no trace of anything, even a scar. Tenebris is Hild. Hild can heal others. It makes no sense to me, because now Tenebris cannot do anything other can hurt others.

Hild winks at the little boy and presses a finger to her lips, a gesture to tell him not to tell anyone. The boy nods vigorously, a huge smile on his lips.

That's when the banging begins. Hild's head snaps up. Someone from outside is trying to get in.

"Mama!" Hild yells. "Papa! The door!"

They both run in from the kitchen.

"They found us," Papa says, pale faced.

"No…" Her mother whispers.

Everyone in the room starts to panic. They run and try to huddle together in the corners. As if that would help.

Hild spots the little boy she had healed and walks over to him quickly.

"Go find your Mama." She says. "Find your mama and stay with her."

"Thank you," He murmurs, frightened.

Hild watches him go to a woman sitting in the corner. She doesn't look sane. She stares at the banging door peacefully.

She is the only one who doesn't look scared, and as she takes her son's hand, Hild hears her murmur to him.

"Don't worry, *James*," She says his name with an accent that can't hide her love. "God is with us. We will be all right. He is with us."

Hild tears her eyes away from them, as the door breaks open.

Soldiers come in. German Nazis that Hild had grown to fear and hate.

"You are under arrest!" They say. "For harboring fugitive Jews. Anti-Nazis. Treacherous."

"We are doing nothing wrong. What is treacherous is you going around killing innocent people." Mother screams. "You aren't supposed to be killing anyone! And yet you do it. You are cruel."

The Nazi soldier points his gun at her head and she freezes.

"It is only a matter of time before we start collecting all of your type. Though we haven't yet, it will come. And since you are helping the future enemies of Germans, you shall be seen as enemies *now*."

"No," Hild murmurs.

Papa steps in front of Mother.

"You cannot take them." He says firmly. "They are innocent and kind people."

Hild holds her breath. The soldiers' gun doesn't waver. Then he moves his arm and points the gun at me. At Hild.

"Your daughter?" The Nazi says. It takes Hild every ounce of her will not to spit at him. I don't blame her. I probably would have spit at him myself.

"Do not bring her into this," Papa says angrily.

The Nazi laughs.

"Protective." He sneers. "She's beautiful. We will keep her though she is not Aryan. She'll be great use to us, won't she?" He addresses his soldiers and they nod with small cruel smiles.

"You will do no such thing!" Hild's Papa shouts.

The next thing happens so quickly that I honestly didn't see it coming. I knew from school that the Nazis' were horrible, but I didn't know that they would just kill people on a whim.

But they do.

The trigger pulls and Papa falls to the ground. Mother shrieks, but Hild is too shocked to move.

Then she sees something. The little boy she had healed has started running towards the Nazi with an angry expression of an innocent ten year old.

He starts banging against the soldier's leg.

"You killed him! You bad man! How could you kill him! Bad, bad bad!" He starts crying.

The Nazi soldier looks down with a look of disgust, moves the gun, aims at the boy's head, and fires.

"*James!*" His mother cries desperately. She is crippled and can't stand up to get him. She falls to the ground.

Still filled with shock, Hild doesn't move. She was a peaceful girl, and this much violence is too much. Hild's mother moves to go to the crippled woman, but the Nazi soldier shoots her too, angered by her movement.

That sends Hild into action.

"Ahhh!" She shrieks with fury and jumps at the Nazi who killed her Papa, her Mother and her little friend. "You monster!" She yells as she strangles the Nazi soldier. He was taken by surprise and that allowed her to get a grip around his neck. Hild is strong, and she has some power, and she is consumed by grief. She wants nothing more than to murder this murderer.

But she is alone. And he isn't. Other Nazi soldiers come and grab her from behind. She thrashes and kicks and bites, not caring if they shoot her but not wanting to go down without a fight.

"Don't shoot her!" The Nazi, whom she had strangled, commands. "She has fire. Lots of men will like her. Good money,"

This makes Hild quiet down. She looks up at the soldier in horror. He smiles cruelly. Then commands his other soldier to move all the prisoners into a straight line. There are enough soldiers that there will be one for each person.

"I want her to see this," The Nazi leader says cruelly. Hild wants to close her eyes but she can't. So she just looks on with horror as each Nazi soldier brings the people her parents had taken care of into a line and aims guns at their heads.

"Please!" Hild shrieks. "Don't! Please, Please please!"

"Hild," A quiet voice says kindly. It belongs to the little boys mother. James's mother. "Sweet child. Do not despair. God is with us. Do not stray from your good heart. No matter what happens."

Hild doesn't know how to answer; she just gapes. Then the triggers get pulled and twenty bodies fall to the floor.

That's all she could take. That was the last straw. Her mind breaks.

She starts screaming and punching and kicking and biting again. The Nazi Leader laughs and slams her against the wall. Her head hits it hard. Weakness fills her.

"You will be fun company," The Nazi leader says against her face.

"Go to hell," She hisses back. Despair, agony and hate rip through her.

He laughs.
"It is not me that will go to hell. It is you all."

Hild spits at him.

"Feisty!" He grins. "You are beautiful for a non-Aryan, love." He presses her arms against the wall, caging her. "I will enjoy you."

He laughs again. Hild can't breathe; his body is pressed too tightly against hers. She looks into his eyes and sees that his pupils are dilated. Disgust fills her.

Then he does something that terrifies her. He orders the other soldiers to bring the bodies out and dump them. To leave them alone. The soldiers comply and within minutes, there is no one but Hild and this awful man in the room.

He throws her on the floor, causing her to hit hard, making her immobile. Hild closes her eyes, not wanting to see what happens next. Not wanting to be there. She can hear unzipping. Then his hands are on her, touching her in places that shouldn't be allowed. Her arms won't work; she can't fight back. She starts crying.

My heart breaks for her. My heart breaks for Hild. My heart breaks for Tenebris Daemon. It breaks for all those people.

Consumed by grief and pain, Hild gives up. The flashback fades out. The last thing I hear is the Nazi soldiers' grunts and heavy breathing, and Hild's soft cries of pain.

■ ■ ■

I expected to be brought back to the present reality. So I am surprised when I am not looking into Tenebris Daemons' eyes.

No.

I am still Hild.

This is another flashback.

She sits on a big bed in a fancy room. Wearing nothing but undergarments. I cringe, fearing for her and knowing what has happened. But something is different... she looks older.

Her eyes are sharp and filled with hate. The hate increases as a man walks into the room.

I recognize him as the same Nazi soldier who had raped her in her dead parents' house.

"We will be at war soon!" He announces and pours himself a drink.

Hild ignores him. Even when he puts down the drink and starts towards her.

"Why do you keep me here?" She asks blankly.

"Because you give me great pleasure." He replies, seemingly amused by her question.

"I hate you." She says. *"Du Hurensohn."* For some reason, I understand the German that she uses. And it is not appropriate.

"Ah," He grins. "I know my dear. But that doesn't change your body. It is still a sight to feel and behold."

"Give me clothes." She demands.

"Sorry, love." He replies. "I like you better without."

Anger fills her, so strong, stronger than when she was first raped that I flinch within her head. But I can't escape. Then something else fills her. I feel it seeping in; it's cold and chilling, turning her passionate anger into something dark. I feel her mind whirling, calculating a plan to escape. But not without killing him. She wants to kill him and she will. She looks around, at his army jacket. No. Hild won't have time to reach for a gun. Then she sees a knife on the dresser table. She looks away quickly. Not wanting to give away her intentions.

"Of course," She says.

He smiles at her comment and removes his clothing. Hild sits on the bed, patiently waiting for the right moment when she would be able to plunge that small knife into his chest. Over and over...

He comes towards her and pulls her on the bed. Hild spreads her arms, making her closer to the knife. The Nazi soldier only sees that as an opening. He lies on top of her. Hild moves up, surprising the Nazi because that gives him a better position.

What he doesn't know is that Hild has gotten her hand on the knife that he so carelessly left out in the open. She smiles as he starts working. His breathing getting heavier and heavier. She smiles in triumph and moves her body and arms.

With the strength of the darkness that has began to fill her heart from the moment her parents and friends were killed, she drives the army knife into the side of his neck.

The Nazi jerks and falls to the side. Blood spills from his wound, but instead of being scared, Hild is pleased and wants to see more. She wants to turn this white mattress red with his blood.

She jerks him over and sits on top of him to get the right position. He stares at her in shock and fear. I see in his eyes that her own eyes are starting to turn red; brighter and brighter until they are the same color as his blood.

"Now, I can send you to hell," She murmurs.

"You'll be dragged along with me," He chokes out.

"No," She says. "I am already in my hell. Now you will go to yours." Hild brings the knife down. Over and over again. Just like she wanted.

Blood spills everywhere, all over the bed, all over the white linen sheets, all over her white skin, over her hands.

When she is done, the bed is painted red with blood, no longer white. Instead of feeling exhausted and horrible, she feels powerful. No one shall ever be able to take advantage of her ever again. She wipes the blood off the knife and looks at her reflection. She sees that her eyes glow, blood red. Instead of feeling revulsion, she smiles.

The darkness that was creeping up on her has consumed her; and she is high with its power. Laughing wickedly, she leaps from the bed and destroys the whole room. Not with her hands, but with her will.

She leaves the building with death. Killing every Nazi in sight. And even though I think it's fine that she's killing the Nazis', since they are bad, I can't help but be scared. This is how she became evil. This is how she became Tenebris Daemon.

35

I snap back to myself with effort. I don't want to see anymore.

Tenebris Daemon stares back at me. Obviously, she had seen whatever I saw.

"I'm sorry," I weep as I drive the dagger forward. It sinks into her chest and pierces her heart. It is nothing like I expected. She doesn't die immediately. A ring of light appears around us. Encircling us. I can feel its power. It will keep everyone out. Only I can bring someone into this ring.

It will help me finish what I want to finish without anyone interfering. I start to wonder whether the voices of the prophecy are actually real, that they are helping me finish my task by creating this barrier of light. I almost forget my surroundings... but then it starts.

The darkness begins pouring out of Daemon. But it doesn't instantly go into me like I expected. It shoots upwards, then starts falling down. Tenebris isn't dead yet, I can hear her gasps. My instinct tells me that I have to stop her heart for the darkness to want to release her. With a cry, I drive the dagger deeper.

"Thank you," She murmurs as light fills her and life leaves her eyes. Then she sags, her last breath leaving her. Her veined face returns to normal. Not the marble white, but the olive white. The redness of her eyes fades, and the light brown ones return. She stares at nothing, but she is no longer a monster. She is Hild again.

Before I can let myself collapse, I remember that I have to take the darkness. So I stand and I summon all the darkness, which now floats through the air, to me. As if it has always been waiting for my call, the darkness attacks me. Instead of fighting it, I welcome it. Part of me is afraid that I will not want to give it up once I have it, because evil always has its lure of great power.

The evil power fills me, making me want blood. The lust for it consumes me. I want to kill everyone. I want to make them suffer. The evil is all consuming. Then I catch a sight of Jake and Angel staring at me with terror. What must I look like? I don't want them to be afraid of me, I want to hug them and tell them everything is fine. But at the same time, I want their blood.

It's like having the little devil on one side of your shoulder, and having a little angel on the other side. They are both whispering in my ear, telling me to do things. Wanting different things, splitting me apart.

But I don't want to hurt the people I love.

That's what makes me different than Hild. Hild had lost everything, and so when the darkness consumed her, she had nothing good to hold on to. Nothing to make her not want to be a monster.

It's different for me.

I have family and friends and people I love. And I don't want to hurt them.

They are frozen. Jake looks like he wants to walk towards me, to shake me out of it.

I don't know what I want.

I want him to come.

But I don't.

Then the last person I want to see steps in front of me.

"Hello, beautiful." He says.

"James," I snarl. Unconsciously, I wonder when he recovered from the beating Jake gave him.

"Wow," He says. "You're scary. You still look the same you know. But your eyes are starting to turn red. It's like the blood of every person that you kill seeps into you and turns your eye color red."

"I haven't killed anyone," I say, not thinking about Tenebris. "But I might reconsider." I glare at him, seeing whether he can take a hint.

He does.

"You just killed Tenebris. And now you want to kill me. You want to kill them too. Including your beloved Jake." He sneers. "That's how strong the darkness it. Give in to it."

"No!" I yell, because he almost had me. He almost convinced me, I am losing my fight for sanity. My head is filling with images of me slaughtering people and I like it. But the light in the darkness keeps me sane, it gives me a way out.

I lunge for James. I am more powerful, but I am too consumed by blood lust to really notice anything else. That's why I didn't realize that I was stepping out of the circle of light. He seems to anticipate my move and backs away, and then runs, with amazing speed, at me. We both crash back into the circle and he is on top of me. I don't know how he got in. I am too shocked, and still too consumed by grief of what had happened to Hild to grasp what James is trying to do. All I know is that I want to kill him. I hadn't stopped to think about what he wanted to do.

That's when he kisses me. I am too surprised and disgusted to break at first. But then, I can't break away. I can't do anything. His mouth covers mine, but he isn't exactly kissing me. He is inhaling me. It is as if he were sucking out everything that went inside me, sucking out the darkness and taking it into him.

I struggle.

No!

This shouldn't be happening. He can't take the darkness.

He can't.

I need to take the darkness so that I can destroy it.

Why didn't I do that as soon as I was filled with it?

Oh ya. I was too busy trying to decide whom to kill next.

The darkness is too unpredictable. And now I have wasted my chance to destroy it.

I can feel the darkness seeping out of me. James is still sucking it out. But now, he isn't just sucking out the darkness, he is sucking out my life too.

That's when the pain begins. If I could scream, I would. But I can't because James has his mouth over mine. My body won't move. There is a strange sensation of being addicted because though his mouth on mine hurts, it also feels good. This is what darkness does. It makes you crave pain.

Then I feel his body jerk. The pain and the pleasure disappear. I am a bit dizzy but I don't know why. James is still on top of me, pinning me down, but he isn't paying attention to me. He is glaring at Jake. Jake couldn't enter the circle of light, and so, judging from James's bloody head, he had thrown a rock.

"Get away from her," He growls dangerously. I want to tell him to back off. To tell him that I can handle it, that he doesn't stand a chance against James. Not when James has just consumed all the darkness. But I can't speak.

"I'm afraid I don't want to do that," James says slyly. "She's quite pleasurable."

Hearing him say that reminds me of Hild and the Nazi man. I grimace and pain slices through my whole body. James looks down at me again. He leans down and kisses me on the lips again, no longer inhaling my power, but just using my body to aggravate Jake. And I can't do anything but let it happen because James has paralyzed me.

"Don't touch her!" Jake shouts, but he can't break the circle of light.

James grins at Jake, then at me. I never wanted to hurt someone as much as I do now. James will *not* hurt Jake. Not through me.

"Get away." I say. "Or I will kill you right here, right now."

"I would love for you to do that," He murmurs against my face. "But not now. And by the time we meet again, you might not want to." He releases me and stands. But I can't move. It hurts everywhere. I almost want to laugh at myself. My threats are no use if I cannot execute them. "It was nice kissing you," He says. "I might get used to that."

"Go to hell," I tell him.

"Gladly," He retorts back. "I have a feeling I'll like it there." Then he turns into smoke and disappears. The light from the circle fades and disappears. There is no longer any barrier keeping Jake out.

"Rose!" Jake says, his face looms over mine, filled with concern. "Rose," He murmurs.

"I failed," My heart aches. "I failed, Jake." My soul cries. "I was supposed to stop the world from falling into darkness by healing Tenebris's heart, by taking the evil consuming Tenebris, but instead, I let it escape. I was supposed to sacrifice myself by killing it." My heart bleeds. "Oh, God…" I cry.

"Shh," Jake soothes me, pulls me onto his lap and rocks me back and forth. As if I am a child. "It's okay, it's over."

"No, it's not," I weep. "It's not over, Jake."

"Rose?" Angel's voice reaches me. I look up at her through my tears. "I'm glad you're okay." She says it so kindly that it makes me cry more. I failed… I failed… I failed…

I'm okay. That means I have failed.

"Rose!" I hear a voice exclaim. I see Cole limping towards us.

"You're okay," I say in relief. My voice comes out coarse. I reach to touch his hand, his clasps mine thinking I needed comfort. I feel my power surge through me and send it to him, healing him of his pains. I want him to be okay. Cole looks amazed. He lets go of my hand and stands straighter, his limp gone.

"Yes, I am now" He says, his eyes mirroring the worry in Jakes face. "And so is Thomas."

"Good," I say.

He clears his throat.
"Are you okay?"

"No," I say. Then I start crying again. "I failed. Cole, I failed…"

"You didn't," Jake murmurs. "You killed Tenebris. You killed her. You didn't fail."

"She w-w-wasn't… the p-p-problem." I hiccup; the sobs make it hard for me to speak.

"What?" He asks, surprised.

"I s-s-saw into her. I saw… flashbacks through her eyes b-b-before I k-k-killed her." More sobs wrack my body. "She had h-h-horrible t-things done to her." I look up at them. "T-t-then she couldn't t-take it anymore. N-n-nothing held her to her s-s-sanity. Everyone she loved was k-k-killed. She kind of just snapped." I bury my face in Jakes' chest. "If I didn't have people I loved, I would have become just like her."

"Don't say that." Jake says harshly.

"N-n-no it's true," Another hiccup. "Her original p-p-power was also to heal people." I tell them, and they look surprised. Again. "That darkness switched it around." I let out a whimper. "It w-w-wasn't h-her fault." I gasp for air. "J-J-Jake. It was h-h-her heart that was b-b-broken. I was supposed to heal it. But I couldn't. I couldn't. I stabbed her. I killed her. I'm horrible," Oh God. I killed her.

I break; because I want to believe that I didn't fail. But it's my own fault that I did fail. I didn't act fast enough, and I had practically let James consume the darkness within me. Anger. Anger. Anger builds up in me towards James, joining the grief and the feeling of failure. The anger makes me stronger, even as I break even further.

"Shh," He says again. "We'll talk about this later." Judging by the sharpness of his tone, it sounds like he had cut someone off.

Silence.

Then:

"Someone's coming." Cole hisses. Cole, Angel and Thomas stand in front of Jake and me. Creating a barrier.

"Don't worry," I tell them. My voice returns to me. "It's not anything evil. I would have been able to sense it otherwise." Even though the dark power was taken from me, I am still a lot more powerful than when I had started. I should have been able to take James on... Why couldn't I?

"Who is it then?" Thomas asks. I look at him. He looks horrible; there are cuts and bruises over every inch of his body. And for a second I'm terrified that he is more hurt than I had originally thought. But when he catches my eye and smiles warmly, I realize that it's just my imagination running wild with me. But still. I reach to touch him, just a graze of my finger against his arm. And his wounds close. He stares at me in astonishment. So do Cole, Jake and Angel. Clearly, my healing powers have amplified.

Two people run into the cave, answering Thomas's previous question and filling me with warmth and new strength.

"Mom," I choke out. My heart freezes. My breath catches. "Dad!" And I start crying again. But this time, my tears are that of happiness.

Cole looks shocked, and then a huge smile breaks across his face. I have never seen that expression on his face before. It makes him look younger. For the first time since I've seen him, Cole actually looks genuinely happy.

Dad reaches Cole and they hug forcefully. Cole clings to him as if his life depends on it. Then they let go of each other and Dad walks to Angel and Thomas and brushes each of their shoulders affectionately. Then he reaches Jake and me. Jake stands, hugs Dad and steps back.

Dad kneels down before me and cups my cheek. I think he's afraid that he might hurt me if he hugs me.

"Dad," I cry, I can hear the love in my voice, and I see it reflected in his eyes. His emotions are churning, like mine. "Dad. You're here. You're okay. You're *here*," My family is whole again. This realization makes me stronger. My friends and parents are looking down at me with emotions of love; their eyes shine with it. It helps me regain control and helps to patch up my shattered heart.

"Yes," He says. "I'm here now." Dad kisses my forehead gently, spreading warmth through my whole body. "You are the reason I'm here." He strokes my cheeks.

"Why did she take you, Dad?" I cry for an answer. "*Why?*"

A pause.
"She took me because of what I knew. And what she thought I would be capable of."

"What did you know?" I ask.

"That you were the one that was going to free us from her dark reign."

"But… how did you know that?"

"Honey," He starts. "Even though 'the gifts', like you have, has passed on in the family bloodline and may skip two or three generations, those of that bloodline are usually born with strange capabilities. This may come as a shock to you, but I, and Jake's father, Tom, are not as normal as we seem."

"What do you mean, Dad?"

"I mean, sweetie, that we also have our own abilities. Though perhaps not as pronounced as you youngsters here."

"W.O.W" I mouth.

"Yes,"

"What's your gift?" I ask. "What's Uncle Tom's gift?"

"Uncle Tom has the gift of speech. He can make people do some things by asking them, things that they may not normally be obliged to do. Most think he's just really persuasive. Many say he has a 'magic voice' or 'silver tongue'. However, his gift is quite weak, and will not work on the strong willed."

"My gift is the gift of sight. I can see glimpses of the future," His eyes twinkle. "And I saw you in my future. I saw you in everyone's future." His eyes hold clarity so deep that I feel like I can almost see the future just by looking into his eyes.

"But more will be said when we get home. For now, lets focus on getting out."

Everyone seems content with that, even though I try to argue about waiting because I want to ask more questions. But it's clear that all the answers will have to wait. Dad helps me up, but when I try to stand on my own, the piercing pain goes through my whole body again. And I can't stand. Jake helps to catch me before I hit the ground.

With Jake and Dad supporting me, I feel relieved.

"Oh dear," I hear my mom say. "Come on! Hurry. We have to get home. Don't drop her! For Christ sake."

Dad chuckles.
"Oh, how I've missed you, Viola,"

"We've all missed you, Alec," My mom replies with a loving smirk.

"No offense," Thomas says. "But seeing as Rose is practically dead on her feet, I think it's best that we save all the mushy stuff for when we are actually safe and sound at home."

"I'm okay," I argue. I like hearing my parents' talk. It's been too long. "And we're safe,"

"Okay fine," Thomas sighs heavily. "But I'm hungry. Lets get home quickly."

"Only you can think about food at a time like this," Angel says, exasperated in the sisterly kind of way.

"I think it's a great time to think about food," Thomas says, pretending to be confused.

Dad and Mom laugh their 'oh you kids are adorable' laugh. And I smile at Jake. I notice Cole looking at me and I smile at him too. His eyes soften and a small grin perks his lips. This is how we're all supposed to be.

One family in different ways. Connected. United.

As we make our way out of the cave, everyone realizes that I really can't walk. That I'm too weak physically and I still can't heal myself. So Jake picks me up in his arms and carries me while the others walk. I still feel a little tainted, but with my face nuzzled against Jake's neck, I drift into a dreamless, healing sleep.

36

I wake up lying on a bed that is not my own. The only thing that keeps me from panicking is the familiar smell of lavender and mint.

My breathing changes from quick silent gasps to slow intakes of the scent. It fills my lungs and makes my head fuzz, but it keeps me relaxed and stops my panic attack.

"Hey there, how are you?" I hear Jake's voice say.

I turn towards his voice and suck in a breath.

He is so close.

So, so, so close.

He's lying right next to me. So near that just turning means that our noses almost touch. This shocks me a little because I hadn't noticed a warm body next to me. Even though I know that I am lying on Jake's bed, and that it smelled of him, I hadn't registered that he was here. Until now.

But here he is. In the room. On the bed. With me.

"I'm great now," I murmur back and offer him a smile. His eyes light up. His hand reaches up gently to let their fingers trace the skin on my face. Each place that he touches leaves traces of fire in my veins. I can feel my body getting warmer.

"I was worried," His blue eyes are warm. "We all were. You were asleep for a long time," His hands stop tracing my face, they stop tracing everywhere but my lips. Warm fingers now touch my mouth lightly. His eyes look down at my lips; my mouth parts when breathing suddenly becomes impossible for me.

My hands somehow find their way to his fingers. He returns my grip and now we are holding hands, lying so close together. It almost seems impossible to imagine a life without him when all I want is to wake up every morning to his warm body lying next to mine.

"I'm awake now," I say. It is true. I've never felt so awake and so alive in my life. But at the same time, I've never felt so... so... dead.

I am happy, but I can sense a part somewhere in my heart that can never be brought back from the shadows. Part of my heart is still left in a dark pit. I try not to let this bother me.

"You sure you're alright?" Jake asks, his eyebrows pulling together in a worried frown. He must have sensed my change in mood.

"Fine," Smile. I touch his face lightly; the worried frown disappears from his face. But even though it lessens, it doesn't disappear from his eyes or heart, I can still feel that.

"Talk to me," He says, the expression on his face becoming serious; his eyes joining in communicating a silent 'Please,'

I sigh. He knows me so well. Too well. He always knows when something is wrong. I try to make myself cheerier, but for some reason, my heart won't comply.

"It's just…" I start; bite my lip. "I'm happy. Don't get me wrong. But for some reason, I'm not into it. It feels like I'm divided. I can feel my happiness that you're here and that you're okay. But I also feel horrible. Like I'm full of life, but I can't feel anything but this dead numbness in my heart."

Jake's eyes widen slightly when I finish. Then he pulls me in for a hug. Almost immediately, I feel better. I never knew cuddles could be cures.

"It's going to be okay," He murmurs. "You're probably just in shock,"

"Probably," I say back. But I don't believe it. This feels different. More permanent.

"Don't worry," He kisses my hair. "We'll figure it out."

I nod my answer. I feel his worry fading.

"Sooo," I say. This mood is too heavy. "How long have I been asleep exactly?"

"Only a few of days, give or take a little," He says, I feel his chin on my head. His warmth is seeping through my clothes, warming my body and chasing some of that coldness out of my heart. I sigh, happy to have some of that unwelcome emotion out of my chest.

"Only…" I laugh slightly. "You say that like it's a good thing,"

"Well, it is shorter than last time,"

"Touché,"

I feel his chuckle as well as hear it. His mood has lightened tremendously, and that darkness that was in my chest isn't so heavy anymore either.

"Jake?" I mumble against his chest.

"Huh?"

"I have to tell you something," I trace the patterns on his shirt. "I have to tell all of you something,"

"Right now?" I can imagine him raising one eyebrow. The picture makes me smile.

"Yes," I close my eyes. "It's important." I want them to know what I know. I want them to realize that Tenebris wasn't all bad, she used to be human, a girl called Hild. She was corrupted by the world that creates monsters out of innocent children. She used to heal, used to love, used to laugh.

She used to be like me.

And I want them to know that.

Because if something were to happen to me as it did her.

I have a feeling that I would end up just like she did.

■ ■ ■

Jake has called everyone into his room. That's where I had slept. I don't understand why we couldn't just meet outside in the living room. It seems more practical. Not that I have a problem with lying in Jake's bed. But it doesn't seem very suitable. No matter. Jake wouldn't have it any other way; he said that I shouldn't test myself. I told him he could carry me outside, and he smiled and said 'I would. But I like seeing you in my bed,'

His comment, though obviously a joke, had made me blush to my roots. It makes me blush right now just remembering. But my thoughts are quickly diverted when the first of my family walks in.

"Rose!" Angel squeals happily and practically jumps onto the bed to give me a happy and tight embrace. Little Simon and Kate rush in right behind Angel, plant baby kisses on my cheeks and settle on either side of me. I can't even express how my chest has expanded at the sight of them. I'm so happy they are okay.

Angel now sits directly in front of me, her legs crossed as though she were a child about to hear a story. Kate and Simon sit on either side of me, snuggling against my body.

Thomas walks in after that and gives me a quick grin, his eyes twinkle and though he says nothing but a simple joking 'Hey, look who's not dead?' the message told by his eyes is clear.

Then Cole walks in. My heart flutters but doesn't take off. Mostly I'm just glad to see that he's okay. He stands next to me and touches my shoulder lightly, obviously not wanting to cause me any discomfort. I smile at him warmly; he returns it.

"Good to see you, Rose," His smile turns into a beam. The sadness I felt in him when he had walked in and saw me so close to Jake has entirely disappeared. However, now it feels like that sadness is in me. As if I had sucked it out of him, but in doing so, it now resides in me. Weird.

"You too," I say with a smile that is… well, sad.

"Don't worry about me," He winks. "I'll be just fine," It's like he can read my thoughts. I was worried about his feelings for me and about causing him pain.

The sadness disappears as soon as it came.

Odd. I swear I am becoming bipolar.

"I know," I smile at him, this time actually meaning it. "I believe in you. You can pull through anything."

He just nods in response. I sense anger and impatience among his love, but as soon as they are there, they disappear. My mouth opens; I want him to answer me, my heart rate increased, making my head feel hot. I am almost going to demand that he tell me that he IS going to pull through, but at that moment, the two people I have missed the most in the entire world come rushing through the door.

My mom lets out a relieved sigh and walks over to my bed with hurried steps. She gives me a motherly squeeze and cups my face.

"I am so glad you are okay," Her eyes twinkle. "And though I am very proud of you, I do not want you to ever do that again."

"Mom—" I start to argue but she cuts me off. My head throbs with anger again. I don't know why I'm angry.

She holds up a hand.

"I didn't mean the destroying evil part. I meant the going off with a completely psychopathic boy who had kidnapped two children."

The anger evaporates.

"I didn't have a choice,"

"I know, honey," She smiles. "But next time, tell someone before you do something like that. Jake almost gave me a heart attack when he told us all you were gone."

"Sure mom," I say, I'm smiling now too. Anger and irritation gone. My mom also looks lighter, less worried.

"Woah, baby," She says, her eyes widening slightly. "You might want to dim down on the happy radiation thingy. I'm starting to feel light headed. All the worry and horrible things that made me heavy at heart are gone,"

"That's good," I smile again.

"She's right you know," My dad walks up next to my mom. I swear if I weren't so weak that I would jump into his arms right then and there. "You are making us all light headed."

"I don't feel like I'm doing anything," I beam. The comforting and familiar way my dad talks returns to me and my heart lightens. It is as if all the dark emotions in everyone around me and all the shadows in the room have disappeared. I felt horrible just a moment before, but now that has passed as well. I do not know what is going on. But I cannot concentrate on anything except for the fact that my dad is here.

Here. Alive. Healthy. And happy.

Tears of joy fill my eyes.
"I've missed you so, so much, Daddy," I give him a trembling smile. My dad's eyes turn so soft, so gentle that I feel like I can just go and melt into his arms.

"I've missed you too," He says and comes to give me a long, heart-warming hug. "I've missed you too," He repeats. I don't realize that the tears have escaped from my eyes until I feel his shirt getting damp. I pull away, wiping at the circular spot of moist shirt.

"Sorry," I mumble.

This makes him laugh. It rumbles through the whole room and I want more. My dad's presence is amazing. Even if he is not special like us. He is special in his own way.

"You have my permission to cry over my whole shirt any day," His eyes twinkle in that way that I can never forget. "As long as they are tears of joy, of course."

"With you they'll always be," I say and sniffle. I try to pull myself together.

"You wanted to tell us something?" My dad asks.

"Oh yes!" I exclaim. The topic at hand had been completely forgotten in the face of my parents.

They all look at me with expectant expressions. I sort through my jumbled thoughts, hoping that what I say next will make sense.

"This is about Tenebris," I say. The tension in the room immediately increases. Then it lessens abruptly but doesn't go away. I feel my own anxiety surge.

I feel as if I am pulling everything dark into me and it is making me feel all the bad things, but making the source that I am pulling the dark emotions from not feel it anymore.

But of course, that's not possible. So instead of dwelling on this, I focus on my family.

No one says anything. They are all waiting for me.

I clear my throat.

"Okay," Pause. "Anyways. I just wanted to share with you what happened."

"We know what happened," Cole says. I don't think he wants to hear this; he doesn't want to relive it.

His annoyance seeps into me.

"No, you don't," I almost snap. Then the irritation passes, leaving me confused but calm. "Sorry." I mumble. "No, you don't." I repeat. "Not from my perspective."

Silence.

I continue.

"When I had the dagger so close to her heart that there was nothing she could do to stop me from killing her, time froze." I freeze. "I looked into her eyes, and suddenly I was looking into her past. I *was* her, I saw through her eyes,"

I tell them about everything I had seen, everything up to the massacre.

"Then when the flashbacks faded and I drove the dagger into her heart. She became Hild again. She even said 'Thank you'," My voice trembles. "I don't blame her for everything she did. It wasn't her. It was the evil living *in* her." I feel anger pour into me. Evil is at fault. "It wasn't her fault. She wasn't always like that. She was actually almost like me. Or I'm like her, whatever..." I'm rambling.

"But the point is," I continue. "I don't want you guys to continue hating her, I don't want you guys to be happy that she's gone,"

"Why not?" Thomas asks. He actually looks curious. He is not doing this out of bitterness.

"Because..." I say, with my own bitter smile. "The thing that committed all that evil is not gone. It was inside me. And then James took it from me."

"That's understandable, I guess." Jake says. "But I don't think the rest of us can be like you Rose. We can't love and forgive someone like that, especially not after she committed so many horrible things." He reaches for my face. Fingers stroking my cheeks tenderly, "But perhaps you can teach us,"

I smile at him, my love for him growing.
"Okay,"

"What I don't get," Cole cuts in. "Is how Hitler could have concealed such a huge massacre. You said it yourself. Hild, Daemon, whoever she was, left dead bodies and bloodshed behind. She killed every Nazi soldier there. Something like that can't be hidden."

"That's what I've been trying to figure out," I say.

"Well," Angel says, her expression turning from confusion, to realization, to wonder. "You can't hide something like that. But you can cover it up."

"Please elaborate," Cole says. I shoot him an annoyed look. Sometimes he can act like such a smart ass. But I don't say anything. My emotions aren't steady; I normally don't get annoyed that easily.

"Well," Angel says completely unfazed. "There was this night. In the history books it is called 'The Night of Long Knives'. It is supposedly the night that the SS, who were Hitler's newer super soldiers, assassinated all of the SA, who were the original storm troopers. It is said that Hitler did that because he thought the SA were getting out of control. And judging by what Rose says she saw, Nazi soldiers had killed Hild's parents *before* the persecution of the Jews, which started in 1939, since her parents and the Jews in the house got killed before the supposed 'Night of long Knives' which was in 1934, hence that shows that the Nazi's were killing meaninglessly even before they were ordered to. So I guess that also adds to history's reason for saying that Hitler said that the SA were out of control, because they actually were. "

In my mind, the picture of Hild slaughtering all the Nazi's in her way came up. It suited the description perfectly. Hitler probably also didn't know what happened. No one would guess that one person, one young girl, could have murdered hundreds of trained soldiers. So instead of trying to figure it out and explain it to the world, he simply 'covered it up' by saying he was the one that organized the massacre.

It makes perfect sense.

"Angel," I exclaim. "You are a genius,"

"Truly, you are," My dad says to her.

"Thanks Mr. Prædixi," She says shyly.

"Please," My dad says. "Call me Alec," He smiles warmly. "You truly are brilliant,"

She smiles at him and shrugs.
"I like history,"

"Woaahhhh," Thomas laughs. "My sister. The nerd. Who would have guessed?"

"Being a nerd is better than being a dumb good for nothing," Angel answers back.

"Hey! I'm good for lots of things," He says.

"Like what?"

"This!" He says and tackles her. Thomas swings his sister over his shoulder, ignoring her screams and laughs. He then, very smugly, walks out the bedroom door. I can see Angel struggling, but I know it will do no good.

I give Jake a puzzled look. He only shrugs. The twinkle in his eyes match Dads, I smile. I hear the front door open.

Dad and Mom, accompanied by Simon and Kate run after Thomas and the shrieking laughing Angel.

Without question, Jake scoops me up from my bed and carries me out the door. Cole follows quietly. I sense unease from him, and can't bring myself to understand why.

We follow after everyone. I laugh when I realize where Thomas is headed and what he intends to do.

And sure enough, Thomas has reached the ocean water. Without hesitation, he drops Angel into the shimmering blue surface, creating a big splash and many ripples.

Between the laughs of my friends and the sound of splashing water, there isn't much else that I am aware of. So, of course, I don't notice until now that Mom and Dad are already a ways down the beach, holding hands and walking on the sand. The sight makes my heart melt; I rest my head on Jakes' shoulder. He's still carrying me, so I tell him to put me down. As soon as my feet touch the ground, I want to run into the water, but my legs won't listen, they seem to want to stay put. So I comply.

I sit down, pouring sand onto my legs and relishing the feel of the setting sun on my face.

"I'm going to miss it here," I sigh heavily. My heart aches just thinking about leaving this place.

Jake settles on the sand next to me.

"We'll never truly leave." He pulls me to him so that I sit between his legs with my back against his chest. "We definitely have to visit,"

"I know," I say. "We will…"

Cole remains standing, looking out at the water as if he could reach home just by thinking about it.

"I don't know about you guys, but I actually want to go home,"

I glance up at him, hoping to catch him with an expression on his face that he would usually try to hide. I do. It's pain.

"What's wrong, Cole?" I ask, my voice reflecting my concern.

"I want to go home," He tells me and looks me straight in the eye. His own eyes hold such sadness that I want to get up and comfort him. He's making me sad. "But there is no home for me to go to,"

"Nonsense," I say, putting as much strength into my voice. "You could live with Jake, or even with my parents! And if you don't want that, you're certainly old enough now to get your own house."

"A house isn't the same thing as a home," He murmurs.

"Well, then you have to make it one," I say. He looks at me with a desperate glean in his eyes. I don't look away until I no longer feel sadness in him. As the last traces of sorrow leave his heart, his eyes lighten with hope. This makes me happy, but I am still devastated. His sadness seems to have entered and infected me. Cole has no family. None at all.

"Yes, brother," Jake says, his voice warm. "You are always welcome."

"Thanks," Cole answers and smiles back. Then he turns and walks back to the house.

"What can we do to help him?" I ask quietly, not sure if the question is directed to myself, or to Jake.

"He'll heal with time," He murmurs.

"And what about James?" I grumble. I had almost forgotten about him. I was too busy feeling wretched about Tenebris and feeling so happy with having my dad back. But now, fire flashes through my soul as I think about the one who stole my chance of getting rid of a corrupt source of darkness. The anger boils through me as I think about his casual, infuriating smile.

"What about him?" Jake asks.

"We have to find him. I have to destroy the darkness that he took from me."

"Well, I don't know…" Jake mumbles. "I don't want you to get any more hurt for the sake of others."

"But that's my job, Jake…" I say to him. "It was my *only* job. I was supposed to heal the broken heart and rid the Earth of that certain corrupt darkness. Only one of those two missions was fulfilled. And now I have to complete the other. I *have* to. Plus, I'm going to get stronger. I won't get hurt. I'll fix this problem." If I am determined to do anything, it is this.

"You can't expect to fix everything, Miss Prædixi," Jake says.

I laugh at his use of my last name, the tension in my veins easing, though my fiery anger lies unforgotten in the chambers of my mind.

"Strange," Jake chuckles and kisses my head and wraps his arms around me. "It's so suitable," I feel so comfortable and safe; I know he's trying to distract me. And though I want to pursue this subject about finding James, I allow Jake to take him away from my mind, if just for a moment. I decide to think no longer of James and what he did. That is a job I will chase after some rest.

My eyes close.

"What's so suitable?" I ask him softly. His heartbeat merges with mine, his skin is warm.

"Your last name. Prædixi, it's Latin for 'Foretold'," He chuckles again. This time sounding amused. "It's like the fates had decided what you were supposed to be born for before even your greatest grandparents were born."

I shrug. What else am I supposed to do if I have no clue how to respond?

"Uncle Dixi! Aunt Dixi!" Childish voices call.

I open my eyes to see Kate and Simon running, dripping wet, towards where Dad and Mom are making their way back to us.

Angel and Thomas laugh at the nickname the kids have already given to my dad and mom. Prædixi can be a mouthful for little children.

Mom and dad catch the kids up in their arms and throw them happily into the air.

"I don't want to leave," I say absently. "But at the same time, I can't wait to go back,"

"Mhmm," Jake murmurs.

"I'm going to miss Angel, Thomas and the kids," I sigh again.

"We'll visit," Jake says. "A lot,"

"Is there a chance we can take our own little vacation out here?" I ask with a smile.

"Alone?" Jake whispers, I can feel my heart thrumming faster and faster.

My voice turns mischievous.
"All alone,"

"That," He says. "Would be perfect."

I tilt my head up so that I can see his expression. His mouth meets mine. His lips are warm and soft, and fit mine without any flaws. This is perfect.

"Promise?" I murmur against his lips.

"Promise."

Made in the USA
Middletown, DE
01 July 2015